MONEY ISN'T EVERYTHING

"Let's be certain we both understand the terms of the agreement you propose." Jonys's expression was amused but harsh. He took a step closer, imposing his body almost against hers. "You want help protecting your sons from the vicar's crazed control. In return, you're offering me the funds to make my estates productive again."

"And to provide for your mother and sisters, yes." Meriel found breathing difficult and her heart bumped her ribs. This was no more than a business arrangement she offered, yet Jonys issued a sensual challenge with his every movement that distracted and disturbed her.

"What makes you think I'll be satisfied by funds alone?" His voice was quiet, entirely reasonable, but his implacable expression and taut muscles invaded her space and senses with heated sensuality. "Can you actually believe money is all I want from you in marriage?"

Meriel swallowed, her throat dried by the blazing twin suns of his eyes.

"Hardly." He flung the notion aside with a sidelong gesture. "I want you in my arms, Meriel. I want the right to make love to every inch of you, to pleasure you and take my pleasure with you. Why should I settle for bank drafts and burn with unsatisfied desires?"

Kept By A Countess

PAT CODY

LOVE SPELL BOOKS   NEW YORK CITY

LOVE SPELL®

December 1997

Published by

Dorchester Publishing Co., Inc.
276 Fifth Avenue
New York, NY 10001

ISBN 0-505-52240-3

The name "Love Spell" and its logo are trademarks of Dorchester
Publishing Co., Inc.

Printed in the United States of America.

For Birkie and Bunker,
Gurran and Ribie,
my adored, re-homed Scotties.
For homeless dogs everywhere;
may they find only loving care.
For each of you who opens
his heart and home to a displaced dog:
Re-homing a dog is always
a love story.

Kept
By A
Countess

Chapter One

"You're close in my heart, however seldom we can be together." Meriel, Countess of Welwyn, murmured the words through a catch in her throat as she wrote the conclusion to her daily letter. In this hushed hour before the household stirred, memories hovered near like a sweet, sad refrain.

Dipping the quill to sign the pressed sheet, she paused, raising her head as the clatter of swift wheels over cobblestones splintered the room's silence. Only dire circumstances, surely, would bring a carriage into Portman Square at that rattling pace.

Meriel dropped the pen and rose, hurrying to the nearest bedchamber window. Slipping inside heavy blue velvet drapes, she looked down Berkley Street. At the speed of a mail coach, a handsome high-perch phaeton and pair bowled aside lurking wisps of predawn mist.

The man tooling the reins must be a blood, an aristocratic rowdy who considered himself a whip, to judge from his choice of a fast carriage that could be easily overturned. Such men had never outgrown boyhood games, in Meriel's opinion.

The lingering chill of the night touched her cheek as she leaned toward the window. A tall beaver hat obscured the driver's face as she looked down at him from the second floor. As he whisked through a pool of dim lamplight and flashed past below her second-floor window, she noted the confident set to his broad shoulders and his chin's forward thrust.

Meriel didn't approve of rowdy bucks treating London's residential streets like turnpikes. But she had to admire a whip who could hold that pace over cobbles in near-darkness.

Leaning farther forward with curiosity, she watched the sporting rig. Perhaps another lady waited at a window on the square, eager to admit the driver to her house, but not to her drawing room.

Meriel grimaced. Sniffing for scandal with such little reason proved that she had lived apart from society too long.

The phaeton slowed near the far end of the square, and she leaned her cheek against the cool glass to keep it in view. How odd. The driver had turned toward the fenced residents' park in the square's center.

Perhaps he had come to meet a maid heading out to market, not a lady at all. Not that Meriel valued a maid's virtue any less; it just provided a less remarkable tidbit of neighborhood news to serve up at breakfast to Hester. Her cousin enjoyed a coze about acquaintances as they looked over the day's letters and invitations together.

Down Berkley Street, the driver climbed off the high box with lithe grace, displaying a lengthy leg with tall boots meeting pantaloons molded to muscular thighs. Pressing her warmest wool shawl against the tucked front of her nightdress, Meriel felt her pulse quicken under her fingers. She folded the shawl and her arms tightly against the flutter.

Ridiculous for a widow of nearly thirty, to gawk at a pair of long legs like a green girl who had never been kissed. If she had good sense, she'd return to her writing table to fold and address her letter this instant.

But perhaps it was her duty to watch a man who had no business being at the square's locked park in the predawn half-daylight.

Reins held high to clear the horses, the man sauntered to the park fence like a prowling tomcat. At this hour the feral night creatures padded about in their final plundering; he was still roving, too. Very likely he was also up to go good.

As the man merged with shadows from the park's trees and shrubbery, Meriel rubbed her clasped arms restlessly. The stranger's athletic grace, as he moved through darkness, brought to mind the faceless lover from the dreams that tormented her far too frequently. Three years in a lonely bed hadn't blotted out the feel of hard muscles moving under her hands, of arms drawing her close against a warm, angular body, much as she had denied those needs since Welwyn died.

Impatient with herself, Meriel propped her

11

hands on the cold windowsill. This yearning to touch and be touched again, aroused by this unknown man's mysterious appearance out of the night, might simply come from too many losses experienced too quickly. Loss made a person feel alone.

Feeble light tinged the border of the gray woolen sky as the phaeton's driver looped the reins over a pointed spire of the iron fence. Her curiosity stronger than ever, Meriel rose on her toes in cold leather slippers for a better view.

With his pair of blacks secured, the man strode back to the carriage, glancing furtively about the square as if he were up to no good. As he searched the space under the driver's box, which was chest high even on his tall frame, he glanced to either side of the street.

Uneasiness tensed her muscles. Then he turned toward the park's lamps again, and Meriel clutched the window ledge. A small dark form, limp and lifeless, dangled from his large hands.

In careening recklessly about the streets, he must have struck a small animal and killed it. Now he appeared ready to dump it in the park. Indignation stirred over the suffering inflicted on helpless creatures by careless people.

The shape squirmed against the hold about its middle. Good. It was still alive, even if it might be injured.

Dread and disgust mingling, Meriel leaned to one side, her view blocked by the man's wide shoulders as he neared the iron rails with the small handful of fur. She couldn't tell from one glimpse whether he held a cat or dog.

As he lifted his light burden over the spikes, a lamp's pale yellow light fell on the ragtag, wiggling bundle—a small dog or puppy. Surely he wouldn't leave the little thing alone, possibly injured, in the park.

Meriel laid a hand over the thump against her breastbone as the pup's paws touched the shrubbery bed's soft dirt. The dog stumbled for a moment on short legs before finding its feet and turning awkwardly. She couldn't tell if it was hurt, but the heartless man had already turned his back.

The pup's soft eyes must be puzzled, pleading, as it watched the man walk away. The image gouged her memory of small faces pressed against a coach's glass as it drove off.

Outrage flared like flames fanned by a bellows. Slapping a palm on the glass, she cried, "Don't abandon that puppy!"

Of course the man couldn't hear her. As if he couldn't see, either, he fumbled at the fence for his knotted reins. Head down, shoulders slumped, he sprang up the narrow step onto the high-perch phaeton's box.

Pushing away from the window as he settled onto the seat, she vowed, "Maybe I couldn't best Osborne, but this man will feel the sharp edge of my tongue."

Running across the room and out the door to the passage, Meriel rushed down the carpeted stairs. She flung herself at the paneled entrance door. Blast it all! The iron key stuck for a maddening moment before scraping through the tumblers.

Dashing out into the square and toward the park, she slipped on damp, rounded cobbles. As she recovered her footing, she looked up the street for the phaeton. An enormous pair of black carriage horses bore down on her like demons on Judgment Day, their iron shoes ringing death knells on stone.

Fright sucked away her capacity to breathe or move.

"Run! Out of the way!" The driver's oaths mixed with shrill whinnies as the wild-eyed blacks fought the bits, harness jangling like fire bells. Time stretched into unreality as Meriel willed herself to move without any response from cold legs and feet. Wanting to close her eyes, she lacked even that control.

Impossibly, the driver held his team together, pulling them to the left at the last instant before they trampled her like straw. The carriage flashed past, its high rear wheels spinning mere inches from her shoulder.

"Safe!" Meriel exhaled more than spoke the word, waiting for it to seem real, for her muscles to unlock. Then relief freed her enough to lurch around, looking for the carriage. The superb whipster eased his matched pair toward an uneven halt far down the square.

Hugging herself, Meriel clenched her elbows convulsively as shudders racked her. She pressed her forearms into her midsection, gulping air as if she had nearly drowned. A chill wind funneled down Berkley Street, flapping her gown against numb legs. The cold shocked her into awareness.

Meriel stood in a public street in a nightdress.

Frantic, she looked about the square for lighted windows. The commotion of the last few moments must have awakened every resident who wasn't deaf as a post.

A few houses gave off a faint glow from under the eaves and basement areas, set back from the street, where servants prepared for the day's duties. Otherwise, only her bedroom window showed a sliver of light along the slit of the drapery she had thrust aside.

How she wished herself back in that safe haven. Word of her hoyden's behavior must never reach her brother-in-law.

A quick glance showed the phaeton had turned in a tight half circle and headed back in her direction. Even now, another early riser might be watching from a dark window as avidly as she had, imagining the worst, eager to write Osborne about her mad rush into the street, stopping a wild buck. Giving way to an impulse could cost far too much.

Dread sent her dashing for the sanctuary of her house.

"Wait! Are you hurt?" the driver called. "Wait up, missy!"

Faint recognition stirred, but she wouldn't wait around to identify it. Why did the cursed man have to develop a conscience now! If he hadn't abandoned the dog in the first place, she wouldn't be in this fix.

Meriel slid on a wet cobblestone again in her thin leather-soled slippers, teetering off balance and turning her ankle just enough to change her sprint into a hobble. When she looked back, the phaeton had gained speed, heading straight at her.

"Wait, I said!" He sounded accustomed to obedience, and that overrode the tight pitch of concern in his tone. If he kept bellowing like that, he'd have half the square out in the street.

Rather than risk facing the neighbors, Meriel

hiked up her hem and ran on, favoring her sore ankle. The driver mustn't see her well enough to recognize her again. If he discovered who she was, the story would be too good to keep quiet and Osborne would hear every outrageous detail.

Hooves clattered close a second time, and common sense abandoned her. One look at the blacks bearing down on her sent her scurrying in the opposite direction, toward the park.

"Quit flapping around like a hen in a storm, little missy!"

The unflattering description was true enough to stop her. Meriel clutched her side, panting from exertion and fright.

Sharp barks from the park snatched her attention. The shaggy pup stood foursquare at the fence, a reminder of the reason she had flown out of the house without a thought for the consequences. Fury swelled anew at a man who could drive away from this helpless little dog.

Throwing the shawl over her hair like a maidservant, Meriel turned.

His tongue was faster than hers, as he wasn't gasping for breath. "You needn't run from me. I won't hurt you, if you aren't already injured. You're limping." The driver leaned from the high perch, his tone solicitous, his face a blur under his tall hat's brim in the dimness before dawn. "I'll drive you to the nearest physician. Though surely you couldn't dash around in circles if your ankle's damaged." The slow dip of his hat brim, down and up, suggested that he was studying her, taking her in from top to toe with insolent thoroughness.

"You had best worry about your own injuries if I get my hands on you," she exploded. "You were driving through a peaceful neighborhood like a drunken coachman."

The phaeton's position shifted toward the light, allowing her an impression of his mouth, shapely and mobile. His face might look kind if she could make it out more clearly; maybe he wouldn't tattle about her folly. But his chin, set like a block of granite, looked stern.

Then a slow, insinuating grin spread his lips. As he looked her over like a predator marking its prey before the pounce, her knees grew more unsteady from his insolent smile than they had from fright and running.

The man looming above her on this empty street might be drunk or mad. He might be out of a nightmare rather than her dreams. Rushing out to confront him had been a dangerous, bird-witted thing to do.

Another yelp from the pup, sounding like a plea, set aside panic and renewed her resolve. Marching on the phaeton, she prepared for battle.

The man swept off his beaver hat, his smile growing audacious, impudent. "What a pretty armful you are, missy."

Outraged at his presumption, Meriel snapped, "You can keep your arms and your tongue under better control than you do your carriage."

His head went back as he laughed, and the nervous pair of highbred blacks shifted the phaeton. Lamplight fell fully onto his face for the first time.

The square, thrusting jaw was echoed by broad cheekbones and a straight nose. Commanding attention, his eyes, set in a forest of black lashes, gleamed as blue as Lake Wendermere.

This rogue was no stranger; no wonder the repeated call of "missy" had rung with familiarity.

17

This was the heartbreaker every parent in Surrey had warned young ladies to avoid.

"Douglas Jonys!" Meriel breathed out his name in mingled wonder and horror.

"Has my fame spread so far that every lovely woman in London recognizes me?" His expressive eyes were teasing, so he might not be as conceited as she had thought him twelve years ago.

"More like notoriety, sirrah!"

Jonys laughed as if pleased by a rake's reputation. He didn't appear to recognize her, any more than he had remembered her name when they had stood up together years before at country assemblies. He had called all his partners "missy" then, and apparently he still used the catchall word for his numberless flirts.

Not that she wanted him to recall her in these damaging circumstances, but she remembered his reputation too well. Even as a youth, Douglas Jonys was a womanizer who lived and loved for his amusement alone.

"Steady there, steady." His tone changed as he soothed his nervous pair of blacks like a fond parent with a fractious child.

That stirred one memory in his favor. Jonys cared about creatures. The entire county knew he had been barred from riding with the Old Surrey after trying to save the fox on his first boyhood hunt. The last act she expected of Jonys was to abandon a dog.

"How can you leave a pup to die in the streets of London?" Meriel flung out the question. Since he had detained her, she might as well complete the mission she had run out to accomplish.

"You might thank me for not running you down, especially when it may have cost me the last asset to my name." He nodded toward his blacks. "If their mouths suffered from pulling them off you abruptly, they won't bring half as much at auction." Then his smile opened a door between them and invited her inside the warmth. "But a kiss from a beauty like you before breakfast would begin to repay the loss."

"A highly improper suggestion, which doesn't surprise me in the least." She clutched the shawl closer, but it felt no larger than a handkerchief under his over-warm appraisal.

"You'll forgive me for hoping, on the strength of that fetching gown you're wearing." His sensual glance kissed her lips lightly and lingered like a tender touch down her body.

"You may hope if you like, but not for me." Indignation was the only possible reaction for a lady to such blatant, suggestive appreciation of her person. The heat sliding over her skin in the wake of his gaze was only natural resentment.

Learning Jonys was a womanizer while she was still a young girl had inoculated her, like the new preventive measure for smallpox, against his irrepressible, dangerous charm. Besides, by deserting the dog Jonys had proved how little a lady should trust him.

Chin up, she called on every ounce of her dignity and resolution, learned along with the duties of a countess. "You can't value horses much, considering you just left that pup in the park."

Gesturing toward the iron railing, Meriel looked at the bereft creature. Bright brown eyes quizzed her. The small dog thrust its long muzzle between two park fence rails like a prisoner at Newgate, pushing back full whiskers that sprang in all directions on the other side. Bearded jaws snapped open as he barked, paws rising slightly off the ground with each sharp sound.

"He isn't mine. Not exactly." Jonys offered his defense like a confidence he could share only with her. "I ended up with him tonight, but I can't keep him."

The answer whetted her curiosity, considering his past protection of even a pestilent fox, but questioning men had never gotten her straight answers. Meriel exchanged looks with the little dog.

Pulling back through the rails, the shaggy fellow collapsed onto his round rump more than sat down. The pup couldn't be a year old, though his whiskered face reminded her of an old man. Head cocked to one side, he stretched his neck toward her as if curious. Meriel longed to gather his sturdy body into her arms.

"I didn't leave the little fellow just to be rid of him." Jonys's smile had lost none of its cajolery after twelve years. "He'll be safe here until someone finds him who can afford to feed him."

"You didn't linger to see that he was found." She mustn't succumb to the friendly, flirtatious assurance of his expression and tone.

"If I hung about, he'd just watch me." Jonys shook his head. "That wouldn't convince anyone he needs a home."

Looking back at the pup, she saw the truth of Jonys's claim. The little dog sat staring expectantly, waiting to be retrieved, the same way two small boys awaited her.

"You might at least have taken him home with you for the night." Her throat was too painful to trust her voice further.

Jonys looked at her closely, but finally nodded southward. "My landlord doesn't let his rooms be used as kennels, or I'd have a few dogs underfoot already. And I owe too many months' rent to dispute the matter. Maybe your mistress could use a good ratter in the stables."

Meriel was taken aback for a moment. Though she meant him to think her a servant, his easy acceptance annoyed her. "I'm very much my own mistress."

His gaze teased her, a twinkle glinting in his liquid blue eyes like sunlight off the sea's ripples. "Then you're perfect for me, missy. I need a woman who can keep herself, for I have nothing to offer at present but my fondest attentions."

"A man who abandons dogs has nothing I want." Meriel poured contempt into her tone and expression. She must send him away quickly and get safely inside, for the wan light was strengthening as she stood bandying words in the street with a rascal.

Looking at him was a mistake, as his seductive gaze on her mouth made her lips tremble. Excited yelps behind her provided an excuse to look at the pup instead.

The rough-coated dog dug energetically at the soft ground under the fence. As he deepened the excavation, he laid his muzzle and shoulder against the fresh-turned earth, burrowing under the iron rails just above the shrubbery bed.

Forepaws and head leading, the loaf-like body wiggled under the fence without a whisker of space to spare. The pup stood, shook briskly from nose to tail, and set off in an odd gait like a seaman's. Making straight for Meriel, he set his forepaws against her knee and drummed for attention.

"Good dog." Bending to stroke the appealing

21

pup, she glared at Jonys. "Don't let men decide your fate." She scratched around the base of a black ear tip pushing out of dark, tweed-like hair. Deep brown eyes begged for more, as intent and demanding as Jonys's glinting blue gaze.

Straightening reluctantly, Meriel said, "Down, sir." The pup just patted more earth-brown paw prints onto her white linen gown, big eyes pleading under overhanging brows.

Meriel didn't need a dog, even one this appealing, leaving dirt and dark hairs on the carpets and cushions in her public rooms. Perhaps she could find him a place with an acquaintance who had little ones at home, or send him to the country. "Sit," she ordered with emphasis.

The dog finally collapsed onto his rear, gazing at her as if expecting a treat for reluctant compliance. He had received training, though not from Jonys. That rake didn't even restrain his over-warm glances.

"He likes you." Jonys interrupted the dog's silent communication with a warm persuasion that probably worked with maids. "Take him down to your kitchens and feed him a few scraps. A small dog like that wouldn't eat much."

"No doubt his appetites are different from yours, at any rate." She wasn't moved by rascals with the easy appeal of sin in their roving blue eyes.

"I wager we like the same things, the pup and I." His infectious grin suggested improprieties. "Both of us would enjoy a cuddle with you before an early breakfast. Or any other time, day or night."

"Thank you, I prefer the pup's company to yours." She mustn't permit herself to think about where he was leading her unruly imagination.

The dog panted as if laughing. Springing up, he trotted toward the phaeton.

"Come!" Meriel swooped down to catch him, but the dog scooted easily out of reach despite his short legs. Jonys wouldn't get him back, not while she could prevent it.

Then she realized the dog's purpose. The shaggy pooch lifted a rear leg on the shiny front wheel of Jonys's polished phaeton. Meriel grinned.

Jonys glanced down at the dog, leg still hoisted, and scowled. "You there! Get away. Stop that!" At the same time, he signaled his team to move ahead a few steps.

"He's just paying you back for your desertion."

Finished anyway, the pup scratched the stone cobbles with one rear paw after the other as if issuing a challenge. Scampering to her, he parted his bearded face to show a length of pink velvet tongue.

"I'd hide behind the nearest skirt, too, if I'd just committed that offence against property," Jonys grumbled.

Stooping to scoop the bushy bundle of fur into her arms, Meriel sheltered him, savoring the feel of a small warm body in her arms again. "I've never understood the fuss about dogs and wheels when you drive through London's filthy wastes daily."

"No one buys a phaeton with blistered paint," he protested, grinning with the perilous charm he'd shown even as a young fellow down from Oxford.

Meriel's curiosity grew at continued hints of penury. His wealthy father must make him an adequate allowance as a second son. Jonys had probably squandered it on a succession of women. "The carriage hardly looks used," she observed.

"I take good care of it." He touched the upholstery with a gloved hand, caressing it as she imagined he would a lover. "Like the terrier, it should go where it can be properly looked after."

His expression lightened. "But I'll have it for a while, until Tat's frees space to take it and my pair for auction. Long enough to take you for a drive in the country."

Meriel shook her head at his quick change of mood and dangerous invitation. It was tempting to learn more about him, just to see if he had changed over the years.

But he hadn't truly invited her to drive out with him. He thought her a maid and expected her to fall into his ready arms like this pup snuggled in hers. "If you're reduced to selling your prads and leaving your dog in the park, you have more important things to do than flirt," she chided him.

"A pretty face shouldn't hide a sharp tongue." Jonys managed to look both injured and winning. At least he would have to an unwary female. "Hand him up and I'll take him away if you like. I want you to have a better opinion of me than you show."

"I have no opinion of you at all." Fearing he would abandon the dog elsewhere, she clasped the terrier closer. The little fellow curved his forepaws over her arm, holding on with flattering determination. "You say you meant someone in the square to take in this pup. Someone has. I'll take responsibility for him now; I doubt you know the meaning of the word."

Heavy black brows drew together and his chin jutted. Though drawled, his reply was as sharp and swift as a stabbing. "You don't know me or my circumstances well enough to judge me. I have too much responsibility, not too little. But you're quite right to say I'm ill prepared to deal with it."

Uncomfortable, Meriel edged away. His easy style had led her to speak too freely, and Jonys had changed in a blink. He no longer presented a picture of cocky ease, but glowered like the hero of the darkest gothic novel. Then his teasing, troubling smile flashed again.

Meriel trusted it no more than his flirting. She couldn't afford to renew acquaintance with a mercurial rake now, of all times.

"You'll have to meet me again so I know the terrier's well." Jonys sounded sincere as he leaned toward her. "Whatever you think of me, I want him looked after. When my circumstances improve, I'll take him off your hands."

Trusting men had cost her too much to count on this one's word. "As if I'd turn him over to you again."

Jonys looked at the dog and away. "His name is Skype, a Scots word for a rascal and wanderer. Most terriers can be rascals, and a wanderer from Aberdeen paid off a gambling debt with him an hour ago."

Appalled at the pup changing hands with so little forethought, Meriel peered under the dog's waterfall eyebrows. "I'm calling him Kept instead of Skype, for he'll be well kept now and never have to wander again." She tucked his head under her chin in a hug. Accepting the salute for a moment, the terrier turned up a broad black nose, licking her cheek. "He'll have all the attention a little dog could wish for."

Jonys grinned, looking at the pup's perch

against her chest with a spark of pure devilment. "I wouldn't mind being a stray myself if you pay attention in that coin."

"Coins aren't safe with gamblers." Kept shifted in her arms, trying to hoist himself over her shoulder. Her light linen gown stretched taut over her breasts as he climbed, and her shawl slipped to her elbows.

Blue eyes glinting, Jonys didn't fail to notice. A gentleman would at least pretend not to see. Turning away quickly, Meriel held Kept under one arm while she tugged the shawl around her.

The corners of Jonys's lips quivered and his expressive eyes sparkled. "If I could teach him to do that on command, missy, I could name my own price for Skype, but he's known to be too stubborn to train as a harrier. No one would take him off my hands, even as a gift."

"Kept shows better breeding than you, whatever his deficiencies may be to a man's mind." Flustered by Jonys's disconcerting stare and anxious about the increasing light, Meriel chose to retreat. "He won't have to earn his keep with me. And now I'll take him in to feed him as you suggested earlier. Good day and good-bye, sir."

Ignoring Jonys's grin, she hurried around the back of the phaeton toward her town house, which reflected the first golden glints of the new day off its yellow brick. A strong sense of his gaze accompanied her, stiffening her spine despite the sore ankle.

At her door, Meriel shifted the terrier, supporting his bottom on one hip like a baby's as she reached for the door latch. Exposed, his pale tummy confirmed that he was indeed male. What a shame.

Males were too aggressive and raucous to allow indoors, besides showing a rude preoccupation with their personal parts. Come to think of it, that description also applied to the rascal whose gaze burned into her back.

Before she could step inside, Jonys called, "Hold a moment. We'll walk our dog in the park on your next day off. When is that?"

"Forget that you ever saw me." Meriel flung the decree over her shoulder. "Kept is my dog now, not yours." Rushing inside, she closed the door on his knowing grin.

Resenting his presumption and insistence, she turned the key in the lock. Jonys appeared to believe he had her as well in hand as his matched pair of blacks. Much as she might enjoy teaching him to treat both dogs and females with the proper respect in future, she couldn't afford to meet him again. Osborne must never hear of this morning's impulsive behavior.

Crossing the entrance hall to the burled wood staircase, Meriel hugged Kept. She couldn't regret rushing out to rescue him from an irresponsible rake. Still, she wished the encounter in the street with its potential for gossip hadn't happened. With luck, she wouldn't meet Jonys again, for he might connect her with the maid in Portman Square.

Jonys represented a serious danger to her, indeed, just not in the way he would prefer to believe.

Chapter Two

Jonys closed the door to his chambers in Albany's courtyard, feeling the unaccustomed weariness that dogged him these days. From habit, he tossed aside his beaver, gloves, and whip. They arched separately through the air and scattered over the hardwood floor, the tall hat rocking on its brim like a plate.

An ebony and silver table rescued from Hadham House's attics normally stood in the center of the entrance hall where his belongings lay. The square table was famous among his friends for its four curvaceous legs, formed by the carved figures of partially draped, dusky beauties. He must be in the wrong rooms.

Looking around, Jonys raised a hand as a shield against the spill of light, bright after the climb up two pairs of stairs lit only by a single lamp. Narrowing his eyes, he glanced through the entry area into the drawing room. It looked like his bits and pieces, right enough, but the entrance hall was bare except for a chest.

"Anson!" The confounded man was always underfoot except when you wanted him.

"Must you shout, sir? I can hardly fail to hear you in a set of two rooms." The straight, narrow figure in black materialized like a specter in the double doorway across the drawing room. Anson still appeared and disappeared as silently as the old earl had demanded, often startling Jonys and his elder brother as boys in the midst of mischief.

"Where the deuce have you put my table?" The old gray-locks didn't intimidate him any more, just irked him at times. "I've dropped my hat and gloves on that table since I went up to Oxford, and I expect to find it near the door where I want it."

"No need to grouse, Master Douglas." All too often, Anson addressed Jonys like a headmaster. Despite advanced years, he crossed the bare boards toward the hall with the dignity of a bishop. "In reality, you threw your possessions at it, and more times than not, you missed the table entirely."

"Would you care to tell me why I'm missing my prized ladies now?" Jonys enjoyed the grace and oddity of the fine old piece. "Don't call me 'Master Douglas' as if I'm an infant in petticoats, when you're the one on the carpet. I should buy you a seat on the next mail back to Much Hadham."

"Yes, my lord." Anson's thin voice wrapped the words in sarcasm, showing how he rated complaints and threats. "No doubt you'll save your groats on your own, my lord."

Jonys retrieved the fallen items, stuffing the gloves inside the hat, and met Anson in the sitting room. Handing them over, he shrugged out of his

29

greatcoat, though without a fire the closed rooms would be cooler than the outside air.

Anson might have known him since he wore skirts, but Jonys had understood his father's vinegary valet nearly as long. The old goat upheld the family honor out of fierce pride in his lifelong service to three earls of Hadham, identifying totally with each master's interests. He meant to whip the latest earl into line, whatever Jonys's limitations.

Exasperated as he was by the old man's autocratic meddling, Jonys recognized a need for support, even from this slim reed. Best learn the table's fate and fall into bed for a few hours' rest.

"Which of my carousing friends carried off the table for a lark?"

Anson's prominent nostrils pinched. "As if I would permit Hadham property to be carted off by hooligans."

"Then you popped the table, I suppose." Jonys found twitting the dignified Anson irresistible, always had.

"Your lordship!" Anson's show of outrage as he repossessed the greatcoat very likely matched his guilt. "I would hardly take it upon myself to flog a valuable piece of Hadham House history for a few pounds, knowing full well you can't redeem it."

Stung by this truth, Jonys ran a hand along his jaw, feeling the rasping growth against his palm. "I could believe you wrestled the table down two flights of stairs and sold it for firewood if you judged that best for Hadham."

"So I did, in a manner of speaking." Anson folded the coat tenderly over his arm, sounding no more defensive than if he'd set out the dustbin. "Though Christie's porters carried it down, of course. Fifty pounds must be found if we're to stay on in Albany's rooms, let alone eat, while you find a better source of funds to set estate matters to rights."

Jonys stared, adjusting to the news that a piece of his life would be auctioned off in a roomful of rich cits as well as his acquaintances. No chance of buying it back someday, when his fortunes improved, from a scion of industry bent on purchasing himself a proper background. Jonys shook his head at Anson. "I should feed you to Old Fanny and move to less costly quarters after all."

"The Tower's lioness is nearly toothless, I hear." Anson jutted his bony chin up from a starched cravat like a turtle. "If you choose an inferior address, you might just as well invite in the bailiffs and set up in debtors' prison. I flatter myself that the tale I spread when we moved back here raised no suspicion. To anyone rude enough to inquire, I remarked that you preferred rooms in the courtyard wing where it's quieter to the mansion's front chamber looking directly onto Piccadilly Street's bustle."

"Which is just what I'd want if I were elderly, objecting to noise instead of creating it." Jonys shook his head, staring up at the plaster ceiling. "Why didn't I insist you stay safely out to grass in your cottage instead of letting you hound me to London? First you tell me to keep mum about estate losses, and then you send a unique table out for auction. Why not stand on Orators' Corner and announce to the whole of Hyde Park that I don't have a feather to fly with?"

Inspecting the beaver minutely for dents, Anson didn't bother to look up. "You accepted me as valet because you didn't know the first thing about how to carry on as earl. No need for theatrics, young sir. As for your table appearing at Christie's, I've told Monk Lewis's man a suitable story in the strictest confidence to cover any hint of the true state of affairs. I said the lawyers have made such a muddle arguing double death duties that funds won't be forthcoming at once."

"The devil himself can't argue with the government and win a question of taxes. Damn it, that table's as well known among my friends as my attachment to it."

Seeming satisfied that the beaver hat had returned to his care undamaged, Anson cradled it in one arm. "Your acquaintances are carousing Corinthians like yourself, who will assume you've lost at cards. Taking steps to settle a debt of honor quickly is the usual manner of a gentleman."

Jonys met Anson's straight stare and critical tone by putting on the face and posture of a top-lofty duke. "In the manner of an earl, you mean, if not to the manner born like Father and Chas."

"You'll not make a mockery of the title in my presence, Master Douglas, if you please. You may not have been bred from the time you were breeched to step into your father's shoes like Master Charles, but you were indeed born and reared as a gentleman. I've never had to remind you of a gentleman's obligations at least."

Accustomed to Anson's left-handed compliments, Jonys entered the bedroom to look out a window onto the covered Rope Walk. The sun's brief effort to burn off the morning mist had fizzled in a threat of rain. Just as his carefree existence had drowned with the loss of his elder brother.

He seldom brooded overmuch, but the loss of

another bit of Hadham, represented by the seventeenth-century table, weighed down his shoulders and spirits. Jonys could almost hear Father lecturing Chas coldly about carving his initials into the second-floor newel post at Hadham House. "This estate isn't mine now or yours later to abuse," the earl had said. "We're only its stewards for a short term, and our duty is to pass it on in a better state than we receive it."

The state of affairs Chas had passed on when he died was destitution. Not that Chas had meant to stick his spoon in the wall a scant year after inheriting the title and its wealth. Nor could Jonys blame another man for indulging in the dissolute delights to be found here in town. What was difficult to excuse was the loss of present and future security for his mother and younger sisters, as well as for estate servants and tenants. And Jonys was Hadham's untutored steward now, without any notion of how to manage an estate or investments.

Heavy-headed from too little sleep and too many obligations, Jonys turned from the bleak view out the window. Sleep wouldn't come at once, not while his responsibilities plagued him. If only he could go to sleep and awaken in the past, before his father's and Chas's deaths, when a wrong choice injured only himself.

Dropping into a wing chair before the empty grate, he closed his eyes and stretched out against the cushioned chair's familiar, sagging embrace. At the sound of footsteps on bare boards, he slitted tired eyes to see Anson coiling his braided driving whip with careful attention.

"Guess I'd best keep my favorite coat on my back, or you'll hand it over to the ragpickers for a few coppers," he twitted the old butler. "Do you mean to sell every stick I own to keep me in empty rooms you consider equal to an earl's dignity?"

Unruffled, the old man laid the whip on a cupboard shelf. "Nonsense. You would look quite undignified if I sold all your clothes."

Despite a grin for the old man, Jonys tasted a bitter mixture of irritation and shame. Anson hadn't expected him to return from a night's cautious gaming with the wherewithal to pay the accumulated rent. And he hadn't.

If that cursed Scotsman hadn't sloughed off a worthless harrying dog on him, he might have brought home a tidy sum today. Not that he was addled enough to believe he could save the estate by gaming. That required fleecing a young lamb of an estate to save his own. Knowing the burden of such a loss, he couldn't shrug it onto a younger man.

Scruples certainly limited a man's options. He could have sold the terrier for less savory purposes. In dark parts of London, ratters brought a good price. But he couldn't bring himself to expose the spirited little fellow to fighting rats in pits for his life while nobs and nobodies wagered on the outcome. The pretty maid in Portman Square would look after the pup's needs, and perhaps he would look after hers.

Thoughts of the square's beauty put him in a better frame of mind. He shouldn't berate Anson for providing the necessities when he himself hadn't done it yet. The old valet would go to any lengths for the estate; could he say the same?

Jonys held up a foot for Anson's help to remove his boots. Instead of hurrying to get the footgear safely into his hands, Anson stood where he was.

"You must know I didn't travel to London in order to set myself against you," the old man said. "If you mean to leave the estate in the mire where your brother drove it, rest his soul, tell me now. I can hire myself out to a rich cit before dinner, even at my age. But an impoverished estate can't provide for the family, let alone its pensioners, unless you find a way to refill the coffers. Have you inquired about the presence of wealthy widows presently in town?"

Setting the ankle of his outstretched leg on his knee, Jonys tugged at a Hussar boot. The valet's help had too many strings attached, for he insisted his way was the only way to retrieve Hadham's fortunes. Anson was an old biddy, pecking at a man every minute. "If you don't object, I'll have a bite and a rest before setting out on a search for a lady of means to marry."

Fetching a pair of cotton gloves from his waistband, Anson scolded him. "You'll leave finger marks on that leather I'll never rub out. Give me your foot, if you please." He faced away, pulling on the gloves.

As the boot slipped into his capable hands, Jonys regretted his quick impatience. "Don't fret, old man. Things always fall into place for me. I'll find a way to fund the estate without selling myself to a rich widow."

Tasseled boot cradled in his hands, Anson faced him, shaking his head. "But you can't deny that marriage is the fastest route to repairing our fortunes."

Jonys agreed with no more than a nod, just to stop Anson's monologue on his duty to the family heritage. "I haven't ruled out marriage. I have to

35

get spliced and produce brats someday. But I'll find another way to get funds now."

"Surely you don't expect to earn the money," Anson said sharply. "Your only marketable skill is charming ladies."

"I'm a notable whip and a bruising rider as well," Jonys quipped. Though gentlemen weren't prepared for a trade or profession by their educations, he felt diminished by his inability even to buy seed for spring planting.

Still, arguing with Anson never changed his mind. Jonys wouldn't give up on his famous luck, which extended beyond the ladies. He would call on Henry Austen again, ask if he had come up with a notion yet to get him over this rough ground, as he had done in the past. Having a banker living at the Albany offered certain advantages.

Anson brushed a mixture of ammonia and turpentine on a stained driving glove, and the scent was as sharp as his sidelong look. "I've posed a few discreet questions at The Running Footman. Two wealthy widows have arrived in town to set themselves up for the season, looking for second husbands, no doubt. Both appear to be younger than your thirty-three years, though ladies will obscure their ages. And their fathers have passed on. You don't want a father negotiating the marriage contracts when you'll need full control of the lady's entire fortune at once."

Revulsion rippled along Jonys's ribs. Fortune hunting sometimes looked like the only practicable path to meeting his responsibilities. But practical wasn't palatable. The more Anson enthused over widows, the less Jonys wanted to hear about them. He had avoided widows, who generally wanted a permanent replacement in their beds, not a diversion. Give him a sophisticated married lady any day, one seeking pleasure in the present, without any more intention than he to nail down the future.

Jonys stared at his feet, one freed, the other still in its boot. After years of playing at love, safe from the need to marry, the boot was indeed on the other foot.

Pushing at the confining leather with stocking-clad toes, he knew he didn't want to wed. Not this way. He hadn't thought much about a wife, as he hadn't expected to marry on a second son's uncertain income. But he wanted more than a convenience, a necessity, a cache of coins for a wife.

"No need to sit about like a bulldog with your face sagging." The remaining boot came off quickly in Anson's expert hands. "You want a nice widow who's already broken to bridle, so to speak. A young lady just making her bows would never do for a man with your experience, even if parents would let you stand up with their young daughters at balls. A reputation for seduction is no help to a man when he wants a wife."

"Doesn't that depend on what the lady wants in a husband?" Jonys leered in an actor's exaggerated way. He was a popular guest at country house parties for his acting in private theatricals, as well as in performances for two. "You'd think a proud title would incline fathers to turn a blind eye to a few peccadillos."

"Only a royal duke might be excused the number of liaisons you're credited with." Anson looked reproving.

"Credit like that brings more advances than a man can handle in some circles, however." Jonys rested his chin on his chest. "Some ladies are actually drawn to notoriety."

"That's the ticket; set your mind on bringing a well-feathered bird to hand. Let me tell you about the two widows, both in command of their own funds and each rich enough to buy an abbey."

Maybe he could annoy the old meddler into huffy silence. "Let's hope neither widow is religious enough to waste good money on ruins other than mine."

Anson gave him an exasperated look. "Lady Helsby is said to be a lively lady, perhaps a bit too lively for *bon ton*, but quite in your usual style. She's bought herself a house with gardens in Berkley Square near Devonshire House. Rumor has it that she's set her cap at the Bachelor Duke himself, but she'll catch cold before she catches him. You might take her eye if you put yourself out a bit."

"A man always ends up putting himself out for ladies." Jonys would marry for money if he must, but he had never needed to plot like a general to woo a woman. He refused to discuss wife-hunting seriously.

"The lively widow is the more wealthy of the two, but the money smells a bit of the shop. Her late husband supplied much of the military's demand for woolen stuff, enough to buy himself a minor title a few years back."

"An action to be scorned far more than selling myself as a husband."

"No one sneers at a good alliance in a bad situation, Master Douglas. And considering your past actions, we can't be overly nice in our requirements for a wife."

"That's beyond enough." Jonys flung up both

hands. "I'm the chap who would wed the lady, not 'us.' You'd have me married to a squint-eyed, horse-faced quiz shaped like a bolster cushion if her fortune met Hadham's needs. I prefer a pretty face across the table, if I must have one at all."

"But the length of the dining table at Hadham House is unusually long. Considering that the damp is ruining the room's fine molded ceiling, surely you could keep your eyes on your plate if necessary." Anson's look and tone reproached him. "Though the Woolen Widow could show a nicer taste in dress, I'd call her face and form pleasant."

"I never suspected you called females anything at all. Sounds like you've actually gone to the length of sneaking a look at the lady. What will you do next, write her love letters stamped with my seal?" Though he preferred to jolly the old man along, Anson was difficult to take this morning.

"Lady Helsby is said to want an old title on this trip to the altar." Anson ignored levity in a way that made a man question his delivery of a bon mot. "The Hadham title is ancient enough to offset your notoriety in her mind, I pray. But never mind Lady Helsby for the moment; she isn't our only possibility. Perhaps the widow who has just taken up residence in Portman Square would be more to your liking."

Jonys sat up, curious. "Portman Square? I just came from that direction."

"I won't ask what you were doing. Let's hope Lady Welwyn doesn't hear of it, practically upon her doorstep."

Anson laid out a nightshirt, which Jonys would pitch on the floor as usual. The man simply didn't

listen, just went on behaving as if you would con-
form to his expectations.

"You can stop speculating on how I spent the
last hours, you randy old goat. I drove into the
square to drop off a dog and almost ran down
the loveliest little maid in London."

Her glossy brown hair had spilled onto her
shoulders in glorious waves, and her gleaming
brown eyes had sparked at him like flints. But her
glowing colors weren't ordinary browns. As light
crept into the square and found her face and figure, the bed-gowned maidservant's hair and eyes
had reflected highlights of the golden stone shap-
ing the house behind her. When her shawl slipped
from her head, the length of her tawny tresses had
lifted in the same breeze that molded her thin
gown against generous curves of breast and hip,
shaped its folds against graceful thighs.

Loose curls had touched her temples and back,
as if she had flown straight down from her bed
under the eaves. That image was enough to take
him back to Portman Square to haunt the park,
waiting for her to walk Skype. Never mind Anson's
widows.

"I know that look from the days the upstairs
maids at Hadham House cleaned your bedchamber far too often." Anson held out a hand. "Your
neck cloth, if you please. Forget the servant girl;
it's the widow you want to woo in Portman
Square. You'll need an excuse to make her acquaintance."

Loosening his crumpled cravat's folds, Jonys
unwound it slowly. He'd like to wrap it around the
maid as if she were a gift and pretend it was his
birthday. The fancy spread through his veins like
smuggled French brandy. How much more pleas-

ant it would be to pursue a beauty than to worry over an earl's problems.

For now, he had to mollify Anson, buy himself a bit of peace. "Perhaps I could show up at the widow's door, inquiring after the terrier I lost nearby." When he dropped Skype over the fence, he had meant to call at every house on the square to learn if he'd landed in a proper home. Jonys settled onto the misshapen squabs again, holding out the linen strip.

Anson stood in thought after he took the white cravat. "That might very well serve the purpose. You can play the part of a considerate gentleman who's searching for a lost doggie, perhaps one belonging to a friend's little girl. That should put you in a good light with a softhearted lady. With the talk she's bound to hear about you, a little white-wash won't come amiss." The valet came out of his brown study. "Your pantaloons, please."

"Confound it all, I *am* considerate. Do you think ladies take lovers who don't know how to make them feel cherished?" Jonys unbuttoned the side flaps and stood to peel off the tight-knit garment, a process that felt too much like skinning a rabbit, especially when Anson carped at him to marry. "Don't answer. I won't have you thinking about my relations with ladies any more than you do." He handed over the pantaloons, which always managed to turn inside out, for they clung to his knit drawers.

Anson took the fawn-colored garment, turning it right side out and closing the flaps. "Your amatory exercise interests me only when it endangers the earldom." He couldn't have been more solemn if his concern was for the Prince Regent's long liaison with Mrs. Fitzherbert.

Sprawling again in the wing chair despite the chill of sitting in footed drawers and shirt, Jonys laced his fingers behind his neck. "I wonder how the terrier is faring; I'd hate to see him mistreated."

Folding the pantaloons, Anson snorted. "Don't think you'll pull the wool over my old eyes. It's that maid whose welfare you're thinking about, not the dog. I advise you to crawl under the covers so you'll be fresh to call on Lady Welwyn before five today. While you still have the phaeton and pair, you might offer to drive her in Rotten Row during the fashionable hour. In that way, you can extend your time with her past the acceptable fifteen minutes for a morning call. With finances as they are, you must move fast."

Sinking deeper into the chair, Jonys slid his hips forward and rested his head against the chair's cushioned back. He shut his eyes against exhaustion and expectations he couldn't meet yet. Somehow, he would set everything right. He must, or send his mama and sisters to sponge off relatives while he closed Hadham House. Jonys rubbed his jaw. "Got any claret in the larder?"

"I'll bring you ale. It's cheaper and better for your digestion."

Jonys listened with relief as Anson's precise footfalls headed for the steep stairs leading to the attic kitchen. He wanted a rest from reminders of duty.

He would think about the lovely creature of Portman Square instead. The tousle-haired beauty sat far more easily on his mind than an entailed estate he couldn't make productive or a couple of sisters of marriageable age without doweries. Though frail little Claire's health troubled him most.

Responsibilities swirled together against his eyelids in a whirl of colors, circling and swooping endlessly without sorting themselves out. Jonys laid his arm over his closed eyes and groaned.

A man needed diversion when the world was too much with him. Or for him. He would go to Portman Square this afternoon, but not to call on a countess. His best ideas came from a contented mind, not a besieged one.

The object of his visit would be a lovely maid who had opened her arms and heart to a shaggy young dog who needed a home. The company of a woman with warmth and compassion would be good for what ailed him.

Chapter Three

"We never would have been allowed to sit in the garden with our feet up in our come-outs." Meriel wiggled her toes in soft slippers, propped on top of the wall in the sunken pergola. Flexing her ankle, she felt only a slight twinge from her early morning misstep.

"We wouldn't have been allowed to sit in our bedchambers with our skirts up." Hester pulled her white muslin dress another inch higher, showing pink stockings almost to midcalf. "I can't think why girls look forward to those first steps in society with such anticipation, when they'll enjoy it far more later as matrons and widows."

Her cousin stretched like a cat in the dappled shade of clematis, which protected their complexions as it grew over the wooden frame covering the walk along one side of the townhouse.

Meriel looked about the garden to see where

Kept had gotten to. He emerged from behind an erica shrub, nosing a white, honey-scented blossom before leaping away. "A season was a terrifying experience I wouldn't want to repeat," Meriel said. "I was afraid of putting a foot wrong, and you feared being found out as you deliberately put both feet wrong."

Hester grinned. "Are we so different now? You still avoid even a hint of impropriety, and I still invite tattle about me. Except for trying not to upset Burchett more than is good for him."

"Poor man. You lead him about like a pug on a ribbon," Meriel teased. Despite her casual air about him, Hester kept Lord Burchett closer than any of her other flirts.

"Ribbons are pretty accessories, not leashes. I only lead where he wants to follow." Hester turned a quizzical gaze on Meriel. "You've gathered a notable number of followers yourself since you returned to town. When will you tie one to you with a ribbon, if not a leash?"

Meriel pushed away the possibility with a sweep of one hand. "Aren't you tired of that topic yet? Though men in general are good company, men in particular treat ladies like personal property from the first moment we encourage them."

Appearing unexpectedly from across the small garden set into the side of the town house, Kept stepped from the lawn onto the wall next to Hester's sandals. Giving her skirts a sniff, he leaped over her ankles.

"Typical male, fascinated by ladies' legs." Hester laughed as Kept sank down next to Meriel's slippers and rubbed his head on her feet and legs, gruffing happy sounds in his throat.

His affectionate display melted a shaving of the

45

ice that encased Meriel's emotions. "Dogs are just as good company and far less bother than men. You know I don't mean to remarry." Kept bounced off the wall onto the recessed walk where they sat and ambled away.

"I hoped you would dismiss your silly notions about remaining a widow once we set up house together and you began seeing people again." Hester leaned on the arm of the elbow chair, looking intently at her. "Men enjoy your company, Merry. You're as beautiful as ever and young enough to bear more children. If you choose, you can make a good marriage."

"Or a miserable one." Meriel watched Kept stand with forepaws against a dogwood's gray bark, staring into its low branches with ears perked. "I thought Welwyn was better than most until his will was read. No, one husband is quite enough experience of the married state for me."

Hester made a sound of disgust as she settled back into her chair. "If Welwyn hadn't been so firmly under the influence of his sanctimonious brother, you might have washed the starch out of him. Do you recall my first exposure to Osborne?"

"You didn't meet my brother-in-law before my wedding day, did you?" The very thought of Osborne shadowed the bright day.

"That was quite soon enough. When we were introduced, the first words he said to me were, 'Immodest dress is an embarrassment to the men you seek to attract and an abomination before God.' And my necklines were far more modest then than now!"

Looking at Hester's pink, indignant face, Meriel imagined the set-down her cousin had delivered in return. Laughing, she said, "No wonder Osborne kept his distance from you the rest of the morning! I thought he was just uneasy with young ladies in general, not terrified by you!"

Hester continued to look offended for a moment, then broke into laughter herself. "Afraid of contamination by my company, more likely. I lost my temper and told him my dress wouldn't embarrass him if he'd look at my face and not stare only below my shoulders."

Meriel was glad for Hester's presence, support, and humor. "He always looked stiff as a gate post any time I begged to have you come stay with me. And he told Welwyn you were an unsuitable influence on me."

"Between them, they put a stop to many visits between us." Anger set Hester's mouth in a grim line. "Considering what Osborne's done since, I'd send him cakes with arsenic sugar tops if I could cook."

Holding out her hand, Meriel smiled past her own resentment at the implacable controls of her married life. "Never mind the past. Osborne can't stop me from living here in my aunt's house with you. Thank heaven for her fortune and Papa's stand on my jointure before I married. They must have meant me to keep my business affairs in my own hands." Like her aunt, Meriel would determine her own future, too.

"You still shape your life to Osborne's peculiar views out of fear he'll deny you visits with your boys." Hester glared into the sunshine. "It isn't fair that he can keep you away from your own children. I'd send him a Stilton with a few veins of poison in it if I could be certain he would be the only one to taste it."

"Should Osborne die, the runners will come for

you at once, as many plots as you've aired to do away with him," Meriel said, smiling without feeling amused.

Her hopeless position in dealing with her brother-in-law weighed on her spirits, even in this sunny garden with Hester and Kept. "Laws were written by men, for men. I suppose I knew Welwyn could leave me without any say in our boys' lives, but it never occurred to me he'd act that cruelly." She clenched her hands against the wrath still aroused by her husband's will three years ago, giving full guardianship over her boys to his brother alone. "Solicitors and judges—more men, of course—say I can only abide by the law and Osborne's wishes."

"I've wondered if that's why you resist remarrying." Hester looked sympathetic. "Though if you found a good man with respect for you, a second marriage could be different from the first."

"I don't require a husband to be contented." The partial untruth made Meriel uneasy, for those unwelcome, heated dreams left her even more lonely when she awoke.

"I'm in no rush to remarry either," Hester said, "though I'm well past grieving Stanford's death in Egypt." Looking out over the lawn, Hester laid her head against the chair's tall back. "I hardly had time during brief leaves to grow deeply attached to him before he was off to battle again." She turned her head to smile wistfully at Meriel. "Perhaps another year or two alone will awaken certain needs, those that make us vulnerable to gentlemen's charms."

"That's not the issue." Meriel knew the dark labyrinths of lonely nights too well. "My needs are little different from yours, I imagine, but indulging them isn't worth giving up my independence."

"Meaning you'd have to marry to enjoy a gentleman's full attentions?" Hester laughed and stroked Kept's back as he wandered under their chairs. "You've lived with Osborne's prudery too long. No one cares how a widow finds solace as long as she acts with discretion. If you're determined not to remarry, you can still enjoy the closest of friendships with a gentleman."

Sitting up, Meriel examined Hester's expression. Concern for this cousin she loved like a sister outweighed reticence. "Are you saying that you and Burchett—"

"Not yet, though I have plans he hasn't considered possible as yet." Hester stared directly at her. "Be honest with me. As you're determined not to marry, have you never even considered taking a lover?"

This was a subject Meriel preferred to avoid. She leaned forward to look for Kept. The terrier danced in the far corner of the garden, leaping at birds in the shrubbery above him as if he had a hope of snatching one off a limb.

"Your silence answers me." Hester never let go of a topic until she learned what she wanted. "Of course you have; don't most of us wonder, even if we shock ourselves, what it would be like to know certain men in the biblical sense? You won't convince me you never have an unconventional thought."

"I don't want to think of men at all, let alone lovers." The effort to master her wayward thoughts about a man's support grew more difficult with every day that passed.

Too often, she considered how comfortable it had been, looking after nothing more than household concerns, without a thought for investments and lawyers or the purchase and health of horses. Meriel didn't want a man to take all responsibility out of her hands, for with responsibility came freedom. Just to have a trusted person with whom to discuss options would ease her anxiety over decisions she hadn't faced before.

Hester touched her arm briefly. "It's perfectly normal in our situation to feel desire, to want to be close with a special man even if we're not ready to remarry."

"Normal feelings, but generally not wise ones to satisfy." This line of reasoning was difficult enough to resist without her cousin supporting it. "Osborne always deplored my worldly tastes and interests."

"What a shame that Osborne can influence you quite as much as he ever did Welwyn. It isn't fair that you can't live as you like now, after years of being judged and found wanting."

"Osborne isn't the only reason I've chosen a quiet style of living." That description of her arid emotional life was an understatement. "Lovers expect at least a pretense of fondness. Emotions eventually end the relationship, or cause it to end in marriage. Since I won't marry, I choose not to hurt others or be hurt myself." The most certain way to avoid falling under a man's sway was to keep away from them all, at least emotionally.

"Surely we ladies can indulge our passions without losing our hearts if men can. You might put that to the test one day. Or night." Hester's smile looked inward, secret.

"No, thank you. Being close with a man even in a meaningful friendship is wearing, and I can't imagine the other kind of closeness without it."

"If I didn't know better, I'd think you don't even like gentlemen." Hester laughed as Kept wiggled on his back in the sun-warmed grass before them. "Men don't cluster around a lady who despises them or vie for a seat next to her after the port's drunk."

"Certainly I find pleasure in many men's company and conversation; they look at things differently than we women. They add verve and challenge to gatherings, just as spices add flavor to foods." Meriel grimaced. "But that doesn't mean I want to tie myself to one, even as a cicisbeo."

As Kept raced under the double bridge of their legs, she put down a hand, wanting to touch, not hold, him. "Too bad a lady can't keep a man like a pet, to cuddle and show affection on her terms, without him taking over her entire attention and life."

As Hester laughed at the absurdity, Meriel felt Kept nose her calf. Unable to resist the eager pleading of his dark gaze, she patted her lap. "Come on up if you like. You can jump up by yourself."

The terrier proved her right at once, leaping onto the wall and balancing on her legs like a tightrope walker until he reached and claimed her lap. He settled, tongue extended, casting a white-rimmed, sidelong look at her as she kneaded his shoulders.

"Perhaps you shouldn't risk taking up with a man," Hester agreed, grinning as she reached to stroke the terrier's side. "If you have no more resistance to human males than to Kept, a lover would twine you around his thumb in a trice."

Meriel hugged the warm pup and he made faint

51

grunting sounds of pleasure. "Men are far easier to resist than Kept. Dogs are everything men too often aren't: loyal, devoted, loving, totally accepting."

"Perhaps," said Hester, showing her disagreement. "But I'd far rather keep a man than a dog, if I could afford to do so. What fun, making them wait on your convenience, as men do all women, not just their mistresses."

The sound of a closing door focused Meriel's attention on the raised side entrance to the house. Norton stood at the top of the steps, staring down the long flight as if he had to march across Spain in full kit.

Behind the elderly butler who had served her parents, Lord Burchett stood looking their way. He bowed correctly as Hester waved at him, but as awkwardly as a wooden marionette, with his long, loose-knit frame.

Meriel looked up at the sun, traveling imperceptibly down the western sky. "Is it four o'clock already? It has to be, as Burchett said he'd call then. He's invariably polite and on time."

"Too mannerly by half." Hester sighed. "I don't know what extreme measures will make him pull me off his silly pedestal and into his arms."

Meriel grinned as Kept leaped off her lap, barking as he ran toward the steps. "I doubt Burchett would think you're less than perfect, no matter how you try to shock him."

Across the lawn, the butler disappeared inside the house again at a sign from Meriel. He was getting past the age of escorting visitors beyond the drawing room; she hoped he would send out a footman with the tray.

"A bit of shocking behavior would do you a

world of good, my girl." Hester's advice sounded distracted, for she watched Burchett as if he were the most handsome man in society.

As Burchett descended the steps, Kept stood at the bottom, legs squared under his boxy frame, barking as if Hester's friend were a house-breaker. His protective attitude warmed Meriel, but she called to him, "He's a friend, Kept. You needn't tree him for us."

Hester laughed, nudging her gently with a sandaled foot as Burchett stopped to speak to the growling guard. "How's your ankle after its sunning and rest? I can hardly believe you turned it, dashing out into the street to bring in a stray pup at dawn. It isn't as if anyone else would take him in before you sent out the porter or a footman."

"You know I act without thinking at times." Meriel's cheeks warmed as she realized that even lies by omission could haunt the teller.

Looking back at Burchett with a satisfied expression, Hester sighed. "I wish you would act impetuously and choose a nice gentleman to entertain you. No, a naughty one would be far more amusing."

Heat crept from Meriel's cheeks over her face and throat. An image of wide shoulders and long limbs, impossibly blue eyes and a suggestive smile, invaded her thoughts. But Jonys had warmed far too many other beds to be invited into hers.

If Meriel ever brought herself to enter into a quiet liaison with a kind gentleman, she wouldn't choose a rakehell and womanizer. Time spent with Jonys would be far from quiet. From the vibrant passion in his gaze, the confident way he moved his big body, the crackling energy that charged the very air about him, she knew Jonys would never be restful company.

But naturally she would do no such thing as take a lover. If a hint of scandal about her reached Osborne's ears, she would be entirely cut off from seeing her sons.

While her mind had wandered along paths leading nowhere, Burchett had nearly reached them in the pergola, led by Kept, casting suspicious looks up at the visitor he escorted. Meriel stood and went forward to welcome Burchett. Smiling at Hester, he greeted his hostess first, quite properly, though his glances at Meriel were a brief formality.

Far from offended, Meriel pointed to extra chairs she'd had brought out for morning callers who might drop by. This one, she had expected. "Sit down here next to Hester and give us the best tidbits from the coffeehouses this morning."

Moving a chair closer to her cousin, he gave Meriel a grateful look. "You always know just what will make a fellow most comfortable."

The gaze he turned on Hester as he sat down beside her left no doubt about the source of his comfort. A keen need shafted through Meriel, a need to be looked at with similar hunger and contentment.

A footman traversed the pergola's path with a small table, and another immediately behind him bore a tray of decanters and glasses. Hester rose gracefully to pour wine for Lord Burchett, joined by Kept, who stood on his short rear legs to sniff toward the tabletop as the tray settled onto it.

"You're far too young to drink wine, and you wouldn't care for lemonade," Hester jested. "Go torment the birds, and Chester will bring you a bowl of water."

The footman nodded and followed his mate down the pergola and across the lawn.

"What an amusing pup he is," Hester said, looking after Kept, who escorted the footmen away. "With those short legs and stocky body, his proportions are far from perfect, but I already adore him."

"That's a stick in the eye for me." Lord Burchett stretched his gangly frame over the scrolled garden bench, looking like a stork roosting on a birdhouse. "I hoped you might admire males with extra length to the leg, m'dear."

Hester blew him a kiss. "Ladies expect perfection only from lovers. Husbands always turn out to be imperfect creatures, for we live with them and see them as they truly are. So my opinion of you will depend on what you choose to be to me."

Poor Burchett might be adept at society's prattle, but he couldn't match her cousin's easy flirtation. His long face reddened as he shifted on the seat. "You—I mean to say I—but surely we're the closest of friends."

Watching quietly, Meriel considered a union between these two very different people. Lord Burchett's nature was like a stolid English oak, while Hester wafted on the breeze like a willow, bending to touch the world reflected at her feet. Surely a marriage would uproot one of them from his natural habitat. Perhaps, at times, taking a lover was better than marrying a man and paying with the rest of your life for the mistake.

Gazing at him through curved lashes, Hester put up her chin at Burchett. "Giving true friendship is far more demanding than mere flirting or wifely duty. If you want to be treated like a brother, you'll have to stop kissing me every time you get me alone, you know."

Burchett looked quickly at Meriel and away, red spreading up his chin and over his ears. Hester's plain speaking before her embarrassed him.

Taking pity on him, Meriel offered a distraction. "Look at Kept, the silly puppy!" The dog dashed pell-mell at a bird in the grass, arriving an instant after it took flight.

Burchett leaped at the change of subject. "He'll never make a bird dog. His legs are far too short for running, and he's too eager to flush the game."

"A show of eagerness can be quite attractive." Hester's sidelong look made Burchett stare uncertainly at her.

Meriel drew her cousin off the chase. "Is the lemonade cool, Hester? I could fancy a glass."

Picking up the decanter, Hester poured out two glasses and brought her one.

The tang of lemons mixed with the scent of fresh-scythed grass as Meriel relaxed on the garden chair. A memory of taking lemonade out to a green lawn where the boys ran in the sunshine raised the level of the constant dull ache under her breastbone. Missing her sons was like breathing during pleurisy. Much as it hurt, she didn't want to stop.

Retrieving her glass, Hester settled beside Burchett and devoted herself to encouraging him to talk.

Her cousin wouldn't, shouldn't, stay with her forever. Ahead of Meriel stretched a lifetime of inviting friends or relatives to live with her, until she was reduced to paying a companion.

Burchett leaned over to speak quietly by Hester's small ear, and a frisson skimmed the back of Meriel's neck and shoulders. She recalled the delightful shivers from a man's warm breath as he murmured messages for her ears only.

From the possessive way he bent over Hester, Burchett was besotted with her, even if he hadn't admitted it to himself yet. How fortunate they were to have found companionship with each other, if nothing more as yet.

Sighing, she turned to watch Kept run about the lawn. She preferred not to see these reminders of intimacy she wouldn't share again. Perhaps once a lady had lived with a gentleman, she must forever after feel isolated in the company of couples.

Shortly after four in the afternoon, Jonys stood staring at the steps the bed-gowned maid had ascended at dawn. If Anson had given him the right directions, the wealthy widow Lady Welwyn lived in the same house as his pretty maid.

Not that Anson ever mistook details. Seizing the brass knocker, Jonys rapped smartly. Only one way to learn about the residents.

As if answering his knock, a dog barked out back, the sound sharp like a terrier. Maybe Skype had been consigned to the stables by an autocratic Lady Welwyn. She might prefer cats for all he knew about her.

By the time the door swung open, Jonys held his curved, chased-silver card case ready. Since his father's name was engraved inside the lid, he hadn't pawned it. Not yet, at least. Handing over a card to the butler in morning dress, he asked, "Is this Lady Welwyn's house?"

The man looked over the card and then him be-

Pat Cody

fore replying in the affirmative. Curiosity edged his impassive expression.

Drat the luck of finding both females in one house. He had best speak with the mistress before inquiring after the maid who had brought in the terrier.

Come to think of it, most mistresses wouldn't welcome either a maid's dog or a member of the aristocracy sniffing around their servants. He must try to save the lass a scolding for taking in Skype. "Tell Lady Welwyn that the Earl of Hadham begs for a few words with her."

The man hesitated an instant. "Yes, my lord. If you'll step this way, I'll see if the countess is At Home." Bowing, he led the way down the long entrance hall past a burled-wood staircase to a door at the back of the house.

A countess. This imposing town house brought home the reason Anson had touted this widow as a possible consort. The Woolen Widow with her ties to trade probably offended his notions of a proper Hadham bride despite her superior wealth.

Taking in the quiet elegance of the furnishings as he passed through the house, Jonys entered what must be a library from the bookshelves lining three walls. Instead of a dark, stuffy apartment, the bright room was cheerful with a sense of purpose about it. One of the fashionable pieced-print paisley shawls lay across a curved chaise longue, and sketching materials sprawled over a writing table. On the cushion of a window seat, a book and jeweled paper knife lay awaiting the reader's return.

His maid's golden-brown hair and eyes would suit the room's green and ivory colors well. Perhaps the chit who had nearly run under his horses' hooves wasn't a servant at all, come to think of it. Her voice had been pleasant and musical, her accent and usage as unexceptional as his own. The little beauty might be a maid who had schooled herself in order to earn the higher position of a dresser.

Or she might even be well born, living with the widow as a poor relation or lady's companion, doomed to fetch and carry in either case. Neither place would make it easy for him to offer her the personal attentions her lissome form and full lips invited.

Jonys didn't seduce innocent, unmarried ladies. Not that this rule limited him much with society's females. He received more signals than even he had energy to answer from young matrons with husbands who turned blind eyes.

Meeting the widow and taking her measure wouldn't require much time. He might find an opportunity to see Skype and the pretty maid who had taken in the terrier, too.

Picking up a carved jade figure that invited his touch, Jonys recognized its value. The smooth surface and deep inner glow of the stone tempted the fingertips to stroke its sensual surface. Unusual for a lady to select sophisticated art like this instead of sweet china shepherdesses. Drawing rooms often made him feel like a dashed toe-dancer as he dodged stands holding china dogs as fragile as lap-mutts.

From the looks of little trinkets like this one, Lady Welwyn's fortune could butter someone's bread on both sides. He set down the delicate piece with care and turned his back on it, wishing he could as easily block out his distaste for marrying his way out of financial ruin. Better men than he had done the same.

From all visible signs, Skype had landed on his paws when the maid carried him in here. Jonys must do as well to provide for his family and his estate people.

But he'd much prefer to take Skype and the lovely maid for a spin through the countryside than force civil conversation with the Widow Welwyn.

Chapter Four

Meriel hardly registered the sound of the door opening onto the garden again. Naturally Chester would bring back Kept's water as quickly as he could fetch it.

Breaking off her conversation with Burchett, Hester looked in that direction. "I expected Burchett to be the last of the day's morning callers." Her tone showed how pleased she was to be wrong. "But here's Norton with his shiny salver this time. If he'll bring the card down those steep steps, the visitor must be worth seeing. Are we still At Home, Merry?" Her expression looked hopeful as she turned to consult on the question.

Though Meriel would rather deny another caller, Hester never had enough company to suit her. "We'll receive them here in the garden. I don't want to take Kept inside until he runs himself into a heap at my feet."

Pat Cody

Reaching her chair despite Kept's leaps at his tray, Norton presented it to Meriel, the small white rectangle centered. He said with faint disapproval, "The Earl of Hadham wants a word, if you please. I've put him in the library."

Waving away the proffered card, Meriel repeated, "The Earl of Hadham!" She couldn't imagine Charles calling on her. If Jonys had somehow discovered her identity since this morning, why involve his brother the earl? If only she hadn't agreed to admit another guest. "Ask him to join us out here, will you, and send a footman with another glass."

Norton made his stately way back to the steps under Kept's watchful escort while Lord Burchett shook his head and frowned. "Didn't realize you and the earl were on visiting terms, Meriel."

"Our families knew each other in a social way as we grew up." Meriel shrugged, hoping she sounded as nonchalant as she didn't feel. "I can't recall that he called on me in the past, but I wouldn't expect a bachelor to enjoy a young matron's society."

"Marriage never stopped this earl's attentions." Hester gave Burchett a look fraught with meaning, and he shifted uneasily. To Meriel, she said, "I'd forgotten the Hadham estate was near your father's. Surely you children were often together."

"The girls were much younger than I, and even the youngest son was almost four years older. Both Hadham's boys went off to school before I was old enough to ride far from the house." Meriel shouldn't have been so combative with Jonys this morning. If the earl mentioned that she had met his brother earlier in the day, Hester would wonder that she had failed to mention it. Even well-

62

meant deception landed her in the briars.

"Perhaps he's assuming the duties of an earl and not just the advantages," Burchett said, looking as if he doubted that. "It's quite proper to call on a former neighbor who's returned to town for the first time after a bereavement." He frowned. "Though three years after a death, a condolence call can't be called mandatory by the highest stickler."

Hester laughed. "Besides, this Earl of Hadham rarely does the proper thing."

What a naughty glance Hester sent her, brows rising and lips pursed. Charles must be as great a womanizer as his younger brother.

The door at the top of the house steps opened, and Meriel looked up to welcome her guest. Half rising from her seat, she sat back again, not trusting her sight or her legs.

This man wasn't Charles, who had been shorter and broader the last time she glimpsed him, perhaps four years ago. The gentleman standing on the steps was excessively wide at the shoulders, tapering to narrow hips thrust slightly forward, and stretching into long, muscular legs with shapely thighs and calves.

Charles never made a pair of pantaloons look half this good—or this dangerous to notice.

When she remembered to look at his face again, Jonys's teasing grin assured her he had seen every move of her gaze. Hot embarrassment spilled over her like tea into a saucer. Here stood the one person who could set the fire of gossip to her reputation, and she had ogled him.

Jonys's tormenting look turned bold, torrid, and brash, even with the width of the lawn between them.

63

Meriel wanted to glance away, gather her thoughts to cope with his call, and couldn't. He held her gaze as if he had seized her in an embrace. Even as he moved down the steps, descending with the athletic grace of a man who conquered physical challenges with ease, he kept the visual connection between them.

Dreading the coming confrontation, Meriel looked about the garden for Kept. If her new furry protector sank his teeth in the man who had left him in the park a few hours ago, it would hardly help her persuade Jonys to forget the details of their predawn meeting.

Kept stood at full attention, ears forward, poised on one paw as if he'd stopped in mid-step. He stared at the newcomer. Then the terrier yelped once, sharply, and streaked across the grass toward Jonys on a plumb line. Thinking of the big-dog set of teeth in Kept's long jaws, Meriel clenched hers.

As Jonys stepped onto the grass, the dog circled him, wagging and leaping at his big hands as if inviting him to play. Meriel relaxed. Dogs usually forgave without reason, unlike many humans, and Kept obviously didn't hold a grudge.

Meriel hadn't even considered forgiving or welcoming Jonys, as she didn't mean to see him again. He had subjected her to the indignities he offered servant girls, but he hadn't seemed quite like the young university man she'd mooned over for a short time as a girl, either. Besides, she needed his gentlemanly silence about this morning, though he didn't behave like any gentleman she knew.

Scooping up the squirming pup and swinging him aloft, Jonys stood laughing up at him. Kept

64

waggled his paws and ruddered with his carrot tail for balance as his tongue lolled out one side of his mouth.

With his boots planted wide in her garden, as he greeted her dog, Jonys looked as if he owned the place and Kept. An urge to go snatch the pup away brought Meriel to her feet.

Across the lawn, Jonys tucked her dog under one arm as negligently as a cane, his gaze locking with hers again. Meriel looked into molten blue flame without flinching, as if this man represented no risk to her reputation and composure.

When he glanced away to find the entrance to the pergola, she released a pent-up breath. Murmurs between Hester and Lord Burchett didn't distract her from watching Jonys's every step. He appeared at the entrance to the sunken walk, and she moved out a few steps to reclaim Kept from him, breathing evenly to prepare for this encounter.

With only an arm's length between them, Meriel leaned forward to take Kept. Jonys's glance made her a quick promise before he walked past to the seated couple.

After nearly melding her to the stone flags with daring, dancing blue eyes, Jonys had just walked by. Indignant and confused, Meriel stared after him. What was he playing at?

"Lady Welwyn," he said, capturing Hester's fingers in one large hand as he bent over them with grace. The charming rogue couldn't even look ridiculous while addressing the wrong lady and bowing with a wiggling dog over one arm.

His smile flashed brilliantly at Hester. "I apologize for intruding on you without introduction. Early today I saw your companion"—he inclined

his head in Meriel's direction with a brief wink—
"kindly carry this pup away from danger into your
house. I called to be certain the little fellow's no
trouble to you. If keeping him is a problem for
your household, I'll find him a home to save you
the bother."

Jonys had the consummate gall to pretend he
could get Kept a home after walking away from
him. And the womanizer had set about charming
Hester just as he had her.

Her cousin sat open-mouthed, but silent for
once. Hester's wide-eyed gaze traveled over
Jonys's manly frame and made too long a journey
of it.

Meriel choked back an irritated admonition.
Admiration wasn't what Jonys needed; he'd had
far too much of that from females already. But she
couldn't afford to be uncivil to him when she
needed his silence about this morning.

Before she could recover her presence of mind
and manners, Lord Burchett had unfolded his
long body from beside Hester, holding out his
hand. "Hullo, Hadham," he said. "Lady Welwyn
said you hadn't called on her before. You've got
the wrong lady by the hand, don't you know. This
is Hester, Lady Stanford, a cousin who makes her
home with Meriel, Countess of Welwyn. Your
hostess is over there."

For a long moment, Jonys stared at Burchett.
Then he burst out laughing.

What a blunder, greeting the companion as the
widow and the lovely widow as a companion. And
now it appeared Lady Welwyn and his little
beauty were one and the same person. His easy

66

assumptions had created a farce worthy of Shake-speare's confusion of identities.

Apologizing to Hester with a grin that won a mischievous smile from her, he added the proper responses to an introduction. Meanwhile, he adjusted his ideas of the pretty maid in a nightdress who looked equally fetching as a titled lady in an afternoon gown. Maybe Anson's notions about him marrying a widow weren't as cork-brained as he had thought at first.

Still holding his dog, Jonys turned to smile at Meriel. "Now I can do what I hoped when I came here, thank you sincerely for looking after Skype. I expected to waste time staring at a fusby-faced old widow without catching a glimpse of you."

Stiff but civil, Meriel addressed his right ear, from the direction of her gaze. "Let me correct another misconception at once. I'm not 'looking after' Kept temporarily; he's my dog, a permanent part of my household." She reached for Skype, but Jonys wasn't ready to hand the terrier over.

As long as he held the dog, he held her attention. "I hope you'll forgive me for thinking you were a maid this morning. Countesses are rarely young, let alone as pretty as you."

"And gentlemen don't take advantage of maids any more than their mistresses." She bit her lip and said more affably, "I'll take Kept now, if you please." Meriel held out her hands.

To thaw her distant manner, he handed Skype over. "Now perhaps you'll believe what I said. I didn't mean to abandon the pup entirely. I've even brought Skype a toy so he won't forget me." Maybe he should have brought Meriel a gift instead, for she acted as if she wished she didn't recall him.

Taking the terrier into her arms like a child, she turned him aside as if she thought he might be snatched away. "Kept has everything he needs here, thank you." Her voice was courteous, distant. "He has a home now, with me, and you needn't worry about his welfare again."

Skype laid his head on her shoulder, the little beggar, looking as pampered and indulged as the most spoiled lapdog.

Failing to provide for the terrier himself was bad enough, without her hinting at it. Her new name for the dog irked him, as if she wanted to forget the pup's connection with him. "I wouldn't have come here if I didn't care about Skype. Won't you let me share him with you? I miss having dogs here in town, you know." Visiting Meriel regularly wouldn't be exactly a hardship.

As he concentrated on showing her his most charming expression, Jonys slipped the simple toy out of his coattail pocket. Remembering pups he'd raised as a boy back at Hadham House, he'd used a generous foot of clean rope, knotting it close to either end and fringing the extensions. His pups had tugged similar toys with him and each other for hours, and Skype should enjoy it, too.

Skype sniffed toward the rope as Jonys held it out, just beyond reach of the broad, black, quivering nose. The terrier's neck stretched and he pushed against Meriel's shoulder with his front paws as he snuffled toward the rope.

Without warning, the terrier surged forward in Meriel's arms, lunging at the toy, and slipped. She stumbled, struggling to clasp the wiggling dog against her waist to keep him from falling onto the stone flags.

Jonys sprang forward, wrapping his arms

around the widow as well as the dog to hold them up. Both went still against him, Skype quiet, Meriel muttering words he couldn't make out with her face buried in his buttoned waistcoat.

Positive he'd enjoy holding her more than listening to her scold him for impropriety, he wasn't in a hurry to let go. But this experience could feel even better without a dog in the middle of it.

Teeth together, she glared up at him. "Let go of me this instant."

"You're quite all right, then? Not going to fall?" He poured concern into the questions, meeting her furious gaze with the anxious expression of a fond uncle. Not that he felt like one of her relations, though he did want relations with her.

"Can you support Skype a little longer after I let you go?" Too bad he couldn't prolong the moment further, but she looked ready to kick him.

"Of course I can hold Kept. I didn't need you grabbing me like a dancing bear in the first place."

"I didn't want him catching his big nails in the fragile fabric of your gown. It's far too pretty to be torn." And holding her in his arms was far too pleasant to give up any sooner than he must.

Every muscle of her glorious body remained tense under his touch, a reaction he hadn't inspired before. "Don't move away as I loosen my hold. I mean to get a good grip on him before you step back."

Though he made the directions matter of fact and his expression bland, he could see suspicion on her upturned face, which was close enough for kisses. "We don't want him to fling himself onto these stones the moment he feels unsupported. He could break his back."

Meriel nodded once and looked down, her forehead touching his chest lightly. His lungs seemed to stretch his chest, even though he hadn't inhaled deeply.

Gently, he relaxed his hold, then slid his hands across her back. She shuddered slightly, not looking up, and he stopped. He'd best get the dog and let her go before he embarrassed himself; blasted tight pantaloons.

Sliding his hands down her sides was just as sweet a torment, feeling the curves hidden by the ridiculous fashion for suspending skirts nearly under the arms. "Keep him braced between us," he reminded her as she quivered.

Now he held Skype's bottom securely in one hand, and the other traveled up the pup's warm body. And hers. A slight movement warned him she was about to move away. "Hold him!" he warned her.

Sounding almost as if her face were buried in his waistcoat again, she asked, "Can't you take him yet?"

"Almost—right, you can let go now." Before the sentence ended, she had sprung away. Good to know she found the connection between them as unsettling as he did.

Bending to set Skype on his paws, Jonys picked up the rope toy he had dropped when he kept them from falling. The terrier pounced on it like prey, shaking and tugging at one end. Might as well give the lady a moment to recover her composure; he could stand to do the same himself.

"I hardly think such extremes were nec—" Behind him, Burchett's complaint ended in a quick intake of breath, as if the pretty cousin had poked Burchett into silence. Otherwise he'd be ruling on the propriety of what had just happened. Jonys didn't mean to be any more proper with the pretty widow than he had to be.

When he'd recovered as much as he would any time soon, Jonys tugged the rope away from Skype's inching, growling hold and sent it spinning down the stone walk. The terrier scampered away after it as Jonys rose from his haunches.

While he had played tug with Skype, Meriel had put as much distance as was polite, and her chair, between them. Golden fire from her eyes aroused warmth he rarely felt for ladies who frowned repressively at him. Undoubtedly she'd comb his head with a footstool now if they didn't have an audience.

Only one way to handle a furious lady forced to hide her temper: Tease her until she smiled or stormed at him. "After such gallant services, a gracious lady would offer me a seat."

"Please sit down, before you find an excuse to force further help on me," she said promptly. Exaggerating a hostess's gesture and tone, Meriel pointed out a chair beyond Burchett.

Bowing with a bit of embellishment himself, he headed toward the chair. As he excused himself for walking before her, Hester beamed up at him like a fond mama welcoming his attentions to her marriageable chit. Not that respectable parents pushed daughters at him.

Straightening her hair and dress while she probably thought him too busy to notice, Meriel said, "Jonys, please explain your position in the family to my friends. Burchett has confused you with your elder brother."

"Difficult mistake to make," Jonys said briefly, picking up the chair by Burchett and carrying it around back of the other couple to her side instead. He wasn't certain what Meriel meant, but he couldn't claim his head was at its clearest after holding her close enough to feel her stays.

Flipping his coattails aside, he sat down, even though she still stood gazing at him as if he had escaped from Bedlam. He smiled up at her, relaxing onto the upholstered chair. "Won't you sit down," he invited her politely. "The view of the garden is lovely from here."

Casting a look upward, she seated herself without a word.

While Hester coughed giggles into a handkerchief, he spoke in a low tone, as if only to her, though his voice carried well enough to reach the others. "Poor Charles enjoyed the title for a scant year before influenza finished him off. You must not have heard about his death. I'm the Earl of Hadham now."

Her slender, lace-mittened hands went still in her lap, and her intake of breath was audible as she stared at him. Chagrin replaced her distant expression. Meriel couldn't find it easy to follow her righteous indignation with an expression of conventional sympathy. Keeping her off balance, as she'd seemed in the street this morning, made her far more attractive to him than allowing her to act the cool and proper lady.

"It's all too easy to mistake who you're talking with, whether maid or mister, isn't it?" He leaned closer, as if telling secrets. "Forgive my error, thinking you were a servant this morning, and I'll overlook yours in treating me like a scoundrel who had no business in your square."

"And keep it quiet?" The rushed query was almost hissed.

"Keep what quiet?" Not that he minded. He

never talked about ladies he favored; society out-
did itself on speculation without any help from
him.

Meriel glanced quickly at her cousin and Burchett as if she had just recalled they also sat
nearby, listening. To Jonys, they didn't look offended or bored at being left to listen to the conversation.

Hester twinkled at him. "I have exceptionally
good hearing. What's to be kept quiet? And why
do you call Kept by a different name?"

"I can't answer your first question, so I'll deal
with the second." Jonys scooted his chair back a
few inches where he could see each of the others.
The pretty cousin seemed well disposed toward
him; he could use an ally in the house. "Meriel
doesn't care for his name, so she thought up one
of her own."

Hester gazed beyond him, eyebrows asking a
question, and he glanced at Meriel. Her cheeks
wine-stained, she stared off into the garden where
Kept tossed his rope and pounced on it as it
landed.

"Thought he said he saw her carry in the dog
just this morning." Burchett sounded confused as
he addressed Hester. "When did they discuss the
dog's name, if he didn't know hers?"

"Never mind now," Hester said. "I'll explain
when I understand that part myself."

"What a tiresome topic!" Meriel looked ha-
rassed, haunted. "Let's find a more general subject, please." She leaned toward Jonys. "Forget the
way Kept came to be here with me. Don't mention
it again, to anyone, I beg you."

Maybe he could guess what she wanted kept secret. Pretty Meriel was embarrassed about run-

ning into the street in her bed gown, as a proper lady would be. He'd dealt with proper ladies so little, he'd forgotten their prudish concerns. Much as he might enjoy teaching her to be less modest with him, he felt a protective urge to keep her propriety intact.

"How could I forget making the acquaintance of a lady as delightful as you?" Jonys scooted down in the chair, stretching his legs before him, crossing them at the ankles in his most comfortable pose. He settled down to watch her.

"I don't understand," Hester chimed in. "Taking in a dog without a home is nothing to hide. You should be proud to rescue a little creature from the streets."

"Indeed." Jonys lounged negligently in the chair, waiting for Meriel to explain as much or as little as she liked to the others.

Meriel's reactions were distinctly odd, giving Hester a slight shake of the head and looking almost fearful. "Let's not bore Lord Hadham."

Hester leaned forward, speaking earnestly to Meriel. "My dear, I know you too well to accept that evasion. You're obviously overset. Lord Hadham already knows what happened this morning, and you know I support you in every way. Burchett has enough influence to help us smooth ripples through society, so you needn't hold back on his account."

"It's Osborne, of course." The little widow looked almost distraught. "But these family matters don't concern the gentlemen."

Burchett nodded at Hester and gave Meriel a look of warning. "Your discretion does you honor, m'dear. You're in a difficult position here in town alone, unprotected by a male relative."

Glaring at Jonys, he continued. "If I can be of the slightest service to either of you ladies, I'm honored to do so. Whatever concerns you, I make my concern, too. Your well-being is as vital to my peace of mind as that of any member of my family."

Jonys, too, was now responsible for an extended family's welfare, and he understood the significance of the implied message. Since Burchett had fixed him with a steady stare during his pontifical speech, Jonys didn't doubt that he had been warned to treat the ladies with respect. From another man, it might have been offensive, a slur on his reputation as a gentleman.

But most men knew Jonys had been among the first to enroll in Angelo and Jackson's academies of fencing and pugilism at the Albany. He'd shattered a fair share of wafers with Manton's pistols as well. Gangly Lord Burchett led society, not sporting men, and his warning showed foolhardy courage. Jonys admired that.

"The ladies won't come to harm through me," he assured the glowering lord. "I'll join you in guarding them, as devotedly as Meriel looks after Kept for me for the present."

Burchett looked unconvinced as Hester clasped her hands. "You see, Merry! Jonys wants to help you, too," she said.

Meriel muttered something that sounded like, "Putting the fox among the chickens."

Rising, Hester stepped over Jonys's crossed ankles to kneel by Meriel. "Now will you tell us what's wrong? You've acted oddly since breakfast, though I didn't like to pry. But if something happened to worry you this much, you should let us all help."

Meriel gave Hester's hands a squeeze as she smiled at Burchett. "You're more than kind. From the way you look after Hester, I know you'll be a friend to me as well."

Jonys waited for a response to his offer of help. When Meriel didn't mention it, he felt disappointed, maybe even hurt.

Giving him a quick look, Hester spoke quietly to Meriel. "Jonys is likely to hear everything from other sources."

Staring at her hands, clasped in Hester's, Meriel nodded. Looking resigned, she spoke with little intonation. "Before dawn this morning, I saw Kept out my window, apparently abandoned. Without thinking, I ran out into the street to get him. In my night rail. Lord Hadham was close by, and we—we talked about Kept for a short time before I brought my dog inside."

Her glancing look glossed over him and Burchett before returning to Hester. "It was silly, treating it as a great secret. I just felt foolish to have taken such a thoughtless risk with things as they are."

Though he might have described the encounter differently, Jonys kept quiet, watching the other three. More seemed at stake here than a little gossip about nothing. Burchett frowned like a magistrate at the Old Bailey, and Hester no longer looked amused. Meriel appeared ready for a sentence of transportation at best.

When no one spoke, he did. "I didn't see a soul in the street while we stood in the square, not even a crier. I wouldn't worry about so small an offense. Lady Welwyn's slippers never left the cobbles, and my hands never left the reins. Surely scandal broth can't be brewed from so little even

76

if someone happened to glance out a window and see her."

A quick look passed between Hester and Burchett. This mystery grew more curious by the moment.

Meriel made a small sound in her throat and straightened her spine. Quietly, she said to him, "They're waiting for me to decide if I'll take you into my confidence. Hester and Burchett already know my peculiar circumstances." Her complexion was whiter than Hester's muslin dress as she swallowed visibly.

Kept appeared soundlessly at Meriel's chair, nosing her without getting a response. He put his paws on the edge of her seat and dropped his new toy in her lap. Making a sound between tears and laughter, she leaned over to lift him into her arms. The terrier nestled against her as she held and stroked him.

"If anybody can be trusted with a lady's secrets, I can." Jonys hoped a touch of humor would buck her up, for by now he felt sympathy with her. "Telling them is the surest way for a man to find a door locked against him."

Managing a weak smile, Meriel nodded. "Three years ago my husband died and left the sole guardianship of our two sons to his brother, a vicar, who made his home with us. I've lived quietly in the country with them until recently, enduring Osborne's set-downs and judgments, in order to be with my boys." As she kissed the top of Kept's head absently, he dipped his ears.

"A few months ago, Osborne informed me that he had enrolled them both at Eton and would live nearby as their tutor." Meriel's jaw tightened before she went on. "He ordered me to remain in the

country. I could see my boys twice a year, when
he brought them to me." Her fingers covered her
lips for a moment. "He prefers that they not be
exposed more to my worldly influence at impressionable ages."

Jonys sat up slowly. Meriel didn't seem to him
like the type who should be set aside as an unfit
mother. Prissy as Burchett was about society's
rules, he wouldn't lend countenance to any such
lady, no matter how highly connected her family.
"What does he mean by 'worldly'?"

"He means to be rid of Meriel at last and rule
his nephews as he did his brother!" Hester's anger
showed in the chops and swipes of her hands.
"Meriel was the only one Welwyn listened to on
occasion, apart from Osborne. Vicar or not, her
brother-in-law was plain and simply jealous. For
example, he said any desire of hers to dress well
or mix with society was female nonsense, a sign
she hadn't a worthwhile thought in her head."

"He might as well condemn the entire ton,"
Jonys said. Despots weren't all in high places, so
he could believe Hester's picture of the vicar. He
knew a few small-minded people who needed
large views of their own importance.

Appalled as he was, Jonys hardly knew what
more to say. He'd rather take action than talk.
"You seem young to have boys at Eton," he said
to Meriel, who looked uncomfortable at Hester's
outburst.

"James isn't yet nine," she answered briefly.
"Little Steven is seven, far too young to deal with
the rough habits and careless cruelty of older
boys."

"Osborne said they needed toughening up after
their mama's spoiling," Hester broke in, clearly

more outspoken than Meriel. "He must have made a large donation to the school to get them in before they're nine. He should be pitched into the midst of a bear baiting, with no one there to save him!"

"A painful and messy end to the problem, no doubt," Jonys observed. This was a side of the dainty cousin Jonys hadn't expected. "But a fair comparison to the situation he's pitchforked the boys into, as I recall my school days. What does your man of law advise?" Hoping to draw her out of a silent retreat, he directed the question to Meriel.

"I've seen more than one solicitor. None of them seems much concerned, patting my hands and saying I must accept that my husband knew best. If you agree, you may find your way to the door, for I don't want to hear again that nothing can be done to get my sons free of Osborne's obsessive control." Despite her obvious unhappiness, Meriel's chin and mouth showed her stubborn refusal to accept defeat.

This lady faced a daft brother-in-law with the legal system on his side. She had interviewed solicitors who had little opinion of female understanding. From personal experience, he knew her concern even for a stray dog. Meriel would love and protect her sons with her last breath.

Besides, he didn't like the notion of any parent being pushed out of a child's life unless serious harm might result to the child otherwise.

"Can't hurt for me to take a hand in this, see what I can do about getting you and your sons back in touch," he said. Three pairs of eyes jerked toward his face, staring, looking equally appalled.

"Don't you believe I can do it?" Jonys felt the

same choleric pain in his gut as from Anson's lack of faith in him to provide funds to pay the rent.

Burchett's long forehead wrinkled as he looked apologetic. "It's not exactly that, old thing. No doubt you have the best intentions in the world." He looked at Hester, confusion and embarrassment plain on his face.

"You can help me most by keeping quiet about this morning," Meriel said, raising clasped hands as if imploring him. "Harmful gossip may already be making the rounds if I were seen in near-darkness beside your curricle, talking with you in my nightdress. The chance onlooker might even wonder if you were—were leaving my house."

He had to admit he had played a part in such a scene, keeping her talking in the street as long as he could. Jonys shook his head. On the surface, things looked grim for his lovely widow. But he didn't like to linger in dark places of the mind, and he wouldn't allow her to do so, either. "Burchett, you've heard no gossip as yet?"

A shake of the head reassured Jonys. "Most tales don't grow moss before they get rolling. That's a good sign."

For the first time, Meriel showed a glimmer of hope in her golden eyes. Jonys wanted to make them shine like guineas.

"You toddle through your clubs and a rout or three tonight," he said to Burchett, "and I'll visit a few of the better gambling hells where ladies are admitted."

"Ladies of the ton?" Meriel's face and tone showed shocked disbelief, the little innocent.

No one could credit that she would act in a way to warrant losing access to her sons. No one but a person ready to destroy reputations for the sake

80

of an *on-dit* to make them feel important in the ton. Unfortunately, that described too many tongue-waggers of his acquaintance.

"Indeed," he confirmed briefly. "If your brother-in-law is blind enough to question your influence on children, he couldn't see his way out of a sedan chair. But most people trust men of God, even false prophets. If a breath of this story is out, I'll come tell you first thing tomorrow. I don't want you to fret about this any longer than necessary."

Meriel looked embarrassed. "When you're offering only help and kindness, I'm truly sorry to refuse it."

"Then don't." Despite common roots in Surrey, she didn't know him as well as she did Burchett. Jonys would have to overcome her polite concern about imposing. "I want to do all in my power to help a former neighbor."

"This is a matter of some delicacy, if you'll excuse me for stepping in, Meriel." Burchett's long face looked grave. "Sorry to be blunt, old thing, but it isn't the best notion for a man of your stamp to be calling here. If Osborne hears about it, her sons will be grown before she lays eyes on them again."

Anger jolted through Jonys and he struck his knee with a closed fist. He'd never hurt anyone on purpose in his life, apart from a few cutpurses and thieves who needed to be put out of commission for a while. "Am I so evil that I can't call on a decent woman?"

Though he didn't expect an answer to his outburst, Meriel laid a hand on his arm. "You aren't evil," she said gently. "But you must admit that the ladies you normally call on don't mind the whispers. They may even enjoy being called one of *Lord Had'em's conquests*. I, on the other hand, must avoid even the appearance of questionable behavior."

At university, his cronies had joked that he might never be Lord Hadham, but he was already *Lord Had'em*. Jonys had never paid any heed to the old by-name before this moment. "Damnation," he said, frustrated and chagrined.

Chapter Five

"Enough, Lewis!" Jonys rubbed his jaw and sat back from the table by his cold grate, littered with ledgers and papers. "Can't you give me one crumb of hope about estate affairs to encourage me? Much more of this doomsaying, and I'll join old Nosy in Spain."

"Can't afford it, sir." The Hadham estate manager gathered up loose sheets covered with neat columns of figures and summaries of needs. "I'm sorry to say you couldn't buy a set of colors, let alone equip yourself with uniforms and mounts, as things stand after the storm."

Hunching his shoulders against the tight ache at the back of his head and neck, Jonys looked at his riding crop and hat, abandoned on a chest. He'd meant to ride to Windsor today, sniffing around Eton for what he could learn about Meriel's boys, until his steward had knocked at the door.

Acting on Meriel's problems would have been easier than hearing about his own. Not that he expected to resolve all her troubles with one visit to his old school, but Jonys meant to learn more about the situation.

Burchett's visit to her yesterday, when he himself wasn't welcome, had rankled. The dandy was Hester's friend more than Meriel's. Yet he, not Jonys, had been privileged to carry the good news that no scandal stirred about their dawn meeting through London society.

"Pensions to be found for five old servants, did you say?" Jonys had best concentrate on his own business for now, even if couldn't do much about it.

"Your brother never made arrangements for two elderly retainers last year who should have been looked after. By now a total of five servants would normally have been found cottages and given a stipend." Lewis pulled one of the pages from the group in his hand and laid it on the table, pointing out various lines as he continued. "Here's the list and figures again. It also shows the pensioners already dependent on you. That's the annual amount required for their support."

The amount wasn't a large sum, considering it would support over twenty loyal lives. Their needs might be met by the sale of his curricle and pair, if the bidding were brisk when they came under the hammer. Too often, a gentleman's breakdowns didn't bring half their worth at auction. Still, selling his carriage and prads would bring in enough to feed these old people who had served his family far better than it appeared he could serve them.

"The damages to tenant cottages and outbuildings. Can't any of the repairs wait?" The storms that had washed London street wastes into low-lying areas a week ago had devastated Surrey, by Lewis's account.

As his man searched the papers once more, Jonys fingered the folded letters he'd laid aside. Once he'd heard the worst his estate manager had to report, he would read his mama's crossed lines, usually a litany of bewilderment. She still couldn't comprehend that the comfortable life provided by his father was lost. Like a pretty canary kept in a conservatory, Mama would never survive being turned out into the real world.

At least little Claire's message would be one of unmixed affection. He could guess at the state of her health by the number of lines she felt up to writing.

His steward pulled two more sheets from his stack, laying them side by side on the table. "These materials would put eleven cottages and the dairy under roof again. The well-house was flattened, and that can't wait. Though the sty roof can be put off, its south wall cannot."

Waving away pages that would loom at him out of the dark, Jonys wished he could escape to Jackson's for half an hour. Just long enough to put on the gloves and punch the bag until his arms ached as much as his head.

It wasn't that he didn't grasp the numbers or the needs set before him by his agent; he understood them too well. What to do about them was a different matter, and staring at marks on papers couldn't cure the estate's wasting illness. He wanted action, not endless pages of problems with no answers at easy command.

"Never mind, Lewis. The numbers mount up to a total that might as well match the Treasury's debt, for all the hope I have to pay it." He rubbed the back of his aching neck under his limp linen shirt collar. The starch had gone out of him, too. "I don't question your figures; you've done an admirable job of sizing up the latest emergency and setting out plans to deal with it. I wish I could find even half what you need to repair the storm's damages and make the estate productive again."

"Thank you, sir." Lewis looked exhausted. Well he might, after coping with the aftermath of the windstorm, maybe a tornado, then riding to London to report it. Nature's insensate destruction had doubled the sum Jonys couldn't raise before the storm. Maybe God was exacting payment from him for every misstep by Hadhams over centuries. No, couldn't be that or the entire estate would have blown away.

Even this grim levity improved his mood. Searching his pocket for a few coins, he passed them over to Lewis. "Anson will give you dinner and make you a pallet for the night. Sorry I can't offer you better fare and quarters after your hard ride, but we're keeping ourselves a little short these days. At least you must drink to the King's health. Do you recall the location of the pub nearest here?"

Looking reluctant, Lewis took the brass. "Indeed, sir. And I'll drink to your health as well, to better purpose, I daresay, God save Farmer George." As he pocketed the paltry sum, Lewis studied Jonys. "Your father never thought it'd come to this, did he, sir? He thought he left matters in good heart."

Jonys nodded. "And so he did. We can't blame him for the disasters brought on by bad weather and poor crops, or by the government's hand in our pockets." Maligning Charles for high living in his short year as earl would be the pot calling the kettle black.

Lowering a closed fist onto the sheaf listing financial obligations, laid on the table again by Lewis, Jonys wished he'd been born a tinker's son. Maybe not that. But before the anxiety of such debts fell to him with the title, he had never realized the weight of a few sheets of foolscap.

Rising, Lewis picked up his low-crowned countryman's hat. "Two more things I'd like to say to you, sir. One, Hadham people trust you. Not a tenant is leaving as long as they can eat. If you provide materials and seed, they'll make repairs and plant winter crops as well as summer. Pensioners have offered to help out, even ones who can barely walk. And none of the servants who should be pensioned off by now has said the first word to me about it."

Mixed pride and grief for his people stuck in Jonys's throat, requiring him to swallow a few times. How could he hesitate to do what he must to pull the estate through these difficult times, when his people showed faith in him?

Lewis came as close to smiling as his laconic nature allowed. "Your father didn't push you to learn estate business as he didn't see the need. I thought he was shortsighted at the time and said so to his face. But what's done's done." He dismissed the past with a backward nod.

"The other thing is this: The old earl would be

proud of you, Jonys. You were closest to his heart, even if you weren't the heir."

Scraping back his chair to stand, Jonys stuck out his hand. A man couldn't answer that speech. It filled a hole in his heart that ached like a bad tooth. His father's affection had been as rarely expressed as his praise, and Lewis had handed him both when he needed the encouragement most.

Their hands, calloused from different causes, met and clung as Lewis continued. "Your father liked a man who faced a fight head-on, and Anson tells me you're doing that. Good fortune with the widow, sir, for that's the sensible step to take in these circumstances. The old earl would approve."

The sense of support seeped away. Lewis assumed Jonys stood at the brink of marrying the fortune they needed. He'd based his claim that the old earl would be proud of him on it. And Jonys hadn't considered it seriously yet, let alone accepted the necessity.

Falling into a wing chair as Anson sent Lewis on his way to a pub, Jonys slumped down with his legs stretched out. He propped his elbows on the chair arms, his chin on folded hands. Maybe he'd best admit a better idea wasn't likely to knock him over the head in time to set the estate right.

Anson closed the door quietly behind himself and came to stand before Jonys. "The end of the ham and a loaf will have to do for our dinner, with apples and cheese after. You might want to wheedle a few dinner invitations next week."

Jonys stared at the empty fire dogs, reminded of Skype's smutty color and eager eyes. The little terrier's company would be welcome right now; a dog always seemed to know when a body or mind needed comfort. "You're right. I have to do it, and do it at once, Anson."

"No need to rush out to your club this instant. You'll do better to drop in on a few routs, as ladies are more likely to ask you to a dinner party than their husbands."

"You mistake my meaning. What you're right about is your widow." Jonys hooked the underside of a chair with his toe and pulled it forward. "I'm not paying you, so you needn't stand about in mock servility when we talk."

Anson lowered himself onto the chair, leaning forward. "Then you'll choose one of the two ladies we discussed to court." His old eyes glinted.

"Past time to be choosy. I've met Lady Welwyn, and the other one can't suit me better." Until now, he had felt distaste about taking a wife for her fortune. As he considered the problems Meriel already faced, guilt tapped him on the shoulder for piling his predicament on hers. But he'd already decided to look into the situation with the brother-in-law, so maybe they could help each other out. If the benefits of the marriage weren't one-sided, maybe he wasn't doing her a disservice.

Knowing what had to be done, Jonys wanted to get on with it. "Just one small rub in the way, but I'll deal with that. Lady Welwyn doesn't care for me to call on her, as my rakish reputation could make her brother-in-law think she's my *petite amie*. Says he's the guardian of her boys and he wouldn't let her visit them at all if he even sniffed scandal."

Anson leaned back, laconic. "That's what you call a minor obstacle, Master Douglas? You've decided to wed a lady who doesn't want you in her house." The old valet looked sour as a green lemon. "Do you plan on wooing her by messenger?"

Jonys grinned, the memory of dappled sunlight on her rich brown curls lifting his spirits further. "No, I mean to get her in my arms again, if you must know."

"Again?" Anson perked up in a way that reminded Jonys of Skype coming to attention, ears perked.

"Never mind that," Jonys said briefly. "First I need to figure out how to spend time with Meriel without harming her reputation. I came close enough to that when she dashed into the square in her bed gown. You're always going on about propriety; you should have a thought or two on the subject."

If he did, the old man wasn't in a rush to speak up. Anson tented his hands. He stared at the shadowed ceiling, his polished slippers, his gnarled knuckles. Finally, he looked over them at Jonys. "Go to church."

Irritation brought Jonys upright. "Doesn't that put the cart before the horse? I have to get close enough to propose before I meet Meriel at the altar."

"If you want to keep company with her without starting unsavory rumors, you must meet her again, as if for the first time, only more properly. Then you'll need a reason to be where she is. Which means going into social circles you've avoided, Master Douglas." The old man sounded certain of his advice. "The most unexceptionable place to meet a lady and mingle with the ton is at the Chapel Royal."

"Just the ticket! Surely being presented to her where God, the Queen of England, and the royal princesses come together would leave even the vicar brother-in-law nothing to complain of." Jonys could also introduce Meriel to a lady of the ton at the chapel who welcomed his calls, which would bring him some small satisfaction. "A lady of social consequence can introduce us, as if for the first time, in the chapel at St. James Palace. Meriel could receive me then, and I could begin meeting her at routs."

"If you can bring about an introduction by a reputable lady." Anson's tone and pinched nostrils showed his doubts about that.

Jonys would show the old man he hadn't entirely wasted his time before inheriting the title. Elizabeth, Lady Melborne, a respected hostess of *bon ton*, attended services at the Chapel Royal as faithfully as the Queen. Among his set, she was known for advising clever young men like Byron on life and love. The vicountess had a soft spot for an amusing rake, and she could be swayed to help promote a sensible match for him.

"I'll wager my best cravat against your worst that two days from now, I'll be sitting in a pew at the Chapel Royal by invitation of a ton leader." Unless lightning struck him down for desecrating holy premises with his presence, he'd reenter polite society again, too.

"This," Jonys assured his skeptical valet, "is something I can do. You see, I know just the lady to help me."

Anson stood and started out of the room. "I'm not daft enough to wager against your success with any lady."

"What better way to spend a Thursday evening than looking at art with two lovely ladies."

91

So far, Burchett had gazed at Hester instead of the paintings, furnishings, and curiosities on preview in these Pall Mall auction rooms. Meriel smiled at the pair, who seemed unconscious of Christie's treasures except as a background to their conversation.

While they admired each other, she would search for the pier glass and table she wanted to lighten the entry hall. Besides, auctions were an entertainment to a lady who had been immured in the country. From the size of the crowd here tonight, townspeople enjoyed them just as much.

The mixture of French, Italian, and Dutch furnishings and works of art lulled Meriel into an entranced state. Oddities of every texture and pattern tempted her on from one item to the next until she reached a corner without her two friends. A waist-high porcelain vase of clamoring colors was large enough to hide in; it would never do for a household with children. Especially boys.

Meriel sighed. Active as he was, Kept could send it tumbling, too, if he bounced against it at full flight.

"I swan, I never saw anything so bizarre," said Hester, somewhere ahead of her.

"Quite," agreed Burchett, adding in haste, "Come along and see this japanned cabinet." He sounded embarrassed.

Among statuary and shuffling gawkers, Meriel located her cousin standing close to Burchett. Curious about what had attracted Hester's attention and appalled him, Meriel edged through the throng to join them.

"Where would you put such a thing, in one of those bathing rooms installed in houses these days?" The ostrich feather on her yeoman's hat swayed as Hester considered the table before her.

"Actually, it's a fine piece," Burchett assured her, tugging on her elbow, "though hardly one I'd expect to see in a house occupied only by ladies." No doubt he was flustered by Hester's forthright talk of personal ablutions in a public place, or by the visions it inspired.

Hester turned to him, and silver flashed from an inlaid table's surface before them. "But no visitors would see it except houseguests, if it held towels and lotions in a bathing room."

Amused by their discussion, Meriel considered the antiquity under debate, now that she could see all of it. The square ebony top was supported by four curved legs, carved to represent the female figure in complete realism and near undress. Silver inlay glinted wickedly in the light of a nearby chandelier with clustered prisms, also to be auctioned from someone's estate.

"This oddity was very likely sent here for sale by a bride who didn't care for her husband's taste in furniture. Not what a lady would choose, I assure you," Burchett said. He urged first Hester and then her to move on. "Come see the Chinese jade carvings instead."

"I rather like it," Meriel said, mostly to tease the staid lord. Living with Hester seemed to be awakening habits from her girlhood that she had lost against the somber backdrop of her married life.

Raising a quizzing glass to study it, he shuddered. "Can't think why. I always thought it was enough to give a body nightmares."

Hester pounced. "Then you know who consigned it here for sale. Tell us who owns such a sensuous work of art, at once."

"Can't say for certain. Might not be the same

Pat Cody

table." Backing away from the sinuous curves before them, Lord Burchett looked alarmed by Hester's playful request.

"Do you expect us to believe two of these oddities might exist in London?" Hester stalked him
step for step. "Obviously it's someone we know, or
you wouldn't mind saying who's selling off valuable furnishings."

Meriel touched the carved curls on one of the
voluptuous table legs. The mention of selling off
personal property reminded her of Jonys selling
his phaeton and pair. This piece was probably an
original commission of a century or more ago,
brought back from a Grand Tour, and not one to
fit into every drawing room.

The exotic table would suit a bachelor's rooms,
a libertine's lair. A picture formed in her mind of
the rake with sapphire eyes glowing dangerously
under brows as black as the ebony table.

"Lord Burchett, is it fair to say that most objects
of this value at Christie's aren't offered for sale
unless the owner needs funds urgently?" Meriel
asked as she examined the silver inlay for loose
bits or buckling and found none. The fine old
piece had been cared for and about, it appeared.
It would make an excellent investment at the right
price.

"Generally that's true." Burchett watched her
with an uneasy air; Hester, with curiosity.

"Without revealing a friend's financial embar-
rassments, can you confirm that we both know the
owner of this table?" Meriel wasn't normally this
cryptic, but people filled Christie's rooms tonight,
jostling past at their elbows as they looked over
treasures before the next auction.

"The owner and I are on visiting terms," Bur-

94

chett said cautiously. "I wouldn't want to call him your friend, just a slight acquaintance. It wouldn't be proper for me to discuss his situation with you, so you mustn't ask me anything more."

"But we know the same dog, the owner and I." His reluctant nod confirmed her guess.

Leaning closer and lowering her voice, Meriel murmured, "Would you act for me in the auction to buy this piece?" She couldn't say what prompted her impulsive decision. Maybe she felt beholden to Jonys for realizing her anxiety about gossip and keeping quiet about it. Maybe she hoped that returning his table would stop him from claiming Kept.

Burchett put a fist to his brow and closed his eyes. "No, Meriel. I can't encourage you in a scandalous action by helping you buy this. You don't want this outrageous table in your town house. What if Osborne comes snooping? Imagine what he'd make of it, and you, for choosing it."

Walking around the table, Meriel stopped to smile at his anguished expression. "Don't fret. The table won't be delivered to my house. I don't have a separate bathing room, and Hester can't think of another use for it. I suppose I'll have to return it to my slight acquaintance."

Lord Burchett flapped his arms like useless wings, then turned to her cousin. "Hester, m'dear, talk sense to Meriel." He looked about furtively and lowered his voice to a pleading hiss. "You're flirting with disaster, buying a table this recognizable and giving it back to a well-known seducer. If word gets out, the worst will be said about the reason behind such a gift."

"Phoo, who's to know she's involved if you handle the transaction entirely?" Hester said. "And flirting is exactly what I've encouraged Merry to do." From Hester's twinkling eyes, Muriel realized she supported the purchase. "Though this gift goes a trifle beyond what I had in mind for a first effort at coquetry."

"Exactly! It's beyond what a lady may give a gentleman, even a close family connection." Burchett looked back and forth between them, when he wasn't whipping around to be certain no one listened. "I'm only trying to keep you from a foolish action for your own good," he assured Meriel.

His concern had made her question the purchase for a moment, until he'd uttered the same claim Osborne had piously intoned to imprison her with his will.

"This is only a gesture of gratitude to an old family acquaintance," Meriel argued, "a compensation to him for bringing me Kept. The table is obviously a family piece from a Grand Tour. His mama would be upset to think it went out of the family; I recall her pride in Hadham's treasures."

Making Jonys this gift wasn't a risk; she was certain of it. Earlier in the week no one had seen her in the square with him, and that situation had been truly dangerous, unlike this one, with Hester's cicisbeo to act for her.

Lord Burchett looked about at the crowd, unconvinced.

"I owe him more than a book," Muriel went on. "Besides, giving a copy of *Childe Harold* to a man of more sensual experience than Lord Byron would be sending coals to Newcastle," she concluded. "I'd rather return something meaningful he's lost. Anonymously, of course."

Hester traced the top of Burchett's clenched hands with one yellow-gloved finger as she looked up at him. "We can find someone else to help us buy the table, if you'd rather not take part."

Burchett groaned. "I never dreamed you would stoop to manipulation, m'dear. I thought better of you."

"Excellent." Hester patted his gloved hand. "Now you're beginning to see me realistically."

Asking for a man's help felt wrong. Besides, Meriel didn't want anyone coerced into an uncomfortable act. "Never mind, Burchett; you have no reason to be involved in this. My solicitor can arrange the entire transaction."

"No, I'll bid it in if you can't be persuaded against such foolishness." Burchett glanced about again and whispered, "But I must warn you that Jonys is being called a fortune hunter among his own cronies. Seeing this table here at Christie's for auction confirms that he's short of the ready."

For a moment the chandelier's light dimmed. Meriel touched her handkerchief to her mouth and tucked it into her reticule. "Is he? I'm not surprised to hear it."

Foolish, to feel a little disappointed in Jonys. He was nothing more to her than a neighbor from the past who had done her a service. She would give him the table and feel no further obligation.

Seeing Hester's look of sympathy, Meriel continued in a dismissive tone. "He's acting sensibly, which any reasonable person applauds. If his brother only held the title for a year, the estate paid double death duties, and coffers can't withstand such a demand easily."

Her friends looked unconvinced but held their tongues.

By controlling her inheritance from her aunt, Meriel understood more about wealth and its management than most women were permitted to know. "If Jonys is reduced to selling off his carriage and furnishings, I feel sorry for his mama and little sisters. I admired Lady Hadham and her lovely flowers as a girl. All the more reason to slip the family a bit of help without making a show of it."

Burchett shook his head and murmured, "I've pointed out the perils of the situation. That's all I can do to discourage you, I suppose. I'm not a male relative, or even a connection by marriage." He glanced quickly at Hester and away.

As she took one of his arms, Meriel took the other. Lord Burchett's concern rose out of friendship, even if he was inclined to be overly protective. Pressing his sleeve lightly, she said, "I'd far rather have you as a helpful friend than a restrictive male relation."

The footman showed Jonys into Lady Melborne's common sitting-parlor. That was a good omen, not being consigned to the formality of the drawing room. Almost at once, he heard a whisper of silk approaching. Jonys walked forward to greet Lady Melborne.

"You utter rascal!" She entered with her plump white hands extended. "When did you last show your handsome face at one of my salons? I shouldn't have been At Home to you today, or any other day, when you can't make time to exchange ideas in my little meetings of minds."

"You know I lose all rational thought as well as my tongue when I'm close to you." He caught up her hands and bussed each in turn.

With clouds of white hair, Elizabeth looked a few steps beyond middle age, but her lovely eyes and shrewd mind made the signs of advancing time unimportant. Her lively interest in people and daily happenings kept others intrigued by her. Like most younger men, he enjoyed her wit and spirit more than the company of many far younger ladies.

Reaching up to cradle his square jaw briefly with a scented hand, she said, "You've never lost anything around a lady, particularly not your heart. I don't know why any of my sex wastes a moment with you."

Putting an arm about her comfortable girth, Jonys guided her to a seat on a sofa that looked into nodding tree branches in the park. "Must be the misplaced female hope of saving the wicked from an ecstatic downfall," he observed.

"Not when the incorrigible man is beyond redemption." Elizabeth still knew how to use fine dark eyes to advantage.

"Don't say you've given up on me now, just when I'm counting on you to redeem me." Jonys pressed her hand briefly as he sat down beside her. Flirting with a lady of wit and intelligence was always a pleasure.

"Reforming your ways at last, my dear?" Shrewd eyes sized him up. "I expected something of the sort from whispers I've heard. An extra watch has been posted on every impressionable young heiress making a come-out this season."

Anson's efforts to squelch rumors hadn't worked any more than Jonys had expected; the ton suspected his pockets were to let. He shrugged. "I'd terrify a sweet young thing as much as she'd bore me. Not that I'm likely to meet one, unless you're kind enough to ease my way back into your friends' good graces."

"That could prove amusing." Studying him from boots to pate, she tapped her full lower lip with a forefinger. "In general, a man who's played on the fringes of society for years doesn't step to its center until he wants a wife. Is that what you're after?"

Rubbing his jaw, Jonys grinned. "I don't know that 'want' is the most accurate way to put it. Maybe 'need a wife' says it correctly. The estate's in serious trouble if I don't find the funds to make it productive again."

"You won't be the first man or the last to rebuild his fortune on his wife's. Have you considered offering your title as an attraction to one of the wealthy papas in trade?"

Jonys shook his head. "I can't afford to rule any possibility out, but I'd prefer a lady who's comfortable in good society. Two of my sisters should have come-outs as soon as they're out of blacks, and Mama's nerves won't stand up to the rigors of a season without support. Besides, she needs to stay with Claire."

"Your youngest sister isn't growing stronger?" Elizabeth's sympathy showed in her expression.

Again, he shook his head. Speaking about his worries for his favorite sister was difficult, even with this old friend. "She's better at some times than others."

"That's usually the way with a weak chest. Summer is coming on, and often the condition improves with that season. We'll have to find you a wife so you can look after your estate and sisters properly." Elizabeth made it sound like a simple matter as she patted his knee.

"With all possible haste." No need to wait about once you recognized an action must be taken.

"You do require a more mature lady," she agreed. "Someone whose first marriage has left her susceptible to an amusing rogue with laughing eyes, perhaps. With a considerable fortune, naturally. Though I'm not well acquainted with either lady, a couple of candidates come to mind."

Leaning back, Jonys stretched out his legs, relieved that he didn't have to take anyone's pig in a poke for a wife. "As it happens, I have a lady in my eye already. We've met, though that information is for your ears alone."

Distinctive dark brows rose. "If she's been exposed to your captivating ways, I can't think why you need my help."

"You give me more credit than I deserve." He made a mocking sketch of a bow. "The lady is proper. And she tells me that my visits can compromise a lady's reputation." That opinion still rankled.

"A lady beyond her first youth, a widow such as I have in mind, wouldn't let a little gossip stop her from enjoying your company."

"My widow would. Not that I don't understand her reasons. She doesn't want to be deprived of visits with her sons, and she believes association with a known womanizer raises questions about her morals."

Jonys slid onto his spine, crossing his arms over his chest. He'd never thought about his reputation as anything but a jest between men, something like calling that old skinflint Jessington by the name Lord Bountiful. He simply appreciated ladies, and they returned the favor.

Lady Melborne nodded. "You refer to Lady Welwyn, of course. I heard talk of the will that left her brother-in-law sole authority over her sons. The other widow who came to my mind, Lady Helsby, is more like the ladies you usually keep company with."

"This is marriage we're discussing, not pleasure. Meriel is just what I want in a wife." How annoying of Elizabeth to agree with Anson on which widow should attract him. He was hardly a boy to be told which mount to ride for his safety and comfort. As many ladies as he'd fancied and experienced over the years, he must know his own mind and tastes now if he ever would.

"Poor thing. I wouldn't like to have the Reverend Lord Lamport's self-righteous eye on me." Elizabeth stared into the distance. "Though I respect your widow's wish to be discreet because of Osborne, I don't see the need to make private choices on the grounds of public opinion."

This philosophy didn't surprise Jonys. Society's guesses about the fathers of Elizabeth's children, apart from the heir who resembled Lord Melborne, had circulated for years. As close-mouthed as she was about her own business, he trusted her to handle his with discretion.

"Since my intentions are honorable this time, Meriel doesn't need to worry. I don't mean to give her a slip on the shoulder." Jonys wasn't such a bad fellow: He didn't despoil virgins or allow a lady to expect anything but mutual pleasure. "A romp in the hay won't put a roof on Hadham's barn. I have to wed her, and at once. If you'll help me back into the right circles, I can talk with Meriel, reassure her that I won't add to her problems with the stern vicar."

"Letting people know that you're now looking for a wife, not an irregular liaison, may reduce gossip about ladies you show attentions," Elizabeth agreed. "But considering the urgency of your need to wed, two strings to your bow would be better than one. Wooing both widows at once shouldn't overexert a man of your talents." She looked a question at him.

"Playing my old games wouldn't even take thought, but I have serious responsibilities now. I'm as duty-bound as any firstborn son to take a wife who serves the family interests. Because the estate's needs can't wait, I can't, either."

Though what he'd said was true enough, he just didn't want to consider the other widow. Something about Meriel appealed to him besides the obvious allure that twisted a man about a pretty little thumb. Maybe it was because she needed his help, whether she admitted it or not. But whatever the reason, he wouldn't waste effort on this Lady Helsby when he meant to have Meriel.

Elizabeth sighed. "If your heart's set on the countess, I'll do what I can to throw the two of you together in proper circumstances."

"My heart has nothing to do with it; my purse is what's empty." Even an old campaigner like Elizabeth had to stick a rose of romance into the middle of a sensible arrangement of pennycress. He liked Meriel more than other ladies who might serve as Hadham's countess, and he could deal with the troublesome vicar. He was proposing a straightforward exchange of favors, not hearts.

A half smile on her generous mouth, Elizabeth gazed at him with an expression very much like pity. "Being a sensible fellow, the fit of a wife into your future doesn't concern you nearly as much as the fit of a coat. Very well. How do you want me to help, by inviting you both to a dinner party?"

"Nothing as riotous as that," Jonys assured her with a grin. "Tomorrow I want you to introduce me to the widowed Lady Welwyn at the Chapel Royal."

Peals of laughter followed a momentary silence. Elizabeth finally fumbled for her handkerchief and dabbed at her eyes. "We'll arrive just before the Queen and make a grand entrance. Everyone will assume I'm quite as mad as poor George, leading you in like a tame pug, but they'll mob us after the services to welcome you back into the fold. Out of vulgar curiosity, of course. I can hardly wait to see the lambs gather around the wolf as he tells everyone what a good dog he is!"

Trust Lady Melborne to secure a pew more than halfway along the wide aisle centering the Chapel Royal, with more people to pass on the way out than in a review of troops. Holding his hat like a shield, Jonys came to attention and marched forward over the carpet behind Elizabeth.

Ahead of them, people stood about instead of leaving the chapel after the royal party's departure. In his wake, the blurred murmur of Sunday voices sank to a sibilant whisper.

Keeping his expression pleasant and his gaze on Elizabeth, he felt raking glances from all sides. He summoned the faces of his sisters, his mama, and Hadham's oldest pensioners as a spur forward. Doing his duty let him feel better about himself, but that didn't make every step toward saving his estates easy.

Elizabeth, Lady Melborne, looked serenely about, singling out acquaintances to remind of their friendship with his father. Jonys responded to words of condolence on the untimely loss of his brother while he endured rude stares of curiosity and parried nosy questions. People who had known his parents well saw putting him through a catechism as taking a proper interest. A sense of humor helped keep a smile on his face.

Fat old Lord Carrington clapped him on the shoulder. "Got to get over rough ground the best way you can, m'boy. Just don't pick a horse with a tendency to take the bit and run with it, if you get my drift."

Lady Carrington appeared to be deaf without knowing it, as she didn't seem to listen anyway. "Never saw the sense in entails, myself," she announced in a voice that reverberated like cannon fire through a valley. "What's the use of land you can't sell without money to make it pay? I hear your mama tried to sell her jewels and discovered they were all paste."

"You mustn't fret over an old friend's disaster that didn't happen," Jonys reassured her. "Most of the Hadham jewelry is also entailed and can't be sold any more than the land."

"Paste!" the lady declared to her husband before facing Jonys again. "Hope you didn't switch them, you young rapscallion. Your poor, dear mama; two sons, both wastrels." Shaking her head until her bonnet shifted on her cap, Lady Carrington seized her husband's arm and steered him away.

If a few people hadn't pulled away and hurried down the aisle to the exit, Jonys would have just grinned and forgotten it. He required all the support he could get, instead of people believing the worst of him.

"Never mind the Carringtons," Elizabeth said to him in an undertone as she turned him toward a bent-over lady who peered up at him sideways.

Pat Cody

"You recall your father's godmother Lady Farlow, no doubt."

"I remember you," the old lady quavered. "Used to cling to my leg when I came to call until I gave you my reticule to distract you. Already knew how to get what you wanted from a lady, you did. And you have no trouble now from the looks of you, fine strapping lad that you are."

Jonys bowed over her hand as if she were a duchess, which she might be, for all he could remember in this welter of names, titles, and faces buzzing around him. Only one face mattered, and he had yet to catch a glimpse of her.

"Go on with you," Lady Farlow said, yanking the strings on her reticule tighter. "You'll be taking away another lady's reticule, I suppose, if you must find over thirty thousand pounds at once, as I hear?" The rise to her voice made it an outright question.

"I'm sure you know more about it than I, for I haven't enjoyed a good gossip lately." He grinned at her.

"Cheeky as ever." Sighing, she patted his sleeve. "Just choose a girl young enough to bear you strong sons. You don't want one with narrow hips, mark my words."

The glint in the old lady's eye tickled Jonys. He bowed. "If you'll have me, I'll wed you at once."

Laughing up at him until she staggered slightly, the old lady said, "Bless you, my boy, that's the best jest I've heard this age." She hobbled away still chuckling.

"Careful what you say, Hadham. You could find yourself married on the spot if you make that offer to the wrong lady." Lord Holland stood smiling at him when Jonys turned.

106

"Expediency is a cruel master." A week would suit his plans nicely, if Jonys could persuade the bride to a special license and a quick exchange of vows.

"Then it's true that you're hanging out for a wife? The rumor's going around the clubs." Holland shook his head, smiling. "What a man will do for love is nothing compared to what he does for money. Perhaps I could help you out with the brass, though not the lady. I might be able to put you in the way of a good investment, if you're interested."

"Very kind of you. I'll let you know when I have something to invest." Feeling his sporting blood rise, Jonys wished he had a few extra quid. He looked past the Whig party whip. "Where's your good lady, sir? And your guests?"

Holland looked over his shoulder. "They were with me, but I suppose my lady stopped to speak with someone."

The crowd shifted, and Jonys caught a glimpse of Hester's smiling face. Surely Meriel was close behind her.

Inside his gloves, his palms went damp. He had best tame the race around his ribs between his stomach and heart, or he'd stammer to Meriel like a youth standing up with a girl for the first time.

"Here come the ladies," Lady Melborne said as she put out a hand. Jonys stood by anxiously while she exchanged greetings with Lady Holland, for he didn't see Meriel in the passing parade of bonnets.

Then the two younger women appeared, looking for Lady Holland. "Little wonder we were separated," the older lady said to their apologies, "with the unusual attendance at service this morning." She gave Jonys a significant look.

At last he was face-to-face with Meriel. Her startled eyes looked more brown than gold in this dim light, and he doubted she heard any more of their introduction than he did. The meeting he'd arranged with the help of the two society hostesses was a surprise to her, as he'd meant it to be.

"I'm delighted to see you again after so many years," he said with emphasis on time's passage. "Your father let me ride any mount in his stable when I was a lad, and your cook gave me cakes. We'll have to catch up on family news one day soon."

Bowing over her hand, he pressed her fingers, caressing them with far more familiarity than a gentleman should. He would only carry this charade of good manners so far.

Snatching her hand away, Meriel inclined her head slightly. "Yes, I knew your mama much better than you boys, of course, and your sisters were still in the nursery. I hope they're all well."

Good. He had inspired a cool tone that no one would hear as encouraging. Let the old biddies write the vicar about that, if they wished. "My youngest sister Claire isn't in the best of health, but Susan and Emily are eager to make their bows."

As Hester offered her hand, she cast him a coquette's look from under long lashes. "I'm delighted to meet you, Lord Hadham. Perhaps we'll see more of you at routs this season, since you've come into the title."

"You may count on it, Lady Stanford. Changes in my responsibilities have altered my style of life considerably." Jonys hoped Meriel heard the truth behind those words.

A stir in the crowd toward the main chapel door led them all to look in that direction. A gloved hand waved above a plumed bonnet.

"I don't believe any of you have met the two people hurrying this way," said Lady Melborne.

This was unexpected. Jonys hadn't planned a second introduction.

A fair lady with a beaming smile pushed through the dwindling stream of people walking out of the chapel, followed by a burly chap who looked lost. "There you are, Lady Melborne," cried the lady, extending both hands. "I feared I wouldn't find you in the crush. Richard and I—he's my *brother*, Sir Richard Dabbs, not my *husband*, for I'm a *widow*—we were late arriving and had to sit in the back."

"Not to worry, you've found me," Lady Melborne said, stopping the flow of words. "Let me tell you who my friends are, for you've almost managed to introduce yourself, Lady Helsby."

Jonys felt he knew the lady indeed, from the glances she poured over him like hot milk over toast. She had made her status plain at once. Widowed and Available.

The name fell into its place of recognition. Lady Helsby. Elizabeth and Anson's second widow, with control of her considerable fortune. Thank God Meriel hadn't been cut from the same cloth.

Grinning at the first sincere prayer he'd offered up since he arrived in the Chapel Royal, Jonys realized that the Widow Helsby held her hand almost under his nose. He must have missed the formal presentation to her. Taking her fingertips on his glove, he bowed above it. "How do you do," he said with perfect propriety.

The pretty little widow seized his hand in both

of hers before he could withdraw it. Her fingers pressed his significantly. "I'm excessively pleased to make your acquaintance," she said, lovely blue eyes sliding up his chest to his mouth before meeting his eyes. "I've heard the most delightful things about you over the teacups, and I just can't wait to discover for myself if they're true."

Responding to a pretty lady's hints from long practice, Jonys pressed her hand more warmly before letting go. He didn't step back as one generally did to show proper respect for a lady, just smiled down into her bright, upturned face. "Never believe anything you hear about a gentleman until you've proved it to your own satisfaction."

A slight stir in the group made Jonys look away from Lady Helsby. Hester cast him a reproachful look. Meriel had turned away, shoulders stiff, elbows tucked tightly against the sides of her pelisse.

Hester touched Lady Holland's arm. "We'll be close by," she said quietly. "Meriel and I want to study this hand-painted ceiling while we have the opportunity, so please take a great deal of time with your friends."

Jonys looked after Meriel. Things couldn't have happened better if he'd planned every event. No one would suspect his interest in Meriel, with Lady Helsby making blatant sheep's eyes at him. Not until he had married the widow of his choice, safe against the vicar's meddling.

That was the only reason he'd played up to the second widow. Her effusions threw dust in the eyes of any spies reporting to Osborne. Meriel would understand perfectly when he got her alone to propose marriage.

Chapter Six

"Are you certain you won't come, Meriel? You know Burchett and I enjoy having you with us." Hester stood near the library door with the dandy, pulling on primrose gloves.

After yesterday's quiet Sunday at the Chapel Royal and at home, Meriel knew her cousin was eager to wander through Oxford Street shops and greet friends. "Thank you both, but no. I plan to read this copy of *The Lady's Monthly Museum* from cover to cover this afternoon. I hope you enjoy yourselves as much as I will." Sitting down to devour a publication all at one time was an indulgence she savored.

Giving her a look over his shoulder as if to reassure her that he would return, Kept escorted Hester and Burchett out into the entry hall. Meriel relaxed into her comfortable chair as the door closed; she needed time alone, unlike her outgoing cousin.

The library door swung open again, and Kept ambled through. The footman grinned at her before closing it behind the terrier. Patting the arm of her comfortable, upholstered chair, Meriel said, "Come, Kept. Come sit on my lap while I read."

Sniffing at the carpet as if he didn't hear her, Kept wandered about the room. The independent little Scots dog rarely obeyed at once, as if he took time to choose what he would do in most circumstances. Completing a loop, he approached the footstool and leaped up beside her feet.

"Come!" Meriel invited again, patting her lap. As he grew more attached to her, he complied with her wishes more often. The terrier turned once where he stood and sat down on the stool, ears back, looking around. She picked up her journal and settled to read it.

Just as she became engrossed in an essay of warning to mothers who read fairy tales to their children, Kept climbed onto her shins. Balancing like a tightrope walker, he teetered up her legs to her lap, pushing the publication aside with swipes of his broad black nose.

Meriel laughed and laid aside the periodical. "I thought getting on with my reading might draw you up here. You can't bear for my attention to focus on anything besides you, can you?"

Turning his head, Kept looked at her, white rims showing under the dark orbs. Meriel scratched his neck first, then rubbed behind his ears until he made breathy sounds of pleasure. Soon he lay down on her lap, turning his tummy up with his head toward her knees. She stroked the soft sides of his bare belly and thighs until he stretched himself, then swiped his paws together over his nose like a baby's fists. Soon his eyes drifted half closed.

Down the hall, she heard the entrance door open, and Kept's ears came to attention. She felt his muscles bunch, ready to leap up if he were needed as a guard or escort. Then he relaxed again. The caller must have left a card and gone away. Picking up *The Lady's Monthly*, Meriel looked for her place in the piece she had begun reading, stroking Kept with one hand.

The library door clicked open. Closing the publication on her finger to mark her place, Meriel looked up as Kept turned his head toward the sound.

Jonys came in, brilliant blue eyes finding her at once across the room, as if drawn by a magnet. Kept's tail thumped her tummy as he looked at Jonys upside down.

Caught by surprise, she said sharply, "Was no one in the hall to see you in?"

"Yes, a footman tried to do the proper thing and escort me here, but I assured him we don't stand on ceremony with each other." His gaze took a thorough inventory of her, as if she might misplace an arm or foot in the intervals between their meetings.

"Indeed. I'll have to speak to that footman." A lady liked a few seconds to prepare her expression and mind for a caller. Particularly one who required her to put up her guard.

"No, don't berate the lad because I insisted on finding my own way." Jonys's winsome smile slipped under her guard too easily. "He tried to do his duty, but I was too fast for him."

"You're too fast for most *hers* as well." Remaining cool with Jonys was impossible when he aimed his captivating smile her way. Besides, she found more pleasure in their repartee with each meeting. "I'll have wine brought in for you if you don't mind ringing. As you see, I'm pinned down by this sleepy pup."

"No, thank you. I'll just drink in the sight of a lady so enchanting she can soothe the wildest dog." He crossed the room with his prowling grace, managing to look languid and poised for action at the same time. His steady, warm regard both unsettled and pleased her.

Glancing down at Kept, he stepped behind her chair and leaned on its back. "What a lazy hound you are, Skype. I could be a thief, entering to carry off your mistress's valuables, and you would sleep through it."

Kept thumped his long tail again, raising his head to keep Jonys in view. Perhaps Jonys insisted on using Kept's old name just to tease her, but it reminded her of embarrassing circumstances she'd rather forget.

"Services in the chapel were well attended yesterday, weren't they?" His tone was conversational, casual.

"Quite. I hardly expected to see you there."

"Do you mean at church, or at that particular place of worship?"

"Both." Meriel wished he would go sit on the sofa, well across the room, instead of standing behind her. She needed to keep an eye on him. "Most men who carouse all night sleep late in the mornings. If you ever made it to services, I wouldn't look for you to appear in the most fashionable places."

"But I'm a changed man; I've given up riotous living," Jonys assured her. "I'm now a stodgy earl, required to show my face before God, society, and Parliament to prove I'll carry out my duties."

"You didn't appear changed in the slightest yesterday." She wouldn't look up at him while he spoke near her ear in that lighthearted, intimate tone. It reminded her too much of his easy manner with the widowed Lady Helsby. Flirting came far too easily to Jonys to pay serious attention when he aimed it at her.

"I don't follow you." He sounded genuinely puzzled.

"You charmed the ladies in church as readily as if you stood in a ballroom."

"I never put forth my best efforts in a ballroom," he protested. "You should see me in a bedroom, my dear."

That mental image wasn't safe to study. Meriel already sensed his nearness as a threat to her peace of mind, equally dangerous to acknowledge or ignore.

"Let's keep this conversation in the library, if you please." Bantering must show him how useless it was to dally with her.

"For now." Jonys reached past her ear to stroke Kept's tummy, his blue superfine sleeve brushing her cheek and throat. "You look comfortable, little fellow." His warm breath stirred her ribbon-bound curls, and her scalp tingled with his nearness. Meriel couldn't draw enough air into her lungs to dispel a sense of traveling at breakneck speed without control over her destination.

Leaning above her, Jonys murmured to Kept as he rubbed the juncture at his rear leg and body with his knuckles. The scent of lime filled her nose, sharp and clean as a wind off the sea. His hands were large, well-tended but masculine, with short-pared nails and strong fingers.

Seeing the gentle way he stroked the terrier made Meriel long to lean her head against his arm, relaxing as completely as Kept. But men weren't to be trusted, particularly not one who had flirted openly in the chapel yesterday with a widow who would never permit herself to be lonely for male company.

Ridiculous to sit here until her lids drooped like Kept's, envying the attentions the terrier received. Deliberately, she moved her shoulders away from Jonys, careful not to disturb Kept. Only a little dog could lie utterly at ease, exposing himself in a position that showed complete trust.

Kept must believe she would protect him, to fall asleep on her lap while Jonys stroked him. No one had protected her but herself, and she wouldn't give a man the option of doing right or wrong by her again.

Curious at his silence, Meriel glanced up at Jonys. His blue eyes blazed as he stared down at her, his expression intense and disconcerting, his strong, tender mouth a mere inch from hers. Quickly, she turned away.

"Did you come to call on Kept?" Without waiting for an answer, she continued. "He seems more than happy to have you here. Isn't he a dear dog?"

Rattling away like Lady Helsby, she must sound like a feather-brained ninny. Enduring much more of his closeness in silence would steam her like a pudding, however. "You must be uncomfortable leaning there, and I'll get a crick in my neck if I try to carry on a conversation with you. Won't you find a chair?"

"If you want to see me, of course I'll come around." A hint of laughter edged his voice, and when he appeared from behind her, a smile tugged at the corner of his mouth.

"Don't flatter yourself. It's just that Kept can make you feel you must go on petting him once you start."

"Touching warm, soft skin is never an obligation to me. I could happily keep it up all night."

Heat suffused her face, throat, and body, but not in a blush. Warmth flowed along her arms to her fingertips, rushed to the farthest reaches of her toes, sensitized all the lonely areas between. Meriel cupped her hands against Kept's warm sides and focused her gaze deliberately on him. She had never known a man like Jonys, who turned innocent comments into velvet suggestions while his eyes made more passionate promises.

His naughty wit didn't insult her, though she would never allow another man to speak half this freely to her. But she mustn't permit this most dangerous of men to say whatever he pleased. Not because she couldn't defend herself against his undoubted attractions, but because she didn't want to do so when he looked at her this way. She should have left him behind the chair.

Kneeling beside her, Jonys trailed his fingers down Kept's soft thigh. "Looks as if Skype is too contented with our company to stay awake. I miss having a dog to warm my hands on." He didn't look at her now, just buried his fingers in the thick coat over Kept's chest, rubbing with the tips in a way that inspired a sigh from the terrier. Kept snuggled his back still more firmly into the junction of her outstretched legs.

Jonys chuckled and leaned closer, looking into her depths as much as into her eyes. "Lucky dog. Skype's found the perfect valley to rest in. I can't imagine a more comfortable place to lie."

She felt an urgent need to shift her hips in the chair, but it was impossible in the languorous state his tormenting stare spread through her. This had to stop before she began making suggestions as improper as his.

Only one talisman against his spell came to mind. Argument. "His name is Kept, as you know very well. If you can't remember it, perhaps you shouldn't come see him again."

"Skype was his handle when I met him. I couldn't call him by another name without losing a part of him I mean to keep. When I care about someone, I hold onto them, you see." He leaned against her chair's side, resting an arm along its back above Meriel's shoulders.

This position brought him far too close. His eyes were on a level with hers, leaving her feeling as if she were drowning in two luminous blue lakes at once. His full lips parted, and she moistened her own. If Kept hadn't been sleeping on her lap, she would have risen and removed herself from overwhelming temptation.

But it would be a shame to disturb Kept when he slept so deeply, warm and heavy on her lap.

Silence stretched between them as Jonys caressed her face with his gaze, the concentration of his full attention setting them apart in a haven of warmth and light. Meriel grew deaf to sounds from the street and household, blind to anything but Jonys's mesmerizing eyes. Outside sensation was suspended, movement impossible, while she drifted on yearnings to know the pleasures promised by his look.

His expression softened, yet grew more determined as he drew closer, filling her vision and senses, yet confusing them at the same time. Again, his mouth was an inch away from hers, this time radiating desire that melted her defenses and called to the cravings she had long suppressed.

Meaning to pull back, she leaned forward, closing the last small distance between them, touching his mouth lightly with hers. Too late, she felt his arm slide around her shoulders, his lips possess hers thoroughly, his passion sear through the aura of reserve she wore like armor.

In a moment, she would free herself, escape the swirling sensations of hurtling through time and space, but for now, Meriel gave herself up to his caress of fingertips and hot, demanding mouth. But she couldn't let go completely.

Tasting and touching his lips, feeling his arm supporting her as surely as had the chair's back, Meriel took what she dared from his embrace and gave what she couldn't hold back. Kissing Jonys, melding even a part of herself with him, felt entirely too good. She couldn't trust herself to feel this good. Leaning back against his arm, she pulled away while she still could, breathless and disturbed.

At once, he let her go. His big hand lingered on her shoulder and slid, as if reluctant to lose contact, across her back as he straightened.

As she couldn't look at him directly yet, Meriel slipped her hands onto Kept's flanks, caressing him gently while she wrestled the torrent of need still strumming within her veins into a semblance of submission. Gradually her breathing slowed, if her pulse didn't. What madness to allow her control to slip with this man above all.

Lifting her hand from Kept, Jonys laid it on the chair's arm, tucking it securely under his fingers. His thumb teased the hollow of her palm lightly, sensuously. Kissing him had been foolish enough; she mustn't look into his eyes again.

His deep, low voice wrapped her close to him, despite her need to distance herself. "I want to talk with you about something important, Meriel. About you and me, about Skype."

Talking was the last thing she wanted to do. If only he would go, without a word, and give her time to erect her defenses again. Kissing him had been a mistake, too much intimacy too soon. A rake used familiarity to consume too much of a woman.

Her voice came out sharp and off-putting, even to her own ears. "You can't have him, if you mean to bring up that tired subject again. He's settled in well with me, and uprooting him would be cruel." If Jonys weren't touching her, she could concentrate more on what he said, what she replied. Meriel pulled her hand free.

After a moment, Jonys rubbed the terrier's chest while Kept played dead. "He's a special dog, more intelligent than most." He twinkled at her. "After all, he took to you at once, too. The only thing he needs now is a man to offset your indulgence."

His teasing tone didn't blunt the sharp offense she felt in his words. "If Kept needs male influence, you may come walk and brush him instead of a houseful of footmen." Jonys sounded just like Osborne, saying her boys needed a man to form their minds and attitudes, as if a mother was expendable.

Jonys looked confused for a moment. "I don't want to deprive you of him. I don't want any of us to lose anything. Skype would benefit from having us both about. We can share him and see that he gets everything he needs, both love and discipline. The two of us can give him more together than either of us alone."

Pushing Jonys away with words was a safeguard for herself. "Considering you were ready to leave Kept in the park last week, your claims of concern now aren't especially convincing."

His expression earnest, he leaned closer. "I never wanted anything but what was best for Skype, and now I want what's best for you, too."

Fire bells clanged in Meriel's mind. When a man said he wanted what was best for you, he meant to treat you like a child, making decisions for you without giving your opinion the same weight as his own. If he even bothered to ask for your opinion.

"I pointed out that Skype is overindulged in this household of ladies," Jonys said. Grinning at her, he radiated his personable charm like a shower of sparks from a grand illumination. "He'll have you and Hester jumping through hoops in no time. You, on the other hand, could use a little spoiling. I can take care of that. Marry me, and you'll make me the happiest of men and Skype the happiest of dogs."

On her lap, Kept sat up and barked once at Jonys. Meriel felt like barking at him herself for following the assault on her senses with an unwanted offer of marriage.

Kissing her had been only a prelude to this. What had wrenched her away from years of suppressing desire had been just part of a plan to coerce what he needed from her.

His proposal hardly came as a surprise, except in its frivolous form. A celebrated seducer might be expected to speak of love, whether he felt it or not, instead of suggesting they marry for the sake of the terrier.

Meriel drew as far away from Jonys as she could without dumping Kept on the carpet. Burchett had revealed Jonys as a fortune hunter. She could never be tempted to agree to a marriage that would benefit only Jonys, erasing her legal existence a second time.

In fairness, that wasn't strictly true. His estate would prosper if he married wealth, and his mama and sisters would be comfortable. Thinking of their plight, she answered him more gently than she had first intended.

"I won't go through the usual speech about the honor you do me, but just come straight to the point. I don't mean to remarry. You'd best pursue the other widow; she seems very well disposed toward you, if her actions at the chapel are anything to go by."

Kept butted her midsection with his head, whining. She scratched his back, taking comfort from touching him. Not that it pained her to give Jonys the negative response he deserved.

Her refusal set Jonys back on his heels. Disbelief widened his eyes. "You wouldn't refuse me because I was pleasant to Lady Helsby at church, surely. She's nothing to me; I don't even know her Christian name. I haven't called on her and don't want to know her any better than I do now. Did my lighthearted proposal offend you? No disrespect was meant; that's just the way I carry on.

After all, Skype brought us together; he could bring us still closer. Please believe I sincerely want to marry you and no one else."

"What you sincerely want is an infusion of funds to make your estates productive again," she said in a no-nonsense tone. "You don't need a wife, you need a loan." The puzzled entreaty in his eyes made it difficult to look at him for long.

"Won't you take a few days to think about my offer, Meriel?" Leaning on the chair arm with the force of his personality concentrated on her, Jonys made her almost wish she could give him what he requested.

"We could be happy together," he said with conviction. "I wouldn't ask you to marry me if I didn't believe that. And yes, you're right. I need money for the estate and its people, my family as well. But I don't mean to bleed you dry so you have nothing for yourself, and I can give you something in return. I couldn't take your help if I didn't believe that."

His sincerity was obvious now, but Meriel had heard assurances of love and protection from Welwyn before he had her signature on their marriage lines. Even if Jonys didn't mean to impose controls on her, the law gave him that right. No man let power lie unused.

"Thinking about it forever won't change my mind, Jonys. I've been certain for several years that I'll never remarry. It has nothing to do with you personally; you're far too attractive, and your family is dear in my memory." She wished he hadn't asked her, and now that he had, she wanted him to accept her answer. Refusing proposals was disquieting. What was a lady supposed to do when she didn't want to remarry, announce that fact when she was introduced to a gentleman?

"I'll speak with my man of business." She couldn't bear the bleakness shadowing his blue eyes toward gray. "Perhaps a loan could be arranged at a bank to tide you over, and you needn't marry until your heart recognizes the right lady."

Rising from his knees, Jonys sank onto the footstool beside her feet as if exhausted. Leaning his elbows on his thighs, he clasped his hands loosely before him. "No chance of a loan; I've already approached every banker in London, hat humbly in hand. None are willing to advance fiddler's money against an entailed estate."

As she suspected, his offer was aimed at her fortune, not her personally. Not that it mattered whether he proposed to marry her or her fortune. She didn't want to love him or any other man. Emotions were too painful to encourage by too close an association.

But she liked his warmth and wit, enjoyed his company. She felt sorry for Lady Hadham and the girls, living in penury, the girls deprived of doweries and hopes of suitable marriages. Without estate funds to support them, how would they live?

Obviously, Jonys could only use a woman's fortune to resolve his impossible dilemma. "What a shame you can't relieve your present difficulty with a less permanent arrangement than marriage," she said to lighten the mood smothering them. "In your predicament, a lady whose feelings weren't too nice to allow it could find herself a protector with deep pockets, even if she didn't want to marry."

Looking up, he grinned, though the lines at the corners of his eyes had deepened. "Is that an offer to keep me?"

Heart pounding and mouth gone dry, Meriel wanted for a mad moment to say that it was. The solution for him was perfect for her, too. Neither of them truly wanted to be married, but each had needs that were normally met by marriage. Jonys required wealth, and she felt the lack of male companionship and warmth more each day.

Besides, he attracted her in a way she had thought only men experienced: desire for physical intimacy without the complications of love and marriage. Shocking as it might seem in a lady, she would prefer to enjoy his companionship without marriage rather than put herself in the same legal position as a child again.

"Would you accept if I were offering to keep you?" Meriel didn't intend to make the outrageous proposition; she just felt curious about how he would respond.

"Would you be as generous in bed as at the bank?" From his tone, Jonys obviously didn't take the notion seriously.

Meriel couldn't decide if she were relieved or sorry. Having a man to talk and laugh with, as Hester did, would be pleasant. But if Osborne learned of a private involvement, no matter how common among the ton, the results would be disastrous. Of course she was glad Jonys recognized the idea as a jest.

"You should have seized the offer without question," Meriel said with an effort at a teasing tone. Best to treat the mad thought as more of the banter that flew between them like shuttlecocks. "It's too late now. But I hope you're able to resolve your financial problems."

"Perhaps I can ask Lady Helsby if she would care to set me up in a pretty little establishment."

His effort at humor sounded as forced as hers, and he looked as if he were coming down with a chill.

Meriel wanted to warm him if only by a small compliment. "Few ladies would be satisfied with a temporary claim on your attentions." The notion of the pretty blond widow leading Jonys about like a prize bull with a ring through his nose disturbed her.

"Thank you for offering that balm to my bruised view of my charms for ladies." Jonys straightened, putting on a smile in the same way he would place a hat on his head. "Will you be uncomfortable if I continue to visit?" He gestured to the terrier now lying crossways on her lap, watching him. "I want to see Skype, if you don't mind, and I like talking with you, little as you believe I value you for your company."

His wistful look tightened her throat. But this same man had dropped Kept over the park fence and all but admitted he proposed out of need for a fortune. "Nothing's changed between us as far as I'm concerned. Call if you like."

"Thank you, I will." He unfolded from the stool, looming to his full height and looking despondent for the first time since she had known him.

When she slid her feet to the edge of the stool to rise, he laid a hand on her slipper. "Don't get up; I can see myself out and you won't have to disturb Skype."

The terrier stood and moved to the edge of the chair. Sharing a hurt look between them, he jumped down.

"Do you mean to walk me out, young fellow?" Jonys asked.

Kept ignored him, walking away from them both toward the window seat. Despite its height, he leaped up and sat down on the padded seat, presenting them with his back. His entire furry body exuded prickly resistance.

"I think we're in his black books," Jonys observed. "I wonder how we offended him. Was it something we did, or something we didn't do?"

"His sensibilities are delicate," Meriel said, smiling. "We may never know." She rose from the chair, grateful to the little scamp. This interview would have been far more uncomfortable than it had without Kept to take their attention off each other.

Smiling as he attempted his usual lighthearted tone, Jonys clasped her hands. "If you change your mind about either proposition we discussed," he said, "just let me know."

Behind him, the library door opened. Hester came in, followed closely by Burchett. Hester looked at their clasped hands, and her expression brightened. "Hello," she said. "What's this about propositions? Anything I should know?"

Burchett looked at the ceiling.

Jonys turned to the pair. "Meriel must decide if anything worth talking about was said. I was just taking my leave, but I'm glad to have an opportunity to see you, if briefly."

Hester looked still more curious, but Burchett forestalled further embarrassing questions, to Meriel's relief. "If you're on your way out," he said to Jonys, "let me take you up in my carriage. I'm just seeing Hester safely inside."

Jonys accepted his offer, making Meriel wonder if Tat's had made room for his carriage and pair. Few men of fashion walked far in London, and his rooms weren't close by. She felt sorry in a way that she had refused his offer, little as she wanted to wed anyone. But he was doing his best to deal with a bad situation he hadn't created, and she must respect that effort.

As he bowed to Hester and her before leaving the room with Burchett, he gave her a last regretful look. She could almost believe he was truly sorry she had turned him down. Though of course he was; he needed funds urgently.

Staring after him, Hester asked, "What's been happening while I shopped?" She turned back to Meriel, examining her face with a thoughtful gaze. "He looks like his best horse died, and you look as wild as a March hare."

Folding her arms across her sash, Meriel paced to the window and back. "The most astounding thing. Jonys made me an offer of marriage!"

"That's hardly surprising, let alone astounding. I assume from his expression that you refused him?"

"Yes, of course I refused him." Surely Hester couldn't think otherwise for one moment. "It was what I said next that leaves me shaking. Hester, I very nearly offered him *carte blanche*!"

In the process of removing her bonnet, Hester stopped with the strings dangling on either side of her chin and sank slowly onto the sofa. "You offered to *keep* him? To pay him for—what exactly did you have in mind to pay him for?"

"I don't think I had anything in mind, actually. I was just thinking about the plight of his mama, whom I like, and his little sisters, and then he mentioned that dreadful Lady Helsby." Now that it was over, Meriel couldn't recall exactly what she had said. Or what he had said. But she was certain she had said far too much.

"Do you think he's off to secure the affections

of Lady Helsby now?" Hester still looked flum-
moxed at Meriel's uncharacteristic behavior.

Feeling her lips and chest tighten at the hateful
suggestion, Meriel strode away from her cousin.
"He certainly needs funds, and I suppose a man
with responsibilities must meet them the best way
he can." Still, she couldn't like the thought of him
selling himself to the brash widow. Jonys was far
too good a person for that fate, even if he was an
incurable flirt.

"In a way, it serves him right." Hester looked
thoughtful as she pulled off her bonnet and laid it
aside. "Everyone knows he's taken his pleasure
with any number of ladies since he came down
from Oxford. It would only be appropriate if he
were at a woman's beck and call, as your kept man
or as Lady Helsby's bought husband!"

Meriel's hands formed fists. The jest wasn't
amusing, though Hester laughed enough for them
both. "Jonys would be miserable with a wife like
her," Meriel said. "If she throws herself at him
shamelessly in church with any number of people
looking on, she wouldn't hesitate to be unfaithful
to him."

"Then I suppose you'll have to take him under
your protection." Hester sat smiling as innocently
as if she'd suggested Meriel take Kept for a walk.

Crossing to the window, Meriel stared out into
the garden with a hand on Kept. Across the lawn,
under the pergola, Jonys had caught her in his
arms and destroyed her comfortable view of the
future. Today, he had seduced her into kissing
him without a word. If only she had never met
him again in the square.

"You know I don't want to remarry," she reminded Hester, scratching Kept between the

shoulder blades. He backed his warm bottom against her and leaned into the caress.

"All the more reason to enjoy an arrangement with a gentleman privately," Hester said, coming to stand beside her. "Which sounds scandalous, but tremendously exciting to me. Just think, you'd only see each other at your best, and he'd never feel so overly confident that he took you for granted."

"I mean to keep away from men entirely, so I don't need to consider keeping one. It's upset me no end to deal with a proposal of marriage when I don't mean to marry again. Avoiding all men is much safer." How much of her agitation was due to Jonys's offer and how much to his kiss, she didn't care to consider.

"Staying away from the whole gender because Welwyn was unsatisfactory makes no more sense than avoiding all foods because oysters make you ill. You've seemed more alive since Jonys and Kept showed up. I think you should consider keeping them both near you. No, don't glare at me like that." Hester giggled. "What better way to ensure that other men don't attract you than to let Jonys occupy your attention completely? And I don't doubt he could do so!"

Agreeing that Jonys could easily put all other men out of her mind didn't make Meriel any less impatient with Hester's nonsense. "You can't be serious. A womanizer like Jonys couldn't limit himself to one lady to gain any sum of money. And if Osborne were to discover I paid a man for—as if he were at stud, I'd never see my boys again."

Her lips quivered as she fought to control the mixed emotions swirling within her today. She felt confused, tired, alone. And remaining alone was the best choice she could make to protect herself.

"That man again!" Hester declared. "I'd like to push him over the highest cliff in Dover." Appearing beside Meriel, Hester slipped an arm about her waist. "Of course you don't want to jeopardize time with your boys, even if it looks like Osborne will only let you see them a couple of times a year at best. But many ladies carry on long-term liaisons with gentlemen without anyone being the wiser. It only takes a bit of discretion."

Leaning back to look at her intently, Hester continued. "Osborne controls your life as completely now through the boys as he ever did when you were married to Welwyn. Yet you seem to fear him more now than you did then. I wonder if Jonys might be able to help you get free from his horrid control over you."

Meriel stared at her cousin. What Hester said made too much sense to ignore. Despite rebelling against her brother-in-law's control by moving to London, she knew Hester was right. Meriel was no more at liberty to make choices that satisfied her rather than Osborne than she had been when she lived in the same house with him.

"You may have a point," Meriel conceded, "but becoming involved with Jonys for any reason is unsafe. I'm not about to marry anyone, and he must wed quickly."

"Not if you pay him for his services." Hester paced about in her eagerness to explain, and Kept jumped down from the window seat to follow, watching every movement. "If he had the funds to build up his estate, he wouldn't have to marry at once. He would be free to help you figure out how to thwart Osborne, and since he'd be around anyway, you might as well enjoy every aspect of his company."

"But my sons." Risk wasn't easy for Meriel to consider, especially where her boys were concerned. "Even if Jonys were willing to take on my problems for a price, Osborne could misunderstand the connection. I can't chance losing touch with my boys, even if I'm allowed to see them just once yearly. Winning Osborne's approval is the only sensible course of action, since I have no legal grounds against him."

Throwing up her hands, Hester wheeled away. "His approval! Osborne has never approved of anything anyone did, unless he first told them to do it. After you live like a nun for the next year, what assurance do you have he won't decide the boys need to be schooled in Switzerland? Or that they should be sheltered from you entirely? After all, you bowed to his every demand after Welwyn died, and he dragged James and Steven off to Eton despite that."

Meriel bit her knuckle, hardly feeling it. Surely the man wouldn't be so cruel. But she pictured with clarity his harsh expression that night when he announced he would drive her boys to Eton the next day. His offhanded dismissal once he'd made his decree had shown his contempt for her, a mere female. She could be certain of nothing where Osborne was concerned.

Across the room, Hester stood watching her. "Jonys seems like a clever man, and Osborne wouldn't credit you with the courage to try besting him after your legal efforts failed. Perhaps you should open your purse and buy Jonys's services. One of which would be finding a way to foil Osborne."

No lady would consider such an outrageous arrangement for a moment. But what if Jonys could help her, perhaps learn something to Osborne's disadvantage and use it to gain her more time with James and Steven?

With his kiss still emblazoned as much on her soul as her mouth, she could never trust the reason she purchased his assistance, even if she could do so. The entire mad idea was unthinkable.

Chapter Seven

The stairs to his rooms were steeper and darker than usual. Or maybe Jonys just thought so after the dispiriting setback of Meriel's refusal within the past hour.

The last thing he wanted to do now was to relive that futile scene with Anson, but going out among his friends, pretending nothing had shattered his hopes for putting the estate right, would be worse. Even responding to Burchett's easy conversation on the drive here had strained his patience. Usually he welcomed company, but not today.

Dragging the door to his rooms open, Jonys stood in surprise. Two burly chaps stood in his entry, shifting a table into place as Anson directed them. Not just any table, but his table of the dusky beauties. He hadn't expected to see it again.

"What's this, Anson?" All three men turned to him.

"Your table, my lord." Anson had to state the obvious.

"Yes, I can see that for myself. What's it doing back here again? Did you have an attack of conscience over stealing it and have it returned?"

The porters stared at the old valet with suspicion and wonder. Anson quelled them with a look before replying. "No, Master Douglas, I had nothing to do with its return. I'm as puzzled as you. These men say they can tell me nothing about who bought it and had it sent here."

"Can't or won't? The prospect of a pint has been known to improve memory." Extracting a few coins from his dwindling horde, Jonys jingled them in his closed hand.

The smaller of the two men spoke up at once. "A lord bid it in, sir. Lord Burford, Burchett, som'at like that. Told us to keep our muns shut about him, but then, he ain't here, is he, sir?"

"Quite." Jonys dropped the coins on the outstretched palm, looking at Anson. If he'd known about this earlier, his conversation with Burchett as they rode from Portman Square would have been far different. He couldn't think why the dandy would do him this favor. Though they were on good terms, their acquaintance didn't justify this.

As Anson saw the porters out the door, Jonys walked around the table, trailing a hand over its silver-inlaid surface. He could be delighted to have it back, if its return didn't put him under an obligation. The interview with Meriel had made it unlikely he could discharge that obligation anytime soon.

Turning his back on another reminder of his failures, Jonys passed into the drawing room, removing his hat. Anson was beside him before he could toss it aside.

Taking the tall beaver, the old man handed over two folded, sealed sheets. "A message by hand and a letter by post came while you were out. Looks like your mother's fist on the letter."

Dropping into his favorite old wing chair, Jonys looked at the two folded sheets. The sight of his mother's graceful looped writing raised the usual stings from his own shortcomings. He laid it on his thigh and looked at the direction written in an unfamiliar hand on the other.

Breaking the seal, he unfolded the thick sheet and read its few lines. "Looks like I'll be going out tonight. Lord Holland invites me to meet him and Lord Murray for dinner at his club. We'll go on to a demonstration of practical applications of gas lighting. I have a few ideas about that process myself. I think I'll accept."

"Gossip has it that Winsor's after investors again." Anson frowned. "Lords Holland and Murray no doubt hope to secure your vote on the next bill before the Lords."

"They might win it, too. You urged me to get myself invited out to dinner more often. I might as well meet Holland." Charles and he had debated the potential of gas for lighting streets and homes since Winsor had shown up in town about five years ago. He had attended a few of Winsor's lectures with Charles, who laughed at the scheme. Wouldn't hurt to see if the Frenchman had come up with anything new.

"Aren't you going to open your mother's letter?" Anson stood waiting, probably hoping to hear the latest family news. His mother and Anson had seen eye to eye on the protection and prominence of the Hadhams.

Expecting the news from his mama to weigh heavily on his spirits, Jonys wished he could delay reading it. He'd had enough blows to his pride for one day. But an earl's duty was to face problems head-on. He broke into the missive.

Aware that Anson stood by, he read quickly. "Lady Donnely stopped in on her way to London. She put up for a couple of nights at Hadham House and entertained Mama and the girls with her plans to visit to a sister in Brighton." No need to worry the old man with the rest of it. Refolding the letter, he shoved it into his pocket. The day was going from bad to worse.

Anson spoke up at once. "Lady Donnely's visit, even if we can't afford to entertain her and her servants and animals in proper style at Hadham, wouldn't make you look that hopeless. Does the letter say something more?" Anson had known him too long.

Jonys set his teeth, not wanting to say it, though denial never had chased away painful truths. "It's Claire. Mama says she's been coughing more, has to be propped up with pillows to breathe at night. Dr. Weston says she needs sea air and warmth to ease her chest. He suggests Mama take a house on a long lease near Brighton where she'll find the best doctors to treat her."

"The poor young miss; it doesn't seem right when she's as sweet as any angel." Anson looked stricken. "We must hope for the best. Maybe Brighton is just what she needs. With the Prince Regent often in residence, you may count on finding excellent health advisors in the area."

Jonys nodded. He didn't know how he would

pay for a house, doctors, and living expenses in Brighton when he couldn't keep his mama and sisters in comfort at Hadham House. But if he had to pick pockets, he'd manage. Little Claire had shown complete faith in him to take care of everything, and he couldn't let her suffer.

"Mama has asked Lady Donnely to have her sister look about Brighton for something suitable for four ladies on their own." They could hardly live in a two-room fisherman's cottage.

"Very kind of Lady Donnely and her sister to help out, as it will save you the expense of a trip." Turning the beaver in his hands, Anson said, "Kind of Lord Burchett as well to return our table. Good friends in times of hardship are a blessing. I'll step around to Christie's and fetch the sum it brought shortly. We'll eat roast beef tonight."

"No." Dropping into his worn elbow chair, Jonys rubbed his jaw. "To take both the money and the table from the man is the outside of enough. Collect the money and deliver it to Lord Burchett's house with my compliments."

Sending back what Burchett had paid for the table was painful, when he needed the money for Claire. Accepting both the table and its price from a casual acquaintance was not an honorable man's act, however. Burchett should have known the double gift was nearly an insult. No doubt that was why he'd tried to keep its source a secret.

"But, sir! Your friend may be offended if you reject his kind action. Obviously he wants to help you through this black spell."

Wishing he could keep the money and table, Jonys wasn't in the mood to argue the matter. "If Burchett were a close enough friend to make me a gift, he'd do it to my face, not hide its source like

138

the act of charity it is. I'll see to returning the money. Perhaps I can sell the table privately."

"Pride is a costly indulgence. Private sales rarely bring as high a price as an auction." Anson looked as sour as dill relish. "The sensible course would be to send him a letter thanking him for the loan and assuring him you'll repay it shortly."

"But I don't know that I can repay him, shortly or otherwise. I don't accept money I can't repay. That's the end of it; I don't want to hear about it again." Knowing he was upset at himself for even considering the possibility of hanging on to Burchett's payment for the table, Jonys tried to hold his quick temper. If Anson didn't take his interference elsewhere very soon, he would be forced to lock the valet in a cupboard.

"You're in a touchy mood, when I expected you to come back from Lady Welwyn's cock-a-hoop. You seemed more than resigned to the marriage; I thought you were set on it." The old busybody didn't mean to budge from the drawing room.

"The lady won't have me. And I don't want to hear any more on that subject, either." What he wanted to do was hitch up his team of blacks and drive them through the countryside like a madman. With his carriage and pair awaiting auction at Tat's, that exercise was denied him. Maybe he should beg Jackson to hire him as a sparring partner to the ton. Gentleman Jackson, proprietor, and Lord Had'em, sparring mate. The grim humor lightened his black mood.

When he looked up, Anson sat on the sofa, the beaver hat on the floor. He must have been hit hard by the news of Meriel's refusal. The old man had aged ten years in a minute.

Jonys rose, ready to assist him if he seemed to

be having an apoplexy. "Don't fret, Anson. We'll come about yet. My luck has to turn at some point."

The valet's head came up; then his shoulders went back. Picking up the beaver hat and dusting its brim, he stood, too. "Of course we will," he said, voice quavering a bit. "I'd quite forgotten about Lady Helsby. All isn't lost."

Jonys had forgotten about her, too. He didn't want to be reminded of her now.

"Perhaps you should call on Lady Helsby at once," Anson said, sounding stronger. "You don't want it to appear she's second choice; ladies are put off by thinking you ever preferred anyone over them. But you made the lady's acquaintance only yesterday, so if you call today, she'll think that meeting her set Lady Welwyn on the backseat of the carriage with you, in a manner of speaking."

The brash little blond widow could never put Meriel in the shade. "Lady Helsby isn't the sort of woman I'd want my sisters to know. She's as forward and fawning as any mushroom of a cit, quite common and vulgar. How many times have you said I must marry a lady who enhances the dignity of the Hadham line?"

"That's a bit harsh, perhaps; the lady is merely overeager, not being as well placed in society as she wishes." Putting on his headmaster expression, Anson added, "Keep in mind that Beggers Can't Be Choosers."

"I'm not likely to forget it." Jonys sat down again and closed his eyes, picturing the two young widows. "Lady Helsby is pretty enough and more than rich enough to attract most men. Meriel is more than a cut above her, though. I can't explain it, Anson. Though Lady Helsby is typical of the ladies

I've enjoyed for years, she isn't the kind I'd want to marry. Maybe I've outgrown my former playmates. Maybe duty has turned me into a staid, respectable old curmudgeon."

"Not even death will accomplish that." Anson spoke as sharply as usual. "If you find wedding Lady Helsby this distasteful, what do you plan to do instead?"

Sitting up, Jonys thought about Meriel's refusal. While he had sat on her footstool like a molting buzzard, she had shown discomfort and concern for his situation.

The lady wasn't indifferent to him; he'd swear to it after kissing her. And being kissed by her. If she felt no response to him, she would be able to meet his eyes easily and her fingers wouldn't tremble in his.

Thinking out loud, he said, "Though she insisted she wouldn't remarry, Meriel made an odd statement. A lady in my circumstances could find a protector, she said, and teased me about becoming a kept man. We treated it as the jest it was. Or as I took it to be."

"Indeed, sir? I take it Lady Welwyn wouldn't normally make such a comment, even in jest, if she's quite unlike Lady Helsby. It shows the lady feels comfortable enough with you to make an outrageous statement in your company. Perhaps that hint of increasing intimacy should be followed up."

"Intimacy? Don't believe it. She's as sharp-tongued as she is sharp-witted, never misses an opportunity to cast my past sins at my feet. If she doesn't think I'm the devil, she considers me his henchman." This was the first time a woman's poor opinion of him had given him an itch to

141

prove himself a better man than she thought.

"Excellent." Anson's old eyes gleamed. "No lady wastes her breath berating a man she doesn't care about."

"Then she must be passionately in love with me." Jonys didn't believe that for one second.

"Ah, well," Anson said vacantly, staring out the window. "She wouldn't be the first lady to take up with you as a lark and fall into love."

"Not because I've encouraged it." Being loved by ladies in the past had felt irksome, burdensome, like responsibility he didn't want. Being loved without demands might be a fine thing, but no woman, even a mother, loved you without loading on endless demands.

"That might be the answer to our problem." Anson still stared out the window in a brown study.

"What's that?"

"You have to admit that few ladies offer gentlemen a slip on the shoulder in any circumstances. Ladies prefer that men do the pursuing. Perhaps a jest about paying to keep your considerable talents exclusively to herself shows her true desires. Truth is often hidden in humor. Perhaps if you went along with the lady's offer as if you believe she meant it, you could use the continued contact to persuade her into marriage."

Jonys sat up, staring at his old valet. "It's been a long time coming, but you've finally entered your dotage."

Did his man want to see him listed in *The Whoremonger's Guide to London* like gentlemen's fancy pieces? What a farce, the Earl of Hadham as another Harriette Wilson, the best known of the fashionable impures. Set up in a little house somewhere, at Meriel's beck and call. Accepting money to take her to bed on demand.

Though that duty didn't sound too onerous. He leaned back in his chair, hands supporting his head. Perhaps Meriel had hoped he would take her up on an offer she could only make as if teasing. Maybe Meriel's first husband had been of little use to her in the bedchamber. Maybe she wanted to try Jonys out before committing herself to the lifelong ties of marriage vows. The same way a man wanted to put a horse through its paces before laying down his blunt for it.

As she seemed proper to a fault, he hadn't thought about her taking an unconventional interest in him. But she had made it clear she didn't want to remarry, and she possessed the normal urges of ladies he had known in the biblical sense. She had kissed him with the hungry demand of a passionate woman. From her harping on his reputation, she must know he was good at satisfying ladies' needs.

Naturally he would prefer a regular arrangement, with the two of them married. But a temporary agreement could lead to that end. Her attraction to him was as undeniable as his to her; he couldn't be mistaken about it with his experience. Perhaps she needed to believe he loved her in order to marry him. Jonys certainly enjoyed her company, and an irregular union would allow her to take passion for love.

Moving to a more comfortable position in the chair, Jonys felt proof of his passion for her stir. Just thinking about the stubborn lift of her chin, the curve of her cheek near his arm, the swell of her full breasts against his arm was glorious torment.

Anson's opinion might be sound. Allowing himself to be set up as Meriel's kept man would provide for Claire's needs at once. It could give him time to work past Meriel's defenses, become indispensable to her. Nobody had complained about crawling into bed with him so far, for his pleasure was heightened by his partner's. He felt more desire to indulge Meriel than any woman he'd ever met, and he would persuade her to wed him yet. No better place to do so than bed.

"Just think about the possibility," Anson urged him.

"I am," Jonys said, pulling at the legs of his pantaloons. "I certainly am."

Since he didn't have an invitation, Jonys arrived at Chiswick the next afternoon about four, when breakfast would be finished. He didn't bother to enter the small Palladian house, strolling around to the gardens instead.

Breakfast, with everyone eating at two long tables in a saloon at ground level, would have drawn too much attention to a long conversation. Outside, he hoped to get Meriel alone where he could speak more persuasively about marriage than he had yesterday in her library.

By now, Devonshire's guests would be viewing the villa's art galleries or gardens, and Jonys's arrival would be less remarked. Not that he expected a friend like the Bachelor Duke to have him thrown off the grounds, but he didn't want to make himself or Meriel conspicuous while he talked with her.

Greeting acquaintances without stopping, he looked along winding paths among trees and irregular beds of flowering plants for her, hoping to find her with Hester.

Along a curved path, he caught a glimpse of a lovely face raised to her companion before a basket hat brim hid it again. He recognized Meriel, though a man's brown-coated back shifted to block a further view of her. Jonys would get her away from the encroaching fellow soon enough.

The man monopolizing her attention moved again, and Jonys noticed Skype sitting as far away from Meriel as a lead allowed, ears back. Around the terrier's neck, a collar and lead had been fashioned from interwoven green, white and yellow ribbons matching those on Meriel's hat. Skype spotted him and ducked his head as if embarrassed at the length he was forced to go to please his lady.

Jonys grinned and called softly, "Skype, come."

Though Meriel didn't appear to hear him, the terrier clearly did. He yanked the ridiculous lead free and bounded forward to meet Jonys, ribbons flying behind him.

At least Meriel wasn't too much the lady to run after her dog, though several bystanders turned scandalized faces her way. "Kept, stop!" she called. "Sit!"

As the terrier reached him, Jonys set a booted foot on the lead and leaned over to tousle the dog's head. "Good boy," he said. "That's the way to lead our Meriel to me."

Seeing her made him feel as if the sun had colored the air with the same yellow glow as the villa's walls. Slowing to a walk, Meriel looked self-conscious as she acknowledged Jonys with a curt nod. Maybe he should have expected her to be uneasy the next time they met after he made her an

145

offer, but he had far more experience with propositions than proposals.

In her white dress with a pale Pomona green spencer and parasol, Meriel looked little older than a girl in her first season. "You're blooming like a mayflower in that toilette," he said as she stopped beside the terrier. "I believe this runaway wild thistle is with you."

Skype stretched his neck, nose quivering between the two of them. Stooping, Jonys retrieved the ribbon lead and handed it to her.

Examining the soiled ribbon where he had stood on it, she finally accepted it with primrose-gloved fingers, wrinkling her pretty nose at him. "Kept took me by surprise, yanking away from me like that. I suppose he caught sight of you and wanted to say hello."

Looking at Skype, Jonys rubbed his jaw. "Could be. Or he may have wanted to run away before anyone else saw him wearing ribbons like a lapdog."

Pink glossing her cheeks, Meriel glanced at the terrier and then back the way she had come. "It does look affected, then, as I feared. Hester thought it would be adorable, to bring Kept dressed in ribbons to match my costume."

Beyond her, Hester and Burchett waited where Meriel had been standing when he first caught sight of her. Returning Hester's wave, he saw that Burchett wore an Egyptian brown coat. His relief that Meriel hadn't been deep in conversation with a flirt surprised him.

"You, at least, look charming," Jonys said, touching her elbow. "You had best find a strong leather collar and lead for Skype if you mean to

146

keep him safe in public places. Shall we join your friends?"

"Kept is an exceptionally well-behaved dog," Meriel protested as they set off to join Hester and Burchett. "He's caused no trouble at all, not even at breakfast."

"Probably too dispirited at being dressed in ribbons to notice the swans Devonshire keeps on his lake."

Meriel gazed in that direction for a moment. "They're well out on the water. I doubt he'll even notice them."

Exchanging greetings with the other couple, Jonys was aware that Hester studied him with a new quality of attention. Very likely Meriel had told her cousin about his proposal. Maybe Hester would support his efforts to get Meriel alone.

"Won't you join us in a stroll about the grounds?" he asked the other couple just to be polite. "I'm not much inclined to stand about when I could be moving."

"Good notion," Burchett replied at once. "Let's walk down by the lake where a bit of a breeze might find us. It's unusually warm for the time of year."

Hester sent Jonys a shrug and sympathetic glance.

Holding Meriel back, he allowed the other couple to lead the way. "This isn't the time for a long discussion," he said to the viscount with a steady look as Burchett passed, "but I want to speak with you about a particular table."

"A table? The table!" Stopping dead, Burchett looked between Meriel and Hester with a hunted expression, then cleared his throat. "Haven't the slightest notion what you mean, old thing."

Hester made a face at her beau, and Meriel gazed out over the lake. Jonys realized that the ladies had to know what Burchett had done, as self-conscious as they both looked. "If everyone already knows the details, we might as well have it out now as later," Jonys said.

Laughing nervously, Burchett said, "I never have anything to do with tables except when I eat or play cards." He looked as if his cravat were tied too tightly as he shuffled his highly polished boots on the grass.

"The two porters who made the delivery say otherwise." Jonys smiled since the ladies were present. From the dandy's reaction, Burchett knew the gift smacked too much of charity to be acceptable between gentlemen, which made his action still more curious.

Poor old Burchett's ears looked wine in color as he turned to hurry ahead down the grassy slope toward the water. "Can't imagine what you mean," he said. "Wouldn't offend you for the world. I like this new way of arranging a garden. Much less stiff than those parterres and fountains."

Hester turned to raise her brows at Meriel. "Should we explain—"

With a warning gesture, Meriel shook her head slightly.

Jonys's suspicions grew. Why would Meriel determine what Hester could reveal on the subject of the table if Burchett had returned the table on his own? The most reasonable answer that came to his mind made his jaw clench.

"You must have acted at the insistence of a lady," Jonys said to Burchett, watching Meriel as the foursome walked on. "Another man would understand I couldn't accept both the table's return and the money paid for it."

Meriel's throat grew pink as her brimmed hat shaded her face from his view. "Though it was a generous notion," Jonys said, "only a shiftless good-for-nothing could keep both, especially as a gift from a lady."

Skype tugged ahead, straining the strands of ribbon that Meriel clutched. She hurried after the terrier, passing Hester as he surged toward the serpentine lake.

Clapping Burchett on the shoulder, Jonys said quickly, "No offense taken, old man. I know who was behind the entire thing." Grinning at the other man's relieved expression, he hurried to catch up with Meriel.

"Looks like you'll need me to take Skype's training in hand," he said as the terrier continued to yank at her arm. "He should be walking calmly on lead by now, if not to heel."

"No, thank you. I can manage him. Kept's just a little frisky today." She still didn't look at Jonys. "What a lovely serpentine lake, in a much nicer setting than the one in Hyde Park."

"The lake is lovely; the garden is beautifully designed." He couldn't resist teasing her. "If no one will talk about your kindness in returning my table, I won't insist on that, but you must realize I can't keep the money and the table as well."

"I don't see why not. After all, you can't prove who bought the table; you're only guessing. I certainly won't take credit for doing you any favors."

"Then I'll invest the blunt at Rundell and Bridge's for you. Perhaps a gold bracelet or brooch to bring out the glinting lights in your eyes."

She flashed him a searing look. "What a waste when I have more jewelry than I wear, and when you could put the funds to good use buying seed for plantation on your estate."

"Or maybe I'll buy you a gold ring to wear until I can persuade you to accept the Hadham engagement ring of emeralds and—" He broke off as Skype pulled free from Meriel's grasp and dashed pell-mell for the lake.

"We mustn't let Kept go into the water," Meriel cried, picking up her skirts to chase the terrier again.

"That dog needs schooling," Jonys muttered, running down the slope after Skype. Just when he had worked up to a neat renewal of his suit, the pup had to interrupt him. The cursed dog scampered ahead, heading for the water's edge. At the last moment, instead of leaping into the lake, Skype jumped into a skiff that had been nosed out onto the grassy bank.

Clambering under the single-board seats to reach the stern of the small rowboat, Skype plopped down, panting and looking pleased with himself, as Jonys halted on the shore. Meriel joined him, calling, "Kept, come. Come out of there now."

"He seems to want to go boating." Jonys stared down at Meriel, flushed and beautiful with tendrils of golden brown hair straying over her forehead and tickling her throat in the breeze. "You might find it cooling yourself to lie back in the skiff and rest while I row you and Skype about."

"That sounds pleasant," she agreed, slipping a handkerchief from her sleeve and touching her forehead and the sides of her throat.

Watching, he wanted to press his lips against

her glowing face and neck, kiss the warm, salty skin until she put her arms over his shoulders and pulled him closer. A tightness in his groin warned him not to follow that line of thought further in knit pantaloons.

Stepping away as she looked about, Meriel said, "Perhaps we should find a larger craft and persuade Hester and Burchett to come out with us."

Jonys didn't want to enlarge the party, not after Skype or good fortune had arranged for him to get Meriel alone. "Not even your vicar brother-in-law could object to your rowing with a gentleman on this ornamental water, in bright daylight with throngs of people walking the grounds." He lifted his brows and lowered his voice into a challenge. "Or are you afraid to trust yourself with me, even in public?"

Sparks flew from the golden-flecked gaze she turned on him. "I won't lose control of myself again, whatever the provocation."

"Then you're safe anywhere with me." Putting a foot on the boat to steady it, he offered her a hand. "Let me help you to a seat with Skype, and I'll shove us off."

When she was settled, he eased the rowboat's prow down the grassy bank into the water and climbed in quickly. As the skiff rocked, Meriel held onto the side with one hand, steadying herself with her parasol as if it were a cane.

While the rowboat glided out in quiet ripples, Jonys tugged at the sleeve of his fitted coat. "Forgive me for taking this off," he said, "but rowing's likely to split the seams. Would you mind holding it for me?"

As she folded the blue superfine, he shipped the oars. He wasn't too occupied to notice how carefully she smoothed the fabric, even bringing it to her nose furtively before laying the coat across her lap. Perhaps she liked the scent of bitter apples which Anson dried and laid among his coats to freshen and protect them from moths.

Dipping the oars, he sent the skiff toward the deeper waters at the center of the lake with long, strong strokes. He meant to keep them well away from other rowing boats and punters.

Skirts spread modestly over her slippers, Meriel put up her parasol and tilted it against the sun. In its shadow, she glanced at him from under lashes as lush as the fronds of water thyme waving gracefully under the boat's hull as it crossed a shallow spot.

Under the sultry spell of the afternoon's warm air, they drifted between long strokes of the oars. Jonys idled more than rowed, moving just enough to keep them in the lake's depths, distant from prying eyes and ears.

Then he noticed Meriel's gaze had settled onto his shoulders and arms, her eyes widening slightly when he pulled at an oar. Feeling like the man who hefted impossible weights at the fair, he stroked the water with long, lazy hauls, putting more movement into the action than was strictly necessary. Amused at himself, he still enjoyed the way her curving lids drifted half shut over eyes that looked languid, sleepy.

Dancing sparks of sunlight flashed off the water's constantly changing surface, dazzling him with dreams of using his hands, mouth, body to inspire that look on her lovely face. Meriel had to become his wife, and this was the perfect, romantic moment to convince her of it.

As he leaned forward, resting his forearms on

the raised oars, Skype set up a series of sharp barks, distracting him. For a moment, Jonys questioned his timing. Perhaps he should wait another week at least, not propose again the day after her first rejection.

As the terrier settled onto his haunches again, growling low in his throat at a distant flotilla of swans, Jonys looked back at Meriel. Twirling the parasol absently, she moistened her pink lips with the tip of her tongue, curving her graceful body to another position on the plank seat.

No. He couldn't afford to wait. Claire had to remove to Brighton at once. After the storm damage, estate buildings must be put under roof again. Jonys gathered his courage with a few forceful strokes of the oars, drawing her flattering attention to him again.

As he searched his mind for a romantic bit of poetry to begin his addresses with, a pair of swans sailed by with exquisite dignity. Scrambling to the center of the small bow-bottomed skiff, Skype set his forepaws on its side and hurled threatening barks at the pair.

The lead swans ignored him as their graceful fellows sailed past in their wake. The sight of more swans set the terrier into a paroxysm of yelps, his whole body lifting with each bark as he warned off the fleet.

Meriel leaned forward, reaching for his lead to restrain him. Skype twitched it away in one of his leaps as he barked. "Hush," she said to him, laughing. "You'll have eight birds with strong beaks over here to bite your nose."

Nearest the skiff, a majestic swan turned its curved head to stare at the frantic dog with an unblinking bead of an eye. It ruffled its wings and stretched its neck toward him. Rapid-fire barks broke loose as Skype scrabbled at the boat's bottom and sides, launching himself over the edge and out into the water to land on his belly near the startled swan.

Shrieking warnings at the bird, Meriel leaned precariously out of the boat to snatch at the terrier swimming after his prey. Jonys leaned the opposite way as water seeped over the side of the little craft.

The fleet of swans came about hard, gliding back to investigate the attack on their rear. Hissing like mad cats, a couple of the large birds shot their beaks at the snapping, snarling dog. Meriel shook her parasol at the nearest swans, scooting to the edge of her seat and half rising in an effort to shoo them away from Skype.

"Sit down or you'll overbalance us," he warned her, sliding further in the other direction to offset her weight.

Trying to impose her parasol between her dog and the nearest swan, Meriel stretched too far. As he reached instinctively to catch her, the skiff rolled slowly onto its side from his added weight, tipping them both into the churned waters. In disbelief, he saw her clutch the parasol with both hands as she sank under the rollicking ripples.

Kicking away from the boat as he went over, Jonys thrashed about, diving to find her quickly before she panicked. He didn't know if she swam, but few ladies learned how. His stomach muscles clenched at an image of her swallowing water, terrified of drowning. He shot to the surface to search for her.

Wiping water from his face, he tossed back wet hair as he looked around, frantic on her behalf. A pair of boots filled with water made the swimming heavy going.

The boat's length away, she bobbed in the water, paddling with one hand and swiping at the swans with the soggy parasol. When she reached for Skype, she sank again, to come up coughing and spitting out the lake's water. Even so, she renewed her protective attack.

The ungrateful terrier swam just beyond her reach, ruddering with his tail and keeping his head well up. He still managed to bark threats at the hissing swans.

Slicing swiftly through the agitated water to come alongside Meriel, Jonys pulled her into his arms. "Get Kept," she cried, pushing him away. "I'll fend off the swans; get Kept safely to shore."

As he pulled her toward him again, she made contact underwater with his thigh, kicking out in her effort to stay afloat under her own power. She flailed at the birds with the parasol, very nearly putting out his eye as he turned her away from the attack.

"Never mind me," she said, coughing as water splashed into her mouth. "Get Kept while I fend off these creatures."

Catching hold of the parasol, he struggled with her for possession of it. As soon as she grasped its handle with both hands, she sank under the water. He pulled her up by the wrist and against his chest, but having her in his arms wasn't nearly the thrill he had enjoyed yesterday.

"Can you swim?" he grated out when she tried to push him away again.

For an instant she looked surprised; then she flung away the parasol and grasped his arm with both hands. "No!" She gasped as water washed over her face again. "But where's Kept?"

"Paddling around behind you like a seal now that the swans have decided that further warfare is beneath their dignity." Exasperated with Meriel for ignoring her own safety to protect her dog, he also couldn't help but admire her foolhardy courage. "Hold on to me and I'll have you ashore in a trice."

Once Skype bumped her with his broad nose as he swam alongside, Meriel was satisfied to accept Jonys's arm about her. Now that the crisis was past, Jonys became all too aware of her sinuous curves moving within his arms, her body warm against him in the cool water. He'd never held a wet woman in this liquid embrace, with sunlight and wavelets washing over their shoulders.

If it weren't for the collection of onlookers gathered at the lake's edge calling to him, he would have taken his time about swimming ashore. Skype paddled nearby all the way in, looking pleased with himself, as if interrupting Jonys's proposal was a proud achievement.

The lake wasn't deep, so Jonys soon touched bottom and stood, gathering Meriel into his arms to carry her ashore. As her hands joined behind his neck, he looked down into her wet face with a surge of tenderness, wanting to save her from every calamity that might befall her.

With water streaming from her clothing, she resettled her ruined hat as he stepped onto dry land and other guests pushed close. "You may put me down now," she said. "I'm perfectly capable of walking."

Ignoring the flurry of questions and advice from onlookers, Jonys let her knees go so she slid down his length, supported against possible faintness.

He kept an arm across her back to be certain she was steady on her feet.

As she stepped away, he saw that her skirts were far worse than dampened, that scandalous practice of fast females of the ton. Furthermore, he didn't want anyone else seeing her in a clinging gown.

Glancing about, he spotted a paisley shawl drooping loosely off a lady standing nearby. "May I borrow this," he said as he lifted it from her elbows without waiting for an answer. Quickly he wrapped it about Meriel to shield her from gawkers.

An outraged "Upon my word!" reminded Jonys that he might have given offense. Distracted, he begged pardon from the shawl's owner with the smile that usually won him forgiveness from females.

As he made an effort to respond to questions about the mishap, Jonys wished everyone would go away and let him look after Meriel on his own. At his feet, Skype barked once and began to shake himself energetically. The resulting shower backed off the crowd in its finery.

Anxious, Jonys tucked the shawl under Meriel's chin. "Do you feel chilled?" Maybe ladies could die from a soaking even on a warm day. Yanking the uneven wrap down to cover as much of her as possible, he glared at a man pushing through the onlookers toward them until he realized it was Burchett, struggling out of his coat.

Hester hurried to Meriel, taking her hands to peel off the wet primrose gloves and chafe them. "Here, let Burchett put his coat about your shoulders, too," she said. "We must get you home at once. Jonys, will you bring Kept?"

"Certainly," he said. Feeling oddly deprived and left out now that her cousin had taken over and begun leading Meriel away, Jonys stood dripping beside Skype. His feet felt as heavy as his spirits, with his toes squelching in wet boots.

Skype barked, and Meriel turned at once, gazing at Jonys instead of the terrier. "Your coat!" she said, looking stricken. "You're just as soaked as I am, and I'm very much afraid I let your coat sink into the lake."

Jonys grinned, enjoying the way she colored as her gaze shifted down his soaked shirt and pantaloons before flying back to his face. "Blame the swans for the entire mishap," he said. "And for pity's sake, don't buy out a tailor's shop over the loss of one coat."

Chapter Eight

"That's his voice in the entrance hall! He didn't send word that he meant to call. I hope nothing's wrong." Hands pressing against flutters in her stomach, Meriel looked from the door to Hester. Beside her, Kept came to attention, ears erect and eyes fastened on her.

"I don't have to ask who you mean when you're as white as my petticoat." Hester laid aside her charcoal and sketchbook. "Osborne comes without notice on purpose, hoping to disconcert you, so it would serve him right if you don't see him. Send him word you're Not at Home."

"But he may have brought word about the boys." James had a tendency to sore throats and Steven had frequent accidents. Her worst nightmare was that one of her boys would sicken and die before she learned they were ill.

Hurrying to a glass, she checked her hair for

neatness. Thank heaven she had chosen to wear a lace tucker and ruff with her walking dress this morning. Would Osborne think this new way with her hair too fashionable? She had washed it after the dunking in the lake three days ago, and it still tended toward unruliness.

A cold bump against her leg assured her that Kept was beside her. He often walked or sat close enough to nudge her with his broad, damp nose.

"You look charming," said Hester, appearing in the glass behind her. "Osborne has absolutely no reason to find fault with your appearance, though he'll probably do so anyway. I'd like to tie his cravat for him, tighter and tighter until he can't criticize anyone, ever again. Don't you dare allow him to unnerve you. Meet him with the assurance that you're living in your own house, taking care of your business affairs quite competently."

Panic shook Meriel. "Does that mean you're leaving me to face him on my own? You must come in with me. Please, Hester."

"Wouldn't miss it," said her cousin, lips and eyebrows drawn into angry lines. "Just let him try his tricks with me present." Kept barked sharply twice. "And you'll help me, won't you, Kept? If we have to, we'll chase him out, with you nipping at his skinny calves and me battering him with the hearth broom."

"No, please, don't make him angry. He might take his temper out on the boys if we upset him." Maybe she shouldn't ask Hester to come in with her.

"I'll try to keep my tongue between my teeth," Hester said with reluctance. "But you encourage his hateful behavior when you allow him to bully you."

A knock at the library door was followed by Norton's entrance. "I've put Lord Lamport in the drawing room, m'lady." The butler waited for further instructions, looking sympathetic.

"Thank you, Norton," Meriel said, acting the outward role of mistress of the house, if not feeling its inward calm. "Tea at once, with as many different cakes as cook has on hand." As Norton pulled the door to behind him, she explained to Hester, "Osborne enjoys his sweets. Maybe refreshment will put him in a better humor."

"That green persimmon doesn't have a better humor." Hester followed her and Kept out of the library.

Crossing the hall to the front of the house, Meriel felt as if she were trudging into battle without hope of survival. She had never learned the right tone to placate her brother-in-law. Just thinking of him depressed her spirits.

At the door to the drawing room, she paused to take a deep breath and felt Hester's hand on her shoulder. Kept looked up at her before putting his nose to the crack in the door. At least she didn't have to face Osborne alone today; she had supporters. Hester believed she was a decent person and good mother, whatever Osborne's opinion. If she was to deal effectively with him, she must believe in herself.

Meriel pushed open the door and entered her drawing room with her shoulders back and head high. "Hello, Osborne. I hope you bring me good reports on my boys and yourself."

Standing, Osborne indicated a sofa beside him as if he were in his own drawing room. "Sit down, Meriel. Welwyn's sons do very well. Lady Stanford, I can't think why you're here. This conversation concerns only Meriel and myself."

Kept walked directly to him, sniffing at the white stockings he wore with old-fashioned knee breeches. With hardly a glance down, Osborne shoved him aside with his foot.

Fury rising in her throat, Meriel hurried to scoop up her dog and carry him away from the vicar.

Hester looked like a banty hen ready to defend her chicks. "You don't seem to realize that this is my home, too, Ossy." Her cousin knew he despised pet names, calling them an affectation of fashionable fribbles. "As two widowed ladies, Meriel and I always receive callers together. You wouldn't want her to closet herself with gentlemen."

Smiling with more than a hint of malice in her expression, Hester chose a chair facing Osborne. Meriel slipped quickly into an elbow chair near her, Kept on her lap. Retribution would be swift.

"Pertness is no more becoming in a lady of your age than in a young girl." Osborne pulled his coat's tails carefully to the side before seating himself with as much ceremony as a bishop. His tone and eyes were cold like the winter's worst wind, chilling and cutting at whatever stood in the way.

"I'll hang on your every word and action, to learn kindness instead," Hester replied instantly.

Kept's tongue fell out of his open mouth, and he looked as if he were grinning.

Even as she regretted Hester's sarcasm, which tightened Osborne's lips and slitted his eyes, Meriel admired her spirit and quick response. Meriel never found the right reply until hours after disturbing conversations.

"You would do better to sit quietly and consider

that I'm a man of God and a brother by marriage to Meriel. No impropriety can attach to my visits under any circumstance."

Osborne made a show of presenting his shoulder to Hester. For him, her cousin was no longer in the room. "You look well, my dear, almost modest," he said to Meriel. "Though you'd do better to show less vanity in arranging your hair. This is why I advised you not to seek out those who pursue only pleasure. I'm disappointed that you ignored my counsel and came to London. When do you return to Welwyn Hall?"

The old sense of wrongdoing fell on her under his sorrowing gaze. "When James and Steven come down for the summer holiday, I plan to be there. Though I hope to have them with me here in London for a few days first, if you'll allow it. They would enjoy visiting Astley's Amphitheater and the Tower." Meriel made a point of smiling. "The boys will be ready to relax from the rigors of school, and I'm eager to be with them."

"It isn't possible for the boys to visit London. You know I don't consider the air healthy here, and I wouldn't want them exposed to unsavory elements of society at their tender years." Osborne didn't look at her as he delivered the ultimatum.

"Most of their schoolmates spend time here without harm," Meriel said. Forcing a cheerful tone, she added, "Though I'll stay at Welwyn Hall whenever they come down from Eton if you require it. I wouldn't miss an opportunity to be with them for any consideration." She wanted to serve him polite notice that she wouldn't be denied time with them.

"We'll both be there." Hester's support was welcome.

As if her cousin hadn't spoken, Osborne addressed only Meriel. "I urge you to return there at once as London's society is no fit place for a proper mother to be. However, the young earl and his brother will use the days between school sessions in a more meaningful way than being indulged by an overly fond mother. I mean to show them every church and cathedral of historical and architectural significance in the south of England."

"But they need time away from study to go back to it with renewed interest and energy," Meriel protested. "And they need days with a parent to know they're loved."

Kept made a sound like a word.

"All children, boys as well as girls, need a mother's guidance and love," Hester added.

"Their dead father chose me to rear them properly in his place." Osborne didn't change his tone or expression, and he didn't so much as glance in Hester's direction. "Mothers can't help but spoil children, though I concede that you want the best for Welwyn's sons, Meriel. You aren't a competent judge of what's good for them, however. My brother's sons will receive the most thorough education available today, and edifying travel during all school holidays will prepare them for responsibility far better than pampering."

Her boys would be kept away from her forever, as Hester had predicted. Swallowing anger in order to speak reasonably, Meriel felt the old despair of being powerless. "All holidays? Do you mean them to be away from home any time they aren't in school? Are we never to be together?"

Restless, Kept shifted position on her lap, looking at her with large, anxious eyes. She put her hands on his round sides to gather comfort from his presence as much as to reassure him.

"This is difficult for you to understand, my dear sister. But you must accept that they're out of skirts and off leading strings. It's past time they put away childish things. They must prepare to serve God and the Welwyn title and estates as is their duty. You'll have to be brave and allow them to grow into the fine men their father expected them to become." Conviction rang in Osborne's voice and showed in his features.

Out of respect for his collar, Meriel controlled her desire to rail against his wrongheaded decisions, speaking with quiet reason and dignity. "James is only eight, and Steven seven. They won't be called on to handle the responsibilities of men for many years. Even if you won't let me see them, can't you allow them time to be boys? Surely they'll become better men for experiencing the usual childhood years."

"I couldn't agree more," Hester said, "except that they must know their mother or grow into twisted, unnatural men like badly pruned trees."

As if her cousin hadn't spoken, Osborne shook his head at Meriel. "A man knows more about—" He broke off as the door opened on Norton, followed by two footmen carrying trays. Setting his lips together, Osborne watched in silence as a table was placed before Meriel and the tea tray deposited on it.

"Put the cakes near Lord Lamport where they'll be easy to reach," she murmured to the footman. Meriel welcomed the interruption. She needed time to breathe, to think, to settle the shudders of fear and anger that wracked her mind and body. Osborne had always ignored her when she showed emotion. If she were to communicate with him, she had to remain calm. She couldn't fail to move him. James and Steven needed her intervention.

Osborne never looked at servants, and he wouldn't speak until they left the room. He had barely tolerated a couple of servants in Welwyn Hall's dining room to serve meals, refusing to allow discussion of any personal topic in their presence.

Meriel didn't want her boys to grow up with this toplofty attitude toward the people who kept them comfortable. She had begun teaching them to treat servants and tenants with respect and consideration, but would they remember her early influence under Osborne's sole guidance?

The vicar stared pointedly at Kept while the servants left the room. When the door closed behind them, he said, "My dear, you can't mean to make my tea with that nasty creature on your lap."

"Don't worry about the dog; you're obviously immune to any threat of death." Hester's disgruntled observation made Meriel want to laugh hysterically, thinking of her cousin's many schemes to finish off the vicar, even though she didn't dare to smile in his company.

Kissing Kept between the ears with affection and defiance, Meriel set him on the floor. He sat down by her slippers and leaned against her leg while she made tea the way Osborne preferred it.

As she lifted an extra cube of sugar for his cup, Osborne rose and said, "I'll do it; you never get it right."

When he was a yard away, hand extended, Kept stood, gruffing in his throat. Meriel placed her hand on his side, feeling the vibration set up as he vocalized his opinion of Osborne. Though she agreed with it, she couldn't allow him to anger the man and be kicked. "Kept, no," she said firmly.

Though he stopped growling, he didn't sit down again until Osborne took his cup and settled into his chair. Kept had become far more protective of her than she expected for the length of time he had been with her. Her heart warmed at this evidence of his attachment to her.

When Osborne had devoured two cakes with greedy pleasure, Meriel ventured a comment. "I hope you'll reconsider your plans for the boys' holidays. Perhaps you could allow me to visit with them during holidays just until they're a little older. Surely they'll benefit more from travel and your good explanations of what they see when they're fourteen and fifteen."

Taking his time about selecting another cake, Osborne set it on his cup plate and brought his cup and saucer to her for refilling. "I appreciate your devotion to the boys," he said as she took the cup. As she began pouring, he continued. "But they're my responsibility, and I can't condone pampering. They'll be reared as befits gentlemen by gentlemen. You mustn't be selfish, my dear sister."

The absurd admonition shook Meriel and her hand jerked, spilling hot tea into the saucer. Carefully she set the cup on a towel to dry its bottom and poured tea from the saucer into the slops. Hoping her voice was under control, she spoke with caution. "I can't think it's selfish to love my children and want us to be together at times."

"I wouldn't expect you to understand complex matters, my dear." Osborne sounded soothing as he took his cup from her nearly steady hands.

"You must leave vital decisions like this to a wiser head, remembering that your husband entrusted them to me alone. Even in his death, you must be guided by his superior judgment as is God's will. I won't lead you or Welwyn's sons off the path he would choose if he could still be with us."

Her husband's lack of faith in her ability to rear their sons devastated her again, as it had since his death. Meriel was too appalled to trust her voice, but her cousin didn't suffer from that handicap.

"You pious, pompous fool," Hester cried, leaping to her feet. "No wonder you don't have a proper parish anymore. You're too busy playing God to lead people to worship Him."

Kept stood when Hester did, rumbling threats like a yodel as she spoke.

Seeing Osborne's face suffuse and his lips tighten, Meriel felt the old impotent trembling wrack her body. "Hester," she whispered as her throat tightened past speaking. When her cousin looked her way, she shook her head in warning and despair. Lesser insults had turned Osborne ugly in the past.

Now he glared at Hester. He set down his cup and laid aside the half-eaten cake. Standing, he addressed Meriel with cold formality.

"You've allowed yourself to be misguided through emotion to take a woman into your house who blasphemes God and His chosen servant. You will cast this creature of the devil into the streets at once, or you won't see your sons while I live." His chin up and his ice-gray eyes frozen on her, he awaited her response.

Meriel rose, looking between Osborne's cold assurance and Hester's expression of guilt and apology. Terrified by a fixed look like madness in his eyes, she tried to summon a reasonable tone. "Sit down and finish your tea, Osborne. Hester responded in the heat of the moment to what seemed like injustice to me and my sons. She'll apologize if you want. Let's be reasonable and forgiving, as our Holy Father expects us to be."

Osborne didn't blink as his eyes became blank walls, as if no human existed behind them. "You're hardly qualified to translate God's will for me. I mean what I said. You can't live with this ungodly influence and be a person I'd allow near *Welwyn's sons*."

His harping on those last two words had grated her nerves throughout this visit, as they had since her husband died. Now they shredded her shrinking control over years of resentment and fury at the impossible demands and interference of this sick, dangerous little man.

Curling her hands into fists in the folds of her skirts, she spoke with diminishing control over the quaver to her voice and the expression of her wrath. "My sons, too, Osborne, my sons as much as your brother's. Keep in mind that Welwyn didn't conceive them alone, he didn't carry them for nine months under his heart, and he wasn't even present when they entered this world from my body. My sons still have a living parent who loves them as much as their father did or as much as you do, Osborne. I know your misguided edicts grow from your love for them, just as your interference in your brother's life resulted from loving him too much. But I can't stand by while you try to twist their minds by your control as you did his."

Osborne stood staring at her as if a pigeon had transformed into a hawk before his eyes and attacked him. His nostrils pinched and his eyes loomed large in his face. An invisible cloud of hostility and rage gathered about him and moved inexorably toward her, engulfing and choking her with its pressure.

His voice was as swift and quiet as a snake's bite. "Thank God you have no legal right to carry on your evil efforts to lead Welwyn men astray. You know nothing about brotherly love that devotes a lifetime to protecting a brother and, now, his sons. You tried at every turn to undermine my place with Welwyn, when we had been together since the day I was born. You won't destroy my place with his sons, for you won't get near them."

Kept answered with piercing barks, standing between Osborne and Meriel. In shock at Osborne's crazed charges, she couldn't think how to reply to mad, senseless statements.

Casting a look of fury at the terrier, Osborne thundered out, "God has given me another chance to keep an Earl of Welwyn's feet on the path of righteousness, and no evil will keep me from my duty. Women are the devil's handmaidens, and you'll not sully those boys further."

Stiff as a poker, Osborne marched to the door of the drawing room with Kept snapping and growling at his boots. The vicar turned to kick viciously at the dog, but Kept dodged away. From a safer distance, but still between Osborne and Meriel, he continued defiant barks.

By now, the vicar's face was as white as his collar, and the look in his empty eyes terrified Meriel. "God will strike you dead if you come within view of Welwyn's sons again."

Yanking open the door, he stomped through and slammed it behind him. Running to it, Kept snuffled loudly at the crack. When the outer door slammed, he dashed back to Meriel, making a medley of sounds without barking.

Meriel simply stared, feeling the charged air of the room swirl around her. Kept's paws bumped her shin and Hester's arm slipped around her waist, but she was hollow inside, unable to respond. Numbly, she waited for the agony of loss to fill her, squeezing life from her heart and lungs. She couldn't think or move as cold cloaked her entire body.

Feeling Hester urge her toward the sofa, she moved in that direction. It didn't matter where she went or what she did. She would never see her beloved sons again. By allowing emotion to get the better of her judgment, she had unleashed her feelings and lost her boys forever.

A cup pressed against her lips and she drank. Hot tea. China black. Lemon and Demerara sugar, two lumps. If she concentrated on insignificant details, the enormous sorrow might not swell and explode within her chest.

Paws pressed painfully into her thigh and a warm tongue washed her cheek. A whimper roused her enough to look down, and Kept's pleading brown eyes brought her gradually to an awareness beyond her frozen spirit. Hester bent over her, dabbing with a lace-edged handkerchief at the cheek Kept wasn't tending. She must be crying, even though she felt no sobs or tears on her face.

Taking the handkerchief from Hester's hand, she put an arm about Kept. Shuddering, she came back slowly to reality. This loss hurt far more than any physical pain, more than she could endure and live. Yet she couldn't escape the horror and

171

have any hope of holding her boys close again. She had to go through it, deal with it.

Hester had her arms about her, rocking her and crooning. Kept was bumping her cheek with his nose. She wasn't alone.

Meriel patted them both awkwardly. "Sit down here beside me," she said to Hester. "We have a great deal of planning to do. Osborne will not keep me and my sons apart."

Chapter Nine

As the footman went up to announce him, Jonys grinned at the terrier's cautious descent from tread to tread down the burled-wood staircase to the entrance hall. With his short legs and heavy chest, the dog could easily overbalance, carrying his weight to the front as he did. Skype must have recognized his voice as the footman let him in and come to greet him.

A muffled feminine voice reached Jonys faintly from above stairs. "Don't tell me someone's come to call, Hays. I don't want to see anyone after yesterday's horrid visitor. Who is it, anyway?" Meriel must be near the stairwell rising above him, on one of the townhouse's three upper floors, for him to make out her words.

A quiet murmur followed while Jonys considered the possible identity of yesterday's caller.

When Meriel spoke again, he stepped onto the

stairs to catch what she said more clearly. "The Earl of Hadham! And me turning out a cupboard in a mob cap. Put him in the front drawing room, and I'll be down when I'm fit to be seen."

The Countess of Welwyn playing at housemaid. Jonys couldn't resist the impulse to see this in more than imagination. He took the stairs two at a time.

Halfway up, he scooped Skype off the tread where the terrier had halted, watching intently with his head to one side. Tucking the dog under his arm, Jonys arrived on the second floor and glanced around briefly. No Meriel. Skype pointed with his nose up the next flight.

Sounding breathless, Meriel's voice came louder, almost over his head. "Wait! Not the main drawing room; I can't face that room again today. Take him up to the drawing room looking into the garden."

Grinning, Jonys slipped quietly up the second staircase as Meriel continued. "Don't serve him claret; I noticed he didn't finish the glass when he called last time. Offer him a choice among hock, port, or—"

Breaking off as he appeared at the top of the stairs, Meriel stared at him in surprise. She stood before a cupboard that opened into the passage surrounding the staircase and held bed linen. Though her headgear matched that of the maid's who stood by her, Meriel's bearing left no doubt which of the three before him was in authority.

Snatching off the voluminous white cap, she thrust it into a stack of sheets in the open cupboard. As she tidied her hair with quick touches of graceful fingers, she looked vexed and disconcerted. "What are you doing up here? Maybe I should be flattered by your eagerness to see me, but your manners disgrace your old nanny."

"The conventions can keep a fellow from having any fun, can't they, Skype?" He set the terrier on his paws. "I couldn't resist coming up to see where you sleep." This floor appeared to be given over to bedchambers from what he glimpsed through open doors.

"If you want a tour of the house, ask for it politely and I'll arrange for the housekeeper to take you around." She was very much on her dignity. "Thank you, Hays, you may see to the wine. Milly, we'll finish the inventory later. Jonys, if you'll bring Kept, we'll go down to the drawing room where I can receive you properly."

"How disappointing." Teasing Meriel might eventually encourage her to relax and take life less seriously.

Bundling a half-folded sheet into the cupboard, she began to close its door.

"No need to leave that job half finished," he said, stopping her and tugging on the sheet. "Might as well put this away since you're here. I'll help. It can't be that different from folding a handkerchief."

As he shook out the sheet again, she stared at him, lips tight and arms crossed. "You shouldn't be up here; and now that my servants have gone below stairs, we should as well. I'll wager you've never folded a sheet in your life."

" 'Should's' are as limiting as conventions, I find. As for folding sheets, I'll never learn how any younger, as my nanny used to say." The linen looked well worn, not what he would expect a countess to keep for her beds. "Look at that, a hole where somebody snagged his toe in a thin spot.

175

Here I've been trying to wed you as a woman of wealth, and I find you sorting out your own sheets, which look ready to be cut up for dusting."

"At least you realize that we won't suit." When she reached for the linen, he bunched it behind him.

Stepping back, she continued, talking a little too fast. "I needed to be busy today, rather than sitting about with useless thoughts chasing around my brain like squirrels through a tree's branches. So I decided to sort out the linens my aunt left me along with this house."

The cursed sheet seemed to billow to twice its normal size as he searched for two corners to match up. Maybe Meriel's visitor of yesterday was the source of her worries. "I call them windmill thoughts because they turn around and around but never get you anywhere," he said. The more he handled the linen, the bigger it got. "This is the first sheet I've seen with no edges to it. It looks worn; why not throw this one out, or give it to Skype to sleep on?"

"The linens were sadly neglected during the last years of my aunt's life. She didn't see as well as she once did, and I'm afraid her servants took advantage of that."

Reaching into the folds on the floor, Meriel came up with two corners at once by some miracle and put one into each of his hands. Another dip into the cascading linen, and she'd found two more. Women were naturally better at this sort of thing.

"And I always thought I was an authority on sheets." He grinned as she ignored him. He'd have to try bigger bait to get a rise out of her. "Can't think of anyone I'd rather have teach me more, though. What do I do with my bits?"

"Just like most men," she said, shaking her head and demonstrating how to match the corners together. "You're much better at muddling things than putting them right again."

"I'm trying to convince you to take me in hand and set me straight," he said with a lewd leer. Coaxing a smile from her seemed more of a task today than usual.

Without comment, Meriel caught up the other end of the folded sheet and held it off the floor, coming toward him. "Hold up your end of it like this and bring it to me," she directed him.

This was an opportunity not to be missed. Lapping his sheet's ends as she had, he met her and secured the corners under her fingers. When she had them in her grasp, he closed his fingers over her small fists, covering them completely.

How delicate the bones of her little hands felt within his hold. How irate the expression of her dark golden brown eyes over the sheet stretched under her defiant chin.

The scent of violets from her hair mingled with faint lavender from the linen and raised a bouquet of desire in his mind and body. Her eyes widened as she tugged at her hands and found how easily he could hold her there, arms wide, with little more than a sheet between them.

If he let go of her hands, he could have his arms about her before she moved away. Could it be a mistake to seize a kiss, when he wanted to do so this urgently?

An unexpected flurry of activity around his feet was followed by a loud ripping sound. Startled, Jonys let go of her hands as he looked down.

The folds of the sheet lying on the floor roiled like heavy sea swells until a hairy paw thrust its way through. Strong swipes enlarged the rip until a long whiskered muzzle, followed by a stout body, emerged. Skype fought his way free of the sheet and turned to bark at it, ripping at it with sharp teeth.

Meriel stooped gracefully to take it away from him. "No, Kept," she said firmly. "No. I don't like it when you tear up things. No. No."

The terrier sat down, looking away, then frisked around her as if asking her to play. As Meriel bent above the dog, Jonys wanted to caress the vulnerable back of her neck where wisps of curls strayed onto it.

" 'No' doesn't appear to worry him," Jonys said, amused by her serious discussion with Skype over his wrongdoing. "But it's only an old sheet, after all. Hardly worth making a fuss about."

"The next item he traps himself in could be Hester's best knit shawl, and she can't afford to replace her things easily. Best to teach him respect for others' property from the start." Rising, she dropped the sheet onto a large basket of linens nearby. "This can be mended and still give good service, if not in the guest rooms."

The hint that her cousin might have limited funds struck Jonys. Meriel was a generous person; he'd have to reassure her that Hester would always be welcome in their house.

Motioning to the basket, he said, "That tear is a yard long; do ladies really think it's worth the thread to mend linens this far gone? If I had a shirt with a hole in it, I'd send it to the rag man when it ripped."

Meriel started toward the stairs. "That's why

178

men have capable wives or housekeepers, to prevent such waste. Let's go down to the drawing room."

As she walked past him, he caught her hand briefly and kissed its palm, looking into her guarded eyes as he released it. "At least give me credit for trying to acquire a more than capable wife, even if you consider me a wastrel. If you'll agree to wed me, you can sort out the linens and the kennels at all of my houses."

"How many do you own?" she asked, holding the hand he had kissed against her stomach with the other. That wasn't quite the area he had hoped to affect.

"Three decent manor houses, a hunting box, and Hadham House," he answered. "The income from the lesser properties provides my three sisters their doweries, or will when they're productive again. So don't get too set on ordering things as you want them in those linen cupboards."

"Your linens are nothing to me," she said shortly. "Take them out to your kennels for the dogs to sleep on, for all I care."

Meriel picked up Skype and started down the steps with his front paws hooked over her shoulder. From this vantage point, he panted at Jonys.

"What a disappointment." Though he kept his tone light, Jonys wished she didn't dismiss his hints that they marry without a second thought. He hadn't found the right approach to persuade her as yet, but he would.

Following her into a long room across from the stairs on the first floor, he looked about it for clues to her nature. The colors were quiet and restful, blues with grays that were cousins to blue, and touches of green echoing the leaves nodding outside near the windows. Across a pretty Axminster carpet, tall windows looked down into the garden where he had sat with Meriel, Hester, Burchett, and Skype in the pergola.

A pergola wasn't a structure you expected to find in a town house's small garden, come to think of it. Jonys glanced about the cool room, quiet and reserved at first glance, like Meriel. Yet a few unusual features suggested more lay waiting beneath her surface.

A cloud ceiling, more subtly painted than the one at the Queen's retreat, Frogmore, he had noticed at once. But the window wall was the room's most dramatic feature. Painted in delicate, shadowed hues as if seen through mist, stylized plants grew from window to window. The veiled garden mural was clever, beautiful, rare. Like Meriel.

The unexpected was what he must expect from her, like the imaginative, unconventional taste she showed here. Maybe he could surprise her, too, give her a better opinion of him.

"Won't you sit down," she invited him.

As the footman entered with a tray of decanters, Jonys shook his head. "I like moving about, if you don't mind." If he sat down in his present eagerness, he'd only spring back to his feet.

To the servant he said, "Pour me a glass of the hock, please. What will you have?" Meriel held up a hand in refusal. "And spirits aren't good for hairy little fellows, Skype," The terrier balanced on his hindquarters to sniff at the tray.

"Kept enjoys having you come to call on him." Meriel emphasized the dog's name, and he grinned at her. She trailed a hand along the back of a chintz-covered chair as she walked away from him. Her pleasure in touching things pleased him, bringing visions to mind of her hands eager to play over his body.

Setting his glass on a side table, he reached into his coat. "Much as I like to see Skype, you're the main reason for my calls, especially today. I brought you a small token of my feelings for you." Giving her something of real significance buoyed him up more than any event had done in a long time.

Rounding a striped sofa, she perched on its edge as if she might need to run away at any moment. "Don't disappoint me by pretending to be lovelorn, Jonys. I can't bear to be that mistaken in your good sense, or in your opinion of mine."

"Perhaps you don't choose to believe that an old dog like me can fall in love, but I want to see you happy. Surely that's a great deal more than many modern couples bring to marriage." As he crossed the room to her, he extracted two folded pages from his slanted inner breast pocket. "Don't misjudge how quickly a man can feel real affection for you, Meriel. Much as I enjoy bantering with you, I say that in all seriousness. I want to be your friend, your very good friend."

As he unfolded the sheets, she said quickly, "You mustn't bring me gifts; real friendship doesn't require that kind of proof."

Jonys smiled; she deserved to be twitted a bit. "This gift isn't as valuable in monetary terms as my table, but I hope it pleases you." Leaning down, he put the pages in her hands and waited, watching her expression.

Meriel glanced at the top sheet quickly, then looked back again. The room seemed to tilt and recede. She smoothed the thick, cream paper on her lap, feeling its faint texture with her fingertips to convince herself it was real.

A childish drawing, stick figures really, sprawled across the page. Impossible! Those looping lines for the leaves of trees were unmistakable, but Jonys couldn't have one of Steven's drawings in his possession. She had every one he'd ever made for her safe in a folder upstairs. Besides, she hadn't seen this one, with a disproportionate tree and two small figures far distant from a collection of roofed boxes that usually represented Welwyn Hall.

Sliding out the sheet underneath, Meriel felt a growing swell of unreality. The down-slanted lines and cramped letters of James's immature fist crept over the page in smeared pencil.

The uneven tops to the sheets looked as if they had been torn from a drawing book, none too neatly, and both the drawing and writing had been done in a rush. They were the most beautiful sight that could meet her eyes.

Rising, she moved in a near-trance to the writing desk under a window and laid down the sheets with great care. She felt afraid to hold them, afraid to breathe on them, terrified they would disappear by some horrible alchemy. A superstitious fear warned her that if she grasped them too tightly, they wouldn't really be there.

"They're from your boys." The unnecessary information came from just behind her. Jonys's reassuring tone startled her; she had forgotten his presence.

When he reached toward the papers, most likely to edge them into full light, Meriel snatched them away. She couldn't conceive how the drawing and letter came to be here, but they felt thick and warm to her fingers as if her boys had just held them. Anxiety over losing this once-removed contact with her sons made her unwilling to have any hands but hers touch them. Even the hands that had brought them.

A chair's edge pressed against the back of her knees and Meriel sat, never looking away from the engrossing penciled lines. Studying the drawing, she could hear Steven's eager voice in her head, explaining what he had drawn in great detail. "That's the tree I'm going to climb when I'm as tall as James, all the way to the top, and I won't fall out either because I'll be big and strong then, strong enough to get a kitten down all by myself without any help, and I'll find a bird's nest, but I won't bother the eggs."

Her blurring vision found the cramped writing James had slanted down his sheet. A quieter, more serious voice echoed the words she read.

Mother I think about you every day. I didn't want to go. I dont like it here even the nursery is better. Uncle Os says I have to study and work hard before I see you again, I'm too big to need a Mama. Wanting isn't the same as Needing is it. Nanny said so when I said I needed another biscuit. When I grow up I'll see you every day. I won't let anything hurt Steven dont worry.

James's letter choked her throat with sobs and blinded her. But it was his signature that burst past the painful barrier and flooded her face with tears.

At the bottom of his letter he had made an effort

to sign the sheet as he had seen his father flourish his name across a page: "Welwyn." In pencil and boyish script, the effect was hardly the same.

But to her aching heart, the single word revealed a boy shoved into a man's shoes before he was a youth, cast into a place where he had to look out for himself and protect his younger brother against boys older than himself.

Instead of complaining or railing against her for allowing him to be yanked out of his familiar home, he tried to reassure her. He didn't ask for help or rescue, just thought of her worry over little Steven. In his effort to shrug on the burden of a man when he wasn't yet nine, he endeared himself to her even more.

Her distress over the weight of such cares on a little boy made her bend above the writing desk in agony for him. Sobs ravaged their way out of the deep dungeon where she normally kept them imprisoned.

Knowing she couldn't stop the wracking tears at once, Meriel held the two precious pages to the sides of her bowed head, unwilling to expose them to one stain of moisture. If she couldn't hold her sons, she could touch what they had touched with their own dear, grubby fingers.

A mental image of those two small pairs of hands sent fresh surges of weeping breaking over her usual barriers. Then big arms folded her against a solid wall of warm support. She held the precious pages out to the sides, choking out, "Don't crease them; oh, please don't let anything happen to my treasures." The plea included, unreasonably, both her sons and these cherished tokens from them.

"I have them safe, and you, too." Jonys's deep

voice rumbled under her ear, reassuring and fierce.

First one sheet and then the other was eased from her fingers, and she pulled away from the warmth to see where they went. Jonys had collected them both in one big hand and laid them on the desk. He knelt to the side of her, but she couldn't think about that right now as he took her back into his comforting hold. Grief for her boys and joy at this contact with them filled her to overflowing.

"I have you. Nothing will happen to you or your sons. I have you." The litany of comfort murmured above her head gave Meriel permission to let go, to let down her guard. She didn't have to be strong right this instant. Big hands alternately caressed her back and patted her, while arms closed her into a haven where she could rest, where she could take strength instead of give it for the moment.

Every sore place of her spirit, scraped bare by the past three years and ripped open again by Osborne's edict of yesterday, ran in a wild river that couldn't be dammed or diverted any longer. Trying to stop her tears only increased their force, and she lost time and herself in the secure fortress shielding her at last.

Gradually the torrent slowed to a stream, then to a trickle. Too spent to move, she leaned into the solid warmth of a chest and shoulder big enough to support her easily. The weave of a waistcoat pressed against one ear, but her stuffy nose caught only a whiff of a cravat's clean starch and sunshine.

Though she needed desperately to mop her cheeks and blow her nose, Meriel didn't want to move. This stolen time and place was filched from mental anguish she hadn't escaped for a waking instant over the past three years. The ache would begin again in a little while, but not yet. Not yet.

Jonys was aware of little by now but his chest, arms, and hands, and his cheek where it lay against her hair. His heart. He could feel his heart weeping with her, for her, at the same time it swelled with tenderness for this brave lady who had stood alone too long.

He had been hunched on his knees too long, twisted in the position he had first taken when he reached for her. Numb prickles warned him not to move quickly or expect support from his legs and feet if he had to rise. He didn't care; he wasn't going anywhere. Not as long as she needed to lean against him, bend her body like a willow from the small desk chair onto his chest, with her head tucked under his chin.

If she wanted him to hold her for the rest of the afternoon and evening, all night, he would. If anyone dared come to the doorway and look in, he would strike them dumb with a glare.

Nothing must break this connection, this flow between them. He could feel them breathing in the same rhythm, and if his heart wasn't bashing his eardrums, he probably could feel hers beating with his, too.

For the first time in memory, he felt as if he was doing something meaningful, giving something where a real need existed. Where he had felt powerless to make things better lately, he could make this moment better for Meriel. It might not be much, compared to the needs of a world starving and at war, but it was everything to him here and now.

Jonys looked up at the painted clouds above them. Comfort must be like a cloud, because the more he tried to cover her with it, the more he felt enveloped by it himself. He wished they were on a cloud, drifting across sunny skies above the needs and duties of a demanding earth. He wished he could hold her above every care and woe.

Gradually, she quieted in his arms, and he cherished every instant, dreading when she might pull away. When she finally moved, it was a tentative drift of one hand down his waistcoat to explore the shallow pocket.

Next her hesitant fingers slid up his side and into his coat pocket, just over his heart, and found his handkerchief. Only the one small hand moved, her cheek nestled against him while she searched.

If only he could give her everything she needed, not just a couple of sheets of paper marked by two small, bewildered boys. Though that seemed to be enough to give now. That and a clean handkerchief.

Jonys didn't release Meriel while she applied the clean linen to her drowned eyelashes and wet face. When she tucked her nose into what must be sodden folds by now, he propped his chin on top of her disordered curls and grinned. If anyone had ever told him that Lord Had'em's heart could flop over like a sleeping hound finding another comfortable spot just because a woman was sheltered in his arms and blew her nose, he would have laughed in derision.

But he didn't feel like laughing about this. Or maybe he did, but only in the most tender, joyful, triumphant way. And only if he could coax Meriel to laugh with him. She had lacked laughter in her life far too long.

When she spoke, her voice was tremulous but eager. "Did you see them yourself? Talk with them?"

"Yes," he said, liking the way her curls tickled his chin when she talked. "I posted down to Windsor yesterday and dropped in at my old school. Hasn't changed much. Had a few words with the headmaster about a cousin's boys, then said I would take them out for a feast. Just casually said I'd take Welwyn's boys along, too."

A sigh rose from the region of his cravat. "That easily you were with them? Maybe it was because Osborne was calling on me at the time. How did they look?"

So that was who had set Meriel against seeing anyone today; he wasn't surprised by the revelation. "They looked like two normal little boys to me, a bit stiff with a stranger, but perfectly polite. Their nanny would be proud of them." Jonys risked a slight hug as he held her and she didn't move away.

"Yes, but did they look healthy, fearful, well fed? The important things, Jonys. I want to hear everything." Now she sounded a bit more like herself, telling him what to do.

"Let me think, then. The little one, Steven, was a bit shy at first, but then I thought he'd never be quiet long enough for his brother to wedge in a word."

Meriel made a sound between laughter and tears. "That's my Steven!"

"Handsome little fellow. Looked like he'd combed his hair in the dark, and one of his buttons was done up wrong. Had a smear of dirt on his upper lip, but he licked it off with the three puddings he had at the pastry cook's."

"Was James starved as well?" Her effort to sound brave was admirable.

"Never met a boy who wasn't. But James was polite enough to have to be begged to stuff himself. He's a regular little man, you know, almost as formal as a duke with me."

"He feels far too re-responsible for his age." Her voice was definitely muffled now.

"They're a bit confused by Eton, but I gave them a few pointers on standing bluff. You don't have to worry about those little fellows; they're game to the ground." He wouldn't tell her about Steven's split lip or James's scraped knuckles. He'd never reveal how James had winced when his back was touched, likely caned by one of the older boys.

The foursome he'd filled with cakes and pudding seemed ready to stand together for the good of them all, once he'd explained how difficult it could be for a couple of older boys to watch four opponents who kept moving all the time. They would manage better until he could sort things out for Meriel.

"Do you think they—they know I haven't abandoned them?" The quiet question, tinged with despair, tightened around his heart.

"They both know you couldn't do that," he assured her, even if he hadn't thought to ask the boys such a question. "When the little one took a breath I told them how much you missed them, and your James said in his proper, grown-up manner, 'Children see more than people think, sir, but thank you for saying so. Steven needs to hear it.' And then they fell into an argument over who had never doubted that you loved them for one minute."

Her chuckle was watery but reassuring. "They

always could argue the least thing for hours."

"Typical brothers. Chas and I were the same. Rest easy about those two scamps. They'll come out of this ears up." He'd pin the vicar's ears back if they didn't.

"I have to see them safe," she murmured as if talking to herself. "I can't bear to think of them under Osborne's deranged control."

Jonys swore by the curls tickling his chin and the sodden mess of his shirtfront and neck cloth that he would banish her demons. Meriel would never cry like this again, for he would win back James and Steven or anything else she needed for happiness.

He would owe her that as his wife.

Chapter Ten

Lifting two of the skins, Meriel took them to the bright daylight streaming in the glover's window. Her movement stirred a bouquet of the fragrances that Atkinson sold and used to scent his custom-made gloves.

Hester joined her, bringing the fabric sample for the new pelisse Meriel had ordered a week ago. Now she had no interest in it. Selecting leather for a new pair of gloves seemed a trifling use of time after Osborne's edict of two days before and then Jonys's visit yesterday.

"I prefer the lilac leather as far as the color itself goes, but it isn't right for the pelisse. The darker blue complements the lilac twill cloth more." Hester studied the three colors in the stronger light at the shop window.

Meriel stared at the three hues. She would have to decide what to do about Osborne, for he couldn't be allowed to impose his crazed notions on James and Steven as he seemed set on doing. "Whichever you prefer."

"Have a pair of gloves made up in each," Hester answered promptly. "When you need lilac gloves, you won't find this hue anywhere."

"The lilac, then." Osborne's virtual imprisonment of her sons took too much of her concentration to care about shopping. She felt edgy and impatient to be doing something significant to overcome the vicar's influence, even if she didn't yet know what might be useful.

Much as she wanted to snatch them away from him and flee the country, to do so might only confuse them, removing them from the familiar settings of home and England. Besides, with the Corsican Monster waging war, no country was safe from his seizure. The Little Emperor was another madman out to dominate others' lives.

Not that she could prove Osborne mad. He had presented a facade of reason to the world, reserving his hateful outbursts for the family. Besides, few people questioned the word of a vicar, a man of God.

Hester fingered the bishop's blue dyed leather. "Do you really like the blue with the Princess Elizabeth lilac? This particular lilac tends more toward blue than pink, I vow."

"Indeed." Keeping her sons anywhere in England left them subject to Osborne's total control.

"But the blue may give too much sameness to the overall toilette," Hester said.

"Yes, blue." If only she knew a man to discuss options with, someone who might understand what boys needed without feeling he could make the decision better than she. Fighting madness and unfair laws on her own left Meriel feeling overwhelmed.

"No doubt three fingers on each glove will be more than enough," Hester said.

"No doubt."

"Ha! I knew you were listening with only half an ear, if that." Hester dropped her voice to a murmur and moved closer. "I asked you to come out shopping with me to take your mind off your troubles, but you'll have to make an effort to think about other matters. Worrying every moment of the day won't help either you or your sons."

"I'm sorry. You're right. I'll try not to spoil your day." Holding up the blue leather, she added, "This one will do, and Atkinson has my measurements already. Did you need anything here?"

"Get them both, Merry. The lilac would be lovely with your blue spencer."

"I don't need lilac gloves at the moment, so why be extravagant? Would you enjoy having a pair made up in that shade?" The small gift would be an apology for her poor companionship on an Oxford Street ramble.

"Thank you, but no; it isn't my color. Cheer yourself up with a small indulgence, though. When I'm blue-deviled, nothing makes me feel more ready to cope than something new to wear, like girding myself for battle." In a wheedling tone, she added, "You deserve good things. If isn't as if you can't afford two pairs of gloves at once. You needn't pick and pinch just to prove you can manage money as well as a man, which I sometimes suspect you do."

Meriel felt defensive. "Caution with money isn't the same as being a pinch-purse."

Though she had kept housekeeping books during her marriage, Osborne had limited even her pin money after Welwyn's death, taking over household budgets himself. Until her aunt's legacy bought her freedom, the vicar had made her plead for every farthing from her widow's jointure as if she were on the dole. She knew the humiliation of empty pockets and begging for a copper. Independence required money, and the funds to hold onto her freedom wouldn't leave her hands.

A stir at the door made Meriel look in that direction as the shop assistant rushed forward to bow in an older lady with ceremony. Though they hadn't met since she lived with her parents in Surrey, in the same neighborhood as Hadham House, she recognized the newcomer at once.

"Lady Donnely!" This old acquaintance had called on her parents many times while staying nearby with Lady Hadham. "Fancy meeting you at a glover's in London. How good to see you."

The pigeon-breasted lady squinted as if she needed a quizzing glass, then bustled over, hands held out. "My dear Meriel, well met indeed. Iona and I spoke of you only a few days ago, for I broke my journey with her on the way here as usual. I missed your father sorely, as I do on every visit to your old neighborhood."

Meriel had to think a moment to recall that Jonys's mother's given name was Iona. As a girl, she would never have been allowed to address Lady Hadham that informally. It pleased her that Lady Hadham still remembered her.

Taking each of them by a hand, Lady Donnely stood beaming and nodding back and forth. "And this is your cousin Hester, I vow, for I remember you, too, you cheeky girl."

"While you're in town, I hope you'll call on us

194

in Portman Square," Meriel said with genuine warmth.

"Thank you, my dear, but this is more a stop to order a few necessities than a visit." Lady Donnely turned to the hovering shop clerk. "Find us chairs in a corner out of the way, for I can't stand long in these ridiculous flat slippers."

To Meriel and Hester, she said, "I can remember when shoes had proper heels, if you gels don't. Fashion isn't often kind to ladies of uncertain years, but you feel such a frump if you don't make an effort to look as if you know what's the thing." She paused to laugh at herself, a quality Meriel had learned to admire from her. "Spare me a few moments so we can exchange news before I rush off to the next shop. I can't leave for Brighton without ordering a dozen new pairs of gloves; my old ones show their age more than I do."

Quickly, Meriel handed the two leathers back to Atkinson's assistant. "I'll have a pair from each, if you'll make a note of that."

Bowing, he took them and bustled away.

"Of course we'll stay to chat with you," Meriel assured Lady Donnely. "Nothing is more important than time with good friends." Far better than shopping, catching up on mutual acquaintances would push her worries to the back of her mind for a little while.

Hester agreed and Meriel continued. "You must be traveling on to Brighton to visit with your sister. Is Lord Donnely with you?"

"Just to see me safely there," said the lady complacently. Her husband had idolized her through more than thirty years of marriage. "Then he'll return here to look after tiresome business affairs. I must get on to Brighton, for poor Iona asked me to find her rooms there, close to the sea and the best doctors. You may recall that her youngest, Claire, always had a weak chest."

Any of Jonys's sisters interested Meriel, because of her past acquaintance with his mama and her renewed acquaintance with him. "I hardly know Claire; she was still in the nursery when I married. She must be almost a young lady now?"

"Turned thirteen, poor mite." Lady Donnelly shook her head and tutted as they seated themselves in the rout chairs set by the window for them.

"Her condition has worsened?" Meriel made a mental note to send books for both the mother and daughter by the post, along with a letter for Lady Hadham. Occupying an ill child of any age was difficult enough for a mother, even without worries about chronic health problems and the funds to treat them.

Lady Donnelly sighed, smoothing her Devonshire brown silk skirts over plump knees. "The poor girl looked terribly pulled down, though she never so much as whispers a complaint. And her cough! Much as she tried to hold it back, it shook her visibly." Leaning forward, she said in a confidential voice, "I wouldn't be surprised to learn that it's consumption, though Iona never used the word. But she said the cobweb pills had done the child no good, so what else could it be?"

Consumption was too often a death sentence, if slow in its progress. With other losses weighing upon Jonys already, how particularly tragic to have his youngest sister suffer from that malady. How would he provide the treatment and sea air Claire needed when the estate was all to pieces?

The three of them discussed the best shops for

196

various purchases since Lady Donnely came to town only occasionally. As Meriel hadn't lived in London long enough to form strong opinions on shops, she considered her problems and Jonys's as the other two talked.

Perhaps it was more than coincidence that both Jonys and she wrestled with circumstances centered on beloved children. He had eased the ache of separation from her sons yesterday; perhaps she could relieve Claire's situation.

At last Lady Donnely patted their hands and rose with effort. "Talking pays no toll. I must have my measurements taken here before rushing on to order new stays from my milliner. When I return to London in a few weeks, I promise to call on you both, however. Donnely always says we might just as well spend two months away from the estate as one, once we have the traveling carriage out and redded."

With warm leave-takings, the ladies separated. Meriel and Hester waited outside the shop while their footman stood by the street to wave down the coachman as he drove past.

"Do you know if Burchett means to call today?" Meriel would be surprised if he didn't.

"He's taking us both for a drive in Hyde Park about five o'clock," Hester answered, "if you'll come with us."

"Thank you, I will. I want to ask him to make another purchase for me, similar to the one at Christie's, and the drive to the park will give me time to persuade him." The news about Claire's deteriorating health had decided her. Meriel would propose to Jonys that they deal with their family concerns together.

Under her straw bonnet's poke, Hester brightened. "Will this request shock him as much as the one to buy the table? Do you want Burchett to invite Osborne for a sail on his yacht and push him overboard? I could help!"

"No, I prefer to deal with Osborne myself." The fewer people who knew her plans, when she made some, the better. "Satisfying as it would be to have him out of the picture, Osborne is the boys' uncle. He's been part of their lives as long as they can remember. I prefer finding a way to lessen his influence without your neck being stretched."

Touching that tender part, Hester pulled a face. "You have a point. I think I'd prefer the guillotine to nubbing cheat."

"Did you pick up that cant term for the gallows from Burchett? With your ghoulish mind, James and Steven will adore you, but you'll be a terrible influence on them." Smiling at her cousin, Meriel longed for the day the boys would have the freedom to know Hester better.

"The boys need a roguish influence to offset their uncle, since you won't allow me to murder him." Hester's cheerful statement drew a startled stare from a well-dressed matron walking past. "What do you need Burchett to do, if we can't burn Osborne's bacon?"

"I want him to go around to Tat's and see if Jonys's team and carriage have sold, since I'm not allowed in." These conventions about what ladies could or couldn't do were the reason Meriel needed help to deal with Osborne. "If it's still available, I want him to buy it for me."

Laughing, Hester said, "Don't tell me you mean to take up driving a high-perch phaeton! Next you'll be snapping a whip over a coach and six like that dreadful Letty Lade."

198

"I do well to keep a pony and trap under control. I mean to give the equipage back to Jonys, of course, in return for learning what Osborne is doing, or taking other actions I can't." As a gentleman, Jonys would be more discreet about her business than any agent she might hire, and have access to more places of business, clubs, and homes as well.

As the footman opened the door to her landau, Meriel moved forward and mounted the single step.

When they were both seated facing the coachman, Hester said, "Burchett feels the greatest sympathy for you, especially after I told him about Osborne's daft behavior. He'll do anything to help you, I feel certain."

"If he'll purchase the phaeton and pair, he'll have done enough," Meriel said. "I can't go on imposing on your friendship with him when the situation could become dangerous. You realize that Osborne isn't acting in a rational way."

"The man is mad, without a doubt," Hester agreed fervently.

"He's certainly not thinking about what's best for my sons." Though she didn't know a great deal about madness, Meriel felt an instinctive dread of being near Osborne, a fear born from seeing him act without reason in many situations over the years. "He isn't an evil man, but more an ill one. It's as if his thoughts don't work in normal ways to let him fit into usual patterns of behavior. Osborne believes he's right, yet whatever he does creates pain and hardship for those closest to him. And he can't recognize the damage he does to people he cares about."

Hester shrugged, raising her parasol against the

sun. "Your view is more charitable than mine. I feel the same aversion to getting anywhere near him. It's true he can't be reasoned with, even when he chooses to hear any voice but his own. He's a dangerous man when he's crossed, and it isn't safe for you to challenge him by yourself."

"My first thoughts about ending Osborne's control over my sons were more illegal than dangerous, but you're right to urge caution." Jonys didn't appear to be a man who would balk at either illegal or dangerous actions he believed right and necessary. Her cousin's beau, on the other hand, was far too conventional to be comfortable with what Meriel might have to do on behalf of her boys.

Bowing to a passing acquaintance, Meriel murmured, "I don't mean to deal with Osborne entirely on my own."

"You could persuade Jonys to any mayhem, just by asking him for help," Hester said. "He's truly taken with you, the way his gaze follows you even if he's speaking with me or Burchett."

The statement spread through Meriel like warmth from a grate, but mentally, she stepped back from the fire. She couldn't risk being burned.

Yesterday's gift of the drawing and letter from her sons had been a kind action by Jonys. It had also been a shrewd one. He had teased her about marrying him in the early part of his visit, showing that he still meant to mend his fortunes with a rich wife. Nothing could incline a mother in her position more to a man than his concern for her children. Meriel credited Jonys with the intelligence to recognize and act on that route into her favor.

Jonys loved all women far too much for his affections toward one to mean much. "He's taken with my fortune, and he makes no bones about it," she assured Hester. "So you needn't talk hearts and flowers where the truth is closer to pounds and pence."

Hester grinned. "My opinion isn't changed, but you'll think as you please. I'm just relieved that you'll ask for his help."

The thought of begging for help like a child disgusted Meriel. "I won't make myself beholden to any man. I'll pay for his services or I won't accept them."

Hester tilted her parasol to shade them both. "One of these days, the iron in that stiff neck of yours will melt like a candle. And you may have already struck the steel to spark the wick."

If her father were alive, Meriel could at least ask his advice. A distant cousin she'd hardly met had inherited his title and estates. Being left alone to deal with an unbalanced person like the vicar made her feel particularly vulnerable.

"Fustian," said Meriel, discounting Hester's silly fancy. But she wished for a man's insight and support.

"If you stop fighting, you might discover that this can actually be pleasant." Breathless from the wrestling match, Meriel struggled to hold Kept in the low-sided wooden tub with one hand and scrub him with the other. The dog looked far too small to be this strong.

Kept threw back his head and howled, the sound reverberating around the stone walls and pavement of the stables behind her town house. While his paws were braced conveniently against the tub's edge, she scooped one up to check the grooves between the large pads for stickers or small stones. Though he tried to pull his paw free, he didn't flinch as if it had cuts or sores.

While she bathed his big feet, he washed her face with long swipes of his tongue. "Kisses won't get you out of the tub, either, Kept." To avoid his face-washing, she turned him to work on his rear paws. He sat down on them in the water, looking over his shoulder with huge, reproachful brown eyes.

"Poor puppy, you look miserable. But you'll survive this, and then I'll give you a lovely treat." As she lifted his rear again, Kept made a lunge for freedom. She fell on her elbows in the large, shallow tub as she caught him. Good thing she'd put back a few old gowns for rough outings with the boys.

Woeful whimpers escaped his throat as Kept shivered dramatically, glancing at her. With his wet hair and whiskers slicked down, his dark eyes loomed large in a surprisingly small face. He concentrated the full force of his best piteous gaze on her, spoiled by shifts into indignation. Wet as he was, she wanted to hug him.

"Small males never want to be bathed, as I recall from being one." As the gate's latch clicked, Jonys spoke cheerfully from the mews entrance to the stables. He must have come around to the back of the house after asking for her at the front.

His unexpected arrival had made her jump and nearly let go of Kept. Two days ago she had talked with Burchett about visiting Tattersal's Livery Stables, and had received a message from him last evening. The letter delivered by hand to Jonys had asked that he call on her this afternoon, not this morning.

The plaguey man would come early, when she looked like her own scullery maid. Nearly as wet as Kept, with wisps of hair hanging in her eyes, she must look a sight in this faded blue printed-cotton round gown, long sleeves pushed up and skirt bunched under her knees.

Wagging his tail frantically, Kept bucked to get free of the bath, splashing still more water over them both. "No, Kept. You may greet Jonys when you're dry." Efforts to hold the wet dog probably made her look as if she had caught the greased pig at the fair.

Jonys shrugged out of his fitted coat and waistcoat in a flash, kneeling beside her on the cobbles. His big hands settled firmly but gently around Kept's shoulders.

"Stay," he ordered.

Jonys meant Kept, of course. He wasn't responding to her impulse to run from his closeness.

Naturally she felt self-conscious in this first meeting after half lying in his arms. Not that he had held her in the usual way a man held a woman, of course, for he had only offered her comfort in her distress as any acquaintance would in the same circumstances.

It wouldn't do to imagine more behind his actions or her reactions than existed. He was an attractive man, a practiced seducer, and she'd been a widow for several years. She was an adult, not a giddy girl to succumb to every rake whose sparkling eyes entranced her.

Shoving her hair back now that someone else had Kept under control, she realized with horror that she'd pushed wet, lathered hands into her curls. Yet Jonys looked her over as if he had found a delectable dish on a buffet table.

Leaning forward over the dog, he recoiled and asked, "What cesspool have you been into, my lad?"

"He found something long dead from the odor and liked it well enough to roll on it. He doesn't want the smell washed off, either." Though Meriel preferred to think that grappling with Kept had made her breathless, she could hardly look away from the bulk of broad shoulders making the fine linen fabric of his shirt look fragile. Comforting as she had found them in the drawing room, his strong chest and shoulders made an entirely different impression now.

"The odor marks him as a great hunter to other dogs, I imagine." Jonys grinned at her. "Think how he feels, coming to you covered in valor and glory, and you plunge him into cold water."

"Hardly that. I had kettles boiled to warm the water, and I won't apologize for despising some behaviors males consider glorious." Keeping an eye on Kept was difficult with Jonys leaning across the dog, near enough for her to count the man's eyelashes. If it was safe to look at him that long.

Damp and disheveled, she glanced at the perfect arrangement of Jonys's crisp black curls, a strong contrast to his starched cravat and white shirt. He was a perfect black and white sketch in the dazzle of direct sunlight, and the combination made his glinting eyes appear still more brilliantly blue.

"Might as well accept the inevitable, Skype." Though he addressed Kept, Jonys twinkled at her as he spoke. "When a lady makes up her mind you'll clean up your ways, you might just as well submit meekly to her methods. The torment won't last as long if you don't struggle, and when you're sweet enough to please her, you'll find it's well worth the misery."

Meriel laughed, the first time she'd felt like it since Osborne's visit. How impossible to imagine Jonys submitting meekly to anyone. "I can manage him, truly. You needn't get wet, too." A splash had already stuck the fine linen against his stomach so that its muscular planes were outlined. Her midsection felt stuck to her spine.

His slow smile began in his eyes, tugged at one corner of his lips, and relaxed his firm jaw. She touched the center of her upper lip with the tip of her tongue. His mouth was generous, curving, tender. She hungered to taste it again.

"Of course you can handle him, or anything else you put your mind to," he said. "But some jobs are more easily done by two, and a dog like Skype is a two-person task. You should have sent word that our dog needed washing, and I would have come earlier."

"If you'd caught that first whiff of him, you would have known I couldn't wait. Besides, Kept is my dog, and I chose to bathe him myself. He'll learn to know and trust me more if I'm the source of what's good for him as well as what he considers good. What he fears now won't scare him later if we face it together in a matter-of-fact way."

"Good of you to instruct me on how to get better acquainted and inspire trust, which I hope to do with you. You'll probably need a bath once we've cleaned up Skype, so I can get started on you as soon as we've finished with him."

The gleam in his eyes teased her, but he also looked more than capable of lifting her into a tub of scented, warm water. And lathering her all over with those big, gentle hands that had stroked her back while she cried. Meriel let out the breath she'd held and soaped Kept's chest, massaging him until she felt his heartbeat slow. Hers raced.

"My groom offered to help bathe Kept, but I like being self-sufficient." Maybe if she ignored the comments that turned her heart to hot butter, Jonys would stop making them. If she really wanted him to stop.

"That's a bad habit I wish you would change," he said, capturing her wet forefinger with his little finger as she rubbed lather up Kept's side. "Too much self-sufficiency can get lonely."

Keeping her head down, Meriel pulled her finger free and turned Kept, standing him so she could wash his undercarriage. The terrier's back bowed higher as she lathered his thighs and tummy. With Jonys holding the dog's shoulders, she could avoid the man's dangerous touch. Today she needed her wits about her.

"What could you know about loneliness?" She smiled up at him. "If you don't want to sleep alone, you just take another lady to bed with you."

"Bedding has nothing to do with loneliness, or it shouldn't." He scooped a handful of warm water to pour over her exposed wrist. "When you take to the sheets with me, I want it to be a celebration and nothing else."

Meriel sat still, watching the last drops of water slip off her skin, as quiescent as Kept had become. Though restricted only by a loose touch of one hand, the terrier didn't move a whisker now except to look between them.

Stealing a glance at Jonys, Meriel found an earnest expression on his features. She preferred him to be only suggestive and playful, the carefree charmer the young girls, herself included, had sighed over in Surrey. How much easier to strike a bargain with him if he didn't show warmth and humor, if he hadn't held her with compassion yesterday, if he hadn't brought her the most meaningful gift she could have received.

The talk she had planned between them grew more difficult every moment. Using a womanizer with no heart, only debts, wouldn't cost her a pang. But then, to seduce ladies, Jonys must make them think he felt something besides desire for them. He had to be good at it by now. And his sister was seriously ill; he would be glad for the money she could supply, no matter how it came into his hands.

Her boys had to come first, but at least she would deal with Jonys as honestly as possible. Scrubbing with renewed vigor, Meriel said, "I'm glad you were able to come. Not just to help with Kept, but because I need to talk with you."

"I always look forward to our conversations." Sluicing water over Kept with one hand, he showed no regard for his wet cuffs. "I think Skype's ready for a few rinses."

"I'll dilute a mixture of olive oil, bran, and white vinegar to keep his skin and coat from drying after the bath. Let's give him a couple of clear water rinses before that final one, though."

Jonys nodded and held Kept up so she could rinse his chest and tummy. How naturally they worked together to bathe Kept. Surely Jonys would make as good a partner in freeing her sons from Osborne's heavy-handed control.

The sun seemed to glance off the stable yard stones with less brilliance as soon as she thought of the vicar. His inner darkness cast shadows over any aspect of life it touched.

Meriel had to be right in her estimation of Jonys. Her sons' welfare depended on it.

Chapter Eleven

"If we take Kept inside, he'll dampen the carpets drying himself on them," Meriel said as Jonys rubbed the terrier with the old linen she had brought out to the stable yard for that purpose. "Will you feel insulted if we go to sit in the garden by way of the back stairs?"

"Certainly not. Besides, we're about as wet as Skype is." Jonys grinned as he held the squirming, indignant terrier against a shirt soaked to his well-formed chest. He looked her over as if her damp gown revealed as much. "Just lead me to a place where I can let this tornado loose without his doing damage to himself or anything else."

As Kept voiced a three-note complaint, Meriel led the way down steps from the stable yard, through a laundry area, and into the kitchen. Pausing briefly, she spoke to Cook. "Will you prepare a luncheon for us, including a treat for Kept, and have it sent into the garden, please."

"*Oui, madame,*" said the cook, who she knew hailed from Yorkshire.

Pretending she didn't see the tidbit of chicken Jonys slipped to Kept, Meriel led the way down the servants' passage to the stairs at the center of her town house's offices.

Moments later Jonys freed Kept on the fresh-shaved grass in the center of the garden. The terrier raced in tight circles before them, snorting and gagging, shaking himself in a violent blur to loosen the heavy curls of his wet hair.

"Skype has a strong opinion of baths." Jonys stood watching the dog, the knees of his buckskins marked with wet circles and his boot toes scuffed.

"He holds strong and stubborn views on most things." Few fashionable men would have pitched in to help her wash a dog in the clothing they had come calling in, and even if they had, they would have rushed off afterward to change.

Jonys would never make her sons do penance for a little natural dirt as Osborne did James and Steven. Surely Jonys would agree that the boys couldn't be left under the vicar's stifling control, no matter what the laws and courts had decreed.

"You'll dry soon, believe me," Jonys said to Kept. "The way you tear about, ten minutes should do it."

"I'm glad you talk to dogs, too." Meriel turned to watch Kept race around them, clasping her hands behind her.

"My manners are excellent, and I'd never rudely ignore anyone." His smile proved he wasn't ignoring her.

On impulse, she confided one of her secret beliefs. "Dogs don't necessarily grasp all the words we say, but I'm certain they sense our moods and meanings. The more I've talked to my dogs, just general chat, the closer we've come to communicating. Partly we learn to read each other's movements and habits, but it's more than that. Like knowing the other's feelings, or putting thoughts and pictures in each other's heads."

"Why not?" he said, rubbing his chin. "That's how animals must talk with each other. Maybe when we're bright enough, dogs teach us to speak with them in the same way. Creatures often show awareness we poor humans lack."

Glad he treated her private notions with easy acceptance, Meriel felt more ready for the serious discussion ahead. She focused on Kept's after-bath capers again, searching for a way to begin.

Kept stretched out his forelegs, rump and tail in the air. Laying the side of his muzzle in the grass, he combed his whiskers by pushing his muzzle along, first one side and then the other, grumbling and emitting sharp barks.

Jonys laughed. "What a little clown he can be."

The early afternoon sun warmed Meriel's shoulders and sparkled in Kept's wet hair, creating a cascade of crystals when he stood again to shake off fine droplets of water. His ears flapped and he held a long growl of protest as his body shuddered in movement from one end to the other.

Jonys watched Kept with a half smile and fond expression. His attachment to the little terrier boded well for his attitude about children. When he reported on her sons, he had chosen evocative images that had helped her to see them in her imagination at least. That showed an awareness of them and of her need to know about them that pleased her. Surely she could find no better ally than Jonys to help her protect her boys.

Her proposal wouldn't come easier for putting it off. She walked away from Jonys into the shadow of a lime tree, needing to lessen the impact of his physical presence. "You were kind to come so quickly after getting my message."

Turning only his head, he stood relaxed, big hands propped on his hips, weight on one well-formed leg. "Just let me know you want me and I'll always come."

Smiling acknowledgment, Meriel cupped a hand about a leaf, feeling its faintly ridged edges against her palm. "You must know I didn't ask you here in order to bathe Kept."

His grin and the warmth in his gaze gave Meriel courage to continue. "I want to put a certain proposal before you which I believe can benefit both of us."

Humor and hope dawned in his expression and he swung to face her. "A proposal? Dare I hope you're asking me to marry you this time?"

"No, of course not." Seeing his smile fade, she wanted to reassure him. "But what I have to say does have nearly the same effect as marriage on your fortunes. If you find my proposition agreeable, you should be in a position to save your estates and give your family what they need without marrying anyone now. Then later, when you discover real feelings for a lady, you can wed from desire and not necessity."

"But I don't find a marriage with you at all distasteful, which necessity nearly always is." Though his square jaw jutted, his mouth curved in a teasing smile. "And desire is a definite part of my plans for our union."

Meriel shook her head and pulled the leaf off

the lime. Looking at it instead of him, she said, "Please don't think of marriage as a possibility between us." She turned the narrow leaf end to end. "Not because you aren't an attractive prospect as a husband in many ways, but because I have no intention of wedding anyone."

As Jonys started toward her, Kept streaked past him, bounding like a deer. "Was your first marriage a disaster?" he asked with quiet reason. "Give me credit for being a different man from Welwyn. I wouldn't be a perfect husband, but at least you'd get a new set of faults with me."

"Welwyn was never cruel; it wasn't that. He was just too much under the control of his brother Osborne, Lord Lamport, for us to have a normal family life with the vicar as part of it."

Jonys's lips tightened. "Burchett told me about his visit here and his odd behavior toward you and Hester. Is the man a lunatic?"

"I couldn't say that, not being properly qualified, but he's appeared unbalanced in his thoughts and actions around the family for years." Just thinking about Osborne's obsessive, staring eyes at times made Meriel uneasy. "Most people wouldn't notice unusual behavior on his part much of the time, but his actions and words create misery for others more often than not. Certainly he's forced an unnatural separation between me and my sons."

"Surely you don't refuse to wed me because you think I'm anything like him." Jonys's expression and tone showed he thought the idea was preposterous.

"No, you're nothing like Osborne," she hurried to reassure him. "I just don't want to remarry and give a husband absolute control over me, our children, my assets. I won't allow any man that control again, so please don't consider marriage with me as a solution to your difficulties."

Striding about restlessly, Jonys looked indignant. "You think I'd take advantage of my position as your husband to order you about and waste your fortune? That I'd keep you away from our children as Osborne is doing with Welwyn's and your sons? I hoped you had a better opinion of me by now."

"It isn't that I think you would intentionally do any of those things." This wasn't what she wanted to discuss with Jonys. "My feelings on this subject aren't about you as a person; they're about what I want and need to be comfortable."

"I'm relieved to hear you say so." His rogue's smile returned. "As long as you don't consider me a bedlamite or an ogre, I can change your mind about me as a husband." He prowled about the lime tree like a fox around the henhouse.

To Meriel, his insistence on marriage seemed unusual in a man. "But I can offer you a way to work out your financial difficulties without becoming a husband. Both of us are in difficult situations we can resolve with a temporary alliance, not a permanent union. One doesn't kill the goose to get down for pillows."

"Why do I fear my goose is cooked when you look at me with that stubborn, determined tilt to your pretty chin?"

If she didn't ignore his flirtatious banter, she'd never get her proposal made. "Most men would leap at the opportunity to earn the funds they need to recover their fortunes and provide for their families, without having to put their necks in a parson's noose."

Halting, he stared at her, his mobile mouth lifting at one corner. "Earn? You've decided to pay for my services instead of marrying me to get them?"

"Yes. No. Yes." Flustered by the gleam in his sardonic, suggestive gaze, Meriel didn't know quite what she meant. "That is to say, I want to pay you for your services. For your efforts to help me get my sons away from Osborne's unhealthy control."

As he walked toward her, Meriel backed away. Though Jonys smiled as he shadowed her, he looked dangerous, a man not to be trifled with.

"And is that the only service you mean to purchase from me? But you can have my help for nothing. I'd enjoy chasing the little church beetle from under his rock."

Imagining Osborne as an insect crushed beneath Jonys's heel was easy enough, with him staring down at her from under lowered lids as he advanced. Jonys emitted enormous energy, barely suppressed. Meriel wasn't afraid of him, as she was of Osborne, but his physical presence could be overwhelming to her senses. Keeping her distance seemed the wisest course.

Dodging around him, she hurried toward the pergola. A little shade on such a warm day would be pleasant. Prickles along her spine warned her that Jonys followed close behind.

"I don't ask anyone to put himself out for me without compensation," she said over her shoulder. "I don't know what might be required to get my boys away from Osborne."

Under the shady pergola roofed with clemantis, Meriel faced him. Above, the vines wove together

215

and swayed off the sides of the wooden beams framing the garden structure.

The natural setting made her statement sound bizarre, even to her. "You must understand that I'm not asking you to escort me to a ball, but to interfere with a legal guardianship. It could be necessary to take steps that are illegal or dangerous."

Jonys stood too close, staring down at her with eyes gone dark in the shadows. "But I enjoy danger."

As he grasped her shoulder, a strong sense of peril impaled Meriel. His touch held her in place without physical force, alarming her far more than if he constrained her. As leaves stirred overhead, light flickered alternately with shadow across his square face. This man's threat lived and must be battled within herself.

"But I won't ask you to take risks for me unless you gain something as well." Meriel had to persuade Jonys to accept her offer. "Neither of us need feel beholden to the other if we enter into a simple exchange."

"The exchange isn't simple. A gentleman can't take money from a lady and remain a gentleman." He shook his head of crisp dark curls and let her go. "Only an unprincipled knave could do that."

Clasping her elbows, Meriel returned Jonys's intense stare. "I'm offering you the funds you need for your family and estates as well as your freedom from a marriage of convenience. I know your youngest sister is ill." She waved away the question he began to ask. "Never mind how I know. Just tell me why honor is more important to you than your little sister's health."

"Perhaps it isn't. Let's be certain we both understand the terms of the agreement you propose." His expression was amused but also harsh. He took a step closer, imposing his big body almost against hers. "You want help protecting your sons from the vicar's crazed control. In return, you're offering me the funds to make my estates productive again."

"And to provide for your mother and sisters, yes." Meriel found breathing difficult and her heart bumped her ribs. This was no more than a business arrangement she offered, yet Jonys issued a sensual challenge with his every movement that distracted and disturbed her.

"What makes you think I'll be satisfied by funds alone?" His voice was quiet, entirely reasonable, but his implacable expression and taut muscles invaded her space and senses with heated sensuality. "Can you actually believe money is all I want from you in marriage?"

Meriel swallowed, her throat dried by the blazing twin suns of his eyes.

"Hardly." He flung the notion aside with a sidelong gesture. "I want you in my arms, Meriel. I want the right to make love to every inch of you, to pleasure you and take my pleasure with you. Why should I settle for bank drafts and burn with unsatisfied desires?"

Seen against the green ceiling of vines above them, his face wore an expression of passion and determination. His blue eyes seared her will with fires that consumed reason.

Meriel longed to step away or laugh, to respond lightly, even to run like the coward she felt she was. But any such response was impossible.

Jonys represented her sons' salvation, but her personal damnation. To offer him what he wanted

217

was to risk losing herself, for he awakened her senses with no more than a look, a touch. He might even arouse more, more than she could survive and remain whole and herself.

If she gave him what he wanted—and, to be honest with herself, what she had come to want with him—a physical barrier must be removed from between them. Meriel would have to retreat behind a barricade of the spirit within herself and defend it against his warmth, understanding, comfort, concern. Or lose herself and her freedom.

Giving him the passions of her body would be all too easy. Protecting her spirit from his demands for closeness would challenge every thread of strength she possessed. While he sheltered her within his arms as she cried for her sons, Meriel had learned how deeply seductive his hold could be. Not just to her body, but to her very essence.

Yet a man could give and take pleasures of the body without emotion or marriage; why couldn't a woman do the same? Staring at him as she summoned defiance against her own weaknesses, Meriel chose belief in her strength of mind.

Most ladies wed to make a suitable alliance, not from love. They produced heirs, even broods of children, without caring passionately for their mates. Without admitting their mates to the secret places of their souls.

In her first marriage, Meriel had done the same. She could give herself without succumbing to love outside marriage, if it meant saving her sons from unnatural manipulation by the vicar.

Deliberately, she held out her hand to Jonys.

"You've always satisfied your desires without marriage," she reminded him. "If I offer you that arrangement, will you help me? The benefits of my bed and purse, but no legal control over me, in exchange for help to free James and Steven from Osborne's influence."

"I'll be damned," he said, surprise wiping sensuality from his face and bearing for the moment. "You are afraid to marry me."

"Fear has nothing to do with it!" Meriel flung her hand down, hating for him to think her a coward. "I don't care to put myself under any man's control again, not just yours."

Jonys studied her from under straight black brows with his chin thrust out. "You don't trust me, that's what it is. You can't let go of your fear of being controlled again to marry me, even to protect your sons from Osborne."

Unable to answer, Meriel turned away. Fear wasn't a strong enough word to describe what she felt about marrying again. Total terror was closer. She could leap off a cliff to her death to save her boys far more readily than live out her lifetime in the bondage of another marriage.

Making an effort to control the tremor in her voice, she finally answered. "If the only way to save my sons is to marry, I'll do it. But I can't bear more children with the threat that they could be taken away from me. And you require an heir."

Big hands touched her shoulders, and Meriel refused their urging to turn. Head down, she waited for his decision, unable to breath for the panic clamoring for her to escape.

Her curls stirred against her neck as he sighed. "You drive a hard bargain, Meriel. Do you think I'd force you into a wedding? A man doesn't want a reluctant bride."

In relief at escaping the sentence of marriage,

she whirled to gaze up at him. He looked weary, resigned. She couldn't feel triumphant if he felt defeated. She couldn't deprive him of everything he asked and give nothing in return.

Placing her hands on his shoulders, she spoke with the greatest need to make amends she had ever experienced. "If I could marry anyone, you would be the first man I'd consider. I'm not rejecting you, but marriage. I want you to take me as well as the financial help you need. Let's help each other."

"I never expected a beautiful woman to have to beg me to take her to bed." Though he laughed, he also grimaced as he slipped his arms loosely about her. "I'd be more crazy than Osborne to refuse your generous offer. Yet I'll be honest with you: I'll do this your way only because I believe I can still persuade you to marry me in time."

"In equal honesty, I must warn you not to depend on it." Meriel could think of little reason why a man would insist on marriage under the circumstances. Perhaps he wanted all of her fortune, even though that did not fit her image of him, and not just the financial help she offered him. Perhaps like most men, he couldn't bear to lose, and saw giving in on this point as losing.

"I have a condition of acceptance," he said, tracing her jaw with a fingertip. "I don't like control any more than you do. Funds disbursed will be accounted for to the penny. The money involved in our exchange will be a loan, to be repaid when my estates are productive again."

"I'll have my man of business draw up an agreement for you to consider." She respected him for insisting on this provision, even if he might never be in a position to honor it. Repayment didn't matter to her as it must to him.

"Put your faith in contracts if you like," he said, drawing her toward him. "I can think of better ways to seal an agreement."

As he leaned nearer, Meriel held onto his upper arms to maintain her balance. Her fingers closed on the fine pleated linen of his shirtsleeves, feeling the faint texture of the weave, soaking up the moving warmth of the muscle underneath.

His lids drooped over his jewel-blue eyes as his square chin jutted above her. "Don't forget that you're the one who insists on this arrangement," he reminded her, grinning wickedly. "If you're going to keep me, I expect to be wooed."

Even as he challenged her, his hands stroked in sweet circular persuasions below her shoulder blades, urging her closer by slow, maddening degrees. As passion softened his features, she sank into the smoldering blue of his gaze, and her heart fluttered against the beat in his chest as naturally as the verdant leaves moved above them.

As in her drawing room, his arms enclosed them in a separate world, a place they created between their beating hearts and bemused gazes, beyond time or thought. His lips were full and shapely, only a wish away, and the wish was hers to fulfill.

Meriel slid her palms and fingers up his arms and over his shoulders, grazing the white expanse of his cravat to push into the crisp curls at his collar. The lively texture of his black hair sprang against her sensitive fingertips, filling her with a sense of purpose and desire. Molding her hands to the shape of his head, she urged his face down and stretched up to meet his mouth.

His lips slipped against hers in a slow caress like the brush of satin. Pressing her body against him as if she could draw his strength and confidence into herself, Meriel wondered at the silken glide of his mouth across hers, like the whisper of a thin garment sliding off her body as passions stirred.

Just touching the contours of his lips with hers was deeply arousing, enough for the moment, yet building a tension that pulsed through her blood and mind and muscles. Anticipation became unbearable desire.

Groaning low in his throat, Jonys gathered her closer into his arms, against the hard length of his body, touching her lower lip with a light rasp of his tongue. Rising onto her toes, she slanted her mouth over his, eager to taste and explore his entire being.

Meriel wanted to give and take kisses with the eagerness of an impatient lover, with the need of a long thirst. As their mouths searched and found, begged and plundered, she wanted more kisses, more closeness, more of this wanton, wonderful desire for still more.

When he pulled free to press his hot mouth against her closed eyelids, temples, throat, she found breathless joy bubbling from the growing pleasure inside. She expressed it in another demanding foray into the swirling depths to be found in his kiss. She felt his lips smile as she tried to capture all his mouth, press it everywhere with fervent promises of more.

The need they had created was too great for a few kisses, a few embraces, to begin to satisfy. She wanted hours and days and weeks of closeness to know him and learn how to enjoy him more each time they came together. Now those weeks, perhaps months, might be possible.

No matter how long a time, it wouldn't be enough.

Sighing, she pulled away to look up at him. Just seeing his face above her, his features softened by the same desire that pulsed deep within her, was pure delight.

A warm, furry body settled against her ankles.

"Go away, Skype," said Jonys, without looking down.

Laughing, she protested, "Kept's only soaking up a bit of the good feelings we're sharing."

"Just don't forget which of us is which and scratch me behind the ears," he warned her, kissing her nose. "We may both be *kept*, but I insist on getting first consideration."

Chapter Twelve

Frowning across her desk at the solicitor the next morning, Meriel held her tongue. Like most men, Trent thought he knew what was best for her and didn't hesitate to tell her what it was.

"Besides being highly irregular, such an arrangement is dangerous," Trent objected. "An unscrupulous man can persuade a lady into the most disastrous financial dealings, and you have no one to protect you since your father died."

Holding up a hand, palm out, she said, "My head leads me into this action, not my heart. I expect you to handle financial details with Hadham, Trent. As difficult as it was to persuade the earl to take the loan in the first place, I want to keep the actual exchange of funds impersonal. I don't mean to embarrass him by handing it over myself."

"Loan, indeed. Ladies should never give money

to gentlemen. It isn't natural." Nostrils pinched, Trent spat the words into the morning sunshine cutting across the desk centering the library. "You had best keep up that pretense with others, but I know from dealings with your aunt what it means when a lady lends money to a man of Hadham's reputation and appearance. You have the same stubborn look about you as Lady Anna when she sat in that chair and ordered me to pay out a stipend as unfortunate as this one."

Meriel studied the irate man who had handled her aunt's business affairs for years. This was the first she had heard of Aunt Anna's irregular past. "Thank you for your concern and advice. I've taken you into my confidence because significant sums will be transferred to the earl, and you're bound to notice such transactions and want an explanation. I consider the money an investment in my sons' well-being and my peace of mind. If your sensibilities don't allow you to do as I direct comfortably, I can use another agent."

Glowering, Trent shook his head. "You're as willful as your aunt. As if I'd consider for an instant allowing anyone else to know the extent of your financial holdings or your folly. If you're set on this course, I'll protect you as best I can. What have you promised the rascal so far?"

Little as she liked his judgemental, over-protective attitude, tension flowed from the hands Meriel gripped together on the desk's mahogany surface. She had come to trust her man of business and didn't want to approach another.

Meriel toyed with the sand shaker, aligning it with the pen tray and covered inkwell. "I prefer that you not refer to the earl in negative terms, for I've chosen him as an ally against Osborne. Whatever the personal nature of our association, you need not concern yourself with it. I'm nearly thirty and responsible for my choices." She smiled at the old man. "And you're an old dear to care about what might happen to me."

Though he cleared his throat and polished his spectacles, Trent looked pleased.

"Transfer a thousand pounds to Lord Hadham's account at Barclay's when the contract suits him," she continued. "Drafts of one hundred pounds each month will continue until I give you further notice." She doubted Jonys would accept more than these amounts.

"The contract will suit him; I'll see to that." Though Trent still grumbled, he made penciled entries in a pocket diary. "Perhaps this course is better than marrying a wastrel and handing over all your assets. I only hope the earl doesn't bring you to grief, and not just financially."

Curious, Meriel asked, "Was that the result of Aunt Anna's loan?"

The old man looked up at her, but he stared into the past. "I suspected as much. A man of title must marry to get legitimate heirs. If the lady he wants won't have him, he does what he must. Your aunt went on a Grand Tour shortly after a certain tonish marriage took place, and she returned an old woman."

Poor Aunt Anna, living alone here while another lady bore her lover an heir. In her later years, she had avoided company and snapped at those who insisted on visiting.

Chilled though she sat in a shaft of sunlight through the library window, Meriel pictured Jonys at Hadham House with a wife and an heir whose eyes flashed as brilliantly blue as his. She pushed away the thought. A son would belong only to Jonys by law, whoever his mother.

Absently, she asked, "Why didn't my aunt marry? Were you privy to the whole story?"

"Your aunt told me only as much as she wanted me to know, and you'll do the same, no doubt." Trent shook his head and sighed. "I drew my own conclusions. The gentleman was nearly twenty years younger than Lady Anna, and she never brought herself to accept the offers from him that society gossiped about."

Startled, Meriel considered the temperamental but reserved lady who had been her godmother. Appearances often gave little clue to a person's private life and thoughts. Knowing that her aunt, who had appeared the epitome of propriety, had conducted an irregular relationship with a significantly younger gentleman made her own choice not to marry seem less odd.

Which reminded her of Jonys's reasons for agreeing to her choice. "Please call on the earl as quickly as you can. His need for funds is urgent."

"It always is."

Trent's sardonic murmur made her feel protective toward Jonys. "Remember in your dealings with Hadham that he'll be guarding my interests, just as you do."

"Like the fox guards the hens, I don't doubt," he muttered, making another note.

"I won't pretend ignorance of the real nature of this agreement between you and my client," Trent said, frowning over his gold-rimmed spectacles. "And I won't pretend to approve of it. Keep in mind that I watch over her interests as closely as I did her aunt's."

Jonys sat in his small drawing room staring at Trent. He hadn't expected to like anything about the business side of the arrangement made with Meriel two days ago, and the reality was worse than his lowest expectations.

"Understand the terms clearly before you put your signature to them. For valuable considerations as outlined there," Trent intoned, gesturing to the document he had laid on the writing table before Jonys, "you will provide Lady Welwyn with personal advice and protection."

"I never heard it called that before." The solicitor's patent disapproval brought Jonys's flippancy to the fore.

Eyes narrowing, the little man continued. "You will act toward her publicly in ways to preserve her reputation and dignity or you forfeit all claims upon her."

Nodding, Jonys said, "That can certainly add titillation to the whole proceedings."

"You will refrain from consorting with other females of low or high degree while you accept funds from Lady Welwyn."

"Does the lady tend toward jealousy, then?" Jonys resented the man's tone, bordering on impertinence.

Trent gave him a long, cold stare. "My lady prefers not to entertain a case of the clap," he said bluntly. Looking out the window as if the sight of Jonys offended him, he continued. "The document further provides that either of you has the right to withdraw from the arrangement at any time without penalty."

"Why would I want out?" He was certain he would not.

"My thought precisely, for the advantage appears one-sided to me. However impossible it may seem to you, the lady might find you . . . incompatible with her expectations. Even an unpleasant part of her life at some point. In that case, you will make no further demands on her generosity."

Surprised, Jonys nodded. He hadn't considered the possibility that he couldn't give Meriel complete satisfaction in every way. He didn't much like it that she had. Though perhaps the provision came from this cold fish, not her.

"Besides, your situation is likely to change," Trent added, sounding grudging, "and Lady Welwyn insisted on providing for that eventuality. At such time as you wish to marry in order to produce heirs, you are to break the contract by written notice, without an interview being necessary."

Frowning, Jonys nodded again. He had to persuade Meriel to wed him, for carrying on the Hadham line was a responsibility he couldn't ignore. Surely he could persuade her once he got her in his arms. The idea of fathering an heir with any other lady left him as cold as Trent's eyes.

Jonys picked up the quill lying ready on the writing table. No need to read the document after this beak had spent the better part of an hour bleating about it. Best to have this whole distasteful part of the business over before he changed his mind.

"You'll find your phaeton and pair returned to the livery stable you patronized before, by the way. Lady Welwyn says you'll need it."

Laying down the quill again, Jonys felt the full indignity of his position. Accepting the funds provided by the agreement chapped him enough, but at least they benefited his family and the estate people in his care. Especially Claire, already on the road to Brighton with Mama and his older sisters. The carriage was an indulgence for him alone.

"I can't and won't accept personal gifts from the lady."

"You may take that up with her, for it isn't a part of the agreement before you. Lady Welwyn says you'll be required to travel extensively over the matter of her sons, and she prefers you to have private means to do so." Trent stared down his thin nose. "Please continue your reluctance to accept gifts outside the compass of this contract."

The man's toplofty attitude was an outright insult. Jonys settled back in his chair, anger spurring him out of his usual careless humor. "Trent, you don't have to like the task you're directed to do. You don't have to like me. But you will show proper respect to the title if not to the man."

A sharp nod was the only visible response from the solicitor. "Very properly said, my lord. I beg your pardon for allowing my concern for Lady Welwyn to overcome my sense of propriety."

"A concern I share. My intentions toward the lady are entirely honorable, so if you don't like the terms between us, you may urge her to make an honest man of me." Grinning at the surprised look on the solicitor's face, Jonys picked up the pen again.

"If you'll forgive a personal observation, sir, I must say that I thought it a shame when I heard you had come into the title." Trent eyed him critically. "However, your tone when you very properly reprimanded me was enough like your father's to bring him forcibly to mind. You have the potential to make as admirable an earl as he, I don't doubt."

Both pleased and embarrassed at the praise, cloaked in terms to do his critical valet justice, Jonys hoped he could achieve half what his father had for the estate and its people. If he was beginning to sound like an earl, perhaps he could hope to fill the responsibilities of one in time, without having to hang on a lady's skirts to do so.

Jonys dipped his quill in the ink pot.

Like raindrops, the orchestra's strains spattered the crowded room with sound from the gallery above Lady Melborne's public rooms. Guests paid far less attention to the music than they would to an onset of rain, in Meriel's opinion.

Touching her arm, Hester murmured, "He's stood up with that insipid chit twice now. Once more and the old cats will have them betrothed."

Meriel peeked over her fan at Jonys, then furled it, stick by stick, to reveal the smile with which she answered his. "Aren't they well matched, with his blue coat just the shade of her ribbons. Do you suppose Miss Rendon planned it that way in hopes he would wear his blue superfine?"

"I vow, you don't seem to care at all who he stands up with or how many times. It's unnatural." Hester shook her curls, twined with pearls and silk petals.

"If anyone's upset, it should be Miss Rendon. While he dances and talks with her politely, he send me glances I hope no one else notices." Meriel turned her shoulder to the floor where dancers in two sets performed a gavotte. His standing up once with Lady Helsby, the pretty, rich widow, had made Meriel far more uneasy than two dances with a young lady with a penchant for the scarlet coats of young officers.

"If anyone had told me a week ago what a co-quette you could be, I'd have stared to hear it." Though Hester sounded severe, her eyes and smile teased. "I don't recall that you flirted at all in our come-outs."

"I've had an excellent tutor." Meriel glanced over her bare shoulder, to find Jonys watching her with warmth, as he more often did than not in company.

"And you're an eager pupil." Hester sighed as they slipped through the crowd toward the card room. "You may be comfortable playing fast and loose with the man, but I'd never allow him free rein to dance and flirt as he likes."

"If he follows me like Kept, we'll be far too noticeable. I prefer to be discreet about my private life." Meriel had been surprised when Jonys assured her last week that he wouldn't make her conspicuous. He had been subdued, for him, in that first meeting after he signed the loan agreement he had insisted on, though he seemed to have recovered his usual good spirits since.

Perhaps he had been as shaken as she had at finding herself in an unfamiliar position toward a person of the opposite sex. Meriel still vacillated between anticipation and doubt over the new footing with Jonys. Seeing him made her feel shy and bold by turns.

As they entered the card room, Hester waved to Burchett, settled at a whist table in a corner. "Would you like to take a hand for a while?" she asked Meriel. "It's quieter in here than in the main assembly rooms."

"If you find an open spot at a table, take it. I feel too restless to concentrate on cards." Meriel didn't know why she felt this inability to sit still these days. In part, she was uneasy about her boys, though Jonys had delivered another round of letters between them, assuring her that James and Steven saw at least some of her missives.

"Then I'll take a hand at silver loo for a while," Hester said. "Look for Burchett and me before you go in to supper."

Nodding, Meriel wandered out. She didn't want to dance again at the moment, either. Weaving through the crowd into the Melbornes' dining room, which it was when the furniture hadn't been carried out for a rout, she found Lady Bessborough arguing the positive effect of Perceval's assassination on the economy, and joined the group's fringes.

When a hand touched her waist lightly from behind, she didn't have to turn to know Jonys stood close. Taking her fan, he waved it gently beside her face so she felt the curls at her ears and nape stir.

These little attentions were a revelation, showing her that the most effective flirtation was the small act of consideration, given without display. No gossip had spread about them so far, tales that might get back to Osborne, yet she never attended the same social occasion as Jonys without feeling like the most admired lady in the rooms.

After a few moments, he leaned over to return the fan and murmured, "Won't you walk about with me, Lady Welwyn? You know my aversion to standing in one place for any length of time."

Leaving the group without stirring any more notice than when she had joined it, Meriel quitted the room with Jonys. Their private arrangement added another dimension even to a stroll through an assembly, as if they had a secret together.

233

Both of them greeted acquaintances, and Meriel felt pleased with her companion. Jonys appeared to know and like everyone, and his manner was just the right blend of elegance and ease. Certainly his appearance couldn't be improved upon, even if his lapels weren't quite the latest cut. His self-confident carriage counted for far more than fashion.

Ladies on all sides gazed at him openly or covertly, but admiration was clear on every face. Though she didn't need that confirmation of his appeal, a private pride welled in her that of all the females who admired him, Jonys preferred to be with her. Glad no one could know her thoughts, Meriel understood why gentlemen vied to win the most sought-after cyprian as a mistress.

"Notice the third potted palm along that wall of French windows." Jonys nodded through a doorway into a saloon.

Glancing across that room, Meriel said, "Quite an unremarkable plant, I should think."

"No matter. If you take your time to cross the room and stand by that particular palm, you'll find it to your advantage." His mouth curved up and his eyes twinkled.

"How much time?" Suspicious and intrigued, Meriel couldn't think what mischief Jonys might be planning.

"No more than five minutes," he said. "I only need time to gather a few items."

Curiosity growing, Meriel returned his bow of leave-taking and watched him walk away. He moved with a lazy grace that suggested leashed energy and restless purpose.

At her side a lady tisked. "As appealing as sin,

but not a man to trust with one's heart or one's purse, would you say?"

Looking around, Meriel found Lady Helsby staring after Jonys with an expression of calculation on her dainty features. "Our families have known each other for generations, and my impression is that Lord Hadham is a gentleman of honor," Meriel said. She didn't like the rich widow's avid face or belittling comment.

Lady Helsby's smile turned brittle as she faced Meriel. "I've heard he was an acquaintance of your youth. That sort can be dangerous to a woman past her first bloom, hoping to fulfill youthful fantasies before it's too late."

Whether the widow sought information or offered spite, Meriel didn't like her manner. "Do you indulge in fantasies, Lady Helsby? I find that dealing with reality requires all my energies. Excuse me; friends require my attention now."

Leaving the widow standing alone, Meriel passed through the doorway and into the saloon. Her heart beat faster after the unpleasant encounter with Lady Helsby, as it did when she had to deal with Osborne.

The widow must have questioned a great many people to learn that the Hadham estate lay near her childhood home. That much talk could call undue attention to her and to Jonys; she must warn him to be still more careful in his public behavior toward her. What a shame that negative people like Lady Helsby and Osborne could make life difficult for others.

Speaking with people she knew here and there, Meriel made a circuitous way around the room by flickering candlelight to the French windows. As she approached the third palm in a row standing between tall French windows with separate curved heads, she looked about to see if Jonys were nearby. Glancing about the room, she wasn't prepared to be seized by the elbow and drawn backward through the opening.

On the verandah outside the window, Meriel found Jonys smiling down at her as he closed the glazed panel quietly. "Come this way," he said, urging her across the flat stones and down a few steps in the dim light from the house. "I don't want someone to steal my other prize."

"Wait. Where are we going? I can't just disappear without a word to anyone." The garden sloped down to St. James Park through darkness, and Meriel wasn't certain she wanted to fade into the night with Jonys.

"But that's the fun of it, going off unexpectedly. Trust me. You'll like it when you get there." His voice was amused, and his eyes in the moonlight were little lighter than the velvet navy sky.

"I don't have my shawl, and Hester expects me to find her before the supper dance." Whatever made her think she wanted a private liaison with this impetuous man?

Without pause, he urged her on across grass that formed a springing, colorless carpet under her thin slippers. "No fear of chills; I'll keep you warm. Hester's an intelligent lady; she can at least guess who you're with. Any more objections?"

"Can't we slow down a bit?" Keeping up with his long-legged stride could make her breathless in a very short time. She felt rushed in a different way, too, hurried into intimacy she wasn't prepared to face yet. She needed time to think, instead of dashing off into the darkness like this.

"Here, let me put my arm about you so you don't

stumble." His hand slid around her back and found her waist, securing her against his side. As he swung easily down the slight slope, she felt his warmth and movement where her hip touched his muscular thigh. "Is that better? We're nearly there."

"Nearly where?" Looking about, Meriel couldn't see a place in particular for them to be near. Then Jonys led her through the darker shadow cast by a tall shrub and into an area of low plantation on the other side. Though the colors were all gilded by the moonlight, she recognized the scent of chamomile rising from low beds.

"Come sit here," Jonys invited, releasing her from his side but retaining her hand in his. Against the background of the shrubbery, iron spears held a garland above a garden seat with wooden slats set into iron end supports in a comfortable curve.

Shadows and textures silvered in the moonlight to form a place of enchantment in the garden. Meriel stood, drawing its peace and beauty into herself.

Meanwhile, Jonys spread three napkins over part of the seat and handed her to it. "It's early yet for dew, but I wouldn't want you to mark that lovely gown," he said. When she was seated, he joined her, placing a bundled napkin between them.

"Have you brought out half the Melborne linen?" Meriel smiled at him as he unwrapped the bundle.

"And not a hole or thin place in it," he said, "for I checked. Elizabeth won't mind. Here," he added, "taste this and tell me it isn't a treasure to delight the discriminating." He broke an end off a slice of pale cheese and held it before her lips.

Leaning forward, Meriel accepted the tidbit from his fingers, feeling their texture and warmth against her mouth for a scant moment. Smooth, rich taste and texture rewarded her tongue. "Double Gloucester," she said with appreciation.

"My favorite cheese," he replied, "followed by a grape." Once more he fed her, this time giving himself a bite of fruit and cheese together.

Juice flooded her mouth as she bit down on the light-colored grape. Its clean taste came perfectly upon the creamy sensation of the cheese.

"Delicious." Breaking off a piece of cheese from the slices lying on the napkin between them, she offered it to him. "The double Gloucester tastes like the moon looks, and the grape gives the sensation of the moon's light."

"Take off your glove," he said, studying the bite of cheese she offered him.

"They're quite clean," she protested.

"But leather leaves the wrong taste in my mouth," he said, one corner of his mouth twitching as he teased her.

Laughing, Meriel laid down the bite and pulled off her gloves. Jonys made the smallest moments special. When she offered him a bite again, he closed his mouth about her fingertips, taking the cheese and leaving tingles to shiver their way up past her elbow to her shoulder.

Nervous about what might come next, she shifted backward on the garden seat.

Jonys raised his brows, eyes reflecting moonlight, but offered no comment. Reaching under the seat, he pulled out a tall bottle and two trumpet glasses that rang with the clarion tone of fine lead crystal as they chinked together in his big hand.

"Our first meal together is a cause for celebration." The cork eased out with a soft pop in his strong fingers, and a light mist rose from the ribbon-necked bottle like the light from spangles.

The excited whisper of the golden wine as he poured it into the glasses told Meriel that Jonys had found champagne for their garden supper. She leaned forward to take the stem from him, touching his hand briefly as she accepted the wine.

Feeling missish was silly in a woman her age, with a man whose services were paid for. Dear Jonys was kindly devising a romantic mood, but she mustn't let herself believe in the magic of moments out of time.

Looking down into the glass, she watched bubbles rise like hope, without visible reason. And they burst when exposed to the air outside the wine, as hopes too often did.

Touching his glass to hers in a pure ringing note, he said, "I didn't bring you champagne so you could watch it like a performance. Take wine with me, missy." He raised his glass, and a shaft of light picked out the spiral up its stem. "To laughter and joy between us forever."

Regretting that he'd used his universal name for ladies at this moment, she felt further saddened by his saying "forever" when that was impossible. One day he would marry and she would drink wine alone.

"To laughter and joy," she repeated before she sipped the wine. Probably he hadn't noticed her omission.

As she drank from the glass, she bent back her

head slightly. Her pale throat echoed the lines of a graceful Elgin marble statue in his mind. Except that she was warm, breathing, responsive flesh, far superior to any artwork he had viewed.

Jonys wanted to pitch the wine glass over his shoulder and lay her on the grass at their feet. A bed of chamomile would be restful, once he'd ignited the fires she kept carefully banked down. But he had already seen in her expression and small movements, heard in the tight tone of her voice that she didn't want him in that way tonight.

Honoring her wishes didn't mean he understood them. Picking up a slice of cheese, he broke it in half and gave her a share. If all she wanted of him at the moment was a picnic in the moonlight, then he'd restrain himself. Though as fitted as these silk knit knee britches were, he would have to stay in the shadows and not return to the house for a while after she went in.

Feeding her a grape, he took one for himself. They tasted better from her soft fingers.

"I expect you prefer that I not visit your town house late at night," he said. Might as well lay his picnic on the ground, so to speak. Beating about the bush never told a man what he needed to know.

Startled, she turned wide eyes on him. "No! I mean, Hester is there, and the servants would be shocked. Surely another place would be better for us to . . ."

Clearly she didn't mean to finish that sentence. He might as well help her out. "You can't come tiptoeing up the stairs at the Albany. One of my neighbors would very likely try to persuade you to come along to his rooms, and I don't mean to share any more than you do."

That reference to their contract made her look away.

Shrugging, she said, "I'm not quite certain what to do. Let me think about it for a while."

"Not too long, I hope," he said as if he weren't about to burst with need where he sat. "Generally in these circumstances, a little house can be found in a less tonish neighborhood, though still a good address. Someplace where the neighbors are accustomed to a great deal of coming and going, but pay little attention to what's going on along the street."

Teeth catching her lip, she looked off down the garden as if she could take in the view in the darkness. "Yes, of course that must be how it's done. How silly of me not to think of it. I'll ask Trent to look about for a suitable place."

He'd just as soon not have that old ice sculpture's eyes frosting their love nest. "Perhaps you could trust me to find a place that would suit you," he suggested. "Men hear of houses coming up for lease or purchase here and there."

Rolling a grape in her fingers, Meriel didn't look at him. "Yes, I suppose you would. Men speak of those things to each other, perhaps, when they set up a new amour in keeping, and then when they cast her aside."

"You aren't thinking about throwing me over before you even have me properly set up!" He pretended horror, hoping to lighten her mood and draw her into the pleasure of finding a place for them to discover each other.

"No, of course not," she assured him, still not looking away from the grape she mauled. "I'm quite happy about our arrangement."

"I can see that for myself," he said, bending over to look up into her face.

Reluctantly, she laughed and drank another sip of wine. "It's just that this is all new to me. I need a bit of time to become accustomed to the idea."

"It's new to us both." Speaking gently, he said, "You may be certain that no other lady has ever had me in her keeping. But you're cheating yourself, having met your part of the bargain at once, then delaying the first installment of repayment from me."

A tentative smile answered him first. When he remained silent, she said, "As long as I'm happy with the arrangement, you mustn't feel any need for repayment. I enjoy your company and sweet surprises like this." A sweep of her white hand indicated the moon and garden. "For a lady, it isn't just a matter of thinking or saying you will, and you do. It's more a mood, a sense of the time and place and person all coming together at the right moment so that it's unquestionably right."

If a moment more unquestionably right existed for him, Jonys couldn't imagine it. But Meriel was his main concern in this joining. "If you need to wait, we wait."

"I'd like us to know each other better." She didn't seem satisfied with her first explanation. "Before we reach that advanced stage of acquaintance, I want to take time to become friends."

Grinning, he said, "Bed is the fastest place to get acquainted, and it's even possible to make friends there. Just give me a chance to show you how friendly I can be."

Taking her glass, he set it down behind him on the bench with his own. When he turned back, she sat with her hands over her mouth. Taking her fragile wrists in his hands, he tugged gently, pulling her into his arms.

"Don't fret," he said. "This is just a small advance to prove I can provide satisfactory service, ma'am."

Her laugh sounded more nervous than amused. He tucked her against his chest, holding one of her small hands to his mouth. "Just look at this sticky little hand," he teased her. "You've played with the grapes until you have juice all over your fingers. Didn't your nanny warn you about what happens when you play with your food?" He licked the soft pads of her fingers, then pulled the forefinger into the depths of his mouth to suckle and tease it with his tongue.

When she caught her breath, he took the next finger into his mouth and tortured it and himself in the same way. Her shoulders writhed in the slightest movement, and he pulled her against his chest, moving against her to feel her rounded breasts beneath her silk bodice. This game couldn't continue long if he were to remain sane.

Needing, seeking her mouth, he sank his hands into the silken coils of her hair and pulled her face to his, claiming her lips without a gentle preamble. His mouth took and clung to hers, wanting all her sweetness, all her womanly touch and taste for himself.

He kissed her with all the passion pent up in the rest of his body, with the whole of his need to give her all of himself. His mouth made love to hers in a promise of passion to come between them, and assured her he wouldn't be denied for long. His lips wooed her to want him, dared her to withhold herself, and too soon, teased her to playfulness while he could still let her go.

Not that he could let her go very far yet. With his mouth against her forehead, her cheek pressed against his chest, he held her while he stared into the sky. This was madness, gazing at moonlight and counting to a thousand in an effort to control your longing for the lady in your arms. He hadn't felt this restrained agony since he was a lad.

After a while, Meriel pushed gently against his chest and sat up, tidying her hair and gown in the fussy way that made little difference to a woman's appearance after she'd been thoroughly kissed, thank heaven. Meriel had never looked lovelier to him than she did sitting there with her hands raised to her rumpled curls, breasts even higher than those cursed stays pushed them, as if she were offering them to him. He set his teeth together and tried to think of Skype.

Looking off to the side, Meriel said in a prim, breathy voice, "If you care to know it, I find your work most satisfactory."

Even as he laughed, bent forward over widespread knees to ease his ache, he knew patience could only be stretched so far. He'd go househunting tomorrow.

Chapter Thirteen

An especially warm day made the breeze atop Primrose Hill more welcome than the view of London, spread out like a paper-pieced quilt below her. Meriel waved to Hester, who was sitting down the hill with Burchett under a stand of trees.

Earlier the four of them had shared an alfresco tea. Lacking Jonys and Kept's restive energy, Burchett had chosen relaxation after his repast, and Hester was keeping him company.

Standing on the summit of the scenic hill with London's smoking chimney pots in the distance, Meriel felt the breeze wrap around her body, enfolding her like Jonys's arms in the moon-brightened garden two nights before. Her lips parted at the memory of his sweet and searing kisses.

"You smile as if you have a secret," Jonys said, returning from a nearby vantage point where he had taken a different view of the city. "Tell me what makes you happy today, so I can supply it forever."

Meriel hugged her elbows, wishing he wouldn't talk about forever, that he would simply be happy with today. She searched for something to substitute for her thoughts of chamomile-scented kisses during Lady Melborne's assembly. With his vast experience of ladies who desired him, Jonys didn't need to know how much he occupied her thoughts.

"The only thing I lack is freeing my sons from Osborne's control," she said, "and you're already helping me toward that. Have you talked with Henry Austen again?"

Kept idled along, snorting down his nose into the grass as if blowing interesting insects out into the open. Though he didn't look directly at the two of them, he worked the ground in an arc about them.

"I've seen Austen, but he has no conclusive information from his banking acquaintances yet. He can't ask them directly if Osborne fiddles the accounts." Jonys looked toward London instead of at her, lifting the tails of his coat as he propped his fists on his hips. "I've also had a conversation with Henry Brougham about the vicar."

"Brougham the radical barrister?" She had read in the *Times* about his opposition to the war with the American colonies. "Wouldn't he consider a case in the Court of Chancery too tame for his efforts?"

"He'll take on any case that might bring him notoriety. But it was his strong sense of family values, like that of most Scots, that led me to consult him." Jonys's eyes were far brighter and bluer than the late-spring sky as he looked down at her. "Your plight caught his interest. He's checking old cases to see what arguments might be put forth to support a plea for joint guardianship of your sons with Osborne at the very least."

Her hopes, which had risen as he described Brougham, sank. "Joint! I'd be content to share responsibility under normal circumstances, but Osborne has proved himself more unreasonable and unbalanced than ever. He's never considered any suggestion I put forward, and by now, I have no reason to trust him to do anything but bully and threaten me."

"I'd prefer you never had to deal with him again. He doesn't sound right in his head, and I don't know how dangerous he is." Jonys looked about them before putting an arm around her shoulders and drawing her against his side. "But Brougham might uncover an aspect of the law that suggests another course of action. It seemed prudent to let him dig away like a harrier, which he looks like with his sharp nose."

"Yes, of course you were right to consult him." Meriel took comfort from being close against Jonys. She hadn't realized how much a simple hug could put heart into her.

When he let her go and stepped away, she felt bereft.

"Another party coming this way," he said briefly, nodding down the slope. "Don't worry. I caught sight of them before they could have spotted us."

"That's good," she said, resettling her cottage bonnet and tying its strings more securely against the rising wind. "I'd rather Osborne not learn that

I have you to help me just yet. He might disappear with the boys if he feels threatened."

"We'll continue to be discreet. Which gives me an opening to tell you I've heard of a house coming onto the market, near Park Lane, which might suit our purposes."

"Park Lane." A rush of uncertainty shook Meriel like a chill. She had put off thinking further about the house where the two of them would meet and make love. "I don't know. The area seems too public to me, next to Hyde Park. Perhaps another part of London would suit us best."

"Think about it a bit before you decide," he urged her, frowning. "The house doesn't front on the park; it's on Dean Street, an odd little byway between Tilney and South Audley."

"I don't recall Dean Street." Her reluctance to inspect a house for them grew. What features could she look for in a house where the two of them would meet? Perhaps small windows and an enormous bedchamber? The state of the kitchens shouldn't matter.

"You wouldn't have traveled along Dean Street. No one of consequence lives in the little houses on that crooked block. Number Seven stands alone at the bend, next to the house of a writer, who probably sees nothing that doesn't happen in his head. Another advantage is that houses are built on only one side of the street, as it's narrow, meaning it isn't overlooked by neighbors directly across the way."

"But it's too close to Portman Square, don't you think?" Watching Kept was more comfortable than looking at Jonys. The terrier pounced on something in the grass and peeked under his paws.

"That's an advantage, too," he assured her. "I don't want you traveling alone any distance through London at night, and as close as this is, I can ride with you to your town house and walk back to our house."

Our house. She barely stopped herself from objecting to the words. To say that the house would have only her name on the deed was needlessly cruel. He would be reminded that she would pay for the purchase, and that wasn't what unsettled her about his statement. His term brought them too close, when holding him at a distance was the only way to protect herself against remarriage, against finding her identity submerged again by another husband and the law.

"It isn't necessary for you to see me home," she told him, stepping away to look at the view in another direction. "I'll be in my own coach."

The other party had arrived on the hilltop with a great deal of laughter and puffing, but they kept far enough away so their presence didn't have to be acknowledged. Kept stopped bug hunting long enough to stare at them, on point like a bird dog.

"It's necessary to me," Jonys said. "I don't send a lady off into the night alone, especially not you." Jonys had joined her, coming too close again, walking about her as restlessly as Kept. She felt a need to get away from him, and looked back down the hill to where Hester sat with Burchett.

"What's wrong, Meriel?" He stepped in front of her, blocking her view. "Each time I try to talk with you about this subject, you shut me out. I'm not sure you even hear me after a certain point."

Glancing at the people a bit farther away along the hilltop, Meriel said in a low voice, "I hear you quite clearly, and others may as well. The times you choose for a discussion aren't appropriate, that's all. This just isn't the time or place to make decisions about a house for that purpose."

"Have you changed your mind? You aren't bound to do anything you don't want to do." A muscle twitched in his square jaw and he sounded angry. "I can't say I'll like it, but I can't force you to accept what you've paid for."

"Please, don't put it in those terms," she objected, feeling he insulted them both. Meriel didn't want Jonys to think poorly of himself for choosing a course that helped a great number of other people. She also didn't want him to be upset with her. Now she truly couldn't look into blue eyes that flashed like beacon fires before he turned away.

Her desire for this man hadn't lessened in the least, and that made her more wary. Still, she didn't want to wound his feelings. She laid a hand on his sleeve. "I haven't changed my mind."

Jonys didn't acknowledge her touch with as much as a glance. "Then why haven't you invited me to share a bed?" Though he spoke roughly, he sounded injured. "Don't you like my embraces as much as you pretend?"

Heat suffused her cheeks, and Meriel bent her head, glad for the shielding brim of a cottage bonnet. She didn't want him to know how much she enjoyed his mouth caressing hers by now, how much she enjoyed his arms about her.

Head cocking from one side to the other, Kept ambled toward them, stepping high over the grass and weeds long enough to tickle his tummy. He wasn't accustomed to hearing this tone between them.

While she fumbled for an answer, Jonys continued to torment her. "What do you expect from me,

Meriel? I can't tell what you want me to do. Did you hire me just as a cicisbeo to escort you in public? I thought you wanted a real man, private services, those I'm more accustomed to giving a lady whose lips and body torment me with longing every time I set eyes on her. I can make you want me just as much, Meriel, if you'll let me be alone with you long enough. I'd start by pulling off that cursed bonnet with a brim that hides your lovely face from me."

As she turned to hurry away down the hill, Kept stood blocking her way. She stopped rather than step on the whining terrier, and Jonys swung her back to face him.

Twisting out of his grasp, she looked quickly toward the party which had joined them on Primrose Hill's summit.

"I don't give a damn who sees us," he said, catching her hand and walking away from the noisy group. "If Osborne gets an earful from some busybody with nothing better to do than gossip, I'll deal with him. Right now, you're going to listen to what I need for a change."

Shocked into silence by the change from his usual easy manner to this forceful mood, Meriel concentrated on keeping her footing as he pulled her along over grassy hillocks. Though he glanced back at her as he spoke his mind, she doubted that he realized he hauled her behind him like a particularly stubborn donkey on a lead.

"I long to push my fingers into your hair and feel the shape of your head in my hands as I pull your beautiful face to mine," he said over his shoulder with intensity and angry yearning. "One day I'll kiss you until you don't care where you are, whether you're standing or lying down, and then

I'll pick you up and lay you across the softest flat spot that will hold us both."

Frantically, she looked around the hilltop, hoping he hadn't forgotten himself enough to take her here and now.

"Then I'll pluck out all the pins one by one until your hair's loose around your shoulders, your bare pale shoulders, naked except for the clasp of my hands as I hold you. I'll taste every beautiful inch of your lovely skin, from your ears to your toes."

Abruptly he stopped, and on the next rise, she saw another group of holiday-makers, taking the air above London. Swinging around, he seized her shoulders while Kept danced around them.

"Hush!" she cried. "Please." Feeling as undressed as he had described, Meriel looked past him at the people opening baskets of food just ahead, far too close for an exchange like this to be taking place.

"No, my dear heart, I won't hush." His expression was both stern and tender, implacable and hungry. "I've kept quiet far too long already. I'll be an old man before you bed me, at the rate you're going. If you don't kill me with frustrated desire first. I'm not a man-milliner, to be treated to conversation and comfits like a lady friend. I'm trying to be patient, but that isn't my long suit."

As he thrust his chin forward, he looked down at her from under languid lids. The timbre of his voice dropped still lower, reverberating through her body like the deep notes of a cathedral's organ. "I thought you wanted to be the huntress, but you're not tracking me fast enough. So I'm giving you warning. You have another week to pursue me. If you haven't caught me by then, I'm turning on you."

Meriel flinched from the intensity of his voice and gaze. He didn't loosen his hold. Horrified as she was by his contrary fit, another part of her gloated that a man of Jonys's experience wanted her enough to forget himself this far.

Tilting her chin with a forefinger, he forced her to meet his assured gaze. "And be forewarned: I take my prey at once. You won't have time to object to being seduced, love, for I'll have my mouth and hands everywhere at once, everywhere that makes you forget you ever hesitated an instant. You'll be mine, Meriel, whichever of us makes the first move."

Letting her free of his touch, he took one step back. His features formed a challenge. "Which way do you want it? On smooth linen sheets in a snug little house, or wherever we find ourselves when I've had enough of your dawdling indecision?"

Meriel felt weak all over, in danger of collapsing at the knees, but not from fear. His blatant male sensuality and the harsh undercurrent to his silky questions made her breathe erratically. She stared at her half-boots as she couldn't answer the question implied by his raised brows.

Now she understood the term "criminal conversation" in a new sense. His insinuating tongue and torrid stare from under scowling black brows had combined with a barely controlled forcefulness that made her want to take to the bushes with Jonys right here on Primrose Hill.

Somehow she had thought of keeping a man as a little like keeping a dog, for companionship. Perhaps she had expected to call him to her when she wanted company and send him off if he grew tiresome. Though Kept had never tolerated that treatment, either.

Just because Jonys had taken her money, he would never come tamely when he was called. Though he'd be there in an instant if she were in real need. And she did need him. She needed Jonys on her side in the struggle against Osborne. Just as important, she wanted him at her side, even if she hadn't exactly defined his role yet.

When she looked up to answer him, Jonys had walked away down the hill, the set of his shoulders and head looking as if he smoldered with pent-up power that excited and alarmed her. Behind him bounded Kept, trying to catch up to his long-limbed stride.

What if Jonys were so disgusted at her missish behavior he no longer wanted her? What if she had lost him before she'd ever gained him? She began picking her way down the slope.

His energy and quickness weren't what she would call restful in a companion. With him, she always felt on edge, as if riding a half-broken mount that might plunge in an unexpected direction any moment. Holding him in check now wasn't possible, and Meriel couldn't recall why she had wanted to do so.

Looking down the hillside after Jonys and Kept, Meriel picked up her skirts and ran. Drat the people in the other party! If they were shocked, they could just be shocked. None of them had seen her close up, and she didn't recognize any of them anyway.

With his long ears, Kept heard her stumbling approach. As he scampered back to join her, his long pink tongue lolled out the side of his mouth.

By the time she caught up to Jonys, she was breathless in two ways. "Wait!" she said, panting out the single word. Kept danced between them, enjoying the new game.

Jonys's face was expressionless, his eyes alive with a glittering, hard light. "No more waiting, I told you."

"That's what I mean," she gasped, holding her side. "I don't mean to wait. Look over the house in Dean Street, and if you think it will do, I'll sign the papers. You know more about what we need than I."

As he realized that she had capitulated, Jonys grinned with dazzling promise. Catching her up in a bear hug, he whirled her about before setting her down again. Kept jumped and barked as if sharing the wild exhilaration that sang through every nerve in her body.

Jonys grinned wickedly, irresistibly. "I know exactly what we need," he assured her. "And I'll see that we get it, fast."

Jonys paused in the doorway of Meriel's dining room. Shy morning sunlight peeked in the tall window where she and Hester sat at a small table laid for breakfast, setting them apart in an intimate space within the large room. Both ladies wore loose morning gowns and pretty caps, Meriel in a light springtime green, and Hester in white.

Holding a blue-flowered china cup, Meriel looked at him over her shoulder, her eyes beaming a gold-flecked glow of welcome. Tightness gripped his chest for a moment as he thought about coming into his own breakfast room each morning to find her waiting for him like this.

Across the table, Hester cut up a slice of gammon under Skype's concentrated gaze. Abandoning the prospect of ham, the terrier capered to the door, ears flat to invite head-rubbing, as Jonys entered the room.

Meriel pulled out the lyre-back chair to her right. "Come sit down if you can walk with Kept underfoot. Do you prefer ale or tea in the morning?"

"Just sitting down with the two of you is refreshment enough." As he took the offered chair, Meriel nodded dismissal to the footman standing by the sideboard.

Jonys had breakfasted already, but he wouldn't miss the opportunity to sit with Meriel as she broke her fast. He hadn't seen her since the outing to Primrose Hill three days before, for he had investigated the house on Dean Street as if he would live out his life in it. Perhaps he would, the part of it that mattered, if he couldn't win her.

"Instead of singing for your supper, tell us the latest *on-dits* for your breakfast." Hester twinkled at him with genuine welcome.

"As you're reading the court news," Jonys said, leaning across the table toward Hester, "you probably know more gossip than I've heard. It's the ladies who spread tales, not men."

"Not true," Hester said, wrinkling a pert nose at him. "Burchett knows the society news before it's printed. After talking with him, I read the paper only to see what version of events was deemed suitable for public consumption."

"Maybe I've been too busy creating gossip to listen to it." Jonys grinned at Meriel, who sat quietly, smiling at their banter. "Now I'm a changed man, of course."

Meriel glanced at a clock on the mantel across the room. "You surprise me, appearing this early," she admitted. "Few men who belong to clubs are out making calls when the sun has barely warmed the cobbles."

"It's hardly worthwhile to lie abed when you sleep alone," he said, watching to see the spread of extra color over her lovely face. Her eyelashes hovered above her cheeks like lacy ferns on a stream's bank. "Besides, I have a surprise for you today that involves driving more than an hour each way, and we need to take to the road soon."

Eyebrows drawn toward each other, Meriel said, "Today? I wish you had given me more notice." Skype stood up, patting his paws on her thigh as if helping Jonys persuade her.

"Have you made other plans?" He might have known that Meriel was the type to map out her time in advance, but he felt disappointed. "We can do it another day. I woke up in the mood to exercise my blacks and thought of taking you to a special place."

"Actually I haven't decided what I mean to do," she said. "It's just that I'm not as impetuous as you."

Relieved, he grinned. "Then come out with me as an exercise in becoming more yielding."

Her lips twitched in a way that showed him she'd heard more than one meaning to his suggestion, as he'd intended.

"Go on," Hester urged her. "It looks as if it will be a perfect day for a long drive." Skype added a sound almost like a word of agreement.

"You don't even know where Jonys proposes to go," Meriel said to her cousin, scratching Skype's shoulders. "His idea of a high treat could be viewing a steam engine installation or a new system of field drainage."

"Quite true, if I knew of something along that line at the moment," Jonys admitted, laughing. "But the destination I have in mind will suit you better than that. You'll be glad you came." He leaned forward, arm on the edge of the table, to coax her. "I'll entertain you well on the drive, and Skype will, too."

The terrier turned in eager circles between them.

Meriel laughed at the dog's antics. "Kept reminds me of you more and more. But I like to know where I'm going. How else will I know what to wear or when I'll be back?"

"Wear your prettiest carriage dress and tell Hester to expect you back by twilight." Jonys would cope with any protests she put forward, he wouldn't let her miss this outing. "To give you incentive to change quickly, I'll tell you where we're going once you're dressed."

"That's better; I'll come." Meriel began gathering up her letters. "Hester can't entertain you, for she's meeting friends in an hour and also needs to dress."

"Skype will keep me company," he said, touseling the terrier's head and ears. "We'll have a man-to-man chat while you dress, so don't hurry."

Jonys watched Meriel cross the passage and take the stairs. Though she might balk over last-minute plans, she entered into them with eagerness once she decided to accept them.

Hester smiled over her cup at him. "Meriel was right; I do need to hurry away," she said. "But I want a few words with you privately. First, I think you're very good for her."

"Because I tease her into being more spontaneous?" He dismissed it with a gesture. "I mean to be good to her as well for her." That objective mean everything to him.

"Make certain you are." Hester regarded him steadily, serious in a way he hadn't seen her before. "Meriel doesn't display her sensibilities as I do, but her emotions run as deep as any underground chasm. She's dealt with enough grief for several lifetimes already, and if another man betrays her, I doubt she'll ever let her feelings surface again."

Shifting on the upholstered chair seat, Jonys joked, "And I thought I wouldn't be asked my intentions since her father's passed on. Why not warn her not to trifle with *my* affections?" Uneasy about discussing Meriel or his feelings about her, he preferred to keep this discussion light. "Everyone assumes that only the lady risks a broken heart when a man and a woman have dealings together."

Skype barked, probably because Jonys had stopped scratching him. "You see?" he continued, grinning. "Skype agrees that we fellows get blamed before anything even goes wrong."

"Just make certain nothing does go wrong where Meriel's concerned." For such a little thing, Hester looked and sounded as threatening as a bear with a cub. "I couldn't love her more if she were my sister, and I won't have you or anyone else take advantage of her good nature and kind heart if I can prevent it."

"I hope to take care of her as my wife one day soon, if that puts your mind at rest." He didn't blame Hester for voicing her concerns for her

Pat Cody

cousin. If he ever got the right, he'd protect Meriel
with greater fierceness.

"That's a start, but Meriel's been a wife already."
Hester shook her head. "I wasn't impressed with
the care shown for her then."

"As I've tried to tell your cousin, her first husband doesn't represent the entire breed." Stretching his legs out before him, Jonys clasped his
hands behind his head.

"And you're the right breed to take care of her,
not just to share certain pleasures." Hester's sense
of humor showed in the smile tugging at her
mouth, but her eyes still showed her earnest intent.

"I'm the best choice she could make." He didn't
have to think about that assurance.

Head to one side, Hester toyed with the handle
of the fluted china cup. "And do you love her?" She
didn't hesitate to put questions to him most ladies
wouldn't ask.

"Who wouldn't love the beautiful, fascinating
Meriel?" Ladies usually needed to be assured he
loved them; affirming it to Hester wasn't any more
difficult. He intended to look out for Meriel, and
surely that was love.

"Once a rake, always a rake, unless love makes
passion more than a game." Shaking her head and
sighing, she placed a linen serviette on the table.
"You probably love her the way you do every
woman you're eager to bed. Perhaps time and
knowing Meriel better will change that."

"No, word of honor, I'm deeply concerned about
Meriel's happiness and want to take care of her."
He sat up straight. A man never knew when he'd
said the wrong thing to a woman until it was too
late to save himself.

Pushing away from the table, she gave him a considering look. "That's an excellent start," she said. "Do you love her enough not to take care of her at times?"

Without waiting for a reply, she left the room, ignoring his demand for an explanation as she hurried up the staircase across the passage. Feeling helpless and frustrated, he sat alone at the table.

If he lived to be a hundred, he'd never understand a woman's mind. It wasn't that they weren't as clever as men; they were too clever by half. Maybe that was the problem, the reason women talked in riddles as often as not. They constantly talked about feelings, about how the men in their lives affected them and each other, considerations a man would be embarrassed to dwell on at length.

As he stared across the table, more than a little peevish, a broad black nose appeared above its edge where Hester had sat, followed by Skype's fuzzy face and button-bright eyes. He must have jumped onto the vacated chair. Intent on the ham left in her plate, the terrier put his paws on the edge of the breakfast table and stretched toward the tidbits.

"Skype, no. Sit." Jonys spoke firmly without raising his voice.

Giving him a look that mingled reproach and guilt, the terrier sank slowly onto his haunches and stared at him across the plate. Leaning over the table, Jonys took a piece of ham and held it out to him.

"Personally, I don't care if you clean off every dish," he explained to Skype as the terrier swallowed more than ate the bite. "But I have a notion

261

that Meriel wouldn't like you to climb up and help yourself. So we'll indulge the lady. In every way possible, whatever Hester says. What the deuce did she say, anyway?"

Staring expectantly, Skype sat silent and on alert. Jonys fed him another piece of ham. "A fine pass I've come to, asking a dog about a lady, when I was always said to be handy with them. If I ever knew anything about women, it doesn't fit this one."

As Jonys motioned upstairs with the hand holding another bite of ham, Skype's head moved, following every gesture. Jonys handed over the treat. No need for both of them to do without what they craved.

"I'm beginning to understand how you feel, old boy," he said to the pup. Skype swiped first one side of his muzzle and then the other with his long, pink tongue, sweeping his whiskers back like a military mustache. "I'm in the same boat as you with Meriel, kept on a leash, told what to do, told what I can't do." It was the last item on the list of grievances that irked him most.

For a woman who had offered to keep him, Meriel had seemed oddly reluctant to get on with the best part of the arrangement. If he hadn't called a halt to her shilly-shallying over the house, they might still be no closer to meeting in an appropriate place for more than kisses.

"Though I'll admit the situation is unnatural." Jonys stopped him with a look as Skype stretched his muzzle toward Hester's plate again. "Pay attention; I'm baring my heart to you, and all you can think about is your stomach. You're in a position to understand me. It's bloody awkward, not knowing what a woman expects of you. On the one hand, I'm eager to plunge right in, so to speak."

Skype barked once, looking from him to the plate of ham.

"No, neither of us can just grab what he wants; it isn't the gentlemanly thing when the lady's shown reluctance."

Giving Skype another bite, Jonys continued. "Why she's reluctant, I don't know. It isn't as if she's a virginal miss in her first season; she's been married and borne two children. I could swear she wants me, too, so why won't she do the usual thing and marry me? Don't shake your head; of course I know by now when a woman's interested in more than conversation and the quadrille."

The Aberdeen terrier looked mulish with his ears out to the side, staring at the plate again. "I've always played fair with ladies, making it clear from the start I'm not marriage material. This time, I've proposed until I've worn out the speech. And she insists she won't wed. Not just me, but anyone. Other women plot and scheme to trap a fellow, and she offers me money and a slip on the shoulder. I'm no better than a pet pooch. No offense meant, old fellow." To make up for the slur, Jonys handed over the largest remaining piece of ham.

"I should have said 'lackey.' I'm just another footman at her beck and call." Frustration rose in his throat like bile.

Skype nudged the plate with his nose and Jonys gave him more ham. "You're right, that's the sticking point. She supplies the bacon. However I approach matters between us, I stumble over the blasted money. No matter how considerately she has funds transferred to my account through her man of business, I'm bought and paid for. As kept as you."

The terrier's ears flipped forward at the sound of Meriel's name for him. "No, I'm not giving in and calling you *Kept*. A man hangs onto what precious little territory he can claim as his own when the ground won't settle under his feet. I feel like I've been reeling about, hardly knowing what to do next since Chas died and forced me into the title."

Propping his elbow on the table, Jonys rubbed his jaw. He might not have known what to do just at first, but lately he'd been feeling an earl's shoes fit better all the time. Maybe he wouldn't be a disgrace to the family honor as the seventh earl after all. And if he could reach one impossible goal, he could manage two. He'd win Meriel as his countess.

Across the table, Skype barked, staring at the plate, on which lay one more bite of ham. "Just so. A fellow doesn't deserve what he won't work for."

Handing over the last of the meat, he laughed as his spirits rose. "I'll charm our Meriel, see if I don't. And sooner or later, I'll persuade her to marry me. In the meantime, it could be argued that my efforts are providing for my sisters and tenants. Maybe the money's no more tainted than if I had fleeced a bumpkin at cards for it. I'm not coming by it dishonorably, even if it doesn't feel right."

A step on the stair distracted him. Meriel appeared on the landing, clad in a willow-green pelisse over a white gown. She'd had the good sense to tie on a bonnet with a helmet crown and narrow brim that wouldn't catch the wind when he put his horses along, once clear of the Kensington Turnpike gate.

Smoothing her york tan gloves as she entered the room, Meriel looked around. "I thought I heard voices as I came down the stairs, and expected to find Hester here with you."

Jonys rose to meet her as Skype jumped down from Hester's chair. "You heard me talking to our dog. He asked if he could come with us, and I said I'd petition you on his behalf. Though perhaps I should beg him to intervene for me instead." Her cheeks and throat were an invitation in silk to his fingertips.

Dimpling at him, Meriel said, "Whatever you want from anyone, you can wheedle as readily as Kept."

"I'll put that to the test very soon." As he turned toward the door, she stopped him with a touch to his sleeve.

"You promised me certain information," she reminded him, looking and sounding reproachful.

"I'm delighted to find you so eager for news about our house." Chin up, he looked down at her. "It looks like the one to me, if you like it, too. Two stories and the usual offices. Stables out back so you can enter the house directly from the carriage without being observed from the street. Clean enough to move into, though I'll get the decorators in at once if you like it."

"You know that isn't what I meant, but since you've brought it up, I mean to leave the selection of the house entirely in your hands. I hope you'll move there from the Albany, as it's a pity to waste the space on a few visits to it. Much better for a house to be lived in."

A weasel gnawed at his gut. Jutting his chin, he

said, "Do you plan to make me a present of the house when you cast me aside in the usual manner of the kept?"

Her eyes widened, and for an instant Meriel looked as if he'd struck her. Then her features smoothed and she hardly sounded agitated. "I'll sell it when you must wed. If you don't care to live in it, no worry. Trent can engage a small staff to live there and look after it."

Rubbing his chin, Jonys felt as if he'd kicked a pup. His hasty temper had gotten the best of his good sense, cutting up rough at Meriel without cause. "Sorry. Too much generosity gets my back up, when I should be thanking you. The Dean Street house is far more comfortable than my quarters at the Albany. Would you let me engage the staff and see to furnishing the house with some bits and bobs from Hadham House's attics, to make up for my grumpish tongue? I'm said to have reasonable taste."

"Thanks are no more necessary than an apology." Meriel spoke briskly, not quite looking at him. "Please, do as you wish with the house. If you're seen bringing in your things, it will cause far less comment than if I run in and out. Now, do you plan to reveal where we're headed today as you promised?"

Jonys wanted to restore the harmony they'd shared earlier, before his surly tongue upset the delicate balance between them in their uneasy alliance. "We'll pass through the gate beyond Hyde Park corner," he said, "and through Kensington's gate as well."

"Richmond Hill provides lovely views," she said in a polite voice.

"It does, indeed, but you won't see them today.

We'll give Hammersmith the go-by and Hounslow as well." Jonys grinned as she began to stare at him, head cocked to the side as Skype did at times. "If you aren't too tired, we'll wait to stop for refreshment on the edge of Windsor."

"Too tired!" Her eyes were huge in her small face, glowing like stars on a perfect summer night, her voice a choked whisper. "Oh, Jonys, my boys. You're taking me to my sons!"

Launching herself at him, arms open, she laughed until it ended in a sob. Jonys caught her against himself, wishing she wore that expression because of him, with her heart's fullness making her lips curve up and a light come on inside her. No matter. It was enough to be the steel that sparked her flame for now.

Chapter Fourteen

Pacing around the limited confines of the inn's private parlor with Kept underfoot, Meriel drew off her gloves and laid them beside her bonnet and reticule on the round table before the fireplace. How impossible to sit still when she would see her boys soon.

Though it made sense for Jonys to visit the headmaster alone, waiting was difficult now that she stood here in Eton's Christopher Inn, so close to her sons. How long would it take him to arrange for the boys to join them?

Hurrying to the window and pushing it farther open into the cottage garden, she looked along the road in the direction Jonys had taken. What if Osborne were present at the school and refused permission for the boys to come out with their friends? He frowned on all forms of self-indulgence.

Pleating her handkerchief between restless fingers, she turned from the window and stumbled over Kept. Stooping, she said, "Sorry I bumped you, fellow. Did I hurt you?"

Looking up with adoring dark eyes, he licked her hand as his tail stirred. Dogs accepted and forgave, even if you injured them. Would her sons realize she couldn't prevent their uncle from keeping them apart? If they didn't understand, she couldn't blame them, but any show of reproach or reserve on their parts would surely break her heart.

As the door opened, she sprang up. In came Jonys, filling the small space with his shoulders alone, or so it seemed.

As Kept sniffed his boots to check where he had been, Meriel looked into the passage beyond him.

"My company isn't enough?" Though his tone teased her, his expression showed his pleasure at her eagerness to see her sons. "The boys will come along as soon as the lesson is finished, all four of them."

Pride showed in his posture and expression, as if he gained in self-esteem by seeing her pleasure in his gift of time with James and Steven. Accepting a gift as a way of giving one was a new notion to her, one it could be important to remember if she were to remain close with Jonys for an extended time. Clearly, giving was important to him.

"What a relief. I had a superstitious fear that, somehow, Osborne would thwart your plan and keep the boys away from me again," she admitted. "I can't thank you enough for arranging this."

"You've thanked me more than enough just by glowing all the way from London to this inn. I like to see you smiling." He smiled himself, looking down at her with his chin up.

As Jonys leaned against the mantel, Meriel moved past him to look out the window, knowing the boys couldn't be in sight already. She paced back again. The fear of missing the precious hour with her boys through some quirk of fate gnawed at her patience. "They know the right inn?"

Taking her shoulders in his big hands, Jonys guided her to the open casement. "Stand here where you'll see them coming long before they're at the door," he urged her. "I told the headmaster to send my cousin's boys and yours to the Christopher. If he can keep a school full of boys straight, he can identify the correct inn to four scamps. They'll come charging along that street in a short time, I promise you."

Kept wandered off to sniff along the baseboards and into the shadowed corners of the small room. He wouldn't find much sport in a space providing guests with a private sitting room and place to take meals. Besides the deal table and chairs, the room contained only a table by the door to hold trays, a plain bench along one wall and a scuttle for coal.

The dark, boxy room didn't compare to the meanest chamber at Welwyn Hall, but James and Steven wouldn't care. For her part, any place she met her boys was a palace.

A slight breeze stirred the textured leaves and smooth petals nodding in at the casement, cooling her cheeks. Meriel breathed in the mixed scents of blossoms, horses, and an ancient inn. The drone of a slow, fat bee underlay the counterpoint played by birdsong, horses' tack, dishes, and voices from indoors and outside the inn.

Jonys had set up this day for her. No woman had ever known this much joy.

Over her shoulder, she said, "This gift of time with my sons is beyond price. How you arranged it without Osborne learning about it, I can't imagine, but I'm grateful."

"If he comes looking for them, your sons are supping with their friends, whose male relative is treating them all to a tuck. That's hardly a rare occurrence." Jonys grinned like a boy up to mischief as he stood with an arm laid along the low mantel, a boot propped on the brass fender. "I may have neglected to mention to the headmaster that a companion waited for me here, but the company I keep isn't his concern."

Laughing aloud with glad anticipation, Meriel said, "You're taking to having a title quite naturally. A toplofty earl would assume exactly that!" Jonys was teaching her to jest.

Turning back to watch for the approach of her sons, Meriel was struck by another concern. "Did you place the order with the kitchen I requested?"

"Stop fretting, everything's seen to," he assured her. "I ordered beef and Poor Knights of Windsor for twelve, and if that doesn't satisfy four hungry boys, we'll have another round until they groan."

"You must have had relatives bring you here for treats when you were a boy," she guessed, "for you seem to know exactly how to manage everything."

"Chas and I were fortunate to have a reprobate uncle in London who stopped by when his luck with the cards was in." Jonys tilted his square jaw up as if watching the memory unfold on the low ceiling. "Though I suspect Mama sent him money for the purpose at times, so he would let her know we were still alive."

271

His tone was fond as he mentioned his mother. Perhaps Lady Hadham had taught him the consideration that led him to help Meriel now. Pray God she would have the opportunity to shape her sons' attitudes in a similar way.

Perhaps being close with his mother had helped Jonys to understand Meriel's need to see James and Steven for herself, her need to touch them and take in the hundreds of small signals that told a mother more about her child than a thousand reports from others. Certainly he wasn't the roistering rake she had once believed him to be.

Recalling earlier attitudes toward him reared feelings of guilt. "I owe you an apology, for in the past, I've thought of you as a careless womanizer, interested only in the next conquest," she confessed. "After today, I'll defend you against anyone who doesn't realize you're an exceptionally good and kind man."

Jonys grimaced. "Don't canonize me just yet. You're better company when you're happy, so I'm doing myself the favor." He lounged at the stone hearth, kicking at a firedog in the empty grate as if embarrassed by her praise.

Kept had given up on finding a mouse, stretching himself on a braided rug before the fireplace. He dreamed, with paws twitching and an edge of white eyeball showing through slitted lids.

Leaning farther over the sill, Meriel felt breathless and buoyant, overstimulated and fearful. If the boys didn't come soon, she might fly out the window to meet them.

"No one else has helped me as you're doing," she pointed out, warmth welling up inside like bread dough rising before the fire. "Whatever happens in the future, I can never repay you for today."

"Most gifts aren't meant to be repaid, just accepted and enjoyed." His gaze wandered over her features as if he were mesmerized, oblivious to the existence of any other world. Uncomfortable with such concentrated intensity, Meriel turned back to the view out the window.

Part of his strong appeal to her was his generosity. A man who acted with decisive purpose, making his own rules without stepping on anyone, excited her. This man, who gave her what she wanted most without making her ask for it, aroused feelings beyond passion.

In holding the pain of separation from her boys to a manageable level, Meriel had also damped down welcome emotions, like the laughter, good feelings, and desire this man evoked in her. Much as she distrusted his levity and impetuousness at times, she could also respect and admire him for those qualities. She sent another glance his way.

As a smile curled his lips slowly and softened the hard lines of his face, the level of energy in the room changed and gathered about her. Meriel felt his longing as clearly as she had ever experienced her own.

Jonys simply stood gazing at her with a message of yearning on his features that reached out to her, though he didn't move a step from the small fireplace. He was the only man of her experience who could kiss her with a look.

Awakened senses told her that his every muscle strained to come take her into his arms. His eyes turned the turbulent blue of storm clouds, flashing a message of desire like lightning through a hot summer sky, and his jaw jutted with the tension of control.

Restraint required extreme effort for a man of

his nature. His discipline on her behalf was a great compliment, for Jonys was a man of action, not constraint.

"If you keep looking at me like that, with the sunlight setting your hair on fire like my blood, I'll lock that door and you won't see your sons today," he warned her, his voice low and grating. "Find a topic to distract me, for I'm not feeling clever at the moment."

Searching for the least pleasant subject possible, she said quickly, "You might consider what I'm to do about Osborne. Hester still wants to murder him, but that hardly sets a good example for my sons on how to resolve problems."

"Hester talks a great deal of sense," he said. "Before we settle for the easy way out and murder Osborne, I'll wait for complete reports on the inquiries I've started."

"Since nothing has come of checking into his financial holdings so far, what other sort of information do you expect to turn up on a vicar?" As she glanced around from the window, Kept turned over in his sleep, rolling against Jonys's boot.

"The same sort of thing to be discovered about anyone. Keep in mind that a man of God is still a man, and he's capable of the same human failings as any of us."

Meriel nodded. "But have you found reason to suspect him of any particular wrongdoing as yet?"

"I haven't learned any reason not to." His mouth settled into a straight line as Jonys rubbed his chin. "His actions prove that ordination doesn't make everything he does right."

Frowning, Meriel recalled a revelation her husband had made about his brother. "Osborne came to live at Welwyn Hall when he gave up a considerable living, I was told," she said. "Welwyn explained that his brother had suffered a nervous storm and needed the quiet of scholarly pursuits rather than the daily commotion of parish life. And I must admit, I never thought he had the empathy to deal with people's ordinary failings."

"No doubt you're right, though it's other dealings I'm having looked into. Something still might turn up once we have reason to review his management of your boys' trust fund and the estate. Few vicars have the opportunity to learn how to manage estates and investments well."

"Osborne had little to do with either while Welwyn was alive," Meriel admitted. Though Jonys had learned estate management by necessity, he'd had little opportunity to know investments. As a second son, he'd never had much more income than a cleric to manage. "So if he lacks the ability to administer the trust for my sons, perhaps a more capable guardian who's also sympathetic to children's needs would be appointed by the court?"

"Something like that," Jonys said briefly, looking down at Kept, who still slept between them. "I've been thinking," he said as if he'd had another idea. "You don't want me and my little cousins in the way while you visit with James and Steven. I'll get a table out in the main taproom and have the Poor Knights of Windsor served there. You and your boys can talk in here. Then if Osborne should show up to find them, we'll have a big table where he expects us."

"How would you explain where the boys are?"

"I'll say that James went to help Steven find the privies and send one of my boys off to fetch them."

Jonys sounded confident of his plan, but he always appeared to believe that things would work out.

On the hearth rug, Kept stood slowly and stretched, leg by leg. He ambled toward her, ears up.

"Steven would be insulted to be cast in a role where he couldn't find his own way to the necessary, but we may not have to mention it," she said. The need for this subterfuge to spend a few minutes with her own children made Meriel feel grubby, but she would stoop lower if forced to it.

Standing under the window with his forepaws against the dark paneling, Kept stretched his neck upward, pointing with his nose as if sniffing the air. The terrier gave two sharp barks.

Coming to look out the window, Jonys said, "I think that foursome in the distance is our crew."

Osborne no longer mattered, with her boys coming this way. Meriel leaned against the sill, looking with all of her senses toward the boys of different sizes straggling in a loose group far down the street.

The two middle-height boys were hers. They might not be close enough for her to make out their features, but she knew her sons by the way they walked and moved their heads and arms.

How small and defenseless they looked, walking down a public road with heavy wagons rumbling by. A dashing curricle could so easily run away from a young whip and crash into them. How could she keep them safe when she wasn't even allowed normal visits with them? Tears blurred her view and collected in her throat.

James lagged behind in the group, and Steven's stocking had come down. He was talking, of course. Steven had talked early and had never stopped, it seemed at times. The closer they came, the more greedy her eyes felt, sopping up the sight of them to store in her head against the long days and longer nights apart if she and Jonys couldn't free them.

Her chest swelled like a hot-air balloon with the grief of parting with them again later today, and she hadn't even held them against her heart yet. Her throat closed down and her nose hurt with unshed sobs.

Touching her arm, Jonys said gruffly, "I'll head off my two in the taproom and send yours on in here." His footsteps retreated behind her.

Meriel buried her nose in her handkerchief. As the door closed behind Jonys, she sank down on the bench under the window, watching until her eyes burned. Kept jumped up beside her, leaning against her as the boys came closer.

James needed to comb his hair and Steven had a bruised shin where his stocking drooped. Both had grown since she saw them last, and both looked far too young to be at school instead of studying at home with a tutor.

As the boys approached the Christopher Inn and disappeared from view, a few tears overflowed despite her intention not to cry and embarrass the boys. Kept stood with his forepaws on her lap, reaching up to lick at the tears. Laughing, she patted his wiry coat, wiped her eyes, and tucked her handkerchief away.

"You're about to meet my sons, Kept." He cocked his head, ears flicking forward. "I hope you'll like them, and I know they'll take to you. They always wanted a dog." Talking to the terrier reassured her that her voice would sound fairly normal. She stood and hurried across the room.

Light footsteps sounded down the passage, and unable to wait, she wrenched the door open and looked out. Her sons walked hesitantly toward her, looking at the closed doors on either side of the hall. James needed a haircut, and his bony wrists stuck out from his shirt cuffs. Steven could do with a wash, for he seemed to have pudding or dirt on his round cheek and chin. They were the most beautiful sight she could hope to see.

"Hello, James, Steven," she said, stepping out into the passage. Trying to sound normal, she strangled on the effort. They stopped a moment, then broke into a run at the same time, James's longer legs bringing him to her a step ahead of his brother.

She knelt, needing to be on their level to meet them, and held her arms open. Her heart opened of its own accord.

As first one and then the other small body bumped against her, Meriel folded an arm around each of them, straining each son against her as if she could absorb them into a safe haven within herself. Though her mouth tilted up with joy, warm tears trickled from the corners of her closed eyes and down her nose and cheeks. She kissed them both without aiming the caresses and pulled them more tightly to her.

James held his breath, arms fastened about her neck, pushing his length against her silently. Steven breathed through his mouth, stirring the hair beside her ear with his warm breath as he burrowed his cheek against her shoulder and clutched the ruff at the neck of her gown.

They gave off the warm, slightly sour smell of boys who had been running, and she bowed her head between theirs, overcome with how much she had missed the special odor of small boys. Her sons were close against her again, each with his own individual shape and feel in her arms, each more precious than her life. Meriel held her boys at last, and she couldn't think beyond this moment of loving and being together, the three of them.

When Steven moved, she let go at once, standing and using her handkerchief. "How good you both look to me. I hope you didn't have to leave an important lesson to come visit with me?" Moving to the door of the private parlor, she waited for them to enter ahead of her.

James shook his head, lips folded tight while his gaze clung to her face.

Laughing, Steven said, "Just maths, and I hate saying those stupid tables. Why do I have to know tables, Mama? Did you ever hear a grown person saying his six-times? When I grow up, I'll never say a math table as long as I live. I'd rather go outside and run. Do you know how fast I can run, Mama? Faster than James."

"You cannot," James stated, frowning. "I warned you about bragging." He looked up at Meriel with an earnest expression. "I try to make him behave properly, but he talks too much to hear what I say to him. The only time he's quiet is when Uncle Osborne tutors us."

"Nobody would talk around Uncle Osborne, the way his eyes look all cold and empty when he frowns," Steven said. He grabbed her hand and hung on it, leaning against her leg. "I'll just go home with you, Mama. I don't like school and I miss my pony. What if the grooms aren't feeding him and currying him every day? What if he misses me, too, and he runs away from home? Why don't we just leave now?"

Looking from his flushed, eager face to James's bleak expression and knowing eyes, Meriel felt the rage of her helplessness anew. She didn't want to make them fear their uncle while she couldn't legally remove them from his care.

Fingering his hair off his damp forehead, she smiled down at Steven. "You know your uncle loves you two more than anyone. He'd be quite upset if you disappeared and he didn't know where you were." She couldn't even reassure Steven that he'd ride his pony during the coming holiday, with Osborne threatening to keep them away from the estate. "Of course you miss Spotted Dick; he's a very fine mount."

Steven's face was crumpling into tearful argument when loud snuffling made him look around. Behind him, Kept stood sniffing the stocking that slouched around his high-buttoned boot. Laughing, Steven crouched, nose-to-nose with the terrier.

Kept stretched his neck to lick at the pudding on her son's cheek, and he laughed harder, hands rubbing the dog's shoulders. "He likes me!" Steven said, collapsing on the floor as Kept dashed around him.

"He likes the food smeared on your disgusting face," James said sternly. Bending, he held out a hand to the terrier. Frisking about, Kept sniffed his fingers and moved closer as James buried his fingers in the fur under his collar, scratching. For the first time, James's serious face relaxed into a boy's easy grin.

Joining his brother, Steven stroked Kept, too. "What a jolly dog. Is he yours? Did you find him on the way here? Can he run fast? Does he have a ball? Let's play with him."

Thankful that Kept had distracted Steven, Meriel said, "His name is Kept. He didn't have a home, so he came to live with me. Let's sit on the carpet before the fireplace, and we'll all play with him."

They moved toward the empty grate, Kept leaping around both boys to their evident pleasure. The boys fell onto their knees while the terrier dashed between them.

As she sank onto the edge of small rug, Meriel removed her handkerchief from her sleeve. "Who has a handkerchief that isn't too dreadful? Kept didn't bring any of his toys with him, but maybe we can devise one."

Taking the reasonably clean handkerchief James brought out of a pocket, she bunched it loosely inside her own, tying the ends into a misshapen bundle. "Maybe he'll fetch this for you," she said, dropping it into Steven's waiting palms.

Her younger son flung the balled handkerchiefs into a far corner and struggled to his feet to dash after them. James stayed beside her, leaning against her shoulder.

Putting an arm around his slim waist, she said, "I've missed you both more than you could ever guess."

"I've missed you, too," James said in his quiet way. "Steven's just a baby, and he truly likes dogs. But he's blubbered about you something fierce."

"I know," she said, squeezing him while she choked back painful thoughts of her boys, homesick in a strange place, not knowing when they might be with her again. "We know, all three of us, how specially we love each other." She caught Steven into a hug as he raced back to join them. "Even if we aren't always under the same roof, or even in the same neighborhood, we feel the same love we always have."

"But I want to be under the same roof," Steven protested, struggling away to reach for the handkerchiefs Kept held down under a large, round paw. "You might forget me like Spotted Dick has."

Snatching up the makeshift ball to capture Steven's attention, Meriel hid it in her clasped hands. While Kept nosed at them, she spoke to her younger son. "Have you forgotten me or your pony?"

Falling onto his knees and flinging out his arms, Steven laughed. "Of course not. I just said his name, didn't I?"

"Exactly," Meriel said, cupping his cheek for a brief moment. "You can't forget Spotted Dick, because you love him. None of us forgets the other for that same reason. If you ever worry that you aren't in my thoughts and heart, just remember that I don't have all the excitement of starting school to distract me, and I think of you even more often than you think of me."

"Do not," said Steven, giggling as he twisted away to run after Kept.

"Do, too," Meriel answered, pitching the handkerchief ball for Kept and her younger son to chase.

A small hand stole into hers. "Do not," said James, looking up at her with a hunger too close to sadness.

This beloved son, only eight years old, knew too much too soon about life's unfairness. Meriel swept him into a hug he returned with fierce young strength. She had to get her boys away from Osborne before James forgot how to play.

* * *

Unable to sit still, Jonys left his cousin's sons at a table in the corner with heaping plates of food before them. Crossing the taproom, he stopped at the end of the passage where Meriel's boys had disappeared. He had heard a faint murmur of her voice, then their footsteps quicken, and he couldn't keep away.

As his eyes adapted to the dimness of the narrow, low-beamed passage, he could make out the crouched shapes farther along its length. Meriel's head was bowed, with one boy's head on her shoulder and the other's cheek laid against hers. He couldn't see any of their faces, but he didn't need to. Every line of their arms and bodies expressed their love for one another, their mutual needs for the reassurance of touch.

Master paintings of the Madonna and Child had make him feel like this. He needed to clear his throat, but he wouldn't disturb the three before him for the world.

Though he didn't mean to intrude, he felt drawn to the reunion taking place before him and couldn't retreat, either. Jonys longed to join them, kneeling to wrap his arms about all three and keep them safe.

Meriel needed her children no more than they needed her. He wanted her to have what she required with an intensity that wracked him and increased his determination.

Protective feelings were nothing new to Jonys; he had wanted to keep his brother, mother, and sisters safe even as a boy. As he grew up, he had fought every threat to the people, creatures, and places he loved. But this sense of wanting to safeguard Meriel and her sons was a tower beside a tollgate in comparison.

This quiet exhilaration welling up from inside him and spilling over into a new awareness was love. Real love, not infatuation that fed on satisfying only his own needs. Much as he felt compelled to protect Meriel, he now wanted to act beyond his desires for her to give her what she needed and wanted.

Hardly daring to breath, he stood watching the emotion more than the people, with his heart slowing to a solid bump against his ribs. Real love's presence in this passage was as tangible as a lantern's glow.

Meriel and her boys must be together in the future. He knew it with the recognition of love's desire for his beloved to have what she most desired.

No longer was it enough to win her as his wife, to gain his happiness by being with her. The only way to honor his love for Meriel was to help her find happiness as she defined it.

If only Meriel might come to love him, too.

Chapter Fifteen

This carriage ride symbolized her life perfectly at present. Bumping along an unseen road in near-total darkness with Jonys beside her, unsure of her exact destination or the long-term outcome of the journey to the Dean Street house, Meriel struggled against a confused sense of unreality.

Nothing had felt quite real for several days now. Before she absorbed one event into her mind, another occasion demanded a new mental adjustment. And Jonys, lounging too close beside her in the swaying darkness after they'd left the ball at Holland House, had prompted every change.

Just a week ago, Jonys had made it possible for her to see her sons. As she sat in the garden early this afternoon reliving that precious hour with them at the Christopher Inn, a note had arrived from him saying the house at Number Seven Dean Street was ready for use—at her pleasure.

Little more than an hour ago, he'd bowed formally and asked her to stand up with him at the Hollands' ball. As they gave hands across in the country dance, he'd murmured, "Tonight is ours," with a passionate look of promise that left her in no mood to deny him or herself. As they stepped back to back in the figures, he'd added, "I'll accompany you to your next engagement when you're ready to leave here."

To anyone who overheard him, his message hadn't meant what it did to her. Taken with his earlier note about the Dean Street house, Meriel knew precisely what engagement would follow the Holland House ball. Every nerve in her body united in anticipation of being with Jonys in a different dance.

As they held hands to go down the set, he murmured under cover of the music, "I'm eager to see how you like our house and its furnishings."

His saying "our house" didn't discompose her as it had on Primrose Hill. This time, the sharing it implied tantalized her throughout the rest of her stay at the ball. She endured the sweet torment of meeting his provocative glance constantly, while he danced and conversed with others, revealing only his usual friendly grace.

Jonys even stood up with the underbred Widow Helsby, who flirted outrageously with him as she had at every other opportunity. Which was going a bit too far in throwing the gossips off their scent.

No one would have suspected his intentions for the rest of the night from watching Jonys at the ball. Tonight he would escort her to the house he had found and furnished for the two of them. He was eager to satisfy his part of the loan agreement he had insisted on, the line that read "for good and valuable services." That knowledge and the seductive glances he sent her over heads and behind backs maddened and titillated her beyond bearing at the ball.

Their single dance had felt different to her from previous ones, knowing what was to come between them. More charged with emotion and significance.

Exhilaration had lifted her above the ordinary social patterns of the next hour like a hot-air balloon. Her interest in the occasion and acquaintances had receded like the ground far below aeronauts.

Now, sitting in the dark confines of her town carriage with Jonys filling up most of its interior, Meriel decided her dresser had laced her stays far too tightly. Had she worn her best chemise and petticoat? At least her hair was freshly washed and this gown was new.

Though she couldn't see Jonys in the deep darkness along this stretch of road, she could feel his slight movements of breath where his shoulder, arm, and thigh pressed against her. He was far too large, too male, too focused on her, to ignore for one instant. Not that she wanted to ignore him.

Her heart thumped too hard and fast under her ribs, at her throat, in her ears. Though she craved this night with Jonys, plus all the other nights possible, she also felt uncertain. He had known many ladies, but her experience had been limited to one husband. Whatever she knew from the marriage bed didn't prepare her to take a practiced lover into her arms.

Tonight, Jonys was as much a stranger as an old acquaintance. As a young girl in Surrey, she had known him mostly by gossip as a rascal who was dangerous to her reputation. Meeting him again twelve years later in Portman Square, she had believed him to be an irresponsible, heartless man who could abandon a little dog.

Over the last weeks, he had proved himself considerate and all too ready to help her meet responsibilities. Which made him the greatest threat of all.

Because she must remain in control of her future to have any say in her life, Meriel had to resist the urge to accept everything Jonys offered her. His clean scent of soap, sun-dried linen, and starch permeated the carriage, reminding her that what she denied herself was good and fine.

Though she would make love with Jonys tonight and, she hoped, for many nights to come, she must never allow herself to love him. Loving him, she would long to give him everything he asked of her, even the marriage that removed her legal existence. Love opened the door to unbearable loss.

As she leaned away from the pressure of his big body, Meriel's chest tightened with panic. Darkness and Jonys's presence loomed larger, filling her coach until she felt as if the air inside it was forced out and used up. Jonys's overwhelming closeness could smother her.

In the same way that sharing the narrow confines of her carriage with Jonys could steal her breath, so could sharing their bodies bring them to a deeper level of mental intimacy. And that proximity threatened far more danger to her legal independence than to her reputation. She must resist Jonys's practiced seduction on every level.

Shifting sideways, Jonys laid an arm along the seat back, enclosing her in the sensual circle of his complete attention. Despite the darkness, she felt his gaze and set her mind to repel its charm. Jonys wooed as naturally as he breathed; she must be on guard against losing too much in gaining the intimacy with him she craved.

A flicker of light from the running footmen's torches fell on his face briefly as they stopped at the Hyde Park tollgate. A devilish gleam sparked his stare before they drove on, casting his eyes into mysterious dark hollows under heavy black brows, then merging his features with the night.

Mephisto might look like that, looming out of darkness in brief flashes of flame to scald your senses with a look and claim your soul. If her Master of Darkness were Jonys, she would dance with the devil tonight and rejoice in it. But she would never sell her soul into the bondage of love and marriage.

As the carriage leaned to the right, Meriel looked out on Hyde Park Corner. The Dean Street house couldn't be far distant now. His hand found hers as if he heard her thought. Leaning over, Jonys grazed his smooth, warm lips up the side of her throat to her ear, and the caress shivered across her shoulders and down her spine.

"Cold?" he murmured, gathering her against his chest.

"Quite the opposite," she replied, hearing the breathless quality in her voice. He noticed it, too, for his low laughter wrapped about her as closely as his arms. Though she allowed her body to melt into his embrace, she fortified a citadel deep within herself.

The carriage turned sharply to the right, and Jonys braced himself against the frame behind her head to hold her securely in place. Here in what must be Dean Street, not a light showed on either side.

"From this point to the bend in the middle, no houses front on Dean Street," he murmured, "so you're less likely to be noticed approaching the house from the direction of Hyde Park. From South Audley Street's entrance, you would pass six other houses, but only on one side. This was the most private place I could find for you to come." His concern for her reputation sounded in his protective tone.

"You gave the choice of a house careful attention. I appreciate your thoughtfulness." Squeezing as much of his large hand as she could clasp, Meriel realized that Jonys, unlike the men in control of her life from her father onward, acted out his consideration for her instead of talking about it as an excuse to impose his will.

"Looking out for you will always be my first concern," he said, lifting their joined hands to kiss her fingers.

The carriage slowed and turned right again, then rocked gently along an unseen route. Meriel might be afraid, on a blind journey into a strange place, with anyone but Jonys.

"We're in the mews alongside Number Seven," he said, his voice sounding reassuring and elated in this deeper darkness, "also behind a few houses on the other side that front on Tilney Street. If your coachman brings you back here to the stables, you can enter the house from the rear and reduce the risk of being seen and talked about."

Meriel peered past the dim glow of the carriage lanterns, seeing little. "Will Kept be inside?" Days before, she had asked Jonys to send for the terrier when she first visited the house. Having Kept here would make her less a stranger to this unfamiliar place.

"No doubt he is," Jonys assured her, pushing open the carriage door and leaping out to let down the step himself. Extending his hand, he added, "Anson said he would see to fetching him personally, so you may be certain Skype's waiting for you right now."

As her foot touched the step, Jonys put an arm about her waist and swung her easily to the cobbled yard. Holding her against his side, he crossed its width with her held close, to a door at the back of the three-story house.

As they approached the door, it swung open, spilling yellow light into the yard like rich cream. A thin, elderly man stood in the back passage, dressed in black and holding himself sternly erect.

Kept shot past his stockinged legs and into the yard, frisking about the two of them as they stepped inside. Looking with curiosity at the elderly servant who must be Jonys's butler, Meriel found his keen eye on her.

Smiling, she said, "You must be Anson. Jonys said you brought Kept here for me tonight, and I thank you for seeing to my comfort so kindly."

Bowing correctly, he said, "Your comfort here will be of first importance to me, m'lady, and to the staff." He turned to motion a woman, two girls, a lad, and two liveried manservants forward from the steep stairs leading down, no doubt, to the house's usual offices.

Just as if she were a bride brought to the front entrance of her new home in state, Anson presented the cook, maids, footmen, and boot boy to Meriel. When she had nodded to each one and repeated the name in hopes of remembering it another day, the old butler dismissed them to their duties with a nod.

This hardly felt like an assignation, being bowed into the house with the full honors belonging to its mistress. Meriel appreciated the ritual, setting her presence here with Jonys above an easy affair between a fashionable couple. Though it couldn't grow into the full commitment of marriage, their association held far more significance for her than a passing liaison.

"Thank you, Anson," Jonys said, turning Meriel toward the front of the house. "I'll give the lady a tour of the rooms on this floor, and you may bring us wine in ten minutes' time."

As they walked down the passage with Kept toddling before them, looking back to make certain they followed, Meriel felt the energy of anticipation rising in her companion. Jonys was eager to show her this little house, and her interest and dread to see his arrangements grew.

The place itself wouldn't matter if its purpose was only discreet joinings of bodies. If she allowed it to represent a setting where they would come together on many levels, her battle to reserve part of herself from him would require heavier defenses.

Opening the first door to the right, he stood back to let her and Kept enter first. "This is the breakfast room, though I'll take all my meals here. I didn't furnish it formally enough to call it a dining room." He walked around to the other side of a square pedestal table near the fireplace. The chairs' pierced-rail backs swept into a graceful curve, and the seats were upholstered in gold wide-striped fabric.

Meriel looked about with as much interest as

Kept displayed as he examined chair legs with his nose and snuffled out of sight under the table. The walls were painted a light green, high above vine-striped wallpaper, and the woodwork shone darkly green against them. The glowing finish of fine old mahogany furniture in flickering fire-and-candlelight welcomed her.

Warding off the mental picture of them sharing breakfast in the lovely space, Meriel said, "What an appealing room. It's a shame you won't be entertaining."

Coming to clasp her elbows in his large hands, Jonys twinkled down at her with a tilt to his eyes and lips. "I plan to be very entertaining, indeed, though not at my best in this room, I hope."

Kissing the tip of her nose, he led her and Kept back out into the passage. Motioning to the door on the same side farther along, he said, "I'll save that room for last on this level. Over here," he continued, escorting her through double doors to the left, "is our drawing room. It extends the full length of the house on this side, except for a small chamber at the back where I'll keep my clutter out of view."

Standing in the center of the room on a lovely old Oriental carpet, Jonys looked at her with hopeful expectancy, black brows raised. Kept sat down beside him, leaning against his white stocking. Turning his shaggy-browed face up, he waited for her response like Jonys.

Meriel smiled at the two of them, chest filling with a sense of her good fortune that they had come into her life together. Turning slowly, she took in the blue-painted walls above white wainscotting, with a cloud-painted blue and white ceiling between the curves of molded plaster borders.

"How light and pleasant it is here. You'll never feel low in this room," she assured him. Her choice of pronoun surely showed him the house was his residence, not hers.

Gesturing upward, Jonys said, "I had it done especially for you, so you would always find a bright sky above you here."

"With that wish behind its plan, I could never be anything but content," she assured him, touched despite her misgivings. Even if she couldn't surrender all of herself to him, to withhold her approval of his efforts to please her would be cruel. "I couldn't have chosen any aspect of the dining or drawing room to please myself more."

Kept ambled to an upholstered elbow chair and leaped up to settle into the faint hollow of its seat. "What splendid old furniture, both here and in the dining room," she added. "It looks as if it's been loved for generations. I much prefer fine old things to modern pieces. So much more comfortable and home-like."

Relief flowed over his features. "I hoped you would prefer it to the current taste for furnishings with parts of beasts for supports. The house is filled with items I chose from Hadham House storage and its less-used rooms. It was a rush getting them to town, but I wanted this place to feel like a home to you from your first visit."

Shifting position as he looked away from her, he continued. "I didn't realize how much family things meant to me until I came into the title and became responsible for keeping them intact. It's important to pass this heritage along to my sons and their sons. This is a part of my place in Hadham history."

Looking at her with fervor, he said with obvious sincerity, "Besides, you should have fine furnishings around you, Meriel, pieces of real quality, with permanence and history to them. That's why I wanted to bring Hadham treasures here, to give you a suitable background where you could feel you belong. I want you here with me as much as you'll come."

His earnest invitation scalded her with regret that she couldn't give him everything he deserved for his efforts to please her. Including the sons to inherit the treasures he loved.

Crossing the rich, glowing colors of the carpet, Meriel linked hands with Jonys, looking up into his broad, eager face. "It feels home-like and even familiar to me already. The writing desk under the window, for instance, is one I recognize from visits with my mother to yours when I was a girl. It stood in a morning room where your grandmother retreated from the household's bustle."

Laughing, he looked down at her, pleased. "Fancy you remembering. I forget that you were often in my house while I was away at school." He glanced quickly about the room. "You may have noticed how few paintings and decorative bits and pieces are in place yet. I've brought things I like from the country, but I want you to decide if you care for them and to place them where you prefer. We'll spend a few afternoons and evenings getting everything just as we want it."

His eagerness to include her in decorating this place both warmed and warned her. Its seductive appeal was designed to entice her here.

Any changes she had suggested at Welwyn Hall had been forbidden by Osborne, if not by Welwyn.

295

As a result, the place had felt like a museum, never a home to her.

This house enfolded her with the same allure as Jonys's gaze. Here, her comfort was as important as his. At Hadham House, he would expect his countess to impress the family home with her personal touches. A shadow of envy for the lady he made his wife dimmed her pleasure in the present.

Now a wreath of fur on the chair's cushion, Kept raised his chin from his four paws. At a sound in the passage, he jumped down and scurried out to investigate.

Slipping an arm about her waist, Jonys guided her from the room after the terrier. "And now for the room set up especially for you."

"From what I've seen already, I can't imagine how you've planned a space to suit me any better," she murmured.

Ahead of them, Kept stood with Anson as he opened the door to the front room on the other side of the passage. The butler set a tray of decanters and flint crystal glasses just inside and stepped back for them to enter.

As Meriel passed through the door, Jonys murmured to Anson, "I'll ring if we need anything else. Don't wait up, and tell the others to retire at the usual time."

Bowing, the man turned to her. "If you'll forgive the familiarity, m'lady," he said quietly, "I wish to express my pleasure that you've taken the earl in hand. His father would have admired you sincerely for it."

"Thank you, Anson," Meriel said, amused and surprised. Lord Hadham had been kind enough to her in an offhanded way when she came to his notice as a girl. "It's more accurate to say we're taking each other in hand."

The butler bowed with a twitch to the corner of his prim lips and left them.

"Anson bestows no greater praise than my father's posthumous approval," Jonys explained, grinning. "You should be highly complimented to earn it."

"Indeed, I am," Meriel agreed. Curious, she looked about the room they had entered. Before the front window stood an ebony table with silver inlays, four carved feminine forms as its shapely legs. Kept stood sniffing the feet of one curvacious beauty.

Muffled footsteps crossed the carpet from the doorway and Jonys slipped his arms about her waist. "That table had to be here, as we've never managed to agree on which of us owns it now." His voice rumbled from his chest where she leaned against it, low and teasing.

Laughter welled from the growing happiness inside her and spilled out, making her feel as giddy as if she had drunk too much champagne.

"How appropriate!" she said, leaning back to look up at him, her head on his shoulder. "It couldn't have a more fitting home than this house, for more than one reason."

"I confess, I hoped it might inspire thoughts of passion in you when I placed it here." As he kissed her temple, she could hear his quiet chuckle and feel it transmitted from his body to hers. She felt more attuned to him every moment.

"I'm glad you approve," he continued. "This room is your personal retreat from the world, but I hope you'll allow me to sit here with you at times."

The chamber was furnished as a library or study, with bookshelves to the ceiling along two adjoining walls. One of the new lounging chairs with a steeply sloped back stood to one side of the fireplace, but most of the room's furnishings showed the grace and beauty of long and useful lives.

Snuffling at its edges, Kept walked around the big overstuffed lounging chair, surely selected by Jonys for his personal use. When he had made a circuit and returned to its front cushion, Kept leaped onto the seat. Turning twice, he settled into an oval shape, nose and paws tucked neatly within its confines, in the center of the cushion. Heaving a huge sigh, he closed his eyes.

"If you selected that chair for your comfort, you may have to get a second one," Meriel said, laughing.

"I plan to lounge elsewhere tonight," Jonys bantered, hugging her close before releasing her. "The chair Skype's claimed and a table are the only new pieces in the house." Moving with long-limbed grace, he crossed the room to a small rectangular table near the largest bookcase. "When I saw this, I had to get it for you. See, it moves on casters."

Pushing it against the bookcase, he folded the table's top over to the floor from one end. "See the steps mounted on the back? And more steps unfold from inside to lead up from them." He demonstrated, propping a folded ladder extension upon the table's frame in an A-line shape.

With as much pride as if he'd built it, Jonys said, "It's a metamorphic table, changing into library steps so you can reach the top shelves easily. Come try it."

Seeing his enthusiasm over the ingenious table,

she did as he asked. What an odd seduction he offered her. After years of inspiring gossip about his suave ways with women, Jonys didn't woo her with wine and passionate embraces. Instead, like a greater whitethroat, he displayed the nest he had fashioned for her before claiming her in a mating dance.

When she stood on the first step of the table-cum-library-ladder, he took her by the waist and turned her toward him. Rubbing her nose with his, he whispered, "Library steps could come in handy for other things you can't quite reach, too."

Sliding her arms across his shoulders, she leaned her body toward him, knowing he wouldn't let her overbalance. Tilting her face to one side, gaze still holding his, she urged him forward with her arms until their mouths met. Her eyes drifted shut as she kissed him lightly and then needed a closer touch between them.

As her lips clung and parted, his arms tightened about her. The precipice she stood on loomed far more perilous than one step up a ladder. She kissed him tenderly, deeply, sharing almost all of herself.

When she eased away, his languorous lids rose on the blue blaze of his beautiful eyes and for an instant his expression was somber. He sighed.

As he lifted her off the step to the floor, Jonys said with a note of regret, "That's been a fantasy of mine, to have you stand on that single step, eye-to-eye with me, and kiss me with your whole heart."

Meriel felt a pang of regret that her kiss hadn't wholly satisfied his fancy. Any shadow cast by their unmatched needs was hers. The realization was as unexpected as finding Jonys's seduction far more personal and tender than that of the Lothario he was reputed to be.

Oddly, she found it far more tender and endearing than passionate poetry and fevered embraces. She could never fear she was only another nameless "missy" to him when the way he demonstrated his desire would fit no other lady's style or tastes.

"I know you like to read," Jonys said, closing up the table again, "so I wanted you to have a room here to fill with books of your choosing. I'm not particularly bookish and read little beyond agricultural and sporting journals." He gestured to a large desk across a corner of the room, its side to a window to light its surface during the day. "I can work on accounts and estate plans as you read."

Hesitating, he gazed at her. "You'll want privacy, too, so when you need this room to yourself, just say so, and I'll stay out of your way."

"I don't know how much I'll be at this house, of course," she said gently, feeling she mustn't make promises she couldn't keep. But his obvious desire that she very nearly live here pleased her.

At the moment, she wanted to give him everything he desired in return for his generosity of spirit, but knew she could not. "We'll share this space when I can be here."

His awareness that she needed time to herself impressed Meriel. As much as he wanted company, she hadn't expected Jonys to notice her difference in this characteristic. No one had ever noticed her nature so minutely, particularly not the men in her life.

"I want this house to be your retreat from the world, your safe haven." Jonys cupped her cheek with his big hand. "When you come here, I want you to find contentment, pleasure, the best hours, and the best feelings."

Turning her face, Meriel placed a kiss in his palm. "Nothing," she murmured past the emotion catching in her throat, "and no one in my life has prepared me for the consideration you've shown me in creating this special place."

"It's all I can give you now," he said. "It's not all I want to give you over the years to come, but it's a start."

She almost said he mustn't promise her years, but she stopped. Why mar the mood with talk of future parting? Their hours in this house would be a time she gave to herself, with Jonys's help, special and apart from any time that had ever been or could ever be.

As he looked down at her, the entreaty in his expression melted the edges of her guard, flowing over her body and through her senses like a warm, scented bath. His gaze showed her a deep yearning that encompassed desire and flew beyond its boundaries. His longing touched a wick within her and lit her fervor to share it.

His brilliant blue eyes invited her to enter into his soul, to share not only this house but himself. Taking her into his arms like the most precious thing he could hold, he gave her a sense of being weak and strong at the same time. She held onto him to anchor herself somewhere between those extremes.

Rising onto the toes of her slippers, Meriel stretched upward to close the distance between their mouths again. Glad passion flared in his expression as he bent to her, and their lips met to give and take at the same time. Neither waited for the other to lead, but each searched out the joy of discovery and closeness. When she swayed with hunger for more of him, all of him, for the touch of his hands and his warm breath on her body, he clasped her more tightly but freed her lips.

"Your mouth makes my hands hungry to touch your skin, all of you," he murmured in a husky voice.

Her eyelids fluttered halfway open, enough to see his molten blue eyes in soft focus. His big, warm hands slid from her shoulders to her waist, turning her and tucking her close against his side. Holding her gaze with a mesmerizing stare, he walked her though the door and across the passage to the steps leading upward to the rest of the house.

Though she didn't know everything that awaited up those stairs, she felt no concern. Jonys had arranged each feature of this lower level to please her, to draw her here again and again, to prove that she was appreciated as a person as much as desired with passionate purpose. The next level would be as much a heaven and haven as this one.

As they stepped onto the first riser, she stopped him, smiling. "I'm going to kiss you on every step," she warned him. "And twice on the landing."

He collected on her promise at once, and lifted her onto the next riser. "Don't want you to get tired before we reach the top," he teased, kissing her again.

Chapter Sixteen

By the time they stood on the second floor of the Dean Street house, Meriel was dizzy with kissing Jonys, breathing as if she had run up the flight instead of being carried up, one step at a time. Four doors opened onto the passage before them, revealed in the soft glow of a night lantern.

"This one," he said, stepping to the right. Nodding over his shoulder, he explained, "When I'm alone, I'll sleep across there. But neither of us is alone tonight."

Pushing open the door, he waited, watching, as Meriel walked in past him. A bouquet of fragrance wreathed her in welcome as she entered the candlelit room they would share tonight, a bower blooming with flowers. Printed chintz draperies, paintings of flowers, and bowls filled with mixed blossoms turned the space into a private garden for the two of them to share.

A fire burned in the basket grate, and paper-white sheets had been turned down on a high, square-framed bed. The massive structure's stiff, flower-embroidered hangings had been softened with filmy draperies.

"Oh, Jonys!" she said, going to lay a hand on its carved natural-oak corner. "This looks as if it was stolen from a castle."

"Then it's suitable for a princess," he teased, removing first his coat and then his waistcoat. In the thin lawn dress shirt underneath, he came to pull her into his arms and back her against the corner support of the bed. "If larcenous thoughts will distract you from lustful ones, you can forget them. The bed's mine by title and inheritance, at least for my lifetime."

Incredulous, Meriel looked up at him and down the length of the sumptuous bed. "You brought the Hadham bed to London from the master's room at the estate!"

His dark head lifted and his square jaw firmed as an ancestor's might have at Agincourt. "Why not? I'm Hadham, and if I want my bed in town, I bring it." Then his hauteur faded into a twinkle. "Besides, nobody's getting any benefit from it at Hadham House in an unused room."

Leaning against her lightly, his muscular frame held back from pressing with his full weight, he traced the curve of her cheek and jaw with the backs of his fingers. When she turned up her face to be kissed, he spoke instead. "Don't you see, Meriel? I want to prove to you that this is different from anything I've ever shared with a woman. I'm different. Bringing the bed here is part of showing you how I've changed."

Kissing her eyelids and temples, he said, "You

were right about me when we met again in town. I was nothing but a womanizer who called every female 'missy' to avoid saying the wrong name. Then it became nothing more than a habit. Maybe you've noticed that I rarely slip and call you that now."

When she nodded slightly, he traced feathery kisses along her cheekbones. "I haven't slept in the Hadham earls' bed myself as yet; didn't feel I deserved to. Lately, I've begun to feel the time is right to claim it. You're a part of that feeling, and you deserve to share the bed with me."

Her chest swelling with affection and laughter, Meriel laid her hands on his shoulders and slid them down the mounded contours of his chest. "My dear, dear Jonys," she murmured, "so much effort to make a point you could simply have stated. You didn't have to go to all this trouble."

Moving against her hands in a way that showed he enjoyed her touch, he said, "I'd go to great deal more trouble for you; that's the point of action rather than words."

"For a man of action, you talk a great deal." Meriel smiled, looking into his eyes as she followed the long line of his body with her hands where it tapered from his broad shoulders to narrow hips. He felt even better than he looked, sleek and strong and pliant.

His laughter was low as he gathered her close, almost lifting her off her feet as he alternately kissed and nibbled lightly at the sensitive side of her throat and down onto her bare shoulder. "Maybe another subject would suit you more. Perhaps moonlight. Your skin looks gilded with moonlight, where I can see it, and I can't see nearly enough of it."

As he spoke, he unhooked her gown, keeping her within the circle of his arms as he did so. Reaching into the back of her loosened dress, he found the ties to her skirts and petticoats with tell-tale ease and undid them. That was an advantage of lovers beyond first youth: Experience avoided small awkwardnesses while they learned each other's particular desires.

"I want to savor every step of undressing you," he murmured. Hands loosely set on either side of her waist, he pushed the garments slowly down her body with his forearms, while he cupped her hips, thighs, knees, calves with his big hands.

When he knelt on the floor before her with folds of fabric billowing around her feet, he looked up the length of her body, eyes glowing darkly in the low light. "Step out." His voice sounded deeper and husky.

Steadying herself with her hands on his shoulders, Meriel complied, raising one slippered foot and then the other as he filched the garments from under her feet without removing his gaze from hers. Rocking back on his heels, he swept her length with his stare, head back to gaze at her openly.

Feeling only a little shy under the blatant pleasure of his appreciation, Meriel warmed at the upward curve of his lips and the downward sweep of his lids. Her body shaped into a sensual, curving stance, one hip forward, in an instinctive feminine invitation to him.

Coming easily to his feet, he crooked a finger into the top of her stays, between the up-thrust mounds of her breasts, and tugged her toward him.

Willingly, she went. Arms about her, he unhooked the lightly boned garment from the bottom up, pressing against her to keep it against her body until he finished.

When he had freed her from the constriction, he slid his hands between them to cup her breasts and allowed the undergarment to fall where it might. Holding her gaze with the wicked glint of his blue stare, he stroked the tips of her breasts with his big thumbs, the fine lawn of her chemise adding an extra edge of delight to the friction.

Arching her back to meet the mounting need his big hands aroused, Meriel held onto his shoulders. The magic of his touch spiraled downward to pulse between her thighs.

Sliding her hands against the fine fabric of his shirt front, she absorbed his heat and the strong pulsing of his heart, not just with her fingertips, but with her palms and a growing inner awareness. Feeling his pulse quicken to her touch and seeing the pupils of his eyes enlarge gave her a deep sense of connection with Jonys.

As he caught his breath at her hands' movements over his chest, she eased her fingers into the intricate folds of his cravat, searching for the secret to unwinding it. Catching her hands, he stopped them.

"So impatient," he said with affection. "But not nearly as impatient as you'll be soon." While he spoke, he removed the cravat deftly. As he pitched it aside without looking, Meriel reached for the buttons at his shirt placket.

Again, he stopped her. "Not tonight," he told her, kissing her hands and fingertips. "Tonight is for you. Another time, you may make love to me as well, but tonight, I'm going to adore you as you've never been adored, and you'll need your whole attention to accept it."

"But I understood that making love requires two participants," she objected, tracing his lips with a finger.

His lips closed around her forefinger, bringing it into his hot mouth to ravish it with his tongue and teeth. Raising his head at her intake of breath from the unexpected sensations, he smiled mysteriously. His eyes gleamed in the dancing flicker of candlelight, as they had in the carriage by a torch's flare when he had reminded her of a devil.

"The way I want to make love to you first requires your full participation," he said, unbuttoning his shirt. "Unless you tell me everything that pleasures you, I won't know what to repeat."

Rising on her toes, Meriel nuzzled the hollow of his throat, laid bare through the placket's opening. Kissing the pulse she found there, she touched his skin with her tongue experimentally, and when his arms closed more tightly about her, she tasted him with greedy tickles along his collarbone. "I want to pleasure you, too."

"Little innocent," he groaned. "If you pleasure me too much this first time, you'll find yourself with a spent old man and nothing else. Your turn will come later tonight. But first, I mean to adore you."

Whatever he meant by adoring her, Meriel didn't argue, just clung to his wide shoulders while he unbuttoned the side flaps to his formal knee breeches and slipped them down. She wasn't accustomed to adoration in relations between husband and wife, just duty that could be pleasant on occasion. Perhaps lovers did things differently.

As he stepped out of his breeches, his muscular

thighs and flanks flexed under the silk knit small-clothes covering him from waist to knees. Stepping close to slip her hands down his hips, she found the curves denting each side of his shapely rear. It felt as good as it looked in fitted pantaloons. The movement of hard muscle under soft silk as he planted his feet wide made her gasp with a surge of desire too strong to identify as anything else.

Hands cupping her bottom, Jonys pulled her against the hard proof of his arousal, a half smile curving his lips. "It's been a long time. I won't be able to endure much of your welcome torture tonight," he said. "Another time, you can tease me until I give in."

"Take them off," she said, surprised at herself. Having had a family of two boys and a husband, she hadn't thought males had much to look at under their breeks, but Jonys inspired a new appreciation.

Jonys unlaced his silk drawers, neither hurrying nor dawdling about the business. His eyes glowing with humor and restrained passion, he slid his drawers down his long, well-formed legs. When they touched his feet, he stepped out of them and away, straightening to his full height in the yellow glow of fire-and candlelight.

Mouth dry, Meriel indulged her curiosity. Contrary to what her mother had told her, all men weren't just alike in certain particulars. Private parts were as distinctive as hands or feet and as recognizable.

"Satisfied?" he asked, sounding a bit strangled. "Though I hope you aren't, in every sense of the word."

Smiling at him briefly, Meriel shook her head

and circled behind him. "Oh, yes," she murmured. "This side is even more beautiful."

"Only women are beautiful," he insisted over one shoulder. "What are you doing back there?"

"Appreciating fine art," she said, grinning. Firelight glanced off the planes and hollows of his body, as angular and sculptured as any of the Elgin marbles. Whatever he said, she would have her hands all over him before the night was far gone.

Jonys half turned, reaching for her. "It doesn't seem right for me to stand here in the altogether while you're still wearing a chemise and stockings." Two strides brought him to her.

Untying her chemise, he eased it down her arms and over her hips. Wiggling to help it off, she laughed, a bit nervous standing there in pink stockings tied at the knees and nothing more. Jonys caught her up in his arms, cradling her easily against his chest while she slipped her arms about the thick column of his throat.

"You'd best not be laughing at me, my girl," he said, striding toward the massive Hadham bed with her in his arms, as if she weighed little more than Kept.

"I'm not." Laying her head on his shoulder, she traced the bow of his collarbone with one finger. "I'm just so very happy, Jonys. So very contented and pleased with you and me and this house."

Standing by the bed, he said, "Before much longer, I want you more than pleased with you and me."

Pointing a pink-silk-clad foot, she laughed. "You've forgotten something; I'm still wearing my stockings."

"So you are," he agreed. "Don't they make you feel like an abandoned woman?"

"Only in one sense of the word." She rubbed her calf against his arm, feeling his muscle flex through the tissue-thin silk of the stocking.

Tenderly, he smiled and kissed her lips once before lowering her onto the vast Hadham bed. "I don't ever want you to feel abandoned in any other way," he said as if taking a vow.

Lying down beside her, he eased one leg between hers and propped his fist on the other side of her waist. He lay against her side, close in a sense she hadn't experienced before.

"You're perfect," he said, leaning over to kiss her in a number of places she hadn't been touched by a man's lips before. "You're beautiful and you say all the right words to make a man feel like the best thing that ever happened to a woman."

Reaching up a finger, she traced the heavy, straight line of one dark eyebrow. "That isn't difficult," she said, "for you are. The best thing that ever happened to this woman, I mean."

Covering her mouth with his, Jonys groaned deep in his throat as he kissed her until she lay giddy and breathless, wondering if the room were spinning, or if they were. "My little love," he said, "I haven't even begun to be good to you yet."

Giving herself up to the dual exploration of his mouth and hands along her body, Meriel pressed kisses against his smooth chest. Touching every inch of him she could reach only added to the pleasure his touch brought her.

And then rational thought merged into sensations beyond definition as Jonys pleasured her breasts with his lips and teeth and tongue until she moaned and pressed herself to him, tumultuous pleasure rising to a level past bearing. Shamelessly, she begged, "Make love with me, Jonys. Please, please come inside."

"Not yet," he crooned as she clamped her knees onto his strong thigh. His fingers played over the sides of her stomach and thighs, making her catch her breath, before he searched for the center of her rising need with his hand.

Slowly, languidly he stroked her moist depths until she flowed with the desire to rise with his rhythm and increase its pace. Then his hand and fingers became increasingly insistent, demanding, and she couldn't endure the sweet agony longer. "I can't bear it!" she complained and begged.

"You can," he whispered when she tried to move away, and she held fast to his shoulders, teeth shut tight against the urgency he built within her and then forced past a pinnacle she hadn't known existed. Crying out, she clung to him, quivering and spent.

As she sighed with the relief of release, he kissed her and murmured, "I adore you."

Once again his fingers began their slow wooing, and his mouth sought her swollen nipple. She whispered in panic, "I can't!" while her traitorous body decided she might.

Almost at once, the combined attentions of his knowing hands and loving lips pushed her toward a new urgency for release, and from a long, hazy distance, she heard her thickened voice chanting, "Please, please, please," as she fell off the edge of the world, still within his arms.

Laughing, Jonys took her mouth with his, his tongue teasing and dancing with hers. For a time the touch of his hands and mouth made her long for the night to last forever as she rose toward the pinnacle of impossible need again. Pushing his hand aside, she reached for his hips, determined and panting. "Come with me, please!"

Then he was above her, his dear face framed by crisp curls dark against the shadowed colors of the bed's canopy, while he nudged, hot and insistent, for entrance where she most wanted him. Pushing against the sheets with her feet, she raised her hips to welcome all of him, and at long last he joined with her, filling her with a deep thrust that left her eager for the next. And the next.

Desire was a rising torrent of rushing need, frightening in its intensity, except that she wasn't alone. Passion drove her into a matched pace with him, feeling his demand and pleasure build, willing to follow wherever he led.

Holding Jonys with her arms, her legs, with inner places she hadn't known to use before, Meriel reached for the summit he drove her toward, heights beyond earlier attainment. She chose to go there with Jonys, for together they could do anything.

Shuddering into pure sensation, she followed Jonys out of herself and back again, feeling for an instant that no boundary existed between them, that they had joined on a level of blinding white light beyond that of their bodies.

Treasuring that sensation of togetherness, missing it when it faded back into their separate selves, Meriel held onto Jonys when he made a movement away from her. "Please,". she murmured. "Stay there a little while."

"But I'm too heavy," he protested, still holding himself above her on his elbows.

"I want to feel your weight," she begged, tugging

him down by the shoulders and holding onto his calves with hers.

Gently, he let himself down, relaxing only when she smiled and nuzzled against his damp neck and chest.

Welcoming the solid feel of him, the man's scent of him, Meriel slipped her hands along his back and waist to stroke lightly over the firm contours of his shapely rear.

"Ha!" he said drowsily, rubbing his head against hers. "I should have known you wouldn't rest until you got your hands on my beautiful side."

Only one dissatisfaction marred her joy in the night.

Jonys roused her by kissing her nape, and Meriel snuggled into the curve of his body. Awakening more fully as she realized this was the real man, not another of her lonely dreams, she turned over on the big bed and opened her arms to him.

Kissing her nose, he laughed quietly in the darkness. "Too late," he said. "You shouldn't have gone to sleep if you wanted more than seconds. I want you home before dawn to lessen the risk you might be seen leaving here."

Groaning, she tried to burrow under his shoulder, but he rolled away, urging her to get up and let him help her to dress.

Slipping into her quiet Portman Square town house from the stables a short time later as arranged, she set a sleepy Kept on the tiles beyond the door to the main part of the house. How lovely it would be if she could lie in Jonys's arms all night and awaken with the morning light touching his face beside her.

Sighing, she took to the stairs alone, except for

Kept's scrabbling claws as he followed her to a cold bed.

No matter what choice she made, she couldn't have it all. To gain the right to be with Jonys every day and night, she would have to be his wife. But she could never risk losing herself and future children in marriage again.

Chapter Seventeen

Staring at the books without taking in their titles, Meriel relived the previous night. And the night before. For the past week, thinking about anything but Jonys and the little house in Dean Street had taken extreme concentration.

Bowing to a lady across Hatchard's who waved, Meriel picked up a book from a table display and pretended to consider it. Reading wasn't what interested her most at present, when living offered her more than enough lively action and compelling drama.

Outside, rain spattered the streets and washed soot from the air, while people scurried about their business instead of clustering to exchange news. They crowded into places of business like this, bringing the faint fatty odor of wet wool indoors. Meriel wrinkled her nose, wishing that an unaccustomed restlessness hadn't brought her out shopping. Though if she had remained at home, she would doubtless wish to be out.

Though it was nearly noon, Jonys might be at home instead of visiting one of his clubs or making the rounds of other gentlemanly haunts. If he was sparring with Jackson, he normally took that exercise earlier in the day. Though he surely had had enough exercise lately without resorting to the science of boxing. Raising the book, she hid the grin tugging at her lips.

This frivolous, flighty mood was totally unlike her—until the last week, at least. Now she hardly knew what to expect from herself next, in emotions or behavior.

Replacing the book she held, Meriel decided to purchase only the slim volume tucked under her elbow. If everyone she met asked her opinion of *Childe Harold*, she probably should read it. Admitting she hadn't read the most touted work of the moment left her listening to hyperbole without any personal opinion on it, which grew tiresome. It wasn't fair to judge Lord Byron's work on the basis of her view of him as a moody boy with a great deal of growing up still to do.

Reading was an excellent way to use a rainy day, if she wanted to return home. Not that she had to read at Portman Square. Even if Jonys wasn't at the house on Dean Street, he had begged her to treat it as her own, which it was in a financial sense and was becoming in an emotional one.

As yet, Meriel hadn't appeared at the house where Jonys lived without warning or in the middle of the day. After all, other friends might have called upon him already, and daylight left her more exposed to the chance that someone might see her come or go.

Joining the shoppers and the subscribers to the lending section around Hatchard's central counter, Meriel made up her mind. When Byron's slim volume of verse was wrapped and tied, she would direct her coachman to Dean Street.

Kept and she could curl up in the library, even if Jonys should be away from home. At least she would be closer to the origin of her thoughts, and she would be there to welcome him when he came in.

Leaning back in the chair at the desk, Jonys moved papers about without noticing what they were. He needed to draw up a plan for which fields to plant and which to leave fallow over the next five years, and make a decision about converting a cow pasture to grazing for sheep.

Going out to his club or a few coffeehouses might turn up talk of the mad vicar that would suggest a course for helping Meriel, as well. He didn't lack for plenty of tasks, and he didn't mind the rain tapping the window behind him, either. This tendency to sit and stare, lost in thought and inaction for several minutes together, was quite unlike his usual self.

Rubbing his jaw, Jonys glanced out the window as the sound of wheels and harness penetrated his unusual preoccupation. Not much traffic used this crooked little street, one reason he had selected Number Seven.

His glance turned into a closer look as the equipage slowed. Though the coachman's hat was pulled low against the rain, those prads were as familiar as his own blacks by now.

Exasperation with Meriel for taking the risk of coming here past the houses from the South Audley Street mixed with exhilaration at seeing her unexpectedly. Pushing away from the desk, he headed for the back of the house.

Out in the stable yard, he had the step down almost before the carriage had stopped. Opening the door, he grinned, unable to look severe when his heart soared at the sight of her beautiful face lighting up for him.

At the vehicle's threshold, Skype crouched, alternately panting a greeting to him, looking far down to the cobbled stable yard where he wanted to be, and pawing impatiently to be set down.

"Hello, love," Jonys said to Meriel as he swung the terrier out of the carriage just before he leaped.

Setting the squirming dog down on the stones, he turned back as Meriel appeared at the door, her color high and eyes gleaming golden warmth at him. "I'm not being rude," he explained, "just prudent, helping this little gentleman out before you."

As she laughed in her musical way, he lifted her out from the carriage, not waiting for her to descend to the step. Holding her against his chest, he let her slide down his body until her jean half-boots touched ground.

"Ah, Meriel," he said, despite grooms or footmen, "I'm glad you're here, and I meant to scold you instead of hug you." He kissed her briefly and turned her toward the back entrance.

"I know you said not to enter Dean Street from South Audley, but I was shopping on Piccadilly, and that approach was easier. Don't fuss. You've urged me countless times to come here, and I have." Warmth twinkled from her eyes, even as she twitched her lips into a prim line.

"I can't deny I'm glad to see you." He couldn't

be severe with Meriel when she looked this happy.

"And it pleases me very much to be here with you on a wet day when we can sit about the library like a pair of old dears, nodding over our papers and books, drinking tea and talking or not as our fancy takes us," Meriel declared.

Jonys smiled. "I can't think of anything I'd rather do, or anyone I'd rather do nothing with." Surely she was coming to care for him, if she was satisfied to spend an afternoon, perhaps an evening as well, with him and Skype in an aimless idyll.

He took the wrapped package she held, a book from the feel of it. "Come inside before you're so damp I have to undress you."

Her head leaned against his shoulder as he walked her into the house with his arm about her, Meriel twinkled with vibrant new life. "You'll have to come up with more of a threat, instead of a treat, to bring me to heel," she said.

"Bringing you to heel doesn't hold any appeal for me," he replied with as much truth as humor. "I'd far rather bring you to heart."

Hearing the entrance door open and close below stairs, Meriel collected her bonnet and gloves, spirits singing at the prospect of roaming Richmond Hill for the entire day with Jonys and Kept, Hester and Lord Burchett. Leaving her room, she hurried across the passage to tap on Hester's door.

Ears forward, Kept stood at the top of the steps, listening intently. Looking back at her once, he set off down the steps as fast as his short legs allowed the descent. With his more sensitive hearing, Kept must have heard Jonys's voice and headed for the ground floor to greet him.

Tapping for her cousin again, Meriel looked inside when she still had no reply. A quick glance showed her the room stood empty. Hester must have finished dressing early and gone on down once she was ready, equally eager to begin the day with Burchett.

Meriel took the stairs with a light step and heart. How fortunate she was to have Jonys as her special friend. If she had ever looked forward to each day with this much anticipation, it must have been when she was a child. Humming, she stepped onto the tiled floor of the entrance hall and turned toward the library.

A series of sharp barks sounded from the front drawing room on the second floor. Wheeling about, Meriel ran back up the stairs. Kept didn't sound like that when he and Jonys played rough games. He didn't bark in that shrill, frantic way except at creatures he considered a threat, including a very few people.

Unwilling to think beyond that, Meriel reached the second floor breathing hard, and dashed to the smaller public room at the front of the house. Wrenching open the door, she burst in.

Hester stood with her back to Meriel, shoulders hunched as if she were cold. Kept danced before her, barking furiously.

"Shut that hellhound up before I silence him for good." The snarling voice matched the face as Osborne wheeled around.

Meriel clung to the door, weak and dizzy. Having her brother-in-law appear so unexpectedly would unnerve her in itself. But Osborne's eyes held the look she had learned to dread most: a blank stare, almost unblinking.

When he looked at her in this state, she wasn't

321

sure if he saw her or some twisted vision of his mind's invention. His eyes were empty, like the shuttered windows of a closed house, deserted and decaying.

The worst reaction possible was to show her fear and disgust at the warped creature he became in this transmutation. Any show of weakness made him worse, while a show of control and co-operation at least kept his aberration near the same level.

Laying her bonnet and gloves on a table by the door, she crossed the room to the fireplace, tugging the ornate iron bellpull. "How are you, Osborne," she said quietly. "Won't you take a seat? Would you prefer tea or wine?"

With a significant look at Hester, Meriel picked up Kept and set him outside the door. Maybe if Jonys came while Osborne was still here, he would see Kept in the passage and realize that circumstances weren't as usual. Dreading the volatile situation if the two men met while Osborne wasn't himself, she hoped the vicar would leave quickly.

Osborne ignored her, prowling about the room while she and Hester took seats near the fireplace. He liked an audience for his performances, even the wordless displays where he intimidated with glaring silences.

"I hope the boys are well," she said neutrally. "The task of tutoring them daily must require a great deal of your time and energies."

He crossed the room to stare at her with those empty eyes, a faint sneer curling his upper lip. "Don't sully Welwyn's sons by speaking of them. You've gone too far at last and I must punish you for it."

322

From the door, scrabbling claws and whines showed that Kept hadn't gone away. Meriel hoped Osborne wouldn't notice and try to hurt him. She couldn't permit that.

"I don't understand what you mean," she said to the vicar in a flat, impersonal voice. He seemed to feed on the emotion he wrung from others, and she didn't want to fuel his frenzy. In contrast, her heart was a frantic fist in her chest, pounding her ribs with the need to escape this threat.

"Once I thought you were only a silly female," Osborne said in his pulpit voice, "wrapping Welwyn about your thumb with your wiles, longing for the useless life of London society." Pointing into her face, he thundered, "Now I learn you're consorting criminally with a man known to crawl between the legs of any slut who will raise her skirts!"

Shocked at his crude language and the speed of his spy system, Meriel kept her tone conversational. "Who in heaven's name said such a thing to you?"

"Never you mind about the source of my information." Striding away, he gestured widely with his arms. "God knows all. Man looketh on the outward appearances, but God looketh on the heart."

Turning back, he said as if imparting a secret, "A man saw your outward appearance of evil, and spoke to his sister. That pious soul reported the evil in your heart. Just as I always told Welwyn, you're neither a fit wife nor mother. He didn't like to think ill of you, but I knew you for what you were then, and now the sordid evidence has come out."

Thundering out the words, he continued. "And

it's up to me to exact penance for your sins and save your soul!"

Jumping at his loud voice, Hester had edged away from Meriel on the sofa. While Osborne's back was turned, Hester reached for the heavy poker at the fireplace, hiding it hastily under the skirts of her carriage dress as he turned.

Meriel's heart thumped harder. Keeping her cousin out of Newgate after a murder wasn't her idea of the best solution to this fraught situation. Now she had two unpredictable forces to watch.

At the window, Osborne faced them, light streaming around his figure and casting his features in shadows. "At least you don't deny your wrongdoing; perhaps I can save you yet, if you do precisely as I say."

Speaking reasonably despite the constriction in her chest and throat that left her breathless, Meriel replied, "I didn't realize you were ready for an answer. I can and do deny wrongdoing. Further, whatever my errors may be, now or in future, they're between God and myself. You aren't my father, guardian, or even my clergyman, Osborne. You must realize that I'm a mature woman, no longer married, and therefore responsible for myself."

She had gone too far. Osborne's face seemed to swell and his shoulders to hulk. One of his eyes drifted slightly off course as he stared, a sign of great agitation with him.

"Shameless. Defiant. Unrepentant." The charges boomed into the room like cannon fire. Legs spread, he lifted his hands toward heaven. "You have been judged, and you are guilty." Arms dropping, he stalked toward Meriel. "However, God is

324

a merciful God, and you may be allowed to redeem your sins."

Meriel nearly spoke, but thought better of it.
Perhaps silence was best. He would rant and
leave, and in a few days the horror of contact with
his madness would recede.

"First, you will end your fornication with the
man, whom I will deal with finally and separately.
You needn't think you'll hide your sin in marriage
with him now."

Hands gripped together in an agony of fear, she
said, "If that's a threat against someone's life, you
had best reconsider. Committing the greater sin
of murder would take James and Steven away
from you, even if you didn't hang."

The grimace that spread over Osborne's face
was terrifying. "The evil can be ended without taking life. Instead, I must take control of certain
lives, including yours, to kill the evil you've loosened on the world."

Crossing the room to stand behind the sofa, he
bent above Meriel. His voice dropped to a tone of
reason. "Which brings me to point two. You will
put all your financial holdings into a trust for Welwyn's sons, for a woman should never be permitted to inherit money in the first place. You're proof
of the folly of it, using your fortune to bind yet
another weak man to you."

Feeling sickened by the greed underlying his
madness, Meriel rose and walked to the front window looking down into the square. She wanted to
be rid of Osborne before Jonys came, for impetuous as he was, she dreaded what he might do.
Not because she cared what happened to her
crazed brother-in-law, but because she didn't

want Jonys hurt or besmirched by this lunacy she couldn't appear to escape.

"You want me to have my man of business draw up papers giving my fortune to my boys through a trust," she repeated. "I assume you mean me to name you to administer that trust."

"Yes, of course," he said as if no other possibility existed.

"My will leaves my sons what I own at present, but Hester is the trustee. I see little advantage to myself in changing those documents as you suggest."

Osborne was behind her again; she could sense him as strongly as a threatening rush of footsteps on a dark street, and the flesh of her shoulders and back cringed with the same sense of personal danger.

"The advantage to you, besides saving your immortal soul . . ." He sounded as if he were musing over a conundrum. "The main advantage as you would probably perceive it is this: If you do as I direct, you'll learn where Welwyn's sons are."

Doused with icy fear beyond that for herself, she flung around to face him. "My sons! What have you done with my boys?"

He chuckled like the fond uncle he probably supposed himself to be. "I'm not the one who's likely to harm them. Welwyn's sons are well protected in my care, which is why he left them to me to look after. My brother knew I loved them as much as I loved him. But I discovered how you and your evil consort hoodwinked the headmaster to get at them, and I've taken the boys away from Eton."

"Are they back at the estate?" she asked with hope, knowing they would have the security of familiar places and faces at their home.

"Hardly." His face was an expressionless mask again. "You had your supporters there, and I won't risk you gaining assistance again. No, my dear, you're about to become a reformed woman. You'll put yourself and your funds in my control, as it should have been all along."

Begging or reasoning was useless in dealing with a man of unbalanced mind. Meriel didn't waste time on either effort. "You realize that I can't do as you direct in an hour or a day," she said with hardly a quaver to her voice. "I'll need a week at least just to determine what can be done to set up the trust you require."

His laughter was a sour sound that curdled hope at once. "Even if I had the patience to give you that kind of time to search for James and Steven, it would do you no good. You'll never find them." He shook his head again and again. "Never. No, your only choice is to follow my instructions. I'll return here tomorrow afternoon at four to meet you and your stick of a solicitor Trent. Have the documents ready for our signatures, my dear. And then I'll tell you where Welwyn's boys are hidden. If you continue to do just as I say, I might even let you see them from time to time. From a distance."

Laughing to himself and shaking his head, Osborne walked toward the door. As he opened it, a tornado tore through, nearly tripping him up. Skidding to a halt, Kept turned on the vicar, making darts at his ankles and barking like an entire pack of dogs at once.

Kicking at him, Osborne shouted, "Call off your vicious dog! And get rid of him before I come here again. He's a menace to life and limb, and I'll not have him walking this earth." Snatching up a spindle-legged chair, Osborne fended off the enraged terrier as he backed out the door and down the passage.

Had Meriel known where to find her boys, she would have let Kept have Osborne to chew on. Needing him in one piece, she caught up a struggling Kept and closed the door, waiting to hear the outer door slam after her brother-in-law.

As she set Kept down, Hester met her, white-faced and shaken, still gripping the poker. The moment Kept was free, he ran for the door, snuffling and barking at this side now, as he had at the other, to get at his prey.

"What will we do?" her cousin asked. "Osborne's all about in the head, the worst he's ever been. Do you know any place he might hide the boys? With friends?"

Meriel shook her head. "If he ever had any friends, I don't know of them. And his few acquaintances were the kind who used him for favors; they didn't return them."

Her mind had raced among possible places Osborne might send the boys since the moment he had revealed they were no longer at Eton. She must try not to think of their confusion and fear, being caught up and hustled off again to yet another strange situation. If she allowed herself to consider all the possible horrors, she couldn't think clearly.

Below stairs, the entrance door burst open. Booted footfalls rang across tile and clattered their way up the stairs. Kept began barking again, this time eagerly, tossing his head back from the door in a pulling motion.

Going to open it, Meriel hadn't quite reached it

when the door banged open and Jonys stood on the threshold. As Kept threw himself at Jonys, he spoke to Meriel. "Thank God! He hasn't harmed you."

Striding to Meriel, he grasped her shoulders, gazing into her face with searching concern. "You're pale as ashes. Have you had a letter from the vicar, too?"

"No, worse. A visit." Meriel leaned against him, taking the solace provided by his broad chest and encircling arms. "He's hidden the boys and I can't guess where to find them. They'll be terrified; I have to find them quickly."

"The bloody bastard! I'd have killed him already except for that." The violence of Jonys's emotional outburst eased Meriel's tension a bit, as if she had expressed the same outrage. "What has he threatened you with?"

"Nothing important. He just demands control of my money by four tomorrow afternoon." She felt weary and unable to focus, heavy with concern for James and Steven.

"Control of you as well, for I know that your funds represent your independence, even your identity, to you." Along with the anger in his voice and features, his concern for her was clear as he bent to study her face.

"Yes, but what's independence without my boys?" Meriel was too tired to think, but that much was clear.

"Did you say something about a letter?" Hester put the question to Jonys.

"It came while I waited for Burchett to come by for me," he explained, rubbing Meriel's back as he held her closer.

Closing her eyes, Meriel listened to the echo of

his voice though his chest wall, as well as through the air. Part of her had retreated to regroup, to focus on something besides the madness pitchforking her life into turmoil once more.

This part of her stood apart and dwelt upon minor details, rather than looking directly upon the horror Osborne had created in her life again. She would have to cope in a little while, but Jonys was here, and she wouldn't have to deal with this horror alone.

Meanwhile, Jonys explained the letter he had received from Osborne to Hester. "He went on with a great load of rubbish about sin and retribution and penance. I was about to throw the thing on the fire when I saw Meriel's name. He used some terms about her that I won't forget when I find him, and he said I wasn't to see her again, could forget marriage to her."

Laughing harshly, Jonys added, "Though he advised me to marry at once, just someone else he named. Quoted something about it being better to marry than to burn."

"Paul in Corinthians," Meriel murmured into his waistcoat.

"What, love?" Jonys ducked his head, trying to see her face.

"Nothing important." She straightened and stood away from his support reluctantly. "Osborne quotes scripture when it suits his purpose, just as the devil is said to do."

Hester frowned, looking at Jonys. "But I don't understand what hold Osborne has over you." She spread her hands. "You asked what he threatened Meriel with, which must mean that your letter contained a threat. You've never met the vicar, so what can he threaten you with?"

Jonys laid an arm about Meriel's shoulders. "He flung the same threat at me he used on her: harm to someone I love. He said if I continued to consort with Meriel, she'll never know where James and Steven are again."

At some level, Meriel took in his statement that he loved her. She didn't know if she was happy or sad that he did, and she didn't have the capacity at the moment to consider that as well as her boys' disappearance.

Jonys was beside her, giving her his strength and support, and she hadn't doubted for a moment that he would be. She slipped her arms about him. They could deal with matters between them later, when they had the leisure to do so.

Hester stood shaking her head and looking between them. "I just don't see how the vicar knew so much about your doings," she said. "You were careful and discreet. I promise you that I didn't say a word to anyone, and I told Burchett that if he so much as hinted that you were more than the merest acquaintances, I wouldn't marry him."

Meriel smiled at her briefly. "Has he finally discovered that he wants a wife?"

"Yes," Hester said with pride. "But I'm not promising him anything yet."

"Of course you'll marry him," Meriel said. Hester wouldn't commit herself while she believed her cousin needed her. That was another subject to shelve until she had the luxury of time and emotion to cope with it.

Jonys caught Meriel's hands and said, "You look like you're about to fall down, and your hands are cold as ice. Come sit down and let me warm you."

Leading her over to the sofa, he sat down and gathered her against him, her head on his chest and both her hands tucked under his big one. Kept followed, and he leaped up beside her, nestling close, his head over her thigh.

Hester said uncertainly, "Maybe I should go watch for Burchett."

"Come sit down with us," Meriel invited, making the most of these moments of respite in Jonys's embrace. "Someone will send Burchett up when he comes. I must decide how to go about finding my sons, and the more heads considering the matter, the better."

"I'd like to push Osborne headfirst into the teeth of a mantrap," Hester said with vicious relish, dropping onto a nearby elbow chair.

"A trap." Jonys said the words slowly, as if an idea were unfurling in his mind. "That's exactly what we need to stop this man before he does further damage to innocent lives. I wonder if I can bait it properly by tomorrow afternoon."

"It's about time someone took me seriously when it comes to Osborne." Hester looked at him with satisfaction and approval. "May I help you spring it?"

"With so little time, we'll all need to pitch in," said Jonys. "Will Burchett object if you charm another man?"

Hester grinned. "If he's over ten and under ninety, I daresay I could accomplish what's needed. Just don't tell Burchett if it involves being naughty."

"No, I just need you to wheedle one a bit. In fact, you can take Burchett with you; he's the very picture of respectability." Jonys raised a brow at her. "I'll have to work fast, for we'll only have tonight and tomorrow morning to gather the pieces to set our snare."

Hester laughed. "Just give me the opportunity; I have a few scores to settle with the vicar."

Staring into the cold grate, Jonys said, "I'll need a number of men to approach a number of schools. A few of the fellows at my club could use the exercise." Looking at Hester again, he continued. "When I know where the boys are, you and Burchett can go fetch them."

Struggling up from his arms, Meriel said, "No, I want to go for them myself."

"Of course you do," he said, taking her shoulders in his hands. "But you have to do the hardest part of all. You must wait here."

"No, I can't do that. I can ask around for my boys at schools in London, at least." Surely Jonys of all people must understand the impossibility of doing nothing.

"Listen, love." His voice, pitched low, soothed and reasoned with her. "Osborne could return here at any time. He's hardly predictable. He could be watching this house to see if you comply with his instructions."

Collapsing within herself to find strength, Meriel nodded. What he said made sense, much as she hated it.

"Besides, it's possible we might not locate the boys by four tomorrow." He spoke faster when she cried out. "You know I'll do everything possible to locate them at once. I know you can't rest until you know they're safe. But Osborne hasn't allowed us much time. He may be mad, but he isn't stupid. He has to believe we wouldn't locate them within the time he's set. So you have to be prepared to meet his demands, and only you can deal with Trent."

Meriel straightened and shoved at her hair. Her

solicitor would fight her about preparing a trust document naming Osborne. Jonys was quite right; she would have her work cut out for her, dealing with his objections.

Kissing the top of her head, Jonys said gently to her, "Are you up to handling Trent, love?"

"Naturally," she said. "I was only regrouping, not giving in to despair. Do you want me to have the papers drawn up as Osborne directed?"

"More or less," he said. "The mad vicar seems well past knowing right from wrong any more. It seems safest to have Trent prepared to give him what he expects if all else fails. We'll have the papers set aside as signed under duress at a later date, if we can."

Ready as she was to sacrifice everything she had for her sons' safety, Meriel was wracked by the outcome of doing so. Not just because she would be left without independence, but because of the difference it would make to Jonys as well.

"If I have to sign over all my assets to Osborne tomorrow afternoon, I won't be able to help you more," she reminded Jonys. "Not with making your estate productive again or providing for your tenants and family. Not with Claire's further treatment."

"Your boys have to come first." Jonys kissed her hands. "The estate will struggle back more slowly without your help, but what you've done already may have turned the tide. And I have another idea about how to get funds."

Feeling deflated by the prospect that he would no longer need her, Meriel asked, "But how? I thought you had exhausted all possible sources of financing."

"At the time, I had." He traced the outer edges

of her fingers as he talked, rather than looking at her. "But I've been thinking about our future, yours and mine. You prefer not to marry anyway, and I won't wed any other lady. So it appears the only legitimate heir I'm to have is my present one—a distant connection in America with a tobacco plantation and a couple of cane plantations in Guyana."

Raising her hands, Jonys kissed her fingers. "If my colonial heir wants his son to inherit more than a ruin, he can help me take care of the old pile now, in exchange for my promise not to wed and get an heir of my body."

Dismay choked Meriel. Jonys was proud of being the Earl of Hadham, the more so because he'd had to grow into the title, rather than being groomed for it as most men were. He loved the land, the house, its furnishings, not just for their value and beauty, but for their place in the ongoing history of the Hadhams.

For her and her boys, he would trade his need and duty to have legitimate issue of his own. To bring her everything she desired, Jonys was willing to give up the great joy of rearing sons to prize and protect the Hadham heritage. Its traditions brought him enormous satisfaction, but he would forgo passing that on to his descendents. His devotion and sacrifice both humbled and elevated her.

Splendorous as it was, the sacrifice was too great for her to accept as his gift. Meriel had to find a way out of this dilemma without allowing him to put her under so great an obligation.

Torn in two directions, she could see no easy solution. She must safeguard her sons, and Osborne's increasing madness made it impossible to leave them under his influence a moment longer than could be helped.

"What about you?" Hester asked Jonys. "What will you do while Meriel sees Trent and I wait to collect the boys?"

"I'll be occupied," he said, looking grim. "I mean to get acquainted with the neighbors in Dean Street as well."

Incredulous, Meriel couldn't prevent a tremor of anxiety and anger from entering her voice. "We only have a matter of hours to work with," she snapped out. "A madman has my sons secreted away, and if I don't stop him or satisfy his demands, he'll disappear with them forever. Is this the best time to go calling around the neighborhood?"

"The necessary time," he said with grave assurance. "When we know how Osborne learned about your visits to Dean Street, we may find the path that leads directly to James and Steven." He squeezed her hands. "Can't you trust me, love?"

Looking at his big hands to avoid his sincere gaze, Meriel dodged a direct reply. "Is it a matter for trust, when finding my sons is very nearly impossible at best?"

"I can do this, Meriel," Jonys insisted. "Give me a chance to prove it to you. You won't have to face Osborne alone tomorrow afternoon, I promise."

Nodding, Meriel tried to smile. She would far rather take a more active part in the plan so she could affect its outcome herself. Though she had traveled a long distance toward trusting Jonys, the effort to put her sons' fate wholly in hands other than her own felt as if it might cost her own sanity.

Chapter Eighteen

Standing beside the window because she couldn't sit down and remain still, Meriel glanced between the men in her front drawing room and the street below. Trent shuffled papers at a writing table, looking incensed and uncomfortable. The man who had come in behind Trent, a Mr. Hill who most likely worked at times as Trent's clerk, hovered nearby.

Checking the ormolou mantel clock again, Meriel prayed fervently that Jonys would appear before Osborne arrived. Jonys had promised her he would be here at four, that she wouldn't have to face her brother-in-law alone. She needed his support after hours of clashing with her solicitor, who demanded to know what Jonys thought he was about when she didn't know herself.

Jonys's messages had been brief and cryptic throughout the night and day. The only part that mattered was the fact that her sons were still lost to her.

Trent had been aghast at her requests for documents placing her holdings in a trust fund managed by Osborne. Even revealing that her sons' safety might depend on it didn't appease him.

Lacking total confidence that even Jonys could find a way to keep the trust from taking effect made it difficult for Meriel to reassure Trent. She knew Jonys would leave no avenue to finding the boys unexplored, but that belief was a product of her mind, not her emotions. Fear mocked faith, and she hadn't known a moment's peace of mind.

As she stared into Berkley Street, her eyes burned with the grit of sleeplessness. Each time she had lain down the previous night, she had snapped awake again, fretting about where her children pillowed their heads. Beyond that concern, she had despaired over Osborne's next mad fit, which might still take her children beyond her reach forever. If only he had acted out his madness before others, perhaps the court would have treated her petition for custody over her boys with more consideration.

Jonys had said she must trust him. Though she believed he would do what he could to help her, she had lost to Osborne's lunacy too many times in the past to believe now in the automatic triumph of right and reason. If Jonys didn't join her in the next few minutes with news of her boys' whereabouts, his madness might win again.

From beyond Portman Square came the sound of a carriage approaching, and Meriel remembered the predawn sounds a few weeks ago that had brought Jonys rolling into her life. Peering out, she couldn't see a vehicle yet. The hands on the painted clock crept closer to four o'clock, and she stared down into the square, teeth clenched.

A pit opened where her stomach had been; and she gripped the sill as her head swam. The vehicle that rolled into view wasn't Jonys's familiar high-perch phaeton as she had hoped.

Instead, a fine town carriage drew up in front of her steps and her hateful brother-in-law climbed down. Inconsequentially, her exhausted mind considered who he knew well enough to lend him a vehicle of this value.

But the only concern that counted was who hadn't arrived. Jonys hadn't come in time, bringing her boys home.

Straightening as she turned away from the window, Meriel ignored the panic that the sight of the mad vicar stirred in her stomach. Her alternative plan to gain time to find her sons would have to carry the day.

Giving in to Osborne's demands would leave her without power to fight him, for funds were indeed power in the real world. Gladly as she would sacrifice every shilling of her inheritance to save her boys, putting herself back into Osborne's total control wouldn't accomplish that. Instead, it would only put her in the same helpless position as her sons.

If even Hester were here, she would feel less alone. But Burchett had come for her cousin a short time ago, raising her hopes that James and Steven had been located. Telling her only that Jonys might have a lead on the boys' whereabouts, he had driven Hester away.

Both had promised to protect her sons from knowing about their uncle's schemes if possible. She didn't want them to be frightened.

Pat Cody

Assuming a serenity she didn't feel, Meriel joined the men at the writing table. "My brother-in-law is on his way inside," she told them as the sounds of the door opening below stairs reached them. Footsteps advanced up the stairs like the march of doom.

Directing a quiet question at Trent, she asked, "You have the papers prepared for his inspection as we discussed them?"

Sighing, he aligned the pages before him perfectly with the table's edge. Lining up his document case as precisely, he said with severity, "Just as we discussed, much as I dislike it."

Osborne walked into the room, looking about the floor furtively for a moment before closing the door. Meriel guessed he was looking for Kept. Though she had no intention of giving her dog away at Osborne's bidding, she had asked the porter to restrain him while the vicar was in the house.

"Good afternoon, my dear," Osborne said to Meriel, coming to take her hand and pat it like any normal family member. "This is a good thing you're doing for your children. A wise move, to put your affairs into competent hands as well."

Nodding curtly, she reclaimed her hand, repressing a shudder at his touch. As usual, Osborne showed enough command of his mental faculties to present himself as a reasonable person before outsiders, but she had known his irrational speech and actions too many years to trust the best of his moods.

Frowning, he nodded to the others. "Two solicitors, Meriel? Surely that's an extravagance on your part we can remedy at once."

Trent looked haughty, but Hill was more of a

diplomat. "Just forget about my presence, Lord Lamport. You won't be billed for my time, I can assure you."

"Make certain I'm not." Osborne bristled at the man's familiar manner. "I check every bill against my notes." Making a show of it, he pulled out a pocket book and penciled in a notation, looking at Hill as he did so.

"Caution is a fine quality, and who can depend on his memory days or weeks later?" Hill had become quite chatty with her brother-in-law, to Meriel's surprise.

"Despite the precaution of noting down the assurance I won't be billed for your time, I find my memory always functions perfectly." Turning his back on Hill, Osborne addressed Trent. "I'll have a look at those documents now." He held out an imperious hand.

Brows coming together, Trent stared at her, waiting for her nod before handing over the papers. Feeling her jaw clench, Meriel gave it. This was the danger point in her plan, when Osborne scrutinized the trust arrangement.

Snatching the document, the vicar took a seat near the window where light fell across the pages, and settled to read them.

The pit in Meriel's midsection yawned wider. She had counted on his eagerness to get her fortune under his control to make him skim the papers. Instead, he looked ready to take the rest of the day to satisfy himself on the terms of the contract. Very likely he would notice the detail she had persuaded Trent to alter.

Unable to watch him read, fearing his discovery of her subterfuge any moment, Meriel paced about the room.

The palpable force of his malign disapproval followed her and grew, billowing around her like a cloud of choking dust from a carriage's wheels. Stopping near the door to the passage, she clasped her hands together, forcing herself to stand still despite her unease. No one else seemed to observe his malevolent stare, but then no one ever had appeared to notice his subtle signs of threat.

Glancing toward him when the feeling of being watched with hatred had subsided, Meriel was surprised to see Hill standing behind Osborne, appearing to read the document over his shoulder. As a colleague of Trent's, surely Hill was already familiar with the papers.

Making a sound of impatience, Osborne shifted forward in his seat and stared over his shoulder. "You, there, what do you think you're doing? Come around in front of me where I can see you."

As Hill bowed and did as directed, the vicar muttered, "Never could abide people skulking about behind me." He settled himself to read again.

In the distance, Meriel heard the door open and close in the entrance hall. Hope and her pulse leaped forward. Perhaps Hester and Burchett had returned with her sons.

Holding her breath, she listened as distant footfalls crossed the hall on the ground floor below. Only one set, so her boys hadn't been found. Hands and throat tight, she tasted despair anew.

Someone had started up the steps, a person with a heavier tread than Hester or Burchett. If only it were Jonys, with her sons in tow. She might not hear their lighter steps on the passage carpet through the closed door.

A few swift steps sounded down the passage,

and Jonys walked into the room, filling it with his confident presence. He was alone.

Exhausted and dismayed, her muscles quivered with the effort of remaining erect. Her boys weren't with him. Jonys hadn't been able to locate her sons after all. Impossible as she had known the task to be, she had held onto a fragment of hope that he would discover where Osborne had hidden them.

Smiling, Jonys sent her a rallying look. "You mustn't worry—"

Breaking into his speech, Osborne sprang up from the chair, pitching the papers he held down on its seat. "See here, man," he raged at Trent, "how many solicitors does a simple trust agreement require? You're trying my patience, I warn you!"

Meriel hurried forward. "Osborne, please. I invited my friend Lord Hadham to be here; he isn't a solicitor." Even with Jonys's appearance to pull his fangs, she couldn't endure one of his insane displays right now, with her composure near its breaking point.

Osborne went perfectly still, the blank look creeping into his eyes. "Hadham," he said on a long, pleased sigh, turning back.

Jonys bowed as if acknowledging an introduction, perfectly at ease. Seen together, the two men offered an obvious contrast in reason and unreason, evident in their different bearings and expressions.

"Hadham here, in my presence?" The vicar glared at Meriel. "You need my direction even more than I believed. Meeting the man away from here for the devil's purposes shows you retain some small shred of decency, but to flaunt him openly before respectable people is the outside of enough."

"The Earl of Hadham?" said Hill in the same overly friendly tone he had used with Osborne. He bowed. "I'm Hill, sir. Very pleased to make your acquaintance."

Grinning wickedly, Jonys bowed in return. "Delighted you could join us," he drawled.

Osborne drew himself up to glare at Jonys. "This is my house. It isn't for you to welcome people to it, especially the lower classes. I'll thank you to relieve me of your company now, and you can take that clerk with you."

Trent came from behind the writing table. "If I may mention a point of law, Lord Lamport, the house isn't yours. It never will be yours. Even if Lady Welwyn had already signed the proper documents, you would only be the caretaker until her sons reach their majorities." His irritation showed clearly in his sharp tone. "A trustee does not gain ownership, however you may have acted in that role!"

Osborne advanced on the slight solicitor, exuding menace from every muscle of his body. Trent removed his spectacles and stared at the vicar with obvious dislike. To Meriel's surprise and fear, he did not back away.

"Hill!" snapped Trent. "Have you seen enough to suit you? If you haven't a medical opinion on this case as yet, I can most assuredly give you a judicial one. And I'd much prefer that you decide if you want him before he takes a fancy to strangle me."

Meriel felt as taken aback as Osborne looked as he stopped and stared at Hill. "Medical opinion?"

she asked Jonys, who nodded, looking grim but satisfied.

Hill bowed to her. "I beg your pardon, coming into your home under the guise of being the worthy Mr. Trent's assistant. Lord Hadham felt you might be safer if you didn't have to put on a pretense about my true identity. I'm George Nesse Hill."

The name meant nothing to her slowed senses.

To Trent, Hill said, "In my opinion the patient certainly has the potential to be violent, but Lord Hadham and I can restrain him if it comes to an attack on your person. And I'm hopeful that I can curb that tendency in time. Yes, indeed. Marvelous things we're capable of doing with these sad cases now. Marvelous." He tilted his head to study Osborne like a prize bull. "No need to shut people away in attics or put them on display like animals in asylums, not with my advanced methods of treatment."

Osborne stood staring at Hill with his empty eyes. "You're a physician?" he asked, jerking out the question. "A great load of quacks and pretenders, the lot of you. Leech onto a man's pocket more often than his blood."

"Yes, yes, old fellow, just as you say," agreed Hill, smiling. "I hope you'll come be my guest at a little cottage I own in the country, where you can tell me all about it."

If Hill were a physician, he didn't resemble any of those in the profession that Meriel had met. Speaking in a low voice to Jonys, she asked in disbelief, "Why have you brought a doctor? Do you believe he can persuade Osborne to stay away from my sons by choice?"

Trent's precise voice cut through the room.

"Hill's a mad-doctor. He'll take Osborne off your hands and keep him safely in the country where he'll do no further harm. Lord Hadham sent him to me with instructions about three o'clock."

For a moment Meriel felt as if she were mad herself. "Osborne suffers from nervous storms; my husband said that. But he never said Osborne was mad!"

"Imprecise term, 'nervous storms,' never use it myself," mused Hill, staring at Osborne with a look of deep pleasure.

Jonys grinned at her. "Would you describe the vicar's behavior as that of a rational person?"

"No, of course not," she protested. "But he's always acted this way; it isn't as if he makes no sense when he talks or chases the maids with a carving knife. I've never been able to persuade anyone else that his behavior is anything but usual."

"But I consider your opinions well worth listening to," Jonys assured her. "If the vicar made you fear for your safety and that of your sons, I had no doubt the noted mad-doctor would find him a candidate for treatment."

Dazed at the swift passage of events, Meriel said, "But I might have been wrong."

"Fascinating," said Hill. "I hope you'll grant me an interview, Lady Welwyn, as your brother-in-law's animosity seems directed at you in particular. As these cases of obsession grow more pronounced over a period of time, others may not notice the increase of mania. I want to gather notes on the manifestations and progress of his condition as you've observed it. I hope to do a paper for the Royal College of Physicians and Surgeons on his form of madness."

"Good heavens!" said Meriel. "Then you truly

think he's unbalanced beyond the ordinary ways that most of us are?"

"Indeed," Hill said at once. "Around the bend. Addled. Wrong in the upper story. Dicked in the nob, if you will."

"Excellent," said Trent. "I'll prepare a statement for Lady Welwyn to sign as natural parent and guardian of the young Lord Welwyn, who is the vicar's nearest relation, authorizing you to confine and treat this man."

"But Osborne is James's legal guardian," Meriel protested, dazed at the rapid development of events.

"No doubt the Chancery Court will determine that a madman can't serve in that capacity," Trent assured her. "Hill's standing as a mad-doctor will satisfy them on that score. As a lady of private property, which you manage, in addition to being the natural parent of the present Lord Welwyn, you'll be the logical choice as guardian over your minor children."

"Surely more is required than my agreement to have Osborne confined." After years at his mercy, Meriel could hardly believe his fate was in her hands.

"The family request for my help is quite enough in the case of a private patient," Hill said, beaming at her again. "If he were indigent, of course, the Poor Laws would apply, and he'd go to the work-house, not come to me."

Osborne drew himself to his full height. "I will not be spoken of in such terms," he said. "I'm not the one who's mad in this company. I'm a man of God, chosen to deal with the iniquitous among you. Like those two," he roared, indicating Meriel and Jonys. "An abomination in the sight of God, unfit to have the care of Welwyn's sons! Fornicators!"

"I'm sorry you had to witness that outburst, milady," said Hill, tutting and moving toward Osborne. "The poor man's obviously becoming distraught, so I'd best remove him from the company. He just needs a quiet place and close watching. We'll be kind to him, never fear. I insist that the chains be wrapped in flannel to protect my patients."

"Wait," said Meriel. "You can't take him away!"

Three men turned to look at her in surprise, and in that moment, Osborne ran. He was out of the room before anyone realized his intention, disappearing through the door and down the passage.

Without hesitation, Meriel ran after him.

Behind her, Jonys called, "Wait, Meriel! Let me stop him."

Ahead of her, Osborne had nearly gained the stairs, and she didn't look back to see who followed to lend her assistance. Mad or not, Osborne knew where her sons were, and he wasn't leaving her house until she wrested the information out of him. Personally.

From behind, she heard Jonys call out again, "Stop, Meriel!" His help would be welcome, but she needed to deal with Osborne at last, for herself and for her boys. Having her suspicions about his mental stability confirmed by the mad-doctor Jonys had found lent her purpose.

With the head start he had, Osborne was on the stairs by the time she reached the top of them. Seizing a large Oriental porcelain vase full of flowers from a table nearby, she leaned over the stair rail and took careful aim. Hurling the vase, she had the satisfaction of seeing it slam onto his shoulder, spilling water and scarlet lobelia down his coat before shattering on a tread.

Looking back with malignity, he bared his teeth, snarling at her, and plunged down the stairs again. His pause allowed her to close the distance between them as they both rushed down the staircase in a reckless chase.

"Kept!" she called, hearing frantic barks from the ground floor. Though she had to watch her skirts, the steps, and Osborne, she had an impression of a frenzied ball of fur dashing back and forth at the bottom of the stairs.

Just as she touched Osborne's collar, Meriel stepped on her skirts and lost her balance. Unwilling to let him escape, she dived forward, falling in a nightmare of confused impressions of color and sound. Crying out in fear and frustration, she turned heels over head.

Though she might break her neck in this fall down the stairs, Kept would delay Osborne until Jonys could capture him. Jonys would learn where he had hidden her boys.

As every bone in her body crashed into anguish, the breath left her chest in a great sucking blow that deflated her lungs. Darkness closed in upon her mercifully, for she couldn't endure the impossible struggle to gasp air.

From a great distance, a voice called her name. It must be true, what Osborne had said, that we were snatched out of life directly into judgment. Should she open her eyes to discover if she must face Saint Peter or Satan?

Peeping through heavy lids, she tried to focus, seeing only a shock of crisp black hair above a blur of a face with too many bright blue eyes. Her vision was a whirl of colors around the dark face bending over her, turning like a pinwheel in a breeze. This face reminded her somehow of the devil, even if she couldn't focus properly. She closed her eyes again. No rush about looking around if that was the afterlife she had earned.

A wet tongue bathed her face, and she murmured, "Yes, and I love you, too."

"Must I lick your face to get you to say that to me?"

Gradually she refocused her sight. Jonys leaned above her, looking both worried and wistful. His hands moved over her, searching and gentle, swift and decisive. Such good, big hands. Meriel reached for the comfort of them.

"Do you hurt anywhere in particular?" he asked her, kissing the hand she extended.

"Mainly my dignity," she said, struggling to sit up on an uneven surface. She recalled the reason for her fall. "Never mind about me. You have to catch Osborne and bring him back, Jonys. He knows where my sons are!"

Slipping his arms under her shoulders and knees, he lifted her cautiously against his chest, cradling her on his thighs where he knelt on the floor. "I don't have to catch Osborne; you and Skype took care of that."

Looking down, Meriel knew why the floor had felt so uneven. She had landed on Osborne when she tumbled through the air.

Lying quite still, he didn't look as if he would get away any time soon. Blood smeared his hand and soaked into his shirt cuff.

Feeling a bit dizzy, Meriel asked, "Did I do that?"

"Most of it, though Skype gets the credit for

drawing blood." Jonys propped her head higher on his shoulder so she could see Kept dancing with impatience to get to her. "The little fellow was so upset at seeing you crash down the stairs with his archenemy, he had to get in one good bite. Can't say I blame him; I wanted to land Osborne a facer myself, but he was already down for the count."

"Considering Osborne kicked him at every opportunity, Kept owed him that much," Meriel said. The vicar still hadn't moved. Meriel grew uneasy. "Is he dead?"

"Not unless Skype decided to finish him off. He's out cold as a crock of butter, though." Jonys didn't look interested in Osborne's welfare as his blazing blue stare caressed her face.

"Good," she said in relief. "Bring him around so I can ask him where to find James and Steven."

"Try asking me, and you won't have to waste the water from another arrangement of flowers," he advised her, rising to his feet with her securely in his arms, showing only the smallest sign of effort.

"You know where they are?" Little had made sense to Meriel for many minutes, even before she tumbled down the stairs. "You might have told me sooner."

"I tried when I came in, but Osborne demanded my attention at once," he protested. "I sent Hester and Burchett to visit with them before I headed here. Don't worry. They're perfectly well, tucked up in a small school in Deptford. One you might even consider leaving them in for a while, as it's meant to prepare boys for Eton."

"But how did you learn their whereabouts?" Meriel suspected she had hit her head hard and was dreaming.

351

"Lady Helsby told me a little more than an hour ago." His smile was smug as he carried Meriel into the library while Hill and two footmen removed Osborne from her entrance hall.

Meriel took her arm from about his shoulder. "Lady Helsby! I don't want to be grateful to her." The widow had pursued Jonys shamelessly, but if the woman had helped locate her sons, she would have to thank her.

"Osborne and Lady Helsby plotted against you together, so you don't owe her any thanks." Jonys flashed her a smile as he settled her on the window seat. Kept leaped up beside her to investigate possible injuries for himself.

"Why would those two get together?" Putting a hand to her aching head, Meriel felt addled. "I know what Osborne wanted, but what benefit would Lady Helsby gain if I put my fortune in his hands?"

"Me," said Jonys, hovering over her. "The lady offered to take me off your hands, with marriage as part of the bargain, in return for telling where your sons were. She was as ready to do Osborne an ill turn as you."

Meriel felt indignant at Lady Helsby or Jonys, perhaps both of them. "You didn't say me how you responded to Lady Helsby's proposal." She leaned away from him, hugging Kept, dreading to hear his intention to wed the widow.

"I told her I couldn't consider marriage with the lady who had told Osborne about your visits to the Dean Street house."

"Lady Helsby had already shown a little too much interest in our acquaintance for my comfort," Meriel said. "I should have paid more attention to that danger, but that was the evening you planned a picnic supper in St James Park." Meriel sat for a moment, thinking. "But how could she have seen me? Her house is in Tavistock Square, a considerable drive away from Dean Street."

"She didn't see you." Joining her on the window seat, he leaned back against a cushion, drawing Meriel back against his chest. "Her brother Sir Richard Dabbs keeps a mistress on Tilney Street, and its stable backs up to ours at Number Seven. Remember the rainy day you drove there from Hatchard's?"

Meriel groaned. "So this horror was my doing. But it was a lovely day; I can't regret it. Especially not since my boys are safe from Osborne forever now. I have you to thank for that, Jonys. What made you certain you could have him taken away by a mad-doctor?"

"That's simple to explain." Setting his chin on top of her head, he said with sincerity, "Anyone who knew you would recognize that you're a wonderful mother to your sons. Osborne had to be mad to think otherwise."

"But this Dr Hill, how did you discover him in time to send him here?" While Meriel believed she had to deal with every problem herself, Jonys had found the fastest way to handle Osborne.

Dropping a kiss onto her hair, he said, "A couple of weeks back, I saw a notice for a lecture by Hill at the Royal Institution. I already had suspicions about the vicar's state of mind from Hester's accounts of his visits here. I went around to Albemarle Street on the night and found myself practically the only person in the audience. After his presentation, I took Hill to a coffeehouse and warned him I might need his help quickly."

Rubbing her forehead on his chest, Meriel murmured, "I needed your help, far more than I'd let myself admit it. Don't marry Lady Helsby or anyone else, Jonys. Let's go on dealing with your problems and mine together."

"Are you certain you aren't still dizzy?" he asked, sounding solicitous. "That was quite a tumble you took. On top of the stresses of the day, you probably should lie abed for a week or two."

"While you go off and marry that dreadful woman? I don't want to let you out of my sight." She felt near to tears, thinking of Jonys in that woman's clutches.

"That's a bit like the dog in the manager, don't you think?" Bending his head to look at her, he grinned. "You don't want to marry me yourself, but you don't want anyone else to."

Leaning against him, she didn't want to let go of Jonys, and not just because she still felt shaky from the fall. "I didn't say I didn't want to marry you; I said I couldn't." If only her head felt more clear. "Please try to understand, Jonys. Once wed, I have no legal existence. A wife is one with her husband in the eyes of our courts, and he's the only one with a voice."

"But I've agreed that you don't have to marry me." His eyes were as intense and bright as Kept's. Putting an arm around the terrier, she took comfort from his warm presence, as she often had since carrying him into her house. This question of marriage must be worked out between them at last. "You must wed; you're the Earl of Hadham. I can't live with the guilt if you never have a son to teach how to become a proper Earl of Hadham."

"No, I'd teach him to be improper, don't you think? So my sons might as well be born on the wrong side of the blanket." Though his tone teased, Jonys looked away.

"Don't make jokes about heirs to the title. Anson would never forgive me if I kept you from continuing the line." Worse, she would never forgive herself. Meriel wanted Jonys to fulfill his dream of passing his heritage on to his sons.

"Providing heirs is one choice Anson must leave to me." Jonys stretched his long legs before him. "I've already told you: If I can't have a heir with you, I'll do without. I love you, Meriel. You're more important to me than heirs."

Her heart aching worse than her head by far, Meriel considered the impasse between them. Losing herself in another marriage terrified her. Yet Jonys was ready to set aside his greatest dream, of sons to inherit Hadham and its treasures, because of her fear. Loving her would cost him far too much.

Jonys hadn't even asked her to love him in return. What would she answer if he did? Taking Kept into her arms, she buried her face in his fur as she faced her personal demons.

Just as she had feared would happen, she had tumbled into love with Jonys as surely and painfully as she had fallen down the stairs. Though she could live on her own and had proved it, Jonys had shown her how much richer and more comfortable her life was when she shared it with him. She felt the same fierce protectiveness toward Jonys's right to his dreams as he had shown when he'd tried to safeguard hers. Both of them were strong, capable people, but each benefited from the other's concern.

Loving a person didn't mean controlling their choices or limiting them. That tumble down the stairs, showing how easily she could have died, had clarified the importance of living and loving while she had that choice.

Much as she needed to be a separate, complete person, she wanted to share in Jonys's strength and concern. She wanted to give him the benefit of her strength and love as well. But she couldn't put limits on him any more than she could accept them for herself.

Love was clearly a form of madness, for she couldn't put restrictions on him. If she couldn't help him to make his life everything he wanted it to be, she had to set him free.

"You must wed someone and have heirs." Setting Kept down beside her, she concentrated on being fair to Jonys. "You can't give up what's most important to you and be content. But you were right when you said I was afraid of marriage."

"Maybe we could find another way to sort out things between us," he murmured, a half smile tilting his mouth.

Near tears, she said, "I hope I'm always reasonable enough to listen to your suggestions."

"I hope so, too," he agreed, leaning forward to kiss the end of her eyebrow. "I could let the American relatives inherit Hadham and we could produce illegitimate heirs to your fortune."

That thought disturbed her. "I don't want to bring children into this world without a father; it wouldn't be fair to them."

"Then you'd best stop seducing me," he advised, nuzzling her throat. "How about this, then. Marry me, and I'll sign an agreement that you'll have full control of your finances and all the children of the union. But I get full say over our dogs."

"You're quite determined to end your stint as a

356

kept man, aren't you?" In wonder at how much this man was willing to compromise in order to live out his life with her, Meriel pushed him away and sat gazing at him. If he truly meant to give up so much, how could she give up nothing?

Jonys nodded. "I can see if Trent's still here to draw up the contract at once. He could probably use the business after being done out of a fee on those papers of Osborne's. What was that about, what he said about a subterfuge with the papers?"

Meriel busied herself with detaching a twig from Kept's low undercarriage without pulling it. "I'm not exactly proud of that now. I was afraid it was impossible for you to find the boys in time. So I made Trent put the wrong year on the papers I was to sign—1817 instead of 1812. Sevens and twos can look a great deal alike in flowing script."

"You didn't expect Osborne would notice he'd have to wait five years to get control of your funds?" Jonys didn't look as offended at her lack of faith in him as she'd feared.

"I thought he'd be in more of a hurry to get my signature," she explained quickly. "And five years gave us ample time to find a way to stop him."

"So you did trust me after all. You just provided for more time to act." He looked pleased as he pulled her against him, an arm about her shoulders. "I'm glad. And you won't have to check the dates and terms if you decide to take me up on the contract I want to sign with you."

"Giving in would be easier than resisting you," she assured him. "Every hour with you has been either a challenge or a joy, and one is as much pleasure as the other. That's when I suspected I must love you, Jonys: when I realized that even

357

our rainy days together on Dean Street were better than sunny ones apart."

Tenderly, he kissed her forehead. "Then let's enjoy many more rainy days in Dean Street. And sunny ones. I'll take you on any terms I can have you, Meriel. Marry me or keep me, but you won't get rid of me. How else can I continue to see Skype?"

"That reminds me of a point I didn't like about the contract you suggested between us. I want a half interest in our dogs, so I suppose I'll have to offer you an equal share in the children and money." She looked up at Jonys so he could read in her expression how seriously she meant the suggestion.

"Keep your fortune for the children; I intend to make my own. You can probably convince me to share the children and dogs, including James, Steven, and Skype." Gathering her into his arms, he said, "I think you should know that I'll only seal our bargains with kisses."

Willingly, she turned up her face.

"Not here," he said, touching the tip of her nose, "for I mean to kiss you all over to be certain you weren't injured in that fall. I thought we might disappear to the Dean Street house for a while."

"It's a dear little house," she agreed, nestling against him. "I want to keep it. Just think, we can escape from our children now and then, always on rainy days, and go spend a lazy afternoon or evening to ourselves. No matter how many heirs you decide you require to safeguard the succession, I want us to remember we're lovers after we're married."

"I'll pray for rain, and not just for the crops," he said, grinning as he pulled her to her feet. Arm about her waist, he walked her toward the entrance hall.

"Wait," Meriel said. "Children may not be allowed at the Dean Street house, but Kept's always welcome. We wouldn't have it or each other if he hadn't brought us together that early morning."

On the window seat, Kept sat on his haunches staring at them, bright-eyed. "Come, Skype," Jonys called.

Kept lay down, still staring without a blink of his brown eyes.

"Come on Skype. Come on, boy."

Kept dropped his muzzle onto his front paws as if settling down for a long snooze.

Meriel exchanged a long look with the terrier, and a thought formed in her head as clearly as if Kept had spoken aloud. "Maybe he doesn't want to be called by his old name. It's part of his past, before he came into our lives."

Standing with his fists propped on his hips, Jonys eyed the terrier. He shook his head. "No, he can't be that smart."

Meriel shrugged.

"However, as a kept man, I can't deny your smallest desire." Jonys leaned forward. "Kept," he called quietly. "Come with us, Kept."

Leaping up from the window seat, Kept jumped down onto the carpet and ran to them.

Shaking his head, Jonys laughed and Meriel joined in. He picked up the terrier and handed Kept to her. Circling his arms about them both, Jonys kissed her for keeps.

Christmas means more than just puppy love.

"SHAKESPEARE AND THE THREE KINGS"
Victoria Alexander

Requiring a trainer for his three inherited dogs, Oliver Stanhope meets D. K. Lawrence, and is in for the Christmas surprise—and love—of his life.

"ATHENA'S CHRISTMAS TAIL" Nina Coombs

Mercy wants her marriage to be a match of the heart—and with the help of her very determined dog, Athena, she finds just the right magic of the holiday season.

"AWAY IN A SHELTER" Annie Kimberlin

A dedicated volunteer, Camille Campbell still doesn't want to be stuck in an animal shelter on Christmas Eve—especially with a handsome helper whose touch leaves her starry-eyed.

"MR. WRIGHT'S CHRISTMAS ANGEL"
Miriam Raftery

When Joy's daughter asks Santa for a father, she knows she's in trouble—until a trip to Alaska takes them on a journey into the arms of Nicholas Wright and his amazing dog.

___52235-7 $5.99 US/$6.99 CAN

IT'S A DOG'S LIFE ROMANCE

Stray Hearts by Annie Kimberlin. A busy veterinarian, Melissa is comfortable around her patients—but when it comes to men, too often her instincts have her barking up the wrong tree. So she's understandably wary when Peter Winthrop, who accidentally hits a Shetland sheepdog with his car, shows more than just a friendly interest in her. But as their relationship grows more intimate she finds herself hoping that he has room for one more lost soul in his home.
___52221-7 $5.50 US/$6.50 CAN

Rosamunda's Revenge by Emma Craig. At first, Tacita Grantham thinks that Jedediah Hardcastle is a big brute of a man with no manners whatsoever. But when she sees he'll do anything to protect her—even rescue her beloved Rosamunda—she knows his bark is worse than his bite. And when she first feels his kiss—she knows he is the only man who'll ever touch her heart.
___52213-6 $5.50 US/$6.50 CAN

Dorchester Publishing Co., Inc.
P.O. Box 6640
Wayne, PA 19087-8640

Please add $1.75 for shipping and handling for the first book and $.50 for each book thereafter. NY, NYC, and PA residents, please add appropriate sales tax. No cash, stamps, or C.O.D.s. All orders shipped within 6 weeks via postal service book rate. Canadian orders require $2.00 extra postage and must be paid in U.S. dollars through a U.S. banking facility.

Name_____
Address_____
City_____ State_____ Zip_____
I have enclosed $ _____ in payment for the checked book(s).
Payment <u>must</u> accompany all orders. ❑ Please send a free catalog.

DON'T MISS *LOVE SPELL'S* WAGGING TALES OF LOVE!

Man's Best Friend by Nina Coombs. Fido senses his dark-haired mistress's heart is wrapped up in old loves gone astray—and it is up to him, her furry friend, to weave the warp and woof of fate into the fabric of paradise. Brad Ferris is perfect. But Jenny isn't an easy human to train, and swatting her with newspapers isn't an option. So Fido will have to rely on good old-fashioned dog sense to lead the two together. For Fido knows that only in Brad's arms will Jenny unleash feelings which have been caged for too long.
____52205-5 $5.50 US/$6.50 CAN

Molly in the Middle by Stobie Piel. Molly is a Scottish Border collie, and unless she finds some other means of livelihood for her lovely mistress, Miren, she'll be doomed to chase after stupid sheep forever. That's why she is tickled pink when handsome Nathan MacCullum comes into Miren's life, and she knows from Miren's pink cheeks and distracted gaze that his hot kisses are something special. Now she'll simply have to show the silly humans that true love—and a faithful house pet—are all they'll ever need.
____52193-8 $5.99 US/$6.99 CAN

Dorchester Publishing Co., Inc.
P.O. Box 6640
Wayne, PA 19087-8640

Please add $1.75 for shipping and handling for the first book and $.50 for each book thereafter. NY, NYC, and PA residents, please add appropriate sales tax. No cash, stamps, or C.O.D.s. All orders shipped within 6 weeks via postal service book rate. Canadian orders require $2.00 extra postage and must be paid in U.S. dollars through a U.S. banking facility.

Name_____
Address_____
City_____ State_____ Zip_____
I have enclosed $_____ in payment for the checked book(s).
Payment <u>must</u> accompany all orders. ☐ Please send a free catalog.

A FAERIE TALE ROMANCE

VICTORIA ALEXANDER

Ophelia Kendrake has barely finished conning the coat off a cardsharp's back when she stumbles into Dead End, Wyoming. Mistaken for the Countess of Bridgewater, Ophelia sees no reason to reveal herself until she has stripped the hamlet of its fortunes and escaped into the sunset. But the free-spirited beauty almost swallows her script when she meets Tyler, the town's virile young mayor. When Tyler Matthews returns from an Ivy League college, he simply wants to settle down and enjoy the simplicity of ranching. But his aunt and uncle are set on making a silk purse out of Dead End, and Tyler is going to be the new mayor. It's a job he takes with little relish—until he catches a glimpse of the village's newest visitor.

_52159-8 $5.50 US/$6.50 CAN

Heart's Magic

Flora Speer

Bestselling author of *ROSE RED*

In the year 1122, Mirielle senses change is coming to
Wroxley Castle. Then, from out of the fog, two strangers
ride into Lincolnshire. Mirielle believes the first man to be
honest. But the second, Giles, is hiding something–even as
he stirs her heart and awakens her deepest desires. And as
Mirielle seeks the truth about her mysterious guest, she
uncovers the castle's secrets and learns she must stop a
treachery which threatens all she holds dear. Only then can
she be in the arms of her only love, the man who has
awakened her own heart's magic.

___52204-7 $5.99 US/$6.99 CAN

FLORA SPEER

Rose Red

A Faerie Tale Romance

Once upon a time...they lived happily ever after.

"I HAVE TWO DAUGHTERS, ONE A FLOWER AS PURE AND WHITE AS THE NEW-FALLEN SNOW AND THE OTHER A ROSE AS RED AND SWEET AS THE FIRES OF PASSION."

Bianca and Rosalinda are the only treasures left to their mother after her husband, the Duke of Monteferro, is murdered. Fleeing a remote villa in the shadows of the Alps of Northern Italy, she raises her daughters in hiding and swears revenge on the enemy who has brought her low.

The years pass until one stormy night a stranger appears from out of the swirling snow, half-frozen and wild, wrapped only in a bearskin. To gentle Bianca he appears a gallant suitor. To their mother he is the son of an assassin. But to Rosalinda he is the one man who can light the fires of passion and make them burn as sweet and red as her namesake.

_52139-3 $5.99 US/$6.99 CAN

An Angel's Touch

Carly's Song

LENORA NAZWORTH

Carly Richards has come to New Orleans to escape her painful past. She certainly has no intention of getting involved with some reckless musician with an overzealous approach to living and an all-too-real lust for her. Sam Canfield is simply the sexiest man she's ever seen, but Carly is determined to resist being mesmerized by his sensuous spell.

Sam thinks he's seen it all in his day. But one enchanted evening, his world is turned upside down when a redhead with lilac eyes stumbles into his path and an old friend he thought long gone makes a magical appearance on a misty street corner. Soon, the handsome sax player finds himself conversing with an elusive angel, struggling to put his life together, and attempting to convince the reluctant Carly that together they'll make sweet music of their own.

_52073-7 $5.99 US/$7.99 CAN